THE APOTHECARY'S CURSE

THE APOTHECARY'S CURSE

BARBARA BARNETT

an imprint of Prometheus Books
Amherst, NY

Published 2016 by Pyr Books®, an imprint of Prometheus Books

Cover illustration © Galen Dara
Cover design by Jacqueline Nasso Cooke
Cover design © Prometheus Books

Inquiries should be addressed to
Pyr
59 John Glenn Drive
Amherst, New York 14228
VOICE: 716–691–0133 • FAX: 716–691–0137
WWW.PYRSF.COM

20 19 18 17 16 • 5 4 3 2 1

Library of Congress Cataloging-in-Publication Data

Names: Barnett, Barbara (Barbara Shyette) author.
Title: The apothecary's curse / by Barbara Barnett.
Description: Amherst, NY : Pyr, 2016.
Identifiers: LCCN 2016013613 (print) | LCCN 2016029865 (ebook) |
    ISBN 9781633882331 (pbk.) | ISBN 9781633882348 (ebook)
Subjects: LCSH: Physicians—England—Fiction. | Pharmacists—England—Fiction.
    | Immortality—Fiction. | Historical fiction gsafd | GSAFD: Regency fiction |
    Fantasy fiction
Classification: LCC PS3602.A77568 A66 2016 (print) |
    LCC PS3602.A77568 (ebook) | DDC 813/.6—dc23
LC record available at https://lccn.loc.gov/2016013613

Printed in the United States of America

To my soul mate and best friend, my husband Phillip Barnett.

LONDON, 1902

PROLOGUE

"**M**y dear friend, hold fast the doctrine: when all impossibilities are eliminated, what remains, however improbable, must be the truth. Nothing could be so improbable that I must now and forever address you as *Sir* Arthur!"

Dr. Joseph Bell stood at the head of the dining table before twenty assembled guests, offering a robust toast to the guest of honor, his student and friend, the newly knighted Sir Arthur Conan Doyle, in London for the first time since the honor had been bestowed on him. His confidante Jean Elizabeth Leckie was at his side.

"Do tell, Sir Arthur," Mrs. Wilder said with a giggle, "is it not true that our dear Joseph is in actuality your Sherlock Holmes?"

"Indeed not, Mrs. Wilder!" The author twisted his mustache a bit more at each mention of Holmes's name.

Miss Leckie patted Conan Doyle's arm tenderly. "My dear, your mustache shall soon be as fine as a strand of silk. Besides, you well know he is! They even smoke the same sort of pipe!" The entire table joined her in laughter, despite Conan Doyle's protestations.

"Ah," interrupted Joseph, coming to Conan Doyle's rescue. "Alas, I do not share Holmes's preference for cocaine, nor does my mind crave the constant stimulation of work. I am quite at peace come Sunday afternoons with nothing to do but read the *Times*."

"I wish my consulting detective could *rest* in peace." Conan Doyle scowled at Mrs. Wilder, as she inquired when a new Holmes story would be published. "Did you not read 'The Final Problem,' my dear Mrs. Wilder? Holmes died at Reichenbach Falls! However, since no one will allow him to be at his rest"—he sighed dramatically—"I can tonight announce a new adventure for the *Strand* come next year. 'The Empty House,' it is called!" Conan Doyle laughed, yet it was darkened with an unmistakable note of vexation.

"But how should you have him come back, Sir Arthur?" Mr. Cranford inquired. "If he is indeed, as you say, dead?"

"Do let us change the subject, Mr. Cranford." Conan Doyle lifted his glass, taking a long draught of his wine, his eyes closed.

Miss Leckie smiled. "Oh! I've something! Have you heard of that apothecary? Lentine is his name. In Covent Garden. The line to enter his shop goes on and on. Can you imagine?"

"And why might that be, Miss Leckie?" Conan Doyle asked.

"Why, his amazing Reanimating Mercuric Tonic, of course! To hear his patter, the medicine 'shall restore life, even in the event of sudden death!' Can you imagine? An apothecary, of all ludicrous things!"

Mr. Cranford laughed. "They should hang them all, the thieving rogues. I've never met one I can trust, always trying to hawk the latest patent medicines."

Gaelan Erceldoune glared at Miss Leckie, his dark, mirthless eyes hard as basalt. Beside him, his companion, Joseph's cousin Dr. Simon Bell, laid a calming hand on his sleeve, an urgent plea to forbear; Gaelan snapped his arm away.

With a peevish edge to his voice, Gaelan steered the topic from the dubiousness of the apothecary trade. "What if your consulting detective *cannot* die?"

Conan Doyle stared him down. "Whatever do you mean—*cannot* die?"

Simon worried a loose thread in his linen napkin, his hands knotted with tension.

"Yes," Gaelan continued, ignoring Simon's disquiet. "Well, after Reichenbach, Holmes is, of course, presumed dead, his body not found. Unsurprising, given the terrain, but I assume your new story finds him quite well. Might you not suggest, therefore, that Holmes's invulnerability extends beyond the intellectual—that he, in fact, *cannot* die by any natural means, improbable though it may seem? Already, you have toyed with the notion—your Sorsa in 'The Ring of Thoth.' You needn't ever be explicit of course; allow your readers to speculate and draw their own conclusions. Holmes's devotees will be so elated that none shall even question how it is possible."

He mimed a vaudeville marquee with his hands high above his head, commanding the attention of the entire table. "The immortal Sherlock Holmes lives on in a new series." At once self-conscious, Gaelan thrust his deformed left hand into his trouser pocket. "He'll live forever, by Jove, your creation shall. Perhaps long after you, sir, have gone to your grave."

Conan Doyle's enthusiasm seemed tepid at best. But Gaelan pressed further. "As well, do you not imagine, sir, whilst giving new life to your most popular creation, you might also draw upon your truest passion—the supernatural world? Would that not, as it were, be killing two birds with one stone?"

"Ha!" Conan Doyle pointed an accusatory finger at Gaelan. "*You*, sir, sound too much like my publisher."

Joseph broke in. "Please, ladies and gentlemen, let us go through to the drawing room. We might continue our conversations there in more comfort—"

But Conan Doyle was not to be stopped. "In a moment, Dr. Bell," he said, holding up his hand to forestall the company. "I've a question for Mr. Erceldoune. Our dear Joseph made mention that you are an apothecary?"

Simon backed farther into his chair, cursing himself that he had disclosed even this small fact to his ever-curious cousin. He twisted his napkin, eyes pleading with Gaelan to be still.

Gaelan leaned toward Conan Doyle, a vague threat in the set of his jaw. "That I am, but why is that of concern to you or anyone here this evening? Do you mean to put me in my place as amongst the same company as Lentine, whom Miss Leckie has just now vilified—and with ample cause, I might add?"

"I mean no disrespect, nor to dishonor you amongst the fine physicians at this table. . . . I am curious, and that is all." Conan Doyle paused a moment, as if to consider something. "I understand, sir, that many apothecaries in eras past were adept in alchemy, even magic."

Gaelan settled back into his chair by a degree, coiled as a snake. "That, sir, *may* have been more the case, say centuries ago—a blurring of the lines. However, Sir Arthur, *I* possess no personal knowledge, for example, of any apothecary or druggist nowadays claiming to hold in his hands the secrets of life through alchemical abracadabra, if that is what you are suggesting. As for myself, I am quite well tutored in chemistry and toxicology, and a disciple of Paracelsus. Many of his dicta still ring true for me. *Sola dosis facit venenum* . . . the dose makes the poison. Paracelsus coined that in the sixteenth century—today it is an axiom of modern pharmacy. He was both an apothecary and an alchemist— and a physician. I would consider myself in esteemed company to associate myself with his understanding of alchemy. He had neither desire to make gold from lead, nor to find the elusive lapis philosophorum, but only to reveal the medicinal science it concealed by its art."

Conan Doyle leaned forward confidentially, as if the rest of the company had vanished. "I have no desire, sir, to offend you. Forgive me if my questions seem more interrogation than polite dinner conversation. I am first and foremost a journalist, but my ardent interest is personal and much to do with my curiosity about the occult, as you may have guessed. I am quite sad to think about how much of the ancient arts were lost or have gone into hiding, along with their knowledge. Our ideas must be as broad as nature if they are to interpret nature, and if ideas—no matter how unusual they seem to our modern sensibilities—are destroyed and visionaries burnt either literally or metaphorically at the stake, we stand not a chance. And by the way, sir. I must aver that you are only one of a very few to have read 'Thoth.'"

"But to your point regarding our natural fear of the . . . unusual . . . On that, sir, at least," Gaelan said, "we might agree."

"Let us, then, if we may, Sir Arthur," Joseph repeated, clearing his throat, "go through to the drawing room. Miss Leckie, would you do us the honor of leading the way?"

"But of course," she agreed, patting Conan Doyle's hand affection-ately. "Shall we, my dear?" She rose, and the rest of the company fol-lowed her from the room.

Gaelan and Conan Doyle found themselves in a secluded corner of the large drawing room as the other guests mingled. Simon stood nearby, gesturing with growing disquietude that they should leave, and quite soon.

Gaelan turned his back on him as Conan Doyle leaned in again. "By the by, sir, I do recognize your unusual name—Erceldoune—I have come across it on occasion in my research into the Otherworld—"

"The Otherworld."

"Indeed. Where the fae folk rule. I've heard of an Erceldoune asso-ciated with legends of old, a certain Thomas Learmont de Erceldoune, a relationship with Tuatha de Danann, the—"

"Fairy folk, Sir Arthur?" Gaelan managed a laugh. "You, sir, hold me in exalted company, and I am sorry to disappoint you, however—"

"It is said that this man Erceldoune had a book possessing great power, given him by Airmid herself, Celtic goddess of healing, a gift for his act of kindness. Have you not heard the tale?"

"My family, old though it may be, Sir Arthur, boasts neither con-nection with the goddess Airmid nor any of her folk—the Tuatha de Danann, if indeed they ever existed. Besides, was not Airmid an Irish fairy? And I am, as are you, sir, of Scottish blood."

Gaelan glanced around the room again, finding Simon's anxious eyes beseeching him to end the exchange. "We'd best join the rest of the company. I see my dear friend Simon is quite unsettled, and we ought soon set off for—"

"It is a book of great healing," Conan Doyle continued. "All the diseases of the world—and their cures—held in a singular volume, said to be written by her very hand."

Gaelan paused, a petulant sigh escaping his lips. "I cannot say I can recall its mention, even amongst family lore." His lips tightened into a tense line as he stood. "Now if you will excuse me, sir, I grow tired and fear it is time Dr. *Simon* Bell and I return to his flat."

"Have you not done enough damage for one visit?" Simon's ice-gray glare drilled into Gaelan as they warmed themselves before Simon's fireplace.

"What do you mean?" Gaelan held his hands up to the blaze, suppressing a wince as a sharp pain threaded through his left hand. Unrepentant, he sighed; yet he understood Simon's displeasure. "I was bored; the chatter of the rich and idle was more than I could handle. I'd forgotten how lifeless it could be."

"It is not what I meant."

"I could not abide that insipid Miss Leckie and her tirade—all their tirades—against those of my trade."

"Do you disagree about Lentine?"

"You know I do not. But to classify the whole of the apothecary trade as a society of rogues and street mountebanks—"

Simon rose from his chair and paced in a small line, hands behind his back, tone clipped. "So for that you had to provoke Sir Arthur at his celebration?" Grabbing a poker, he stabbed at the hearth as if it were a dragon and he St. George.

"Had I not gotten them off that subject, I do not know what I might have done." The warmth of the fireplace, the aromatic burning of tinder and cigars did nothing to defuse the piercing pain that throbbed along the edge of his knuckles and beyond them, into the empty space where long ago existed three fingers. Eyes clamped shut, Gaelan sucked in a breath, trying to ride out the relentless assault he knew was but a phantom. "You might think after all this time it would not bother me still, but it does, oddly, as if the fingers were yet attached."

Simon's annoyance dissipated as he came near to examine Gaelan's hand. "And suggesting that Sherlock Holmes is somehow immortal was an improvement?" He prodded the smooth stump with his thumbs, and Gaelan grimaced with each touch. "I've some fresh ground ganja powder. A cup of tea from it might make it more bearable, unless you'd prefer something stronger. The kettle should be ready by now."

"Thank you; tea would be fine." The mere anticipation of relief began to soften the knife-sharp pain.

"Given that Sir Arthur is a journalist *and* has a particular interest in anything that seems to defy the laws of nature," Simon continued, returning from the other room with the tea service, handing Gaelan a delicate China cup, "I must say his line of questioning triggered by *your* own provocation was disquieting, to say the least."

The warmth of the cup permeated Gaelan's hand as he savored the tea, more soothing than the finest whisky. "Thank you, Simon. Already, the pain dissipates. It seemed quite fitting to offer the idea—about Holmes. I am, in fact, quite curious about how Sir Arthur intends to wrest his hero from that watery grave. And just because I made some oblique suggestion, must you forthwith believe I've painted a scarlet letter upon my forehead?"

"I speak not just of the Holmes. He came a hairbreadth from—"

Gaelan cut off Simon's next parry with a wave of his arm. "Indeed," he said, anticipating. "I must confess that his interrogation about my legendary ancestors unsettled me, as did his reference to that book."

"What if he has some knowledge of it? *Useful* knowledge. God knows the trail has long since dried up, and he is, after all, a journalist—a rather clever one. You might wish to inquire further for what he knows—"

Gaelan slammed his fist into the arm of the chair. "No. He knows no more than you or I. He was fishing, and that is all." There was no more to be said on the matter. Full stop.

Simon grabbed the poker again, and sparks flared as he drove it deep into the hearth, his patience clearly at an end. "Perhaps it is time for you to go. More than a week has passed since my sister's funeral, yet you are still here. Had you been so steadfast whilst Eleanor was yet living and breathing, she might have been happier, but because of your fear—"

Gaelan flinched, stung by the truth of Simon's words. But Simon, too, was grieving. Yes, he'd had no choice but to leave. But what of the intervening years? Might there have been an opportunity for a reunion with her? He sipped the last of the ganja tea and set down the cup.

The clattering of iron startled Gaelan from his seat as Simon hurled the poker into its holder.

"You're a bit skittish tonight, I daresay," declared Simon. His voice was now devoid of all anger.

Gaelan retreated to a far corner of the room, his back to Simon, mustering the scattered remnants of his composure. "Perhaps I was more unnerved by Sir Arthur than I considered. As for your sister, I *could* not stay in England at the time, and this you well know." He turned, now facing Simon: his enemy, his lone friend in the world.

His combativeness dissipated as excuses failed him. Simon was right; he had to get away—from Simon and from England, where too many memories haunted too near. "Yes, you have a point. And perhaps it is time for me to reinvent myself, as it were. I think I'll repair to Scotland for a bit. Perhaps Aberdeen." He could predict Simon's reaction before a word more was spoken.

"Do not dare!" Simon roared. "Do not dare set foot anywhere near Aberdeen. You shall bring my niece nothing but misery."

Gaelan considered his limited options. "I cannot go back to America. Not now, and perhaps not for a long time to come."

"Why in the devil not?"

Gaelan dropped his voice to a bare whisper, sitting again. "I was nearly discovered, and I fear . . . There was an incident, and I—"

"I have never quite understood, Erceldoune," Simon replied, pouring himself a cup of the tea, "why you yet live in the shadows, even now, well-nigh a generation past the time anyone would care you'd eluded the noose. You were certainly enough in plain sight tonight!"

"It is not that sort of discovery I fear. But I yet live in abject terror each time I spy an advertising poster for one of those wretched freak shows come to town."

"I hear they have all but vanished in America. Too distasteful."

"Indeed, that may be the case, yet not so much as you think." Gaelan had hoped to keep his temper in check; Simon was grieving for the last of his close relations. Yet, how could the man be so obtuse? Gaelan sprang from his seat again, striding across the room, his hands clenched into tight fists before wheeling on his companion. "Tell me, Bell," he said finally, his tone sharper than intended, "what do you think would transpire should my condition . . . our condition . . . come to light? How can you not comprehend? The fortunes of wars, the balance of power world-over shall forever alter if one side or the other possesses such a secret. One to which we both hold the key?"

Gaelan seethed, but stopped before the discussion devolved into vicious argument. Simon well knew that men with naught but greed in their hearts yet coveted the elusive Elixir of Life. Why, then, this shallow disregard for . . . ? Gaelan fought against further provocation on the matter. He pinched the bridge of his nose, applying pressure to forestall the gnawing in his forehead.

"Do not worry, Simon. I shall not play the interloper—in Aberdeen. This I promise you." Restless energy propelled Gaelan from one window to the next, despite the headache, as he paused at each but a moment to look up into the starlit sky, hoping it might settle him. "But I can and shall also know that my daughter and her family are happy, and at least observe, if only from afar, their accomplishments. How can you reckon what my heart yearns for, and how it tears me to shreds knowing I must live ever in exile from my grandchildren and great-grandchildren, shall never feel their tiny hands ruffling my hair—" He turned away.

"It is far too late for that, for all your words of regret. There would have been ways to manage it—as I have!"

Simon's harsh words hurt far worse than the cruelest physical torture. "I had *no* choice," Gaelan insisted. "And is it not also true that I saved her life? Perhaps I was a coward to stay away for so many years, but the very thought of discovery . . . It is only now, sixty years hence, that I feel safe to return here."

The weight of solitary exile bore down on Gaelan's shoulders and crushed his throat until he was unable to breathe. Yes, Aberdeen would be a risk, all the more now, since he had come face-to-face with his daughter, his dear Ariadne, a woman who knew him solely as an acquaintance to her "cousin" Simon.

"Yes. You speak the truth, and I have always been grateful for what you did for us both." Regret suffused Simon's countenance. "Nevertheless . . . the sight of you is more than I can stand, the representation of all I have lost, and now with Eleanor's death . . . She is the last, you know. I am as alone as you on this earth, despite what you might believe."

"Aye, I do know that. So let us drink to Eleanor a last time."

Simon poured two tumblers. They drank down the fine Scotch without another word.

Gaelan peered into his empty glass. The emptiness and loneliness, the unrelenting pain that ever emanated from his disfigured left hand: a precipitous burden that threatened to crash down upon him. He strode to the mantelpiece and stopped, scrutinizing the facets in his crystal tumbler before slamming it into the wood. It shattered, slicing into his hand; he watched the blood flow down his arm, darkening the ruffled shirtsleeve. "I shall bid you a good night then."

By morning, Gaelan was gone.

CHICAGO'S NORTH SHORE, PRESENT DAY

CHAPTER 1

Three hours and 125 autographs later, Simon Bell emerged into the unexpected heat of the late-March afternoon, flexing his cramped right hand. His pseudonym, Anthony C. Danforth, swam across his vision, a ghostlike image in red Sharpie; blinking did not vanquish it. His latest novel, another Holmes pastiche, had risen to number fifteen on the *New York Times* best-seller list. "Holmes resurrected in the style of his times! Danforth channels Conan Doyle with a rare authenticity—again," read the review. Simon might add, *Victorian mysteries written by a Victorian mystery.*

The Gingko trees along the Evanston shoreline were already green; their cloven, odd leaves provided a momentary distraction as he wove his way through the baby carriages, skateboards, and bicycles. But there it was again: indelible.

The warm breeze washed over him as he dusted off a sandy white boulder above the beach. Simon draped his trench coat over the rock, and he sat, attention riveted on a pair of noisy gulls rowing over a discarded ant-infested hamburger.

Simon reveled in his well-deserved "reclusive writer" moniker, and it was a rare occasion for him to venture into so public a space. The brave new virtual world made for a handy castle keep, with moats constructed of Twitter feeds and Facebook postings manned by battalions of publicists and their minions. None of his affair.

A familiar figure meandered the beach below, silhouetted in the glare, and Simon did a double take. As if reading his thoughts, the man turned, shielding his eyes against the sun as he peered up from the sand. What the devil was Gaelan Erceldoune doing down there at the water's edge?

Simon loosened his tie just a bit, but thought better of laying his bespoke suit jacket beside him on the guano-stained rock. He thought of calling out, but Gaelan was already climbing the boulders, a rare smile creasing the corners of his eyes as he waved.

Breathless and smirking, face flushed with exertion, he dropped to sit cross-legged on a nearby rock. "Typical of you to dress like a bloody CEO on a fine spring day! Decided to descend from your mountaintop to rub elbows with the masses?"

Simon brushed off the remark with a scowl. "What, no warm greeting, then? And you embody, I suppose, the perfect model of a man?" Gaelan appeared much worse off than Simon had seen him in a long, long time: blown pupils, dark smudges below each eye, a slight tremor in his hand, unshaven . . . worn and washed out. Lank, greasy hair hung loose to his shoulders; his jeans were threadbare and faded almost white; the last vestiges of a cigarette burned between his lips. His expression, though, was as penetrating as ever.

"I suppose I don't have to point out that you look like hell." A pang of guilt—should he have checked in? Made sure Gaelan was all right? Was he living rough here on the beach, one of those gray, stooped vagrants pushing shopping carts along the park paths?

Gaelan plucked the cigarette from his mouth, holding its nearly burned-out remains precariously between his thumb and index finger. Ash drifted from the stub, glowing red, before fading to gray as it fell to the rocks. He shrugged, staring straight out into the horizon. "You just have. Bad night."

Shorthand Simon knew well.

Gaelan sucked in the last of the hand-rolled cigarette before crushing it on the boulder. "Might I nick a fag off you? I'm out."

"You *are* aware they're bad for the health?" That drew a raucous laugh. Simon handed him his pack of Silk Cut Purple.

"Filters?"

"Want them or not?"

"I asked for one fag, not the whole bloody pack. I'm fine, Bell. And I *don't* need your bloody charity." Gaelan noticed a battered paperback on Simon's knee, quickly snatching it up. "*Scandal in Bohemia.* Rereading Holmes? Or pinching his ideas for your next best seller?"

"Just reading."

"Have you not yet committed the entire canon to memory after all these years?"

"It gives me pleasure—nostalgia of a sort, I suppose, like having him nearby again. And you are clearly not 'fine.'"

"These fags are shite." Gaelan stared down at the beach, ignoring Simon's assessment. "Will you look at them, those lads down there? And that kite! I've never seen anything its like. And they say dragons are extinct! Brilliant!" He fished a gold-edged iPhone from his jeans pocket and snapped a photograph. "Have you got one of these things, Bell? They're fucking marvelous."

Simon snorted. "How can anything still be marvelous for you? After all you've been through . . . *we've* been through."

"Do you know what your problem is?"

Besides the inability to die? Besides the fact that I am daily tormented by my dead wife? Simon knew what was coming next. "I'm *certain* you're going to tell me."

"Your imagination is mired in the nineteenth century. You, my dear friend, are two centuries behind the times."

"Says the man with the antique shop."

"Antiquarian *books. And* I'm quite good at the trade, a noted scholar in some circles." Gaelan thumbed the fragile yellowed pages of the paperback, half-separated from the spine, before fixing his gaze once again out toward the horizon. "The shop is a brisk enough business. With the Internet, eBay . . . Even Sotheby's has an online auction with which I've made a fair penny. I still teach the odd class at Northwestern, do a lecture here and there. I more than make ends meet."

"Then what? You look like you've been *living* on the beach, not just taking a stroll." Even as he asked the question, Simon cursed himself—after seventeen decades, one thing he should have learned was that it was never a good idea to get sucked into Gaelan's chaos.

Gaelan scrubbed the heels of his hands into his eyes, his voice so soft Simon could scarcely discern it above the beat of the waves below. "It's getting worse again. I'm trapped in a fucking labyrinth, and I cannot figure a way out—"

Compassion nibbled at the edges of Simon's irritation. "Nightmares?" He was aware that much of Gaelan's often-acerbic attitude was smoke and mirrors. How many late-night calls had there been over the years when Simon would find Gaelan hiding in the dark of his flat above his shop, cowering beneath a table or in the corner of a closet, panicky and shaken? He would seem better, almost normal for a time, and then something would trigger another bout. What was it this time?

"My hold is slipping these days, more and more. Can't sleep; can't eat." An unbidden admission, and certainly not without cost.

"Why have you said nothing to me? You've not rung me up in more than six months—"

Gaelan shrugged, brushing it off. A harsh breeze rattled the branches, dropping the temperature by ten degrees as tendrils of dark gray cumulonimbus overtook the sapphire sky. Swirls of black-green clouds edged the steel gray above the horizon to the east.

"Bloody hell!" Simon jumped, almost slipping down the steep incline as lightning shredded the sky and hail pelted them, icy marbles lobbed by the clouds. The air froze as the wind blasted, and incongruously, it began to snow. Hard. They made a run for Simon's BMW.

"Drop you anywhere?" Simon asked between gasps.

"My shop will do."

The doorbells jangled as they entered through the door below the sign: "G. Erceldoune—Rare Books and Antiquities"—a threshold back in time. Simon only wished that Gaelan had not located the shop beneath the Brown Line elevated tracks.

Simon surveyed the shop, its wood and bronze not much different than the apothecary where he'd first met Mr. Gaelan Erceldoune. But instead of jars and bottles were bookshelves; instead of the aroma of cinnabar and citrus, mint and jasmine petal tea, there was the musty fragrance of old vellum and leather.

Booksellers or not, Erceldoune's shop evoked the bitterest of memories—images better left to the cobwebs of time.

Simon drummed his fingers on the counter. "I might have a line on the book. *The* book."

Gaelan flinched just enough for Simon to notice.

"What? Did you not hear me? I might have located your book."

"Yes, I heard you. How many times is this, then, and each time futile?" Gaelan stepped behind the counter and rolled a cigarette, his eyelids fluttering closed as he lit up and took a deep drag. "Ah. So much better than that shite you smoke."

Simon expected dismissive, but this was complete disinterest. "Really, Erceldoune! What's wrong? I can't help but notice—"

"You will tell me I'm overreacting, Simon. I know you. But it's . . . There was an article. In the *Guardian*. They're renovating the London Imperial War Museum. In Lambeth Road."

Simon was confused, anxiety ratcheting up a notch. "But what has it to do with the book?"

"Nothing at all to do with the bloody book. The Imperial fucking War Museum. Do you not remember . . . ?" Gaelan drummed his fingers on the counter. "They've torn the place apart—"

Recognition dawned.

"They've unearthed *diaries*, Simon. *Handley's* diaries—in the bowels of Bedlam. *Extensive* journals, dated early 1840s."

The name alone sent a chill through Simon. And Gaelan, even nearly two centuries later, was still tormented by years of torture endured there, under the mad doctor Handley's "care." "So what? There's not the remotest chance they'll—"

"You're not fucking listening. They describe—in detail—experiments and 'private freak shows,' as they are called. You want to know why I'm fucking falling apart? Now you do. And how long will it be, do you think, till they come calling?"

LONDON, 1837

CHAPTER 2

The damp night air stank of death, horses' leavings, decayed fish, and disease . . . so, so much disease. Dr. Simon Bell ignored the rising bile in his gut as he strode through the streets of London toward his destination.

Sad-eyed waifs tugged at his greatcoat, their hands trembling in the cold November air. He fled past them, vaguely aware of their presence as he pulled away from their grasp. "Not tonight; I'm sorry." Waving them off, Simon sloshed through miniature rivers on the cobblestones, remnants of the afternoon's rainstorm.

Breathless, shoes soaked through, and trouser cuffs dripping, he stopped, uncertain, lost among the buildings and market stands, each resembling the next in the maze of Smithfield Market. His head whipped one direction then the next through the yellow haze of the streetlamps until he recognized his destination.

Ornate lettering edged in gold sat atop the double-bowed windows: "Gaelan R. Erceldoune, Apothecary."

He'd not seen Erceldoune in many months. The apothecary had long been a popular choice among physicians: clever and well-read—and a bit of a legend. Extraordinary medicines, it was said round the club in hushed and admiring tones, were concocted in Erceldoune's back room and found not in any modern pharmacopeia. Cures long since considered magical nonsense, conjured with herbs and rare metals out of books with odd-sounding titles. More effective than any in current usage.

Simon knew the apothecary was as skilled at modern chemistry as he was at grinding standard salves and dispensing medicines, inventing the most exquisite of preparations months before they would be discussed at the Royal Society. They'd been cordial, never friends exactly, but for ten years they'd shared a mutual fascination with the latest discoveries, no matter the discipline: science, philosophy, literature, languages. Simon had always looked forward to their late-night conversations over a good whisky and a game of chess in Erceldoune's laboratory.

But in truth, Simon knew little about Gaelan Erceldoune, who would never, for all his apparent brilliance, be a part of his society—not someone to introduce round the club, nor ask to dinner. At the end of the day, Simon would return to his London mansion and Erceldoune would retire to his tiny Smithfield flat above the shop.

Then Erceldoune's wife passed away, and the apothecary slammed his door to physicians. He'd refused all requests for the filling of even the simplest of prescriptions, yet his shop remained open to all others—the wretched souls of Smithfield. There was speculation aplenty as to why Erceldoune would so abruptly forsake so lucrative an income source, but Simon never inquired, however much he'd missed their discourse. There were plenty of apothecaries in London eager for the trade.

At times, Simon had wondered why a man as clever as Erceldoune dwelled amid the vile zoology of Smithfield Market. No doubt, he could afford a better abode, away from the reek of animals permeating the air and filth that ran like a river through the streets.

But at this singular moment, Simon's sole thought was the hope that Erceldoune would not refuse him now. He must make the apothecary comprehend the dire nature of Sophie's situation. For if *she* died, Simon knew he would not be long for this earth. Sophie was his anchor, his entire life.

Week by week, Simon's grip on the frayed end of his oil-slick tether slipped further and further as Sophie's tumor grew, a malignant evil upon her breast. Then he noticed the second one, grotesque and purple-red, protruding from the hollow beneath her arm. And his heart stopped, for he knew there was little else to be done for her—by anyone.

Erceldoune's shop was dark—not a surprise for the lateness of the hour. But the dim light filtering through a curtained window above the shop gave Simon hope that the apothecary might be at home and awake. But was it right to disturb him at home, after he'd closed for the night? Urgency dictated he ignore propriety and the stack of returned, unopened letters. How could the apothecary refuse him in the darkest hour of his desperation?

Simon pounded on a door at the side of the building. It rattled, old and tired; slivers of peeling green paint fell onto the wet pavement. "Mr. Erceldoune! I've need of your assistance, if you please, sir!" For several moments, he continued slamming his fists against the desiccated surface, certain he would break either the rotting wood or his hand at the next turn.

Simon stayed his fist at the welcome clang of a turning bolt, and then the door opened a crack. Simon held his breath as a finger of light slipped through, too bright in the dark alleyway. "Shop's closed for the night. Come back tomorrow, if you please. We open at eight sharp." The door rasped as it closed, leaving Simon in the drizzle, stunned. Had Erceldoune not recognized him? Perhaps it was too dark to have seen him properly. He pounded again.

"Mr. Erceldoune! It is Simon Bell come to call. Please, sir, it is urgent. For some weeks now I have been endeavoring to contact you and—"

The hinges creaked as the door opened again, this time wider. Dark, apprehensive eyes, luminescent in candlelight, scrutinized him; their wary gaze penetrated deep within Simon's resolve, forcing him back a step.

"What is it, then?" The inquiry was frigid as the November night.

Simon pressed on, ignoring an urge to flee. "Do you not know me, then? It is Dr. Si—"

Erceldoune replied with a sneer. "I know who you are, have known since I saw you from my window, before you took to breaking down my door. Now please, if you would be so kind as to leave! I've nothing to say to *any* of London's *gentlemen* physicians. Not even Dr. Simon Bell!" The words rasped, bitter poison droplets.

"My wife is ill . . . dying. Even tonight, she . . . I think she may be . . ." Simon did nothing to conceal his anguish. Would it be enough of an appeal to gain an audience, after camaraderie had come to naught?

After a long moment, Erceldoune stepped aside, allowing Simon to pass beyond the threshold. They climbed a rickety, winding staircase, entering a spacious sitting room at the top. The room—comfortable, even elegant—seemed anomalous here in Smithfield, so like its owner.

The sour-sweet smell of ink and old books, whisky, and dying embers permeated Simon's nostrils. He sank into a faded chair, noticing the brimming shelves lining three walls of the room—thousands of volumes reaching to the corniced ceiling, piled high on tables and chairs. In the amber glow of candlelight, the room reminded Simon of a Baroque painting: organized chaos, shadows and light, great stillness, yet activity teeming beneath the surface. But there was a jarring untidiness about the room as well. Papers, quills, and open jars of ink were strewn among the books. Jars of herbs, dirty brass pestles, and broken crucibles littered the floor. None of this fit the meticulous man Simon had known for years.

Erceldoune balanced a tumbler half-filled with amber liquid on his knee, making a game of keeping it steady there. "Why have you disturbed me this night, Dr. Bell?"

Simon shivered from the iciness of the apothecary's welcome, so unlike their cordial relationship had been.

Erceldoune scooped up his glass with a deft move, downing its contents in a single gulp. He poured another, emptying the faceted crystal decanter. Simon noted the tremor in Erceldoune's hand as he thrust his fingers through his hair, the tremble in every word, the almost nervous way in which he threw back another whisky. He had been the most reliable apothecary in London, whatever it was worth, for most of them were reprobates, enriched off the misfortune of others. But now?

Could it have been the drink that changed him thus? Simon hesitated a moment, wondering if he had been wrong to come here. No. This was his last chance, the only chance, to save Sophie—and himself.

"My wife has cancer of the breast. It has now spread. I . . ." Simon was unable to urge another word past the clot of tears in his throat.

Erceldoune held up a hand, pinning Simon with his steely eyes. "Then she is dead. Had I a cure for that, I should be a famous and wealthy man and not living thus in cramped quarters above a shop. If that is what brought you from your warm home and into the night, I am afraid you've wasted your time—and mine. We are therefore done. I bid you a good night, sir." He poured another whisky, downing it in one, before rising shakily, urging Simon toward the door.

The corrosive finality to Erceldoune's words burned through Simon's chest, leaving him breathless. Simon vaulted from his chair, pounding his fist on the armrest. How could Erceldoune dismiss him, with nary a shred of compassion? "No! Hear me out! Are we not friends, at least? How can you—"

Erceldoune's hand was on the doorknob, knuckles white. His cheerless laugh stung with the precision of a saber. "Friends? We were never that. *Never* that!" Anger and the slur of liquor tinted his words with a deep brogue Simon had never before noticed.

He'd been through this so many times the past year, searching for something—anything at all—to give him hope, but each time brought only disappointment. A long row of failed cures lined Simon's laboratory bench, experiments from the workrooms of esteemed colleagues and patent cures from street-corner hucksters. Pitied by friends and laughed at by professional rivals, Simon had become somewhat of a joke around the club. But he cared not a jot.

"But do you not recall those evenings when we—"

"Aye, I do. That you, a gentleman, *deigned* to associate yourself with the likes of me—that is, beyond the fulfilling of your instructions. I should be grateful, then, for that, should I?" he snarled, quiet and dangerous. "And for that I now owe my services at this late hour?"

Simon was dumbfounded by the venom punctuating each word. "No! Of course you do not *owe* me a thing, my dear Mr. Erceldoune. Why ever would—"

Erceldoune continued the tirade. "You and your physician brethren—*fine* gentlemen all, sauntering the vaunted halls of Oxford and Cambridge and Edinburgh. You know naught of healing but leeches and laudanum, opium, and bloodletting. How many times these years have I'd the presence of mind to alter the prescriptions of reckless physicians whose cures would otherwise be poison? Yet *I* am unqualified to treat the unwell?"

"Mr. Erceldoune, to speak true, I do not understand—"

Erceldoune's countenance softened from bitter rage to resignation. His shoulders slumped, and his eyes misted over. He let go of the doorknob and moved to the window, looking down into the street for a moment as if to compose himself before turning back into the room, blinking as if he were seeing Simon for the first time.

"Forgive me. Where are my manners? Please, will you not sit a spell?"

Simon sighed, relieved. He sat. "I—"

"In truth, there is nothing I can do for her." Erceldoune threw up his hands in an exasperated gesture. "Your wife has cancer. It is a piteous tragedy, but one for which I can be no help to you. Women die; wives die. It is sad indeed, but what can one do?"

The finality of Erceldoune's pronouncement ran cold through Simon's veins. He shivered. Was this to be the bitter outcome? Nowhere to go, nothing left to do but stand by helpless as Sophie died . . . Simon struggled to maintain his composure as he stood to take his leave. "Is there *nothing*, then, you can do for my wife? Nothing at all?"

"No. I am sorry, Dr. Bell."

A gilt-framed miniature portrait on the mantelpiece caught Simon's eye: a woman posed in a garden adorned in white roses, her yellow silk dress twirling about her. *Caitrin Kinston?*

"That is Lord Kinston's daughter, is it not? Why have you got—" And then it dawned on him, the pieces fitting into place. He'd heard Kinston's daughter had died of typhus a year before, in the 1836 epidemic. He remembered it now, the whole sorry tale, how she'd run off with someone well beneath her station ten years past, infuriating her father. The match had astonished all of London society. "Mesmerized," he'd heard back then. "By some scoundrel. How else would that inferior sort have his way with her?"

Had that been Erceldoune? How could Simon not have realized, even after ten years' acquaintance with the apothecary?

"Caitrin—my wife, and yes, Kinston's daughter. So? What of it? She died of typhus last year, as did our wee babe Iain."

"My deepest condolences, Mr. Erceldoune. I should have known—"

"So you see, Dr. Bell. I am of little help to the dying. I could not even save my own wife and child." He clasped his hands behind his back, his eyes cast down as he drifted from door to fireplace and back as if wrestling with something deep within.

"But," Simon offered, "you realize it could not have been your fault, your wife's death. I am quite certain you did all you could do . . . within your limitations as an apothecary. But perhaps even had she been treated by a qualified physician—"

"Aye, she *was* 'treated' by 'qualified' physicians," Erceldoune spat, "the lot of them her father's retainers. Yet for all their medical diplomas, memberships in the Royal Society, and titles, the earl's physicians could not save her."

Erceldoune was shaking now, hands balled tight into fists. "But *I* could have. And of all the fools about London *practicing* medicine, I reckoned that you might have been the one to understand that. Yet it seems I have vastly overestimated you." He shook his head in disappointment, collapsing into a chair. "Had her father not meddled, had he not *stolen* her from her bed, my *son* from his cradle, they would both be yet alive."

"How? How do you know that? No one can know that, not with typhus. It's—"

"I *do.*"

CHAPTER 3

Gaelan considered Simon Bell: the eyes rimmed in red, the bruising beneath them suggesting a lack of sleep, the pallor of his skin, the grim set to his mouth all spoke of desperation, a companion Gaelan knew too well.

A tremor of empathy flared up the skin of Gaelan's arms and back. Bell had never been one of those incompetent fools populating far too much of London's posh medical fraternity. He was, after all, grandson to Benjamin Bell. Gaelan revered the grandfather, a brilliant Edinburgh physician—a surgeon as well, and a man who knew his way around a diseased body, unafraid of dirtying his hands in the blood and guts of it. Had Gaelan been too hasty in severing his tie with the grandson, cutting him off along with the rest of the dandies displaying their Oxford diplomas as pretense for knowledge of healing?

Contrite, Gaelan stood and ushered Simon back to his chair before sitting opposite him. He recognized the haunted look on Simon's face from each time he had caught his own reflection this past year.

"My father-in-law—your Lord Kinston—sent his men for Caitrin and wee Iain whilst I was out attending to a young boy, also suffering of typhus." He shook his head derisively at the bitter irony of it. "And now? That lad runs about in the streets, robust and wild, whilst Caitrin and Iain molder beneath the ground. I knew how to purge the fever, vanquish the rash. I'd studied the disease well, fashioned a medicine that would have—" His hands clenched, fingernails digging into the soft flesh of his palms.

Simon was staring at him, observing, judging. *Why does he not leave this place and attend to his dying wife?* Gaelan scrubbed the heels of his hands hard in his eyes, trying to erase the gathered tears. "Had she been not so weak by then, my Caitrin would have fought them off, a protective mother hawk, she was. She knew I could help in ways they never could, believed in my . . . my skill . . . my . . . deep knowledge of the

29

healing arts. But for typhus, the dose had to wait for the exact moment when . . . or it would do nothing—or worse. But before . . . before I had the chance to—" Gaelan's words lurched past the bile burning in his esophagus. "Before I even had the bloody chance, Kinston's men came. I failed them both—all I had in the world, my beloved Caitrin and wee Iain." Telling it aloud drained Gaelan of all energy.

"Might I ask who treated her?"

Gaelan looked up, realizing he wasn't alone. He needed more drink, but the decanter was now dry. "*Sir* Phillip Rivers, a ridiculous fop with the good fortune to be born to a title, but not enough good fortune to be firstborn. So medical college for him, then on to an esteemed career as Kinston's toady."

"Sir *Phillip*? But he is quite able—and a most excellent reputation; he is no fop, sir. You could not wish a finer . . . And with typhus it is impossible to know—"

Furious, Gaelan leapt from his chair, sweeping the empty decanter from the table. "Have you not been listening, Bell? Under his *so-called* care, they *died*. Had he but left to me—"

"I beg you to see reason, Mr. Erceldoune. But can you not put yourself in her father's place . . . understand that he wished for his daughter only the best of care. From a physician with the best university education. That she died under his care is, to be certain, a terrible shame, yet—"

Gaelan had little stomach to continue this debate, but futility failed to rein in his frustration. "How dare you presume to know anything of my education, my training? Indeed, when the residents of Smithfield Market fall ill, where are the Sirs Phillip and Drs. Bell then, hmm? Would he come calling? Would you?"

He would delight in testing his mettle as a practitioner against any and all *gentleman* physicians. "Yet," he said, pointing his finger in Simon's chest, "you come to me, and *not* one of your peers. Forgive me, sir, if I find no small measure of irony in this situation."

Gaelan glanced at Caitrin's portrait, then at his guest. Bell had not come to debate the state of medicine, not this night. And it was unfair to challenge him thus. Bell had come as a desperate husband, a man not much different than himself a year past: frantic and terrified. "I believe I can help you," he whispered, and Simon exhaled a long, deep breath.

"Have you truly something that can drive away the demon cancer?"

That was the question, then, was it not? There were so many professed "cures," volumes of them lining two bookshelves, and not one of them worth the effort of concocting. There was but one possibility, and that in a book so extraordinary, so dangerous, it had long ago cost his family its lands and fortune, his parents and elder sisters their lives. Then there was his own life, altered forevermore by the power contained within its extraordinary pages. Should he now presume to take it up once again? What then, should something go wrong, an incorrect measurement, an instruction misapprehended? Either, or both, quite possible with a manuscript of such infinite complexity.

Tendrils of icy fear crept up his neck as he contemplated the decision. An opportunity, perhaps it might be—should the medicine cure Bell's wife. The demonstration of his true skill so much in contrast to the polite distance of the physician's impotence: laudanum and leeches. Vindication for him and all of his trade, too often maligned, the object of derision for the few frauds among them.

Gaelan scoured the bookshelves, searching the titles, although he knew exactly where to find what he sought. "I have an ancient pharmacopeia," he explained, unable to think of a better description for the volume. "But the recipes in it are unusual. I have used the book only rarely and, I confess, not for cancer. But if there be at all a cure for medicine's most ruthless enemy, I venture it would be in this remarkable book."

The volume he had hidden high on the topmost shelf, away from his sight. Placed there after Caitrin and Iain died, it was too much a reminder of what might have been had he the opportunity to use it to save them. The steep ladder groaned as Gaelan mounted the rungs. Reaching the top, he stretched his arm yet higher, finally dislodging the large leather volume.

"*This* is your miraculous book?" Bell called up from the base of the ladder, startling Gaelan as he descended and nearly causing him to lose his balance.

He ignored the derision in Bell's tone, sweeping past him as he brushed his shirtsleeve across the cover; a swirl of dust erupted between them. Then with a rag pulled from his trouser pocket, Gaelan burnished the cover with meticulous, minute strokes, revealing the engraved image of an intricate tree. Emerging from deep within the leather, its bare branches entwined and diverged into snakes, each consuming its own tail—an ouroboros. The snakes merged, transforming once again into an elaborate border of interconnected and twisted helices. Gaelan beheld the marvelous engraving, considering the complexity of its design.

The hawthorn: sigil of balance between life and death. A reminder that all medicines were a paradox, curative or poisonous and, as Gaelan well knew, too often producing unexpected consequences. And then there were the ouroboroses—they were alchemy's symbol for the circularity of life: life from life, life from death, from death to living in an eternal chain. For what was the true nature of medicine's practice? To lift the dying, to forestall death's knock at the door, and recommence life. But Gaelan knew, more than most, that the ouroboros also signified life eternal . . . immortality, alchemy's *eternal* quest.

"This volume, indeed, dates back many centuries, Dr. Bell. It was, I am told, a gift given to an ancestor of mine." He leaned in conspiratorially, whispering into Bell's ear. "It is a unique book of healing, said to have within its recipes the cure for all sickness that might befall man, no matter how dread." Gaelan continued to polish the leather, bringing forth colors as vibrant as fine stained glass. Every engraved line radiated metallic inks: ruby, lapis, emerald, gold, and silver.

Standing close by, Simon thrust a finger at the volume, a sneer curling his lip. "What is this, then?" he demanded. "This is no medical book; it seems more alchemist absurdity than anything. And I *suppose* it contains magical incantations to be recited whilst conjuring these 'ancient' recipes?" Bell spat the words, disdain plain on his features. "Do you forget, apothecary, to whom you speak? I am no peasant awed by pretty pictures and talk of ancient remedies."

Gaelan pressed down on his ire, difficult as it was. Bell had come to him, not the other way around. But he understood that Bell was at his wits' end, much like any other patient. "I assure you *this* is no book of sorcery, no fraud. All is of this natural world. Its *magic*, if such a word signifies at all, is solely within the elegant and inventive, but proper, combining of herbs and elements. Magic is a relative term. What is now known scientific fact was once feared as sorcery, its proponents exiled, executed, ripped from exalted society, and thrust—" Gaelan halted himself from going further, cutting too close to his own truths.

The book originated, Gaelan knew, with a people out of myth, a goddess of healing long ago vanished from the face of this earth. But who was to say their knowledge was any less than the greatest of the Enlightenment's science, yet called by another name?

This he could not say to Bell, for then Bell would walk out without another word, thinking him mad or one of those street mountebanks who sold curatives from horse carts in the marketplace. "Please allow me, Dr. Bell, to save her as I was not able to help my dear wife and wee son."

"Is there a harm in trying it?" Bell pleaded.

The question should have been expected, yet still it took Gaelan aback. There was too much of the manuscript beyond his grasp, and some amount of fear. Yet he was confident he could comprehend one recipe, at least, down to the last letter, and used well, the medicine would, in fact, cure Mrs. Bell.

After all, he explained to Bell, had his own wife and son been left to his devices and not taken from their beds, he would have used this very book to prepare a medicine. "There is potential harm in any medication, as I am certain you know, but if you heed the instructions I write out for you, it shall be fine. But," he warned, emphasizing each word, "the recipes from this book require a unique sort of care; there can be no improvisation, no room for even the minutest error in handling or dosing."

Simon nodded; he seemed resigned to the risk. "I ask you, sir, what sort of consequences might befall a woman already written off as dead by every physician in London? None will touch her; no remedies remain, no medicine." Almost to himself, he added, "I have little choice but to trust you."

"Good, then. It is settled. I shall prepare it for, shall we say, ten o'clock tomorrow morning? Now if you would not mind leaving me to my work—" Gaelan led Simon down the stairs and out through the side door, watching as he tried to hail a carriage, recalling the last time he'd employed the ouroboros book.

CHAPTER 4

Simon staggered through his foyer, clothes soaked through, barely noticing his cousin Dr. James Bell, hands behind his back, awaiting him, foot nervously tapping on the marble tiles. But Simon could not fail to miss the disapproving glare examining him head to foot as he removed his sodden coat and boots.

"My God, Simon! You are a sight. You'll do Sophie no good if you collapse! And where the devil have you been in the pouring rain?"

Simon had taken far too long with Erceldoune, and it had started to rain again. With no carriage to hire, he'd slogged the two miles home in the downpour. A brandy and blazing fire was needed, but it must wait until he'd seen Sophie.

James was perhaps the last person Simon wished to see at the moment. In a different family, his politically astute cousin might by now have a seat in the House of Commons, but he was a Bell. As other families cultivated politicians and barristers, bankers and explorers, the Family Bell cultivated physicians: successful physicians, respected physicians, invariably well-connected physicians like James, who was newly appointed to serve the young Queen Victoria.

"Stay if you wish; *I* am going up to my wife." He had no time for James and his searching expression, ever judging him these past months. Simon refused to countenance any discussion regarding his whereabouts—or Sophie.

"Then let us go up together."

"As you wish." He shrugged, too weary and anxious to argue.

The portraits of Simon's ancestors stood in judgment as he mounted the stairs—generations of Bell patriarchs. His mettle as both physician and husband strained beneath the oppressive weight of their stares. But would they have fared any better in the face of such a monstrous medical villain as cancer?

Dread knifed through Simon's chest as he approached the gallery—as it had these past months whenever he neared the top of the stairs. Would he find his dear Sophie dead and cold? And what then? How long would he survive without her by his side? Not a month.

The threshold to Sophie's boudoir had been, for the fifteen years of their marriage, an open invitation into her private niche—an anticipated delight. Now the room held not the fragrance of her rosebud bath salts and jasmine perfume, but of pall of disease and impending death: putrefied flesh and lye soap. First one step beyond the doorstop and then another until he fell to the mattress and at her side.

For now, Sophie slept; at least she looked at peace. A lock of blueblack hair had fallen across her eyes; Simon brushed it gently aside, kissing her softly at the temple. She was feverish again. He dampened a small cloth in a bowl of cool water, wiping her face with it before placing it across her forehead. He felt James's presence at the door, the man watching his every move, his reproving eyes bearing down on Simon like his ancestors'.

James stepped forward, placing a hand on Simon's shoulder. "She's not likely to improve much. You need to prepare yourself, cousin."

As if there were a way to prepare your heart to be cleaved in two. "I cannot simply wait and do nothing. Watch her die a little more each passing hour, and this fever . . . it consumes her; I fear it will hasten her demise." Sophie's chest rose and fell, slow and even breaths—a deception. For just beneath the surface lay the truth of it.

James sat upon the other side of the bed; quietly, he removed the brocade blanket, exposing Sophie's chest. Small beads of perspiration were joined there by gooseflesh as James prodded the swelling prominent upon her breast, repeating the task in the pit of her arm. She did not stir from her sleep.

"The cancer has weakened her; you know that, cousin. She cannot fight off fevers of any sort. And this latest illness . . ." He gently replaced the bedcovers, rising to place a hand on Simon's back. "But we should not disturb her rest. Come, let us speak out in the hallway." He led Simon out into the corridor.

"I do know she is weak, and the fever has not helped her cause—" Simon barely caught himself as he faltered, nearly collapsing as he reached for the doorjamb. No longer possessing the strength to remain upright, he slid to the floor, face buried in his hands.

James could not be right; all could not be lost if only they refused defeat. Simon knew he could convince James, despite his infuriating skepticism—he must. Rallying, Simon pushed himself from the carpet, dusting off his trousers. "James. There might yet be a way to save her. A friend—an acquaintance, to speak true—who shall this very night create for me a medicine that could save her. I have been to see him—"

"And this is where you have been? Dear Lord, not again! And a friend, you say? What sort of . . . ? You cannot be serious! *Simon!* What manner of patent hokum is it this time? A poultice? A tonic? A *magic* pill?"

Simon would not back down. "This apothecary . . . Erceldoune of Smithfield . . . his reputation is without blemish. I have known him for several—"

"Mark well my words, cousin. Do not pay heed to one of these apothecary fellows, no matter how well you may think you know him. They lure you in with promises from antiquity and deliver nothing but false hope. He shall only do you—and our dear Sophie—ill!"

CHAPTER 5

The world had much altered, grown, since the seventeenth century when Gaelan had used the book to cure himself of plague. Late autumn, it had been, October 1625, and plague had ridden into London like the Pale Rider himself. Death everywhere, in every home; on every street people were dead or dying: in pesthouses, in plague pits, dropped dead in the streets or forgotten in their beds, rotting as the rats feasted on their remains. No one—no physician, surgeon, apothecary—had the ability to face it down and win. Gaelan's few successes, he'd realized, had likely not been plague at all, but some lesser pestilence.

Then one morning he awoke from a fitful sleep, and there they were: swellings in his armpits, his groin—unmistakable signs. Fever consumed him; the tips of his fingers had gone dusky and then began to blacken within the span of a day, and Gaelan waited for the disease to rob him of all thoughts but welcome death.

As he lay in bed, shivering and drenched, he saw it—a shimmering vision of the hawthorn tree with its odd snakes. He remembered his father talking of the 1574 plague that had decimated Edinburgh. Yet, his father, Court Physician Thomas Erceldoune had saved the lives of the boy king and half his courtiers with a tonic from the ancient volume.

Clawing at the book like a lifeline, Gaelan found the page, but in his delirium, he could barely follow the instructions. With trembling hands, he ground, distilled, and mixed, nearly dropping the crucible twice as he toiled. Finally it was done, and he hungrily drank it down, ignoring the metallic taste and foul smell. He'd little enough chance of surviving, and his last thought before losing consciousness was a prayer that death take him quickly should this effort fail. But it did not, and miraculously, before two days had passed he felt right enough to venture outside. His thoughts turned to rescuing others from the scourge of Black Death—perhaps all the afflicted of his Shoreditch street.

Yet his neighbors had recoiled at the sight of him, fleeing across the cobblestones, calling out one to the next, "He'd the plague! And now it's vanished! Magic . . . sorcerer . . . always knew it . . . suspected him from the start! Something not right with that one. . . . Must be a witch!"

Gaelan shuddered at the memory, and sighed, his thoughts returning swiftly to Simon Bell and the matter at hand. He hauled the book up to his laboratory, footsteps echoing through the narrow, windowless turret and into the large room above his flat. A full moon lit the room through high-arched windows. Seldom had Gaelan reason to come up to the laboratory at night—except to gaze upon the stars, count the constellations he'd known by heart since he was a lad—but tonight the moon rendered the sky too bright. It was just as well, with only until morning to fix Bell's potion.

Young Timothy Gray entered behind him, kindling a fire in the hearth while Gaelan lit glass orbs about the room. Their phosphorescence subdued the shadows and bathed the workbench in luminous daylight.

"Ah, much better than candlelight, Timothy. You would do well to remember that! Now, off to bed with you, lad, and take with you my pharmacopeia to study before you fall to sleep—and do not neglect your Latin verbs either. I shall be quizzing you on them tomorrow!"

Timothy was a good lad, an able apprentice. A fast learner, too, knowing when to inquire—and when to hold his tongue. Gaelan listened for Timothy's footfalls on the back stairs, then the clang of the door to his rooms behind the shop.

Gaelan ran his hand over the hawthorn tree engraved into the book's cover, the leather smooth as velvet beneath his fingers. As he opened the volume, the fragrances of antiquity wafted up: grass newly shorn and the tang of acid mingled with the mustiness of aged paper and vanilla soaked through him, evoking memories of childhood and family long forgotten. He breathed it in, the finest brandy sneaked from his father's chalice. The illuminations glimmered above the page to which he'd opened—an illusion, its colors a kaleidoscopic bending and merging.

Fanciful script framed and formed the images, curling into shadows and tucking into the spaces between illuminations. Gaelan turned one page to the next, pausing occasionally to take in the beauty of the drawings, the colors of the inks, the sense of history, of memory . . . of family, nearly causing him to weep.

Ah, there you are. Karkinos. The crab. Its claws reached out, tentacle-like, grabbing hold and never letting go of its prey.

His father's voice whispered into the shell of his ear; Gaelan could nearly feel his presence at his shoulder. "The crab possesses a kinship with this most tenacious of diseases . . . cancer, it be called."

A woman shimmering in silver and black, holding no weapon but an emerald tree branch, vanquished the crab's claws, which faded into a trail of pewter dust to the edge of the page. A ruby and gold-leafed ouroboros bordered the entire image.

The text was as difficult to navigate as the North Sea, only partially in recognizable English. Latin and Greek, Gaelic in a florid hand, and other languages barely remembered rendered the interpretation thorny at best. But he must get this right. Perfect.

The hour grew later, and Gaelan nearly had it, squinting past burning eyes to match the bottles lining his bench to markings and glyphs in the manuscript text: quicksilver, antimony, lead, nitrates, chromates, sulfates, crystal salts, and viscous liquids. Simple enough, but what of the glyphs in the manuscript for which he could find no match among the assortment of chemical compounds? These must be referencing fine herbs, for the medicines were not only made of elements but of botanics. Gaelan possessed many, used daily in his trade, but these symbols were unfamiliar. Perhaps at one time he'd understood, but it had been too many years. . . .

The glint of a rounded flask flickered in the periphery of Gaelan's vision, the light reflecting and bending around its shape. The glassblower's art of molten lead, fine ground oxides, amorphous and unknowable liquids formed like magic to crystal, to glass. Elements and heat, chemistry and physics, art and science in perfect harmony, so like the creation of medicines conjured from nothing even remotely recognizable to the end result—strong and fragile.

Then it came to him; Gaelan remembered where he had seen those glyphs before. It had been in his father's apothecary case, hidden away on that same shelf, its rotted wood suddenly catching Gaelan's eye through the convex form of a beaker.

Eighteen amber glass jars, each bearing a symbol matching those on the Karkinos page of the manuscript, rested in the rotting velvet-lined box. Beneath the jars lay several animal skin pouches tucked away and knotted securely . . . more glyphs.

Text to ingredient, instruction to symbol, the process was slow and arduous, careful and tedious. Embers of splintered sleep burned sharp as broken glass in Gaelan's eyes as the sky turned from black to the dusky pink of predawn. He needed to be quick; time grew short until Bell would return.

Gaelan tapped the ingredients into a large stone vessel, grinding them anew at each step—the pestle a magician's wand in his skilled hand. Candle flame would do well to heat the spacious crucible, and Gaelan's hands trembled as he watched it brew and bubble, sputter and flare. Finally he added the common salt and water. *Finished!*

Dawn's first dim awakening bled red-orange through the windows, the wood in the fireplace long since turned to ash, the globes of light paled to dull amber. Breathless from hours of concentration, Gaelan waited a moment for the elixir to rest before decanting it into a small cobalt bottle, stoppering it with a ground glass bung.

Running his index finger along the curves of text on the page, he identified the dosing guidance. Inked in scarlet and set apart from the other text, in Latin, "Once prepared, bottled and sealed, do not open until prepared to administer, lest the contents be oxidized and altered prematurely, irrevocably, thus rendering the contents hazardous to life and limb."

With a skilled hand, Gaelan copied the words onto a parchment, carefully rolling it before affixing it to the bottle with glue. On a separate label, and with scarlet ink, he drew the skull and crossbones, and below that, "POISON."

CHAPTER 6

Timothy Gray was already about, dusting the shelves, when Gaelan finally found his bed. An hour's rest and he would be revitalized for the day. Weariness tugged at him, dragging him toward sleep.

A noise broke through his drowsy haze. A rat skittering across the floor? No, the distinct crackle of fire pricked his ears. *Was the shop ablaze?*

Gaelan could not see; he was surrounded by blackness, when only a moment before, the night had been brightening into dawn. And now it was not exhaustion that blurred his vision, but thick smoke.

No flame scorched his skin, yet he recognized the pungent, sickly sweet stink of burning flesh. He retched thin bile.

A whisper ricocheted against the walls and echoed through the distance of time. He well knew that voice, and it terrified him. No longer an adult, Gaelan was but a frightened eleven-year-old boy.

"You are to come with us, young Erceldoune. His Majesty demands your presence." Gloved hands, brutal as a cur's jaws, gripped Gaelan's arms; already he could feel the bruise arise, purple and tender.

At last accustomed to the dark, he saw them—palace guards, two of them towering over him. Black mail covered their faces beneath iron helms that could not keep from his nostrils the reek of their rotting teeth.

The bright light of the palace courtyard blinded him, but he well knew this place, this time. And the disquiet of sickening anticipation prickled at the back of Gaelan's neck.

Edinburgh Castle. A fleeting thought of happier times there as a lad at play and study quickly shattered in the midst of the yard. Gaelan tried to look away from the platform, which arose like an altar from the center. Where was his mother? Where were his sisters, Isobel and Margaret? He could not see them for the crowd.

With all his heart he wanted to scream for them, to cry out, but

Father had told him he must have courage, no matter what he might be asked to do or say.

"You must watch, lad. It is His Majesty's desire—his command." Gaelan's head jerked up as one of the guards pulled back on his hair and the other braced his narrow shoulders, forcing him to gaze upward. King James glowered upon the scene from a high window, no longer friend and benefactor to his family, but executioner.

Shouts arose—his father's name cursed as rotting fruit sailed over Gaelan's head toward the wagon upon which his father stood, upright and still, searching the crowd. "Father!" he heard himself shout before the guards yanked harder on his hair. The crowd swam in and out of Gaelan's vision as his scalp burned.

"Silence!" they growled.

Gaelan shouted again, ignoring the pain in his arms and head, hoping his father would know he was there. No longer courtier and alchemist, physician and friend to the king, Lord Thomas Erceldoune, stripped now of title, lands all forfeit to the Crown, looked down from the back of a wood cart, his gaze fixed on his son. Relief flooded briefly through Gaelan's veins as Thomas nodded once in his direction. But Gaelan could neither forestall the tears nor the terror, knowing what lay ahead for his dear papa—for them all.

Had it been only a fortnight ago they had celebrated his eleventh birthday right above this courtyard, in the palace nursery?

Thomas was shoved, bound and shackled, onto the platform, but he did not fall, remaining upright, proud, and defiant as his accusers addressed him.

"How the mighty have fallen, Erceldoune—sorcerer, betrayer of the very one who has been for these years both sovereign and protector. Do ye not know the magical arts are outlawed?"

Gaelan's father only stared ahead.

"You have been condemned to die for magical healing, a capital crime against the Crown. Witness upon witness has testified to 'miraculous' recoveries after the touch of your hand and the potions of your cauldron. What say you, Erceldoune?"

Gaelan's father stood unmoving, defiance, not fear, in his countenance.

"Answer, prisoner!" The executioners, dressed in black from head to toe, bound Thomas to a lone pike in the midst of the platform, surrounded by bales of straw.

Gaelan tried to pull away from the guards, run to his father, do something to help him. He searched the crowd again for his mother, his sisters, but could not find them as the guards forced his face forward toward his father. The crowd grew precipitously louder, more insistent in its taunts. Finally, his father spoke, and Gaelan knew he was speaking directly to him, voice even and calm as ever it was.

"It is for all men that come into the world to die, and after death the judgment! Death be a debt all must pay; it is but a matter of small moment what way it be done. And aye, I am come hither to die. Providence having brought me hither, it is upon me to clear myself of some aspersions laid upon my name for the sake of my children—my young son and his sisters, and for my goodly wife and my father's good name.

"It was the king called me to such vaunted estate, to be his physician and counselor. But I have offended my prince, for which I humbly ask him heartfelt forgiveness. I beseech you, my sovereign, and pray to God Almighty that he will forgive me my offenses. Ne'er it was my intent to commit offense, magical or otherwise, as it has been my sole purpose to serve His Majesty, my Lord, and see to his well-being. Many have called me a purveyor of magical healing, sorcery, and I say here that this is untrue. Yet I am not without sin, and I am ready to die and go to my Lord God. But as I do so, I desire with a full heart for my son, my daughters, my wife, and all who gather here today to witness this death, pray as do I for the king's grace, that he may long live with you, may long reign over you."

Gaelan did not understand his father's words. Why was he begging the king's pardon, asking for forgiveness? Confessing guilt? His father was guilty of nothing.

He heard the shout from the platform. "Enough of this!"

Gaelan fought again to pull himself from the guards' grasp, clamp shut his eyes as torches appeared from nowhere, fierce orange banners of flame as they bent to touch the pallet of straw and wood. Now the inferno filled his vision; the crackle and spit of the fire drowned out all else as his father melted into it, indistinct from the hellfire that consumed him whole. . . .

Gaelan gasped as he focused on the familiar quiet of his bedchamber, no longer in the palace courtyard. The orange of the flames faded, replaced by beams of yellow sunlight snaking through window blinds. It had been a dream . . . *that* dream.

Fighting for air, he tried to still the trembling in his hands. Cold beads of sweat skated down his back, and Gaelan pulled the bedcovers higher. It had been many years since those images had plagued him, yet they were vivid and fresh, seeming but days, not long centuries since . . .

The book must have resurrected that accursed day from the farthest regions of his mind.

When he was burned, Thomas had only just begun tutoring Gaelan on the peculiar ouroboros book. "It is your legacy, my son," his father had told him with great seriousness and pride. "We shall turn it and turn it, and turn again until you know it as I do, as did my father and his before that. In it are held all the laws of medicine and nature, and only when you are ready, you shall use it. But it will require of you years of study, perhaps five, perhaps ten, perhaps a lifetime."

Thomas turned the pages slowly, not reading—not yet, he'd explained—but pointing out the images, their significance, the languages, and the weight of their history. And then his father was ripped from them with a summons to the palace brought by two of the king's guard.

It was not uncommon for Thomas to be called, even late at night, to King James's study. But this time had been different, leaving his mother trembling, his sisters weeping and gripping Gaelan's hands so tightly he could feel it even now if he concentrated.

"You must go, Gaelan, to my father's house," Mama sobbed, holding him to her bosom. "It is the only way. Quickly. You know how to get there, and he will take you where it is safe."

He'd not wanted to leave them; he did not understand at all. "But, Mama—"

"Wait. Take this book; show it to no one, not even my father, who will seize it from you and burn it. Say no more, my lovely son. Your grandfather will keep you until—"

She placed the ouroboros book in a satchel along with his clothing and his study books, shepherding him from the door and into the night. It was the last time he had seen any of them safe.

Gaelan scrubbed the tears from his cheeks as he observed the morning light casting the book's cover in an almost unearthly glow. It would not be long now until Simon Bell appeared at his door for the elixir.

The dream left with Gaelan an uneasiness he could not shake. Unanswered questions from the night before hung before him. What if something should go wrong? What if this was not cancer, but some other disease ravaging Sophie Bell's body? He'd neglected to inquire of other intervening issues. A poor constitution? Fevers? Yet surely Bell would have mentioned it. But could Bell be trusted? Could any desperate man?

Gaelan dispelled his doubts as he descended the stairs to the shop. After placing the cobalt blue phial on the counter, he opened up and waited for Bell. Breathing in the scent of drying herbs, aromatic oils, and teas, Gaelan assured himself that all would be well.

The doorbells jingled, and he looked up from his *Times* and into the hard-eyed countenance of Lyle Tremayne. He was an intimidating presence—not big, but tough. A well-attired monster in frock coat and cravat. He was too near, his heavy breath oppressive, and Gaelan struggled not to gag on it.

Gaelan had run into the Tremaynes of the world far too often—bullies all. This one owned half of Smithfield, and more than half the merchants and tradesmen cowered in fear of him, paying him handsomely just to stay in business and stay alive.

"And what might I do for you this fine morning, Mr. Tremayne? I've a fine new—"

Tremayne's gaze roamed the counter, resting upon the cobalt phial. "Shut it, Erceldoune. You know what I want. I want you to leave my girls alone. Fix 'em up; send 'em back to me. That's it. No sweet-talking them, no trying to convince them to go back home to their folk. You cost me plenty, apothecary, and I've good mind to see you ruined."

Gaelan refused to be daunted by either Tremayne's tough talk or the gang of ruffians that followed in his wake. "I keep them in good health, best I can, Mr. Tremayne, have done these past ten years and more—as promised. But if you work them when they're diseased, they'll only worsen—make your . . . patrons . . . ill, as you well know, especially if they're plagued with certain—"

Tremayne took another step forward, now mere inches from Gaelan's face. "You just mind your own bloody business. I've got my eye on you, apothecary. I know a bit about you, what you conjure up in that laboratory of yours—" He scooped up the cobalt phial, turning it in his large fingers, stopping to closely examine the skull and crossbones.

Gaelan froze. It was a provocation, nothing more. "I've nothing . . . nothing here but goodly medicines, as you well know—"

"Is that right? Not what I've heard. Plenty of rumors round 'bout how you bewitched Lord Kinston's only daughter that night so many long years ago. Gave to her potions and such—" Tremayne set the phial emphatically on the counter. Point made.

"I've no idea why you might think it so. I—"

"You are not what you seem, if you catch my drift. I'm no fool, Erceldoune, but I've held my tongue all these years for the good you've done me and my men . . . and ladies. However—"

A threat dangled in Tremayne's unfinished sentence. Gaelan exhaled shakily, determined to stand his ground against the thug.

Another customer entered the shop, and Tremayne backed away quickly. "Mind my words, Erceldoune."

CHAPTER 7

Simon awoke at Sophie's side. He had collapsed in her rocking chair, their hands yet entwined. Morning brought little change, for good or ill. Still she slept peacefully, the rise and fall of her chest a comfort.

After untangling his limbs, Simon crossed the room to her bureau, the sight of her hairbrush leaving him nearly undone. Infused with his favorite fragrance—Eau de Sophia—it called out to him with memories of better times. He brought it to his face, running his fingers along the polished walnut, the soft bristles . . . How many times had he sat beside her and brushed her long, dark hair?

She would grow impatient, admonishing him with mock anger and a seductive grin. Firm strokes with the brush would evolve into caresses, soft and sensual, his fingers meandering through her curls. Soon enough she would surrender with feigned irritation, hairbrush tumbling to the floor, a forgotten prop.

Their marriage was something rare and beautiful—friends *and* lovers, she would say with some pride, when women were prized possessions but seldom equals. She would ever blush when he'd proclaim to a room of dinner guests that her brilliance far exceeded his own.

Simon loved to watch her from the library threshold as she perused his collection with the delight of a child on Christmas morning. History, literature, philosophy: her appetite for learning knew few bounds. The thrust and parry of their debates were always a singular joy, even when she challenged his ideas of medicine and science, society, theology.

"Oh God, my Sophie. What shall I do without you here to keep me tethered? I cannot let you leave me, my love. I cannot!" A sob escaped him, evaporating into the chill morning air of the boudoir as he bounded once again for her bedside, burying his face in the bedcovers. Her skin was hot as a boiling kettle as Simon raised her hand to his lips, kissing her palm. Would this tenacious fever ever subside? He did not want to leave her side, but he'd an appointment with the apothecary and, with it, the faintest hope of keeping Sophie alive.

"I'll return soon, my love," he whispered, placing a final kiss on her temple before leaving quietly for Smithfield Market.

Simon's abdomen gnawed with doubt as he crossed Smithfield, watching his footing in the muck and dung of market day. He had a hard time believing Erceldoune a fraud after all the time they'd known each other. But he must stay on his guard. What if James was right and this exercise was but another futile, foolish bit of false hope? And what of it? Doing nothing at all meant her certain death, and soon. That was the cruel truth.

Erceldoune was engaged in animated conversation with an elderly woman when Simon arrived at the shop. Brushing straw and coal dust from his frock coat, he was grateful for the quiet—a stark contrast to the market day commotion with its cacophony of cows and pigs, lambs and goats, street sellers hawking their miracle cures and sticky buns. Although, the walk had done him good. The rain had stopped as well, and the sun had tried all morning to make an appearance through the haze.

The woman took a small sack from Erceldoune's hands. "Good day, then, Mr. Erceldoune, and thank you for the poultice. A miracle, indeed, you conjured for my Eddie." She nodded, bowing slightly to Simon as she scurried into the autumn morning. A new customer entered the shop. *Too bad.*

Erceldoune glanced up from his ledger, setting down his pen. "Ah, good morrow to you, Dr. Bell. You look much improved this morning. If you don't mind, let me see to Lil's needs and then I shall close up the shop that we might speak in private."

Good. Hopefully it would be quick. "Indeed, Mr. Erceldoune, but I am in quite a hurry, as you might imagine, sir."

Erceldoune held up a hand, motioning the young lady to a curtained area behind the counter.

"A moment, sir! I'll be but a moment." Erceldoune turned away from Simon, ushering the girl behind a threadbare curtain.

Simon roamed the shop, anxious, trying to find a distraction in reading the Latin labels on bottles of colorful liquids and jars of aromatic herbs. Erceldoune and the girl spoke in hushed tones, yet it was impossible not to overhear them.

"Ah, Lil, what have you got yourself into now, lass?" Erceldoune admonished the young woman, who could not be more than fifteen or sixteen years.

"Mr. Erceldoune, I'm sorry to bother you, sir, but Mr. Tremayne, he—" The girl sobbed as she explained what this "Lyle Tremayne" did to her.

Simon's patience waned as the minutes ticked by, no longer distracted after two circuits around the small shop. "Mr. Erceldoune," he called through the curtain. "I must forthwith return to my wife—"

Erceldoune reprimanded the girl, not unkindly, and not, Simon thought, for the first time. "Please, Lil, you must heed me, lass. I shall give you this remedy, but each time the medicine works less and less well. You must allow yourself time to heal. Lyle Tremayne is an evil bastard, and you should run as fast as you can to leave his influence. An aunt, a cousin . . . *anyone* would be better than staying under his roof. I fear you should not be long for this earth should you insist on working for him and his monstrous lot."

As they emerged, Erceldoune removed a pair of gloves, setting them in a basket behind the counter. The girl nodded, her hand on the doorknob before the apothecary stopped her, handing her several coins.

"Mr. Erceldoune, I . . . It is I should be paying—"

"I worry about you, y'know, lass. This should tide you over a fortnight, until you might again be able to work. If you've a need I can give you more—even enough to leave this place, if you would only allow me—"

She nodded, taking the coins. "Thank you, Mr. Erceldoune."

"Help yourself to a cup of my special tea; kettle's hot. It'll do you a good bit of good, but mind you keep the door locked as you leave."

"I will, Mr. Erceldoune, and thank you."

Erceldoune hung the "Closed" sign and led Simon through a door and into his private office.

"Forgive me," Simon whispered, certain the young lady might hear them through the door. "I could not help but overhear . . . ?" Time was short, but he was curious.

"Ah," sighed Gaelan. "Lil is a good girl. She got herself into some trouble with her family, and now she's come to this merciless paradise, run away from a drunken father and an indifferent mother. She's no choices, no future. Hundreds like her out here in these streets. Quite disheartening. But I do what I'm able." He shook his head. "Now she's got herself in with a very bad sort. Lyle Tremayne is more than a whore-monger; he's a ruthless, murdering scoundrel, but do not allow me to get started on that blackguard."

"Why is he not in prison?"

"Ha! Indeed, Lyle Tremayne possesses much influence for all his foul deeds—friends in Parliament, at court—a clientele, which, as it were, he keeps in a small ledger. None dare take him on; he's the means to wreak much havoc in many in high places. As for myself, I stay out of his way and keep his girls healthy as I'm able. For that he leaves me be to ply my trade—for the most part, at any rate."

Simon sat in a faded but comfortable wing chair alongside the small oak table where they had shared over the years many an ale, many a conversation. He'd missed Erceldoune's company, and perhaps if . . . when Sophie was again to rights, they might again be friends. But now he must get down to the business at hand.

Producing a small cobalt glass phial from his pocket, Erceldoune explained, "It shall work quickly on the tumors; the cancer should be gone within three to four days." Setting down the bottle, he went on, his gaze fixed directly on Simon. "The potency of the elixir is such that especial care must be taken in its handling. I pray you heed my instructions—*to the letter*." Erceldoune tapped the attached parchment scroll. "Do not vary from them by a single word. If you do, I shall not be accountable for the consequences!"

The dire warning alarmed Simon as he pocketed the blue phial. "And you're certain it is safe?"

"To erase a cancer, you cannot simply administer laudanum, bleed her, and pray, sir! Danger oft times goes hand in hand with strong medicine, but if you take care—"

"Thank you, Mr. Erceldoune. Might I, in happier times, when my wife is again full of vigor and free of her cancer, visit you here? I do miss our conversations."

"Aye, I think it would do me good as well."

Simon took Erceldoune's proffered hand. The girl was yet in the shop, sipping from a bone China cup.

"Good-bye, then, Mr. Erceldoune." He gave a slight bow before exiting into the bright street. He vowed to try the elixir this very day.

CHAPTER 8

"**A**h, Dr. Bell, just in time for luncheon." Mrs. McRory's broad smile was puzzling, as Simon came through his front door, heading toward the stairway. There had been precious little to smile about, especially these past few days.

He paused at the first step, handing her his greatcoat, his heart thudding. "You seem happy this morning. Is there—"

"Oh yes, indeed, and I am overjoyed, Dr. Bell. Overjoyed. Mrs. Bell is awake and much improved. She's had a nice warm bath and downed a hearty breakfast: oatmeal, toast, and jam. I can hardly keep her abed. She insisted upon taking her meal downstairs and eat 'not like an invalid.'" Her laughter radiated an optimism incongruous with his mood.

Might it be that Sophie had at last turned the corner, her fever broken? His legs foundered to jelly as he stumbled, relief merging with disbelief. Bracing himself on the banister a moment, Simon waved away his housekeeper. "Do not fuss with me. I shall be fine . . . I *am* fine." Recovered, he bounded up the stairs two at a time.

"She has been asking for you!" Mrs. McRory called up to him.

"Yelling, more like, I imagine, to be free of her cage!" he called back, rounding the sweeping bend of the staircase. "We'll take luncheon in the gallery!"

Simon paused just beyond the threshold of the boudoir, tamping down on expectation. Despite her improvement, little enough had changed: the fact of her cancer yet remained.

Sophie gazed out the window, her neck craned toward the garden. The late-morning light rendered her face luminous in profile, her glossy dark hair incandescent, and Simon was content for the moment only to gaze upon her. Her forlorn sigh beckoned him into the room.

She turned, and Simon sucked in a breath as she looked up into his eyes, tears falling unabated down her face.

"I crave my garden, Simon. One last time, I wish to walk its paths, sit amongst my roses. Who knows if I shall ever . . . ? Winter shall be upon us soon and I—" She turned back to the window, her shoulders slumped with the weight of impending death.

Simon swallowed hard past the knot in his throat as he crossed the room, drawing her into an embrace. "My . . . my darling," he began, the tremble in his voice belying the smile he only barely managed. "My . . . my heart is light as *air* to see you awake and alert." He was not persuasive, even to himself.

She was frailer than the last time he'd held her only the week before, her skin ghostly, her cheeks hollow. Her eyes were sunken and bruised. But the fire had returned to them. He brushed his lips across her forehead, breathing in the rosewater and honey of her bath soap. "You must be patient, my love. Indeed, it seems, yes, the fever is at last broken! But the November chill is the last thing you need right now, my darling."

She appeared so much more herself, but he refused to be deluded. He only need pull down her gown for the truth to stare him in the face. "You shouldn't be about, my dear. Not yet." After escorting her to the bed, he sat beside her, taking her hand in both of his, pressing a kiss into each finger before gathering her into his arms.

Breaking free, she protested. "My darling! I am much improved. If not the garden, then perhaps something else; I cannot stay abed forever—unless you stay with me," she added with a sudden playfulness that caught him off guard.

Pressing him back against the pillows, she held him down with openmouthed kisses, her tongue gliding across the inside of his lower lip. "You see?" She pouted, holding his gaze.

Simon fought the wildfire of his desire, which surged like a tempest. "I do, my love, but you are yet too infirm to . . ." The beads of sweat on her brow evidenced her fatigue from just this small exertion. "It . . . it is nearly time for luncheon."

Sophie wobbled to her feet. Perhaps the dining room was not so keen an idea. "Look, darling, rather than the both of us taking a tumble down those steep stairs, let's take luncheon out on the gallery. You love it there this time of day, and best of all, no stairs needed! I shall even carry you there, like a new bride!"

"No. I wish to walk, on my own," she snapped, gently swatting away Simon's hands as she led the way down the hall toward the second-floor gallery.

"It is all arranged, my love. Mrs. McRory shall bring up our luncheon shortly." Breathless, Simon dragged a heavy leather chair across thick carpet to sit beside his wife.

Miniature rainbows refracted from the chandelier's crystal prisms to every surface, and Sophie studied the two-story gallery as if to commit it to memory. "I have always loved sitting up here," she said with regret. "It reminds me, especially at this hour, of fairy stories and enchanted castles, and soon I shall no longer be able to . . ."

Erceldoune's elixir weighed heavily in Simon's waistcoat pocket. The immediate crisis had passed; there would be no better time to confess the plan, and beg her to understand.

"My darling, since you are faring so much better, I wish to broach . . ."

She waved him off. "I wish only to sit peaceably with you. I know you are desperate for the means to help me, but my dear—"

Her protestations would do no good. Not now. "Before you utter a word in opposition, I ask you please to listen." She would take it as James had: not well. But he would not keep it secret from her. "You recall the apothecary in Smithfield, of whom I have so often spoken, yes?"

"But not for months have I heard you mention him. What of it?"

"I have been to see him, and he has prepared for me . . . something—" With trembling fingers, Simon withdrew the phial. "I have acquired, my darling, a . . . medicine, powerful enough to treat . . . to vanquish . . . the tumors."

Sophie rolled her eyes, holding up a hand. "Simon!"

They had been in this place too many times. He strode to the railing and gripped the wood with both hands, looking out over the central foyer, turned away from Sophie's gaze. "Please, love, hear me out at least."

"Oh, Simon. Don't be nonsensical," she said, an indulgent mother admonishing a little boy bearing a gift of flowers stolen from her own garden.

He pivoted to face her just as she stood, stumbling in the attempt. Two steps and he was kneeling by her side, setting her in the chair. She cradled his face in both her hands, lifting his face to hers.

"I have, my love, made peace with my death, as I beseech you to make yours. I would rather my life end now than for you to continue this futile search for something that exists only in some misguided fantasy realm."

"Do *not* say this! If anything remains at my disposal to forestall . . . I must at least consider it, as outlandish as it may seem to you! Or to James! Please allow me this occupation, lest I go completely mad." Her willingness to leave him was too much to bear.

"Stop," she said, tender but resolute. "My love, hear me! False hope does me little good, and you less. I know you feel impotent to save me. Simon Bell of the celebrated medical family, honored and knighted, peerages for service to the Crown since the Tudors reigned. This I know! But an apothecary's tonic? Can you not comprehend how profoundly ridiculous the idea?"

He had no desire to row, to waste what little time they yet had. But she failed to comprehend the elixir was for *his* sake, not hers. Yes, it was selfish, but what if it worked? They would then have years, not days, or weeks, but a lifetime!

"Simon, my darling," she whispered, her strength waning. "It is my time; acknowledge it, so when it finally comes to pass, be it tomorrow or next month, you *shall* be prepared."

He refused to hear her. Cupping her cheek with a trembling hand, he drew a thumb down the arch of her cheek, confessing now to her the earnest truth. "When I beheld you lying in your bed this week, so still, so weak, my mind could only evince the end, an end I am with little power to forestall. If you die I shall be lost, and my only and most ardent desire shall be to join you in the grave."

Sophie dropped her head into clenched hands. "Do not *dare* say this to me, Simon Bell. You—" She rose, her rebuke dripping with indignation. Tripping on her gown, she swooned into Simon's arms.

He carried her back to the boudoir. "My God, love, you're light as a feather," he whispered into her hair.

She must take the elixir—and soon. It was the only chance remaining to save her. Yet, in the end, could he trust Erceldoune? Indeed, the apothecary had changed; he was so very bitter and angry. Perhaps due to the deaths of his wife and young son. Or had it been something harbored through the ten years they'd known each other, only now come to the surface?

Simon withdrew the cobalt phial, studying the label, its small, neat script, his thumb coming to rest upon the scarlet skull. Simon pushed from his mind the notion that Erceldoune would determine to get his revenge on the whole of medicine by harming an innocent woman, yet suspicion gnawed at the edges of Simon's thoughts. *No, Erceldoune is honorable amongst his fellow tradesmen. Surely, he would not . . .*

Yet . . . the cobalt phial and its elaborate label obscured the contents. Why? What did Erceldoune not want him to see? Simon bounded the stairs from the gallery to his laboratory to examine the thing more carefully—before giving it to Sophie.

More than the library and even his study, the laboratory was Simon's private retreat. So many years as a boy, he would follow at his uncle's elbow like an obedient pup, as Dr. Samuel Bell, lion of medicine, tinkered and mixed, much to Simon's fascination. "One day, Simon, this laboratory, this home, this *legacy* shall be yours to preserve," Uncle Samuel had promised. "Your brother shall inherit your father's lands, but this is for you, Simon."

And now the remote and unadorned space in this grand home was both sanctuary and shrine for Simon, a place to reflect on the course of a patient's illness—and consider the great Bell legacy bequeathed to him. When a case was particularly thorny, Simon would pace the aisles between long, polished basalt benches and ask his long-deceased uncle for inspiration. And there were times, though rare, when Uncle Samuel obliged: the glimpse of a caliper, the label on a chemical jar neglected since Samuel Bell's days would enkindle an idea, illuminate a course of action. Samuel would surely disapprove of Simon's most recent pursuit. Or would he? Simon clutched the small phial.

What is this tiny powerful miracle, the ink-blue bottle no taller than my palm, not the width of two fingers? Had Simon spoken the question aloud, or had that been Samuel's voice echoing in his ear?

Simon rested the phial on the bench, and the instruction scroll fell away from the glass, unfurling before him, almost of its own volition. The writing was in a clear but ornate Latin, in a hand more suited to another, bygone, time: "*Caveat actor*: All things are poison, and nothing is without poison; only the dose permits something not to be poisonous—and respectful handling of the substance of it."

Simon could not drive from his head gnawing doubts about Erceldoune, which wove through every thought, every glimpse of the phial. And what was this warning about poison? *Caveat actor*, indeed. He took hold of the small bottle again, rolling it between his fingers, turning it this way and that as the wax seal holding in place the stopper turned soft from the heat of his hand. Half flaked away in his palm. He should set it down before the stopper came away entirely, read the instructions carefully, and carry them out to the letter.

The mullions rattled with a gust of wind. Simon jumped at the unexpected noise, and his grip on the phial slipped; he barely managed to rescue it from shattering on the floor. But then, a flash of pain seared through his left palm as the glass suddenly turned hot as a smithy's iron.

Somehow, he managed to set down the blazing vessel, staggering away from the bench, stunned, confused. But where had the top gotten to? How had it come undone? Squinting through tears of agony, he saw the stopper—or what remained of it—useless shards scattered at his feet. *Damnation!*

Blistered and raw, Simon's hand burned like the flames of hell. *What manner of poison is this, which transforms its container to a boiling cauldron?* And how could he give this to Sophie? Would it not burn down her gullet, consume her from within?

He wrapped his hand in bandages made from his blouse, soaked in witch hazel found on a high shelf. It would be days until the sting abated.

Simon searched the long benches and drawers for a ground glass stopper that would fit the small phial, locating one that would do for the moment. He turned his attention again to the small scroll. There it was inked in red: "Handle only with gloved hands or toweling. Rapid oxidation upon exposure to the air will cause phial to heat quickly. Allow elixir to rest for exactly one minute and twenty seconds, then administer within five minutes after that. Discard remains."

So that was it, a simple chemical reaction. The phial had already begun to cool as the reaction stabilized to equilibrium. But had the oxidation altered it? Rendered it useless? He read the balance of the instructions with care, finding in them nothing else but the dosage.

Perhaps he should return to Erceldoune forthwith, beg from him a second container of the stuff, explain what happened. But Erceldoune had been reluctant in the first place, and Simon doubted the apothecary would be at all sympathetic to his plight. Perhaps it was a sign, and he should simply abandon the plan entirely. The idea gnawed at his intestines. *No. I cannot give this up. Not yet.*

As he descended the stairs, phial safely in his waistcoat pocket, Simon paused at the Cluny hanging from the third story down to the gallery floor. He'd always felt a kinship with this ancient tapestry, an incongruous piece of art among the portraits of his forbears, just as he fit equally ill among the distinguished generations of Drs. Bell. Simon knew he was no brilliant physician, able to distinguish one disease from the other with a single glance as they had ever been. And he was no James, politically astute, supremely confident, and socially skilled. But, preferring literature to anatomy, philosophy to chemistry, the breadth of Simon's interests forged within him an open mind, not contemptuous to possibilities unimaginable by more conventional peers, James included.

The Cluny was a metaphor for perfect synergy between myth and science. Uncle Samuel had long ago revealed the mysteries of the intricate needlework: "*Mon seul desir.*" The unicorn, the lion, the grand lady poised in front of her star-splashed pavilion—the master controlling the elements through science, yet unwilling to wholly surrender the magic of legend.

"The design signifies 'understanding,'" Samuel had explained. "We have come so very far from the days of sorcerers and alchemists, magic and its like. But we cannot afford to dismiss their legacy. Who can know for certain what might have been in the mind of antiquity's alchemist and wherefrom his craft derived? What scientific secrets were held in journals and experiments between the lines of a capricious quest for the Philosopher's Stone and elixirs of life? This is why the tapestry hangs here, guiding the way, seemingly so out of place alongside a stairway—to honor the past, but not dwell within its confines."

Why might it not be that an ancient manuscript enshrouded within its pages inestimable knowledge long ago dismissed by modern medicine?

And then he heard the scream.

CHAPTER 9

Sophie's scream ricocheted through the three stories of the central foyer. Simon leapt down the remaining steps to the gallery in a single bound, flying down the corridor to the boudoir.

Breathless, Mrs. McRory entered behind him. "My God, Dr. Bell!" she wheezed between ragged breaths. "I heard her from below stairs, sir, and rushed up as soon as . . . What can be wrong with her? Such a turn, and so suddenly—"

Simon sat close by Sophie's side, trembling hands gripping her shoulders, trying desperately to still her wild thrashing. "Do be seated, Mrs. McRory," he said, unable to wrest his gaze from his keening wife, "before you swoon, and I've two to attend. Sophie, my love?" She did not respond, though her eyes were open and frantic.

Slowly, her wailing weakened to faint bleats.

"Sshh. It's all right; I'm here," he cooed, brushing back her hair, plastered now to her forehead. She looked right through him with the vacant stare of a lunatic—no sign of recognition within them. But she was calmer at least.

Years of experience fled, along with all knowledge; he was rudderless, lost in the tidal wave of this latest crisis. This was no resurgence of the fever; neither her hands nor brow were hot.

Gingerly, he peeled back Sophie's gown to reveal her left breast: terrible, angry red-purple, twice the size of the other, as if any moment it would burst. "Little wonder, my beloved, you suffer so in pain—even in your slumber," he murmured into her neck. Cradling her within his embrace, he kissed her hair, vowing vows he could not keep.

He had one weapon remaining in his arsenal, but ambivalence forestalled its use. His singed and throbbing hand exhorted him from beneath its bandages. How could he? Yet how could he *not*?

Sophie broke free of his embrace, sitting upright, looking into the distance. "Anna, is that you? Oh, Anna, my dear sweet sister." She laughed—a delighted, girlish giggle. "It is so good to see you. Come let us go into Mama's garden and pluck the lavender before she can scold us, and we shall make delicious tea!" Sophie's beatific smile, beaming ear to ear, fractured Simon's heart as she called out in her delirium to her younger sister, dead since childhood.

"I can hear them, I think, Anna. Can you? The fairies! Oh! There is one; I can see her, for she cannot hide her light from us out here." Sophie giggled, a child again. To another world she had gone, a place he could not follow; she slipped away from his hold, rainwater through his fingers.

He could not sit passively by not a moment longer. "I am sorry, my love. I cannot let you go—not yet." Apprehension growled in his belly; the relentless chill of fear throbbed through his veins along with determination to carry through with the plan.

"Oh, Simon!" she said, her gaze fixed upon something outside his ability to perceive. "Do not look so grim and stodgy! Come, play with us. We're having a walk beneath Mama's heather trees—they are so full of flower, and the fairies dance within their branches as they do in the lavender. Can you not see them? Come! Hurry, or we shall lose sight of them!" Blindly, her hands reached out toward him, pulling at his sleeve.

"Please my love, there will be time enough for that, but you need to heed me now." Slowly he removed the stopper; this time, the phial did not heat as it had done before.

He filled the attached dropper, the liquid an oily amber. "I need only give you a small amount. Do you understand me?" She nodded, but was she acknowledging him or someone only *she* could see?

Sucking in a breath, Simon slipped the dropper between Sophie's closed lips and released the medicine in the exact amount indicated in Erceldoune's instructions. "Come, my darling, rest easy against my chest." He settled himself in beside her, nestling her in the crook of his neck.

"Yes, Simon. Much better. Please stay with me."

Simon blinked in surprise. Was it possible that Erceldoune's elixir had begun to work so quickly? Had it chased away her delirium? "I shall. Of course I shall." He forced hope back to the far reaches of his consciousness, until it was faint and hidden away . . . until he knew for certain.

"My sister Anna, did I imagine her here with us just now?"

Simon nodded into her hair, kissing it. "Yes, my love. I—" All she needed now was to sleep. Just sleep. "Hush now. Now let us rest, beloved, both of us, and you shall be much improved when we waken."

Finally, he turned to Mrs. McRory. "I believe we may have seen the worst of it. Please take your leave now and rest whilst you might. I shall call you when she awakens. There will be much to do."

"Your hand sir?"

Simon had nearly forgotten. The reminder of it once again started up the throbbing. "It is of no matter, a small scrape; I shall attend to it later."

"Very well, sir."

Mrs. McRory closed the door to the boudoir, and Simon was relieved to finally hear her slow, plodding footfalls on the stairs.

The fading light of late afternoon painted the walls in flame, doused as evening's darkness descended. The dying embers cast long, dull shadows as Simon waited. Seconds became minutes, a half hour. Nothing—a good or bad sign, he knew not. Just nothing. Sophie's light breath upon his arm tickled, and he savored each tingle as if it were the most precious caress, lulling him to sleep.

And then she tensed, arms splayed, back stiff, arched like a bow— the unexpected movement nearly knocking him to the floor. The suddenness of it caught him off his guard; he recoiled, dazed by the sudden turn. Then just as abruptly, she fell backward, no longer rigid, but convulsing, her movements erratic as her limbs shuddered and kicked. Drawing a candle near, he saw it: spittle gathered at the corner of her mouth foaming and pink in the dim light.

Realization dawned as he spied the cobalt phial on the night table. This was poison's signature, confirmed as convulsions wracked her petite frame.

"My God, Sophie. No. Please, dear God, no!" Leaping upon the mattress, he tried to still her. "Please, Sophie, stop. Stop!" A string of desperate curses intermingled with prayer—to God, to the devil, to anyone and anything that might stop the relentless havoc of bone and flesh. She fought with the bedcovers and with him, and he only hoped the blankets would twist about her enough to tame her chaotic movements.

He climbed astride her, arms bracing her shoulders in a feeble attempt to quell her anguish—and his own. He comprehended too well poison's progression to keep hold even a thread of hope. The pink spittle darkened to red-black, a steady stream down her chin, staining the bed, staining his shirt.

"Do not leave me, Sophie. Do not! Do not—" An inarticulate sob swelled from deep within his chest. "Please awaken, my princess. Please do not leave me alone. Please—"

And then her shuddering stilled, and she lay finally quiet beneath him. Rivulets of sweat ran down his face, mingling with her blood and his tears. Panting from exertion, he wiped his face with cool water from the bedside ewer as he tried to calm his breathing. At least Sophie was quiet now, asleep once again.

Mrs. McRory entered the room without knocking, a candle in hand. "Dr. Bell!" She crept to his side as Simon released a long breath. His housekeeper would make too much of his bedraggled appearance, try to coax him downstairs to dine now that Sophie was resting.

Her fingers curled about his upper arm like a vise. He patted her hand, his voice gentle. "There, there, Mrs. McRory. You see? She's fallen back to sleep. All will be right when she wakens."

"No, sir, I think—"

Simon's heart stopped as his gaze fell upon Sophie's ashen face—and he died inside.

CHICAGO'S NORTH SHORE, PRESENT DAY

CHAPTER 10

Gaelan slammed the front door of his flat, rattling the blinds along with what remained of his composure. The air was stale, a smothering fug of cigarette smoke and old paper. Letting his battered leather rucksack drop to the parquet tiles, he collapsed into deep cushions of a well-worn sofa.

Visits with Simon Bell were never easy. And with a line on the ouroboros book, Bell would be relentless in its pursuit until he'd be once again disappointed. Gaelan appreciated Bell's singularity of purpose, which lasted long past any hope Gaelan possessed of ever locating it. Gaelan had given up; Simon never had.

And what then, if the book should actually be found? Gaelan recalled very little of it. The irony being that every other horrifying detail of his life plagued him in high relief. They invaded his dreams, his waking hours as well. Unexpected flashes of his past would bleed into his vision at inopportune moments, obstinate, defying every attempt to thrust it all from his mind. And it had gotten much worse these past few days.

He could still visualize the cover of the book; how could he not? But all detail inside was in perpetual shadow, images, writing, color . . . all a blur. And this he had never disclosed to Simon. How could he hope to reverse what he no longer understood?

Gaelan punched a button on the remote control, and a large flat-panel screen illuminated on the far wall, painting it with a mural of the cosmos: constellations, planets, stars near and distant. *Tubular Bells* enwrapped him in a sedative soundscape, transporting him far from the turmoil of his life.

Gaelan never considered immortality quite the calamity Simon had done all these years. What extraordinary events he had witnessed— brilliant. Motor cars and space exploration, electricity and computers, Mozart and Billy Bragg. And Mike Oldfield. Television and video games were magic beyond the wild imaginings of his mortal era. Simon was fixated on his never-ending quest to die. To be with his beloved Sophie. What a terrible waste of an extraordinary life—a rich life, and a comfortable life. A hell of a lot more comfortable than his own.

If they managed to locate the ouroboros book—*and* he could find in it a way to reverse their immortality—would Gaelan choose to end his life? He'd considered the question from time to time when living had grown especially unbearable. But it was a useless game; the book was lost forever.

And now . . . those fucking diaries. Of course fucking Dr. Handley would have documented every last experiment, every scream, every cut, every . . . Memories of Handley were always too near the surface, ever vivid, but more or less consigned to the land of dreams. But now . . .

The distant snap of breaking bone echoed in Gaelan's ear, a harbinger; he braced himself for the attack of images sure to follow, as once again he was forced to relive it. That he knew it was coming, and that it wasn't real, made little difference as he watched the index finger fall away from his left hand, severed. Gaelan blinked hard, and the image disintegrated, leaving him breathless and raw.

Dear God, my name! What if that was in Handley's diaries as well? He'd never thought to change it, as he'd moved place to place, never thought it a necessity.

Gaelan retched, and the taste of bile and cigarette smoke rose along his esophagus; he reached the bathroom just in time to lose the scant contents of his stomach. Sinking to the floor, knees drawn to his chin, he rested his head on the cool porcelain of the toilet, wondering if there was a point to leaving the dark comfort of the tile.

Restless, he hauled himself from the floor unsteadily. He should read it again, that article; perhaps he'd misread the time or the place—perhaps he had imagined the entire thing. It wouldn't be the first time his imagination had led him astray.

Pushing the mop of hair from his forehead, he sat at a large, cluttered antique desk and opened his MacBook. The article immediately popped into view:

> *In the midst of a major renovation of the Imperial War Museum at Southwark, workers unearthed a set of diaries in an underground section of the building untouched since it was transformed from Bethlem Royal Hospital (Bedlam) into the museum that now stands in its place. It is believed a physician there maintained the diaries, a so-called "mad doctor"—a sort of proto-psychiatrist—under whose care mentally ill patients apparently suffered many indignities, including possible torture. The finding is important documentary evidence of a time not so distant, when mental illness was treated, not as disease, but with lurid curiosity, even by those calling themselves medical practitioners.*
>
> *In a surprise turn, the documents and other artifacts have been given over to a British medical research concern for study. It is unofficially reported that the firm, whose name was not disclosed, have contributed a large donation to the museum's renovation efforts for being granted exclusive access to one diary of particular interest to their area of research.*

Simon's reassurances had been far from persuasive. "Think about it," he'd said. "You 'died' in 1842 on the gallows—as mortal as any man. How would they even make a connection to Mr. Gaelan R. Erceldoune of Evanston, Illinois? In the bloody twenty-first century! And, might I add, thousands of miles from London!"

Gaelan needed a drink. The good stuff. "Ah, there you are," he purred, falling upon the bottle of Lagavulin, its beguiling amber-green curves beckoning. He poured a tumbler-full, letting it slither down his throat, followed by another, and a third, draining that one as well, until none remained of the bottle but glass and Scent de Islay: iodine and peat. Lag a'mhuilin—hollow by the hill. It fit him to an infinite degree. Perhaps not *by the hill*, so much as *under* it.

He fell boneless into his chair, not yet resigning the battle to remain awake. No sleep. Not until he was numbed up right and proper, transported into a dreamlessness that would endure the night. But Gaelan could no longer fend off the growing fatigue as he drifted between wakefulness and sleep, too exhausted to move, powerless to thwart the inevitable plunge into a surreal conflation of past and present as his eyes slipped shut. . . .

In horror, Gaelan watched himself slice a sharp blade through his arm, elbow to wrist—a demonstration for the punters. "You see? I cannot die! I am impervious." Francis Handley hooted as he approached from the front of the audience, egging him on.

"Do not come near me, Handley. I've the upper hand now. Not a freak anymore. I'm a fucking superhero—genetically enhanced with high-test telomerase, don't you know? This is the fucking twenty-first century!"

But the gathered punters were not listening, instead, encroaching on him five, then ten until half the audience rushed toward him, horrified concern on their faces. "Someone call 911!"

"No, I'm fine, no need to call. I'm only just joking. See? It's a magic knife—pure fakery—" His shirtsleeve fell away to his elbow—not a scratch where blood had just poured from an open wound! "It is magic. Ancient, ancient magic, my dear punters. Wrought of the fairies and elves a millennium ago. Do not be fooled into thinking it is anything else. Science is a lie. . . . It is all magic." Now Gaelan sliced his other wrist, observing it close with detached interest until the only remaining evidence of a wound was the red-black of congealed blood on his white shirtsleeve. . . .

The pounding of his heart jolted Gaelan from the dream; he was gulping air and soaked through to the skin. Shivering, he willed his pulse to slow until its rhythm matched the steady beat of his ancient mantel clock. He must've slept; three hours had passed since he'd last noticed the time.

Post-traumatic stress disorder. PTSD—a nice, sterile self-diagnosis; he remembered when it had been called shell shock or just plain fear. He needed neither Freud nor Jung to name it. Whatever it was called, Gaelan had not been free of its clutches, not in more than 170 years.

Nothing worked for very long: not cocaine, not even heroin, nor any manner of concoction he might conjure in his private workroom at the back of the shop. What he wouldn't give this very minute for a sip of laudanum to still his trembling hands, chase away the pounding in his head, each beat hurling a pitchfork of lightning through his temples.

The empty Lagavulin bottle was a problem. He'd not consumed nearly enough, and he had neither the reserves nor motivation to go out into the snow for another.

He massaged his brow, thoughts meandering to the familiar place where fragmented memory had played in an incessant loop since he'd read the *Guardian* story. "Stop! Just fucking stop!" he wailed, certain he would burst every blood vessel in his head. "Please just bloody stop!"

For a long time, life had been palatable: three hours of undisturbed sleep a night had been more than adequate to face the morning, followed by siesta at three for the remainder. For years, he had been comfortable in this little corner of the world called Evanston, and he'd enjoyed it. And now?

With an angry sweep of his arm, Gaelan sent books, papers, and his computer flying across the room—a sea of paper and gadgets, his laptop sitting at the top. "Well that bloody helped," he mumbled. "Fucking hell."

Disgusted, Gaelan surveyed his handiwork. *Pathetic. Bloody pathetic.* Retrieving from the chaos a small packet of Rizlas, he flicked out a thin rolling paper. *Ah, there you are. . . .* An ounce of the best *Cannabis sativa* money could buy, better than his homegrown. His shaking hands could barely manage rolling the herb into the tissue. Three strikes of his ancient flint lighter later, Gaelan collapsed into the waiting arms of a wasted refuge.

LONDON, 1837

CHAPTER 11

Gaelan Erceldoune worried a corner of the ouroboros book, wondering whether Bell had by now administered the elixir—and if it worked. He would inquire in a day or two, ready to stretch out a hand in friendship. Grief had robbed him of life beyond the confines of his shop, and it was time to rejoin the world. He had Bell to thank for bestirring him from this woeful lethargy.

Now that the book had come down from its nook at the top of the bookcase, Gaelan had a mind to bury himself in it, scrutinize each page to truly comprehend the application of its odd and ancient science. Especially if Sophie Bell had been cured.

Allowing himself a moment's quiescence, Gaelan remembered the stories Papa would tell to him at bedtime after long hours of study and recitation....

"The Tuatha de Danann had amongst them great healers—fairy folk, they were called," his father had explained. "Dian Cecht, god of medicine, had two children: Miach, the god of surgery, and Airmid, the goddess of healing. They knew all of healing, every cure, but Airmid was the most skilled. All the herbs and minerals, elements, for all of medicine's ... science's magic she concealed in her magnificent cloak. This was her book—gift to our ancestor Lord Thomas Learmont, a gift to us for all time.

"Yet it possesses a dangerous knowledge for these times. But some day, when you are ready, long after I am gone, which I fear will be soon, given the change of wind in the kingdom, you must, my son, study it thoroughly as you ply your trade. Do not fear it as others shall, yet use it only when you are absolutely certain it is necessary, and even then only with meticulous care. Its recipes are as fragile as the illustrations are intricate, but more powerful than the strongest medicines known to men."

The flames burned bright on the hearth, providing warmth and light, but as with all of earth's elements, fire could be used for ill—just as any medicine. These were but things without motive, clay in the hands of the skilled tradesman. And whether good or ill came of them was in the hands of the maker.

Gaelan sighed, setting aside the book, his thoughts random and unsettled, alighting now upon Sophie Bell, curious how she had fared. Should he presume to stop by Bell's home on the morrow and inquire after the patient?

Restlessness gripped him as he wandered the sitting room, halting hearthside. Propping his elbow on the mantel, Gaelan stared into the blaze, finding comfort in the crackle of wood as the flames licked and sputtered.

The roar of shattering glass came from below, jolting Gaelan from his thoughts and frightening the dogs of Smithfield, whose howls echoed through the streets. Had a stall crashed to the cobblestones, disrupting the quiet of the marketplace?

Another explosion of glass, this time closer. The shop! And now footfalls thumped heavily on the stairs. *Tremayne or his blackguards!* Of course, come to hector him about Lil or some other matter. Four times this year alone they'd bullied their way past the door after hours, laying wreckage to the shop. But never had they broken the lock to the back stairway.

He would not give into Tremayne's bludgeoning; the scoundrel might tyrannize the whole of Smithfield, but Gaelan Erceldoune would not surrender. There was little that could be done to him—physically—from which he would not recover, and no damage to the shop was irreparable.

Gaelan could afford to ignore the threat and the attempts to intimidate. Yes, the shop would be in ruins again—windows smashed and bottles askew, hundreds of pounds' worth of herbs and chemicals strewn about. None of it signified, and Gaelan would persevere to aid Tremayne's whores, treat their maladies, insist they take the time to heal, urge them from the scoundrel's nefarious influence, even if only to find a less brutal employer.

After swiftly tossing the ouroboros book in his messenger bag, Gaelan flung it to the bookcase just as the door splintered in two.

"I hear tell you've taken up with my Lil, Erceldoune!" Predictably, there was Tremayne, flanked by two men, each dragging a cudgel.

Sucking in a breath, Gaelan stood firm, unmoving. "Not taken up, Tremayne, fixed up, and from what *you've* done to her!"

"Ain't none of your bloody business to tell my Lil she shouldn't be working. You cost me, Erceldoune. Every bloody time. Lil's my best girl, and she refuses to work this night or the next, or the one after that, till you say it's bloody all right!"

This was different from the usual—rarely would these encounters evince conversation. *What is he up to?* Staying calm was his best ally. Aggression was as pointless as trying to appeal to whatever feelings Tremayne might have toward a girl he housed and clothed. "Lil is sick. She shall grow sicker still if you force her—in any way—to work or anything else, if you catch my drift, Mr. Tremayne."

"Ah, never mind all that, Erceldoune. Never mind at all. My sweet Lil has told me a lovely little tale about some sort of special concoction you've made up for some highborn gent, something to cure . . . cancer, is it? And from what I've heard, nothing can cure that scourge. So I have to think, what are you up to, a reputable apothecary like you? You're no street mountebank, and I've got to thinking that you've got something might make me a pretty penny, more than the girls do, I venture. I could retire in fine fashion, wash the stink of this place from my clothes at last!"

What had Lil overheard? Gaelan shoved down a growing panic. "I've no bloody idea what you're talking about. You're not making sense, sir!" Gaelan stared straight ahead, hands balled into fists, trying to recall what she might have been privy to while sipping her tea. And even if she had heard—and understood—any of his conversation with Bell, she would never betray him to Tremayne. Unless he'd beat it from her, or . . .

"Ahhh. Go on!" He laughed. "You know exactly what I'm talking about. They know it too." Tremayne gestured to the men at his side. "Were right there with me, listening to Lil squeal like a gutted pig."

Gaelan knew this was not to end well. "To speak true, Mr. Tremayne, I do not know what you're talking about." He ventured a step back, then another, until he felt the smoothness of the wall behind him.

"No? More's the pity. I can only assume, then, that Lil was lying to set me off her and on a merry little worthless chase to you. Well, she'll pay for it; make no mistake. As for you, I've warned you 'fore this many a time to keep your bloody hands off my girls. And apparently, you place no value upon your life or business." Tremayne's soft sing-song belied the menace in his voice.

Gaelan shuddered, remaining silent, his gaze fixed upon one of the cudgels, as he waited for the first blow. Instead, the men doused the clubs with pitch and oil before touching them to the hearth flames; a suffocating-sweet haze filled the room.

Gaelan smoothed his hands along the wall behind him until he reached a small bronze knob beside the bookcase. Counting his breaths, slow and steady, without taking his gaze away from the silk window curtains now ablaze across the room, he pressed the knob. The book-shelves slid from view, replaced by a masonry wall.

Done. *Now to escape . . . somehow.* But the broken door was many feet away; the only other exit was in the next room.

Tremayne smirked. "*Clever*, Erceldoune. I've a mind to get me one of those; never know when it will come in right handy. However, your books, wherever they have gone off to, will not be safe from fire. Paper burns, just like wood and silk, only quicker. I thought you would know that, being you're a very clever man an' all!"

Little time remained until the entire building would be engulfed in flames. Once the fire reached his laboratory . . . Gaelan held up his hands in appeal. "Tremayne. Hear me. Hear. Me. Now. There yet remains but a small window through which we may back away from this precipice. I serve you and your men, repair their wounds and treat their ailments. There is none other in Smithfield. If you destroy my business—kill me—"

"You think much of yourself, Erceldoune. Enough talk." Tremayne nodded, and instantly the floor was ablaze. "See you in hell, apothecary!" he called out as they fled.

Alone at last, Gaelan withdrew to his bedchamber and down the back passage toward the alleyway. *Timothy! Oh, dear God.* Black smoke followed him down the stairs as fire crackled and spat out burning embers of paper and wood. In moments, the conflagration would spiral through the turret and up to the laboratory, transforming it into a noxious cauldron of chemical reactions.

The blaze had not yet reached the shop, but already smoke billowed through the ceiling from above as Gaelan made his way through the sea of shattered glass, rousting Timothy from his sleep.

The entire building shuddered as they escaped into the street. People shouted, screams muffled by the fire's roar as the laboratory went up, sending flares and flames like rockets into the night sky before the entire structure imploded. In the end, there was naught left of Gaelan's home but steam and smoke, smoldering wood and fused glass.

Gaelan led Timothy to a small iron grate set into the cobblestones. "Come quickly, Tim." A steep ladder carried them from the street down into a deep cellar. The choking, acrid stink of burned wood and smoke faded from their nostrils as they descended farther into dark, stale air, the grate fast fading from sight high above them.

Perhaps this is a sign that it is long past time to depart this place.

They emerged into a large stone room, air chill and breathable, a welcome relief from the smoke and ash. Gaelan edged his way along the wall in the dark to a table. The room was bathed in a soft light as he touched a match to a filament inside a glass globe.

Across the space, Gaelan spied his bookshelves, slid into place from the flat above. Pleased that his bit of ingenuity had actually worked, he allowed himself a moment to admire the achievement.

"You see, Tim . . . ?" Gaelan turned around, ready to explain just how several hundred books managed to travel from the second story of the building into a hidden cellar—a lesson in ingenuity for his apprentice. But Timothy had already found the straw pallet, long ago prepared, and was sound asleep.

Exhausted as he was, sleep was not something Gaelan could afford—not right now. Some unfinished business, and then he must depart London, soon as he was able.

CHAPTER 12

Simon refused to believe it as he stood in horror over Sophie's prone body. She could not be dead. *She cannot be dead. She cannot be dead!* Simon reeled backward, staring in disbelief. *It is not possible.* "No! No, no, no!" he howled again and again, as if saying it would make it true.

The contorted rictus smile pulled the white-gray skin of Sophie's face tight—a skull wearing a mask. The line of red-black blood was dried and sticky on her chin and down her neck.

Hands a vise, Simon shook her hard, the burning in his left hand a vague nagging. He prayed for a return of her convulsions—any sign of life at all. His entreaties echoed through the room, by turns plaintive and thunderous. "Do not leave me, Sophie. You cannot! Please, love, open your eyes for me! I promise I shall go out into the garden with you. I shall!"

He'd forgotten Mrs. McRory was still in the room, and now she was at his side, pulling at his fingers to wrest them from Sophie's arm. "Please, Dr. Bell," she addressed him, a kindly grandmother. He shoved her away, sent her staggering into the armoire.

"I am sorry, Mrs. McRory. But please leave me. Leave me now!"

"Come with me, sir; we shall call your cousin. . . ."

No, that would not do. He could not leave her side. Climbing into the bed beside Sophie, Simon brushed the long curls from her eyes, which stared, accusing him, wide and blank, from sockets already beginning to hollow in her lifeless face.

"Oh my God, Sophie. What have I done? My love . . . you cannot be . . . You are only sleeping; I am sure of it. You *shall* awaken. Do *not* leave me!" he bellowed, even as he forced her eyelids shut with his hand.

"Dr. Bell, if you cannot bring yourself to leave just yet, allow me to settle you a bit."

Simon had no desire to be "settled" at all, but he let her guide him into a rocking chair. He was only vaguely aware of the blanket draped around his shoulders as he stared ahead unseeing.

"My God, Dr. Bell. I am so very, very sorry. I will take my leave, but only to prepare you something to eat. You must keep up your strength, sir!" The door closed behind Mrs. McRory, and finally he was alone with her.

There was *something* he ought to be doing, was there not? Calling for someone to come? But he could not reckon what to do or whom to call. The undertaker, certainly. James, perhaps. *No! She shall awaken. It is only a matter of having patience.*

The full moon washed the room, glinting off the cobalt phial, which still sat upon the night table. He should hurl it across the room, shatter it into a million pieces. What a fool he had been to trust Erceldoune. *My God, Sophie. What have I done? What have I done?* How might he face James, Sophie's parents, even his poor housekeeper, who had witnessed the act?

Time ticked and the hours chimed, one bleeding into the next as he sat in the dark of Sophie's boudoir.

"I've set out some supper for you, Dr. Bell. You must be starved, sir, and you *must* eat."

Simon heard her, muffled through the heavy mahogany door. The mere mention of food made him queasy, and he ignored her plea. "I beg of you, Mrs. McRory. Do go away and leave me be!"

Simon was not surprised to hear the doorknob turn and see his housekeeper once again at his side. "I hope you don't mind that I sent for your cousin to come; he awaits you in the dining room."

No. Not James. But who else might be called? "Let me be a while longer . . . with her, would you be so kind? Tell my cousin—"

"That I cannot rightly do, sir," she interrupted. "You are in a terrible state; you should not be in there. Not like this. Not with her lying there. Please come with me downstairs."

"No. I *cannot.* What if she awakens? What then? She should not be alone." *What if the medicine works oddly and this is simply the way . . . ?*

Mrs. McRory placed a hand on Simon's shoulder. "I know, Dr. Bell. It is so hard to believe. But you must come now. Please." She gently took his hand, guiding him from the chair. He recoiled from her grasp, standing upright as the blanket slipped from his shoulders into a pile at his feet.

He mustered a poised and formal tone. "Tell James I'll be down presently, Mrs. McRory, *after* I have washed." She remained, unmoved, unconvinced.

Simon puffed out a breath, acknowledging her concern with a nod. "You needn't worry. Truly, I shall be down in just a moment," he said a little too lightly. "If you would be so kind as to place a jug of hot water in my dressing room—"

"Very good, sir. But mind you do not take long, or I shall send your cousin to fetch you himself."

Simon knelt again at Sophie's still body, which had already gone stiff. All medicine is poison, and he supposed the more potent, the more venomous. Had his simple act—opening a bottle, exposing the contents to air—so altered the elixir as to make it poisonous? It *was* possible, this much he knew. Or had that been Erceldoune's intent from the start, his worst suspicions about the apothecary proved tragically correct?

With trepidation, Simon pulled back the bedcovers a last time for a final glance. He faltered, stunned and disbelieving. *Impossible!*

The tumors had vanished!

CHICAGO'S NORTH SHORE, PRESENT DAY

CHAPTER 13

S imon reread the e-mail:

> Dear Mr Danforth, I believe I may have in my possession the book about which you advertised on the Antiquarian Online site. Might I ask further about your interest in it? Might it be for your research, perhaps? A new Holmes? BTW: I am quite the fan, and would quite like to think I may be of assistance in this way if it is.
>   Yours, Paul Gilles, DSc

How many inquiries had Simon made over the years? Fifty? Seventy? All had led him to pay a small fortune sight unseen for interesting volumes, alchemy texts with the promise of hidden formulas and obscure language, most of which now sat in Gaelan's shop, cluttering the shelves. And all of which Gaelan insisted were his in the first place, lost when he was arrested oh so many decades ago. But neither he nor Gaelan had ever turned up the ouroboros book.

Gaelan believed Simon had long ago lost his mind pursuing a phantom that likely no longer existed. But he couldn't give up. He owed that much to Sophie, no matter how spiteful, even malicious, she, or rather, her spirit, had become over the years.

She'd scuttled every attempt he'd made at having a normal, intimate relationship with a living woman, turning up at the most inopportune moment possible. It was bloody maddening.

"Malicious? Me? And who was the one rousted me from my eternal rest? And you have audacity to call me cruel?"

Sophie stood inches from Simon, hands poised on her hips, expression haughty, but with a twinkle in her eye. More the seductive mockingbird tonight than the shrill shrike. She was attired in red this night—Victoria's Secret—and her hair was drawn up in a jeweled feather comb.

But how many minutes would it be before impatience and pure spitefulness ended this respite, changing her into the malevolent, shrieking specter he'd come to expect? But even then, she was, and ever would be, his beloved Sophie.

He stopped suddenly as if to avoid her, knowing full well he could walk right through her. "Please, Sophie, not tonight, my dear."

Her fingers fanned, reaching out toward his cheek, her nails scarlet daggers. If she'd been real, his face would now surely be in shreds.

Her lips pursed into a pout. *"You insult me with your little betrayals. First, you summon me from beyond the grave, then you try to bed every young woman you meet!"*

"My dear, it has been nearly two hundred years, after all." He'd given up on women of any sort a long while back. He might as well be living in a monastery.

*"Your friend Mr. Erceldoune seems to fare all right without...
entanglements—"*

"Living like a monk in a small flat. Half out of his mind, hardly a life worth living."

"As if either of you has a choice!"

"Soon, love. I'll put it to rights, I promise. And we both shall finally rest, and on the same side."

Sophie laughed. It was a dissonant, deafening cackling. The vixen had vanished, transformed into a hideous wraith. Simon clamped his hands to his ears to stifle the terrifying sound, squeezing his eyes against the sight of her. And then she was gone, suddenly as she'd appeared.

His footsteps echoed on the oak flooring as he strode angrily from one end of his study to the other. Halted by an inconvenient wall, Simon slammed his hand against the plaster in frustration and reversed course, considering the Bedlam discovery. All those years he and Gaelan had eluded exposure. Could those bloody diaries at last be their undoing?

He'd once proposed to Gaelan that they reveal it themselves. It had been New Year's Eve 2000, the turn of a new millennium, and after much to drink. "Out with it already. So what if the world knows? It's the twenty-first century, and you've bloody discovered the secret to immortality. You'll be rich beyond your dreams—a celebrity. What have you to fear?"

Gaelan had been in the midst of an especially bad patch just then, and Simon didn't know what else to do. It had been impulsive—and exactly the wrong thing to suggest. Gaelan had gotten that haunted, hunted expression—a rabbit about to bolt—insisting that Simon couldn't possibly understand what sort of Pandora's Box they'd open. And then Gaelan disappeared. Again.

It had taken two years for Simon to find him, this time on a remote island off Vancouver. And he suspected that Gaelan was found only because he'd wanted to be found, grown exhausted of living on nightmares and loneliness. He'd been in desperate straits, beyond gaunt, sitting outside a run-down caravan in a rusty lawn chair, barely recognizable, stoned out of his mind.

Simon hadn't been serious about disclosing their not-so-little secret—not really. He had no desire for discovery either. When he'd been too long in a place, he would relocate to the Continent, to Africa, to Asia, only to reappear years later with a slight change of name, a descendent with a claim to Simon's legacy: great-grandnephew, fourth cousin twice removed, great-great-grandson, and always bearing a copy of the will, guaranteeing his inheritance of Simon Bell's fortune. He'd become as adaptive as one of Darwin's tortoises, but never venturing so far from himself as to get lost in the maze of time and age. This most recent occupation of writing Holmes suited him, connecting him to home, his time and place. It kept him grounded, like Gaelan and his antiquarian books.

With the discovery of the Bedlam diaries, Gaelan would likely withdraw entirely into himself, then slip away one morning, departing without a word. Simon could not let that happen, not again. Not now. Not with this strong feeling that the ouroboros book was finally within their grasps.

"You tell me he is not your friend, yet here you are, living not ten miles from his home! And when he disappears, you follow. Spare no expense to find him."

"I need him to translate the book if . . . when . . . I recover it."

Sophie's icy glare sliced through him; she was inches from his face. At least the banshee had vanished for the moment. She would not be moved until he confessed it.

He sighed. "I owe him."

"For what you'd not the bollocks to do yourself."

Pressing his head against the cold, hard window pane, he allowed the cool moisture to release the tension in his brow. Sophie's reflection appeared just behind his shoulder, in the darkened window. He pivoted, about-face, but she had vanished.

He blinked and turned back toward his desk; there she was again. He hated when she did that.

Now perched upon Simon's writing desk, Sophie caressed his uncapped fountain pen. *"How quaint."* She giggled girlishly. *"Quite the tip on this. How the ink must flow—so viscous and smooth as silk."*

Simon collapsed into his chair, feet up, lighting a Silk Cut. She was going to have her say. He'd learned her moods over the years. She could be quite reasonable, sometimes, and if he was patient, she'd gift him with a flicker of her old self. But then, a perceived offense, and she would turn, shrieking in his ear until he could stand no more. He would run from the house to the edge of the bluff and hope the waves below crashed loudly enough upon the rocks to shut her out. It almost never worked.

It hadn't always been thus. For years after her death, Sophie existed only as a recurrent vision, sweet and lovely as when she was living until Conan Doyle dragged him to a séance just after the Great War. The night was still vivid in Simon's memory. . . .

"*I know, old chap, you are sorely missing someone dear.*" *Conan Doyle had worn away at Simon's denial for months. "I am acquainted with quite a marvelous medium, and she is skilled at this sort of—communication. It has quite comforted me to speak with my dear son Kingsley, who died just last year. It is nothing short of miraculous; I have spoken with him several times now, and it has done my heart a great joy to know he is alive on some other plane. It would do you as well, I think, a modicum of good.*"

Protests fared not well against Conan Doyle's insistence, and then Simon found himself in a dark room at a table full of believers—dupes, one and all, including Conan Doyle. Simon hoped the medium was, indeed, a fraud. If she was genuine, and truly might see into his heart and soul, she would be privy to far too much. Simon riveted his eyes to the woman as she swayed and keened, her voice transmuting at will.

He was caught off his guard when her gaze suddenly latched onto his, her lids flying open in surprise. Simon found himself caught in her unyielding stare, unable to extricate himself, waiting for her to proclaim to the room the secrets of his heart. But the battle between them finally ended, and he felt his mind loosen as the room brightened. Exultant applause erupted, drowning out the gasps and bewildered murmuring—inquiries about what they'd witnessed between the medium and Dr. Bell. But the medium, now pale and very quiet, declined all questions. "I was mistaken," she stammered, her eyes haunted with something not there before.

The medium had touched something elemental within Simon and dragged Sophie to him from beyond the grave. It was the final time he had encountered the now-elderly author. And even in the dim light of the séance, and with failing eyesight, Conan Doyle had *not* failed to notice that Simon was looking "not much older" than when they'd first met.

Now, nearly one hundred years later, Sophie draped her long legs across Simon's, leaning back in a seductive pose, one shoulder bared. "*If you want me gone, my dear Simon, just wish me away. You have pined so long, you know no other way, even when I wail and moan in the midst of night, depriving you of sleep, of any semblance of a life. Why do you not simply find an occupation and push me from you? Do you not know 'The Unquiet Grave,' my love? 'Make yourself content' and perhaps someday—*"

"I am long past the remotest hope of a 'someday' at your side, a day that shall never be, I fear. I cannot die; I cannot live. I dwell here in purgatory, neither heaven nor hell. When you are here, it is better, I confess, even when you are your most cruel self, but why must you ever harangue me? Your sharp tongue lacerates my heart. And then when you turn banshee and your soul aims only to terrify me—"

The red satin of her long skirt fell away to reveal the black fishnet of her stockings. *"And yet, my love, you refuse to supplant me. Admit it."* She laughed a demon's cackle, incongruous from her scarlet lips. *"It is a bit warped and more than slightly masochistic, but you do not really want me gone."*

Simon picked up a paper clip, tapping it on the desk in annoyance. "Please leave me," he pleaded. "I've enough to contend with—"

Sophie drew nearer, and Simon could almost feel her breath on the back of his neck, making the sensitive skin tingle with anticipation. He reached for her, grabbing air, pounding the table in frustration. She was gone. Head in his hands, he thrust his fingers through his short hair, breathing with relief.

He needed to reply to Dr. Gilles. But what to tell him?

CHAPTER 14

Gaelan awoke to the smell of freshly ground coffee. At least he'd somehow remembered to set the machine to auto-grind—better than a fucking alarm clock.

One eye, then the other, opened into the too-bright sunshine leaking through the blinds, reflecting directly into his bleary vision. *Bloody hell!* He winced at the entropy of papers, folders, books, and electronic paraphernalia sprawled across the floor. When had he done that?

Clearly, it had not been one of his better nights. At least he'd slept well—a rare enough commodity: no flashbacks, no nightmares, no dreams at all . . . the first time in the four days since the *Guardian* piece. *Thank you, god of tetra-hydro-cannabinol!*

Gaelan's joints cracked with the release of tension as he unwound his limbs from the sofa, yawning his way through the mess. Coffee. Strong, black coffee. Dark roast, thick and rich—no sugar, no milk. He set his mug in place and pressed "Brew." The fizz-pop-pop of the machine and the aroma of Sumatra Reserve absorbed the thundering in his head.

He stepped into the shower and let the hot liquid, sharp as needles, cascade through the knots in his shoulders and arms until the headache splintered into insignificance. He could easily spend the morning here until the water ran cold. But he had a business to run. He retrieved the steaming mug, glancing at the empty Lagavulin bottle with regret, and headed into the shop.

Simon was right. It was ridiculous to think that the pharmaceutical company would make a connection to him by studying insane asylum diaries of an insane doctor. His thoughts drifted to the ouroboros book. Was it really possible that Simon had located it after all these years?

That book had caused nothing but grief for him, for Simon, even for Simon's poor dead wife, who, but for the elixir, would be long at her rest, along with her husband. For all his interest in antiquarian books, for all his buying and selling of texts nearly as opaque and fascinating as the ouroboros book, all his searching for it, part of him recoiled from the very idea of ever seeing it again.

He opened the blinds, dusted the shelves, and opened the shop. Any occupation to distract his thoughts from the book, from Handley's diaries, from ... A quicksilver flicker of a memory slithered through his mind. His toes curled instinctively as it took hold, and he told himself it wasn't real even as invisible flames penetrated the thin leather of his sandals. Exquisite agony burned into his soles, into his soul, unbound, blistered and festering. He was held down, shackled, impotent to stop it.

The doorbells jangled, and the vision was gone. "Good morning," he breathed shakily, forcing a smile. He nodded to the young woman perusing jars of tea on a low shelf. "They ... they are all dried in-house. Fresh each week. Select what you fancy, and I can bundle them in silk sachets for you, or if you like ... bulk is nice too; I've a good selection of infusers, and—" He hoped she would take it in bulk, not certain his trembling hands could manage the dexterity needed for the sachet ribbons.

She paused at a large, inset bookcase, removing an eighteenth-century volume: *Antipodean Art and Artists*. "Are you all right, Mr. Erceldoune?"

Gaelan blinked. Mrs. Frayn. Of course! Where was his mind this morning? The glare—he'd not seen her for the glare. That must be it. Either that, or he was finally losing what remained of his sanity. "Yes, luv, of course," he said too quickly. "A late night." He winked as he managed a knowing grin. "I've your order right here." He fetched a brown bag from beneath the counter. "Tangerine-spice tea, three ounces. Perhaps you'd like a cup now. Kettle's hot—"

"Is this a first printing?"

"It is at that, Mrs. Frayn. The plates are in perfect condition—"

"My husband's birthday is Sunday—"

"The art history professor, of course. It's a handsome gift, if a bit pricey ... but for you, luv, three hundred dollars."

She didn't flinch. "Can you put it aside for me? I'll pick it up tonight while Charles is teaching—"

"Of course. Sure you wouldn't want to stay and . . . ? I've another book, even better . . . upstairs." She paid for the tea and the book, turning to leave. How might he delay her departure, at least for a bit? The vision had vanished when she'd entered, and he'd really rather not be sucked into it again. As long as he was not alone . . .

"Sorry, Mr. Erceldoune. Class in half an hour, and I need to finish grading way too many exams before my students descend and demand their inflated As. You sure you're okay?"

"Yeah. Fine. Let me know how you like the tea."

By noon, the too-vivid flashes of memory had yet to retreat. An endless horror movie in short cuts that would have chased Guillermo del Toro under the bed trembling with terror. A new vision materialized, this time a flail slicing into his arms, his legs. Horrified, Gaelan observed as his skin peeled away, and then muscle and sinew flowered open, revealing the white of bone, before it, too, broke away to expose the black gelatin of his marrow. He heard a scream, not knowing whether it was memory or imagination . . . or real.

Oh for Chrissakes, Gaelan, get a grip! No one will come for you. Don't be such a fucking twit! Who would care now about a man, no matter the overblown claims about him, hanged in Newgate nearly two centuries ago?

A walk. He needed a walk, the fresh, clean, cold air courtesy of yesterday's snowfall. Gaelan flipped the sign in the window to "Closed" and stepped into the midday throng of Northwestern students, surprised to feel the warmth of the sun, as if yesterday's freak blizzard had been a momentary meteorological memory lapse.

The remains of snowdrifts had melted into puddles and slush; water dripped from the L tracks. A train clattered overhead, leaving in its wake a wall of mist and steam embedded with rainbows of bent sunlight dangling midair. Gaelan reached out as if he might capture one in his hand.

Sandaled college students hurled dripping snowballs at each other, like late-season skiers in sleeveless tank tops, enjoying the paradoxes of a Chicago spring. He barely noticed them, blurs in a post-Impressionist painting, as he wended his way through puddles, skateboarders, and bicycles.

He needed to drown the visions, the screams, the memories from his mind; for that he knew the perfect place: a secluded patch of rock and sand up the shore near Simon's house. He'd spotted it a year or two ago, beneath a high bluff as he'd hiked along the beach, not realizing how far north he'd ventured, surprised to spot Simon's promontory one hundred feet above him and ten miles from home. There, he could lose himself to the crash of waves upon the rocks, and dive into the bracing chill of Lake Michigan in spring. He fetched his Triumph Sportbike from its parking space, and took off north along Sheridan.

The alabaster gleam of the Baha'i Temple loomed to his left as he rounded a turn, the shoreline snaking westward. He stopped the bike, picturing the temple's gardens edged with snow as they surely would be. Maybe he'd end the ride here, and lose himself in the great seven-sided hall, surrounded by centuries of wisdom echoing with each footstep, expansive as the building itself. Gaelan aborted the idea as a school bus pulled up to the building—a tour. *Damn.* What if he lost it there right in the middle of all those kids? *Bad idea.*

The terrain changed dramatically, and now he rode high above the lake through bluffs that wound into blind curves, steep rocky ravines on either side. He could hear the wind-whipped waves crashing sixty, eighty feet below, into the base of the cliff. Stopping at the top of a bluff, he looked down, watching the last vestiges of snow clinging to the boulders melt into waterfalls cascading down to the beach below.

Gaelan dismounted the bike and picked his way through trees and rocks, descending a forested embankment, thinking better of it when he lost his footing on the ice, one sandal slipping from his foot. He'd have to bike it.

Carefully, he climbed through brush and loose boulders and back onto the Triumph. He started it up and put it in gear, about to make the turn down a narrow dirt road to the beach. Startled by a sound close by, Gaelan turned, and then he saw it: a hand, disembodied and wielding a jagged knife, its metal gleam blinding him. *Bloody hell!* Spooked, he slammed on the foot brake just as the bike began to roll down the sharp incline, skidding badly on an icy patch. And then, he was in freefall, no longer on the bike. The sudden exhilaration of flight was soon replaced by the realization he was plummeting down the embankment.

Rock and ice, sharp as daggers, sliced through his clothing as he tried reaching out with his good hand to gain purchase on the slippery outcropping or grab onto a tree branch. The Triumph followed, hurtling through the bluff, hitting it, not five feet above him, bursting into flames, shrapnel raining down on him as he continued to descend the steep rock. The pounding of his heart thundered in his ears and melted into the crackle of flames and the roar of the waves as he plunged the rest of the way to the boulder breakwater below.

An echo from high above floated just beyond his ability to protest, "Someone call 911!"

LONDON, 1837

CHAPTER 15

Daylight seeped through a small crack at the cellar ceiling as Gaelan awoke, groggily realizing where he was, his small refuge beneath the ruins of his apothecary, his home. How long had he slept? An hour? Perhaps two? Fatigued and weary, he glanced at Timothy, still asleep on his pallet, before creeping up the ladder and into Smithfield. Despite an early-morning rain, the smoke yet clung to the market, the acrid perfume of charred wood and smoldering straw intermingling with sweet aroma of fresh breads and pastries and the foul stench of raw meat, diseased water, and horse dung.

Morning revealed the extent of the fire's damage. Twelve stalls reduced to piles of smoldering, steaming matchsticks, along with the apothecary shop, and Gaelan had no doubt that Lyle Tremayne would walk away from it unscathed, his connections too highly placed, his clientele too well-connected. Already vendors were rummaging through the mud and ash and charred remains to salvage anything not burned to cinders. Silently, he headed to the livery stable to retrieve his horse. The gentle Fell had been Gaelan's gift to Caitrin just after Iain's birth; they'd loved riding through the countryside together, but Caitrin didn't care for hired horses, and had missed having her own mount. He seldom rode anymore, leaving it to the stableboy to keep the horse fit and well cared for.

"Here ya go, Mr. Erceldoune," said the stableboy, handing Gaelan the reins. "It's a relief to see you alive this morn, sir. After what happened last night with the shop and all. Dad and I thought for sure you were done for. The horses were restless all night long, but your Fell will do right by you. Not very big, but he's strong and quick as the devil."

Gaelan managed a weak nod, unable to form a coherent sentence. Time to move on, he knew. Leave this place and recommence life elsewhere—maybe America this time. But he couldn't leave England without saying good-bye to Caitrin and wee Iain.

Following the Thames westward, Gaelan flew down the road, thankful for the swift, agile horse. The brisk wind restored his energy as city gave way to countryside, and the smoldering stench of Smithfield gave way to the freshening aroma of the riverbank. Yet every strike of horseshoe upon the gravel throbbed through his exhausted body, and into his head.

The horse protested at the relentless pace, slowing periodically despite Gaelan's efforts. He'd no choice but to grudgingly acquiesce, lest he tax the Fell beyond its endurance.

The last time Gaelan had been to the Kinston estate was after Caitrin and Iain had been ripped from their beds to be "treated" there by the earl's personal physicians.

"Bled with leeches," he'd been told upon arrival, the door then slammed in his face. He pictured his wee son, just a few months old, frightened and alone, screaming out in pain with no understanding. Gaelan had stood in the wind and rain for hours praying for a kind-hearted servant, or the vicar perhaps, to come to him with news—any news. He'd shouted their names until his tongue was parched and breath left him, and Kinston's men dragged him away at the point of a sword.

Gaelan spied Kinston House looming near: battlements and towers high above the surrounding landscape. After dismounting, and tying his horse at the tall iron gates of the graveyard, he gazed through the locked bars and past hundreds of aged and mossed-over stone markers toward a small hillock, wondering whether the gleaming white monument at its foot marked the resting place of his small family, of Lord Kinston's only child and her son. A gentle tap on his shoulder startled him in the quiet of the churchyard. "Might I help you, sir?"

Gaelan wheeled, coming face-to-face with an old man, well dressed in cleric's garb. "Good morning, vicar." How much did the vicar know? "I was just coming to your door. I shall be taking my leave of England for a while and should like to lay a flower at a particular gravestone before I do. If you would be so kind as to open the gate, then direct me towards—"

The old man smiled. "You are here to see the Lady Caitrin, of course. She was your wife, was she not?"

The vicar scrutinized him like prey, and Gaelan forced himself to remain emotionless and calm, wondering whether there would be trouble. *Be you a man of God or Lord Kinston's lackey?*

"You look as if you might do with an ale, sir. Do come in."

Gaelan had little desire to drink with the vicar. "Forgive me, but I've ridden two hours after a near-sleepless night, and I've no mind to delay—"

"All the more reason, sir, for you to sit a moment. If not drink, food perhaps. If you don't mind my saying, I am dreadful sorry about Lady Caitrin. I knew her since she was a babe in arms—" The vicar hesitated a moment, worrying a thread on his sleeve. "And your son, of course. All the more so for the way . . . Indeed, it was wrong of Lord Kinston to refuse you last year when you wished to attend her—" He blinked. "*Their* . . . burial. I . . . I assure you . . . I advised him otherwise."

There was little regret in the vicar's countenance. Beads of sweat welled on his doughy face. He was afraid, but of whom?

"Forgive me, sir. I have not come here to harangue you. Have I your leave, or shall you have me thrown off these lands as Kinston did a year back?" He would brook no small talk, no sympathetic platitudes from this sniveling toady. Gaelan gauged the height of the fence, contemplating how he might vault it, if need be.

The vicar nodded, blowing out a breath. "Very well." He unlocked the high gate and pointed in the direction Gaelan had been looking before he'd been interrupted. "You'll find her grave at the base of yonder hill, beneath the acacia tree."

Gaelan approached the hillock, listening for footsteps in pursuit, hoping the vicar had not lost his nerve. The alabaster stone was polished and new, set amid the fragrance of new-mown lawn and the moist decay of autumn.

"Lady Caitrin Arianna Kinston, Beloved Daughter and Mother."
Gaelan bit his lower lip, rage flooding his grief. The bond between
them—ten years of marriage and a son, the earl's own grandson—
severed by a stonemason's awl. Not even the anticipation of such cold-
heartedness mitigated the blow.

He ran his hands across the deep carving of the headstone,
engraving it upon his soul. But where was Iain's grave? He ran from one
marker to the next, frantic, crawling through the damp grass and debris,
but it was nowhere to be found. *Why would they not . . . ?* Then, from
behind, hoofbeats! There was no time! He whirled to find Kinston's
men surrounding him, rifles at the ready.

"You shall leave, sir, and never return," said one. "The next time we
discover you on these lands, we shall call the magistrate. Be gone."

With little use in confronting the heavily armed men, Gaelan was
forced to abandon all hope of finding his son's gravestone. The family
had gathered before the great house to witness from a distance his
humiliation. They were all there—Kinston, his wife, even a serving girl,
holding in her arms a young child—all staring at him derisively as he
was marched off the estate.

The midafternoon sun filtered dull orange-red through the dissipating
smoke of Smithfield as Gaelan arrived at the White Owl Inn. The
boisterous crowd was still buzzing about the blaze, uttering, "Thanks to
heaven," that no one had been killed and the injuries mild. "Ah, but you,
Mr. Erceldoune! What of your shop? And what's to become of you?"

The publican Sally Mills stood in the midst of the crowd, three
mugs in each meaty hand. Gaelan approached her, taking three of the
brimming vessels from her. "Have you a room to let, Sally? And have
you seen Tim around yet today?"

"Thank you, Mr. Erceldoune. Yes, he's yonder," she said, gesturing
with her elbow to a corner table as she shifted one of the mugs to her

other hand. "Too bad about your shop; I've seen the ruin, but of course you'll rebuild." He followed her to a large table, distributing the mugs among the customers. "Meantime, consider the White Owl to be your home." She placed a gentle hand on his arm.

"The room's not for me, Sally, but for Tim. I mean to leave London, quickly as I may."

"Leave? But why? Whatever shall we do without you? Lyle Tremayne will bring in one of his own—some charlatan to fleece us all and line his pockets! You *can't* leave us. I'm more than happy to put you up on the house till you're ready to rebuild."

Gaelan nodded. He well understood what would likely befall the good people of Smithfield if Tremayne had opportunity to put in an apothecary of his own choosing. "That I know well, my dear friend, but I'm afraid I cannot stay. I shall put in a word at the Apothecary's Hall and find Smithfield a proper practitioner—perhaps better than me!"

Timothy had spotted him and was now excitedly waving his arms. Gaelan smiled and began to make his way to his table. "Now, my darling Sal, bring us round bowls of that wonderful stew of yours, which even now intoxicates my senses. And pints of your finest."

"Shop's a ruin, Mr. Erceldoune," Timothy said, shaking his head slowly. "I don't know how we're to rebuild—"

"We cannot."

The food arrived, and Timothy devoured the stew quickly. Gaelan had no appetite, no matter how enticing the savory aroma. He pushed his bowl toward his apprentice, and finished off his ale in three gulps. After withdrawing two envelopes from his leather satchel, Gaelan set them on the table.

"I'll be gone in three days' time, lad. And you shall return home to your father's house. I've here a letter of introduction; you shall have no difficulty in finding another apothecary with whom to apprentice. You're clever, and you're an able assistant; you would do well to study the surgeon's art as well, as I did long ago. The other letter is for your father and a return of monies not used, for he paid me ahead three months."

"But, Mr. Erceldoune, where shall you go? I can certainly follow wherever you set up a new shop. You shall need an assistant, of course, wherever you resettle—"

Gaelan looked away. "No, Tim. I mean to leave England forever. Perhaps away to America." Indeed, he had been in Smithfield too long by far. Soon enough, neighbors would take notice; no doubt Sally already had. They had all aged, Sal, Timothy, Tremayne—all but him. No wonder Tremayne suspected something peculiar. "No, my lad. Fortune be with you, but we shall never again cross paths."

Pulling Timothy into an embrace, Gaelan regretted severing himself once again from all he held dear. But there really was no other way. He gestured toward Sally, now arguing with a customer from behind the long bar. "Now mind her, and she'll take care of you until it is time for your coach on the morrow. I've arranged your fare already." Simon closed his bag, adjusting it over his shoulder and across his chest. He patted it, feeling within it the ouroboros book, determined never again to let it venture too distant from his grasp.

"But—"

Already out the door, squinting into the sun, Gaelan sighed, one task complete and his thoughts drifting to the next item on his list.

"Gaelan Erceldoune?"

He looked up; five men formed a semicircle before him, pistols raised. He took a step backward, tensing. *What's this about, then?* It couldn't be Kinston's men chasing him all the way to Smithfield, and yet . . . Not Kinston's, he realized: Tremayne's men, sent to finish the task forgotten in their haste to flee the blaze.

Perhaps this was a stroke of luck. They would shoot, and he would fall. Fifty witnesses would swear to his death, and he'd be carried off. Morning would come, and he would vanish, the body undoubtedly snatched by resurrectionists.

Over his shoulder, the White Owl quickly emptied, the patrons watching with curiosity as the armed men approached. "I am Gaelan Erceldoune. What do you want of me?"

"Gaelan Erceldoune, you are under arrest for murder, by order of the magistrate. You are to accompany us to the Old Bailey." One advanced, shackles unlocked and at the ready.

Arrest? Coiled and wary, Gaelan stepped backward toward the White Owl, his hands flat in front of him—a gesture of surrender. "I've *murdered* no one."

"That is not what it says here!" Another of the men approached with a rolled paper. "You will answer, sir, for the death of Lillian Mason, found poisoned late last night."

Incomprehensible. *Lil dead? Poison?* It could not be true. Gaelan's knees buckled; he fought to remain upright, facing his accusers eye to eye. He refused to believe it. Tremayne. Had to be. Who else would do it—murder an innocent girl and then come after him to hang for it? Gaelan shouted the scoundrel's name, as if he would have the courage to confront him directly.

"Mr. Erceldoune!"

Tim. Gaelan startled, yet remaining mindful of the armed men, now nearly upon him. "Timothy! Please. Come no closer, lad. All will be right." He held up an arm, waving Timothy away and addressing his captors, begging reason to prevail. "Surely, the young man is no threat to you."

Gaelan held up his satchel, still slung across his chest. "This bag contains nothing but items of sentimental value. I would give it into this young man's safekeeping. You may look inside if you wish, but I would ask—"

One of the men took it, ripping the long strap from Gaelan's shoulder. He opened it. "Fine." He threw it into the dirt.

Gaelan picked it up, beckoning Timothy closer. "Tim, my boy, there's naught to give you a fright. I shall be fine. Only just take my satchel; I'll have no need of it for a while." His voice dropped to a whisper, forcing Timothy closer still, but the men continued to draw nearer. "Be sure to take care with it, and keep it safe for me. Do not let it out of your possession, wherever you go. Someday you shall return it to me."

"But, sir! Your books—"

Gaelan nodded. "Yes, them as well. I—"

The men had lost patience, forcing the shackles around his wrists and ankles. "No more small talk!"

He neither fought nor helped as his captors dragged him off to the mortifying cries of "Murderer!" in his wake.

CHAPTER 16

Two weeks later and still Simon could not believe that Sophie was dead. Life passed as if he were a spectator standing alongside a moving stage. The funeral at his in-laws' estate, recalled only in flashes of distorted faces, lips mouthing unintelligible platitudes. He'd been home three days, refusing all visitors and swathed in a blanket of laudanum, which did little to stem his tearless sobs.

And now his mother awaited him, the most unwelcome caller of all. He sighed, opening the drawing room doors, knowing he could not avoid her forever. Her hard gaze ambushed him immediately.

"I must have a word with your housekeeper. You are a fright, Simon. James told me you were in a bad way, but I refused to believe him."

"Mother, I have just lost my wife." So it began. There was little she could say that had not already been said several times over by James— and even Mrs. McRory.

"Yes, and from what James has told me, it is more blessing than curse that she is gone; she was in terrible pain, he told me, and on death's door. And what is this business of an apothecary? My *God*, Simon." She shook her head slowly side to side. "My dear son, I thought you were more reasonable than this! Look at you! Is this any way to greet a visitor, in mourning or not. Really!"

"You must allow me to grieve in my own way—"

"What? By starving yourself, refusing to bathe or shave?"

"Mother, you know nothing. I—"

"To speak true, Simon, I came because dear Mrs. McRory was fearful for you. She sent word that you had deteriorated both in health and in deportment. I did not believe her, owing it to exaggeration and her own sorrow. Now go, dress properly for luncheon. I have no intention of returning home to Cheshire until I am satisfied you have recovered your good senses!"

Simon was grateful to leave his mother's presence, anxious to reprimand Mrs. McRory for going to Lady Elizabeth, although she'd warned him. But there was nothing Mrs. McRory, James . . . or Lady Elizabeth Bell might say to him.

He'd avoided Sophie's boudoir, the one place he feared more than any other on earth. Now he was pulled there as if tethered to it by an invisible strand of twine embedded beneath his ribs.

Simon opened the door and stood at the threshold, holding onto the frame to steady himself. Her wardrobe was open, and he wanted nothing more than to lose himself in the folds of her gowns. Two steps and he fell upon them, holding his face to the velvets and satins, brocades and silks. He breathed in her scent, her bath salts, her perfume, which lingered on the fine fabrics. She was almost there, so very close, caressing his hair, whispering to him that all would be well.

"Simon . . ."

An airy voice wound through his mind, calling out to him. He turned in its direction, heart pounding, knowing it was only the voice of his own despair calling out from the depths of the abyss. But there she was.

"Oh my God, Sophie! How . . . how is it possible?" Staggering to the bed, Simon beheld her standing before him, corporeal, more than a vision; he reached out to touch her, exquisite in sapphire velvet, dark hair cascading about her shoulders. Was he mad or was this a ghost come to haunt him? He was terrified and elated.

"The apothecary should not die, Simon. And certainly not because you refuse to speak up on his behalf."

"It is not for my silence that he hangs, but for the murder of that girl." In truth, Simon could not imagine the apothecary murdering anyone, much less that particular girl. Yet he was little disposed to get involved despite three letters from Erceldoune's lawyer begging his assistance. He'd watched them burn on the hearth, ignored.

"It was his poison, after all, that killed you, Sophie. He hates physicians, all of us; he blames us for his wife's death. Perhaps he was taking his revenge upon me as proxy for my brother physicians!"

"You don't really believe that!" She sat beside him on her bed, so near Simon could smell her lavender bath salts. He massaged the bridge of his nose. He was so bloody exhausted and had little inclination to argue with a figment of his imagination, ghost, or whatever this specter of his wife might be, however pleasing her countenance, how demurely she glanced at him. . . .

"Are you so certain it was Erceldoune's elixir that killed me? Perhaps it was simply my time or your error. A relapse of fever or a hundred other things?"

Simon had thought of all those things, especially after the accident with the bottle. "I know poison's footprints, Sophie." But the argument was weak, and he knew it. "The doubt shall always live in my mind, love. I am certain there are plenty of others in Smithfield will speak up on his behalf—those that know him and can give real testimony, not the eavesdropping of a conversation. And what if I should be questioned about your death? Would that not go worse for him? As for me, I've nothing left to live for. Now you're gone, I shall drink down the remainder of the terrible elixir and end it!"

Sophie stood and stalked across the room to her escritoire, arms crossed, tapping her foot. Simon was well acquainted with this pose.

"Suicide is against God's laws, Simon, as well you know."

Simon tried to will her away. "Go. Please?" It could not be normal to be speaking thus to an apparition.

"You then shall be condemned to burn for eternity and never be with me."

"It is not suicide, Sophie; it is judgment. And it is just. What I did—"

"Was out of love for me. I would have died soon enough anyway. Listen to me, Simon!" She propelled herself from the desk, coming to light in front of him as he sat, head in his hands. *"Yes, love, you hastened my death—perhaps—but do you not see what a slow and dreadful ending it might have been for me? I thank God Almighty that my suffering is at an end!"*

He felt in his pocket for the smooth lines of the apothecary bottle, which he'd kept close at hand since that dreadful night.

"Dr. Bell!" Mrs. McRory pounded her fist on the door. Simon jumped at the unexpected sound. Sophie had vanished. He went to the door, opening it a crack.

"Are you all right, sir? I've been knocking for minutes, and your cousin has arrived to join you and Lady Bell for luncheon. And you know your mother, if I may be so bold; she grows impatient at your absence."

"Tell James..." What? Just what should he tell his cousin that would not send him bounding up the stairs two at a time in panic? "Tell them I shall be down presently... and leave me be. And please serve; do not wait upon me." Simon listened as Mrs. McRory's footfalls grew more distant. He withdrew the phial, clasping it in his palm.

Now my love, it is time for me to join you. Simon searched the room, but Sophie had not returned. He settled into her bed, breathing in the scent of her that now had nearly faded away.

Simon considered the cobalt phial, turning it in his hand. Carefully, he slid away the glass stopper and placed the bottle to his lips, spilling the entire contents down his throat. A metallic taste lingered on his tongue. *Mercury? Silver, perhaps.* The bitterness of bloodroot and the anesthetic numb of opium and clove... garlic. *Arsenic?*

Simon waited for death to take him as his thoughts decayed into chaos, fragmenting and rearranging themselves into random particles. He observed them caught in the sunbeams that played across the ceiling, radiant dust motes as the drug worked through him. He followed them from his place on her bed, enraptured; colors he had never before experienced swirled before him, then shattered on the floor.

He sensed the poison working through his organs, an evil imp sliding astride the twists and turns of his blood vessels and organs—alive and hungry. How long would it be? Arsenic worked fast, but what of this oxidized elixir? Would it course through to his liver and lungs? Or would it set its sights on his heart and brain?

"Dr. Bell!" Someone was jostling him, shouting his name. "Dr. Bell! Waken up! Waken up!" *Mrs. McRory?* The yelling echoed distantly, yet she must have been nearby. The shaking stopped, and then the soft sound of a closing door. Peace at last.

Simon awoke into darkness. When had that happened? It had been light when . . . so very bright. Halos of color now traced in an ellipse around the periphery of vision in the dark, evaporating as he emerged into painful clarity. The door opened.

A sharp pain lanced through his head before traversing to his stomach, where it pawed and clawed until he retched. He attempted to move his hand, the one that didn't feel like a bar of lead, flexing his fingers.

"Simon, thank God. What the devil happened?"

"James?" he groaned, his parched throat refusing to cooperate. When he ventured to sit up, his head pounded, forcing him back.

"Easy there, Simon. We've been trying for hours to rouse you. Your poor mother is beside herself—"

James helped him to sit. Still, the room swam as he forced himself to focus on the steady horizon of the window frame until another round of nausea passed.

"What is this? Is this what you drank, Simon?" James retrieved the elixir bottle from the floor where it had fallen, holding it up for Simon to explain. "Tell me what it is, so I might understand what in damnation you were attempting here!"

"It is of no matter, James, I—" Simon swung his legs over the mattress, testing them; they were rubber. The room again spun, and Simon fell through the cool, dark chasm of nothingness.

CHAPTER 17

Gaelan scoured the half-empty courtroom, searching the noisy crowd in the heated haze. Two weeks, and finally the travesty of a trial would be over. It would be but the start, Gaelan knew, of an uncharted journey into purgatory. Tremayne, leaning against a wall, glowered at the jury, his arms folded as he stood guard lest anyone might come forward to plead on his behalf.

None but one man might do him some good before the black cap appeared upon the judge's wig. Bell was invulnerable to Lyle Tremayne, but nowhere to be seen. And why should he be? Sophie Bell was dead, and, from what he'd heard, by poisoning. Gaelan would not have been surprised to see Bell himself standing in the dock shouting, "Murderer!"

Again, and again, Gaelan replayed it in his mind, recounting each step taken to create the elixir. He'd made no obvious mistake, yet Sophie Bell was dead. What slight askew turn of his pestle or half second too long in the crucible might have turned this healing elixir into a deadly poison? Or had Bell corrupted the elixir some way? Had he failed to follow the directions? There was no way to know.

Gaelan glanced up toward Sally Mills, handkerchief in her hand, dabbing at tears as she stood in the front row of the gallery. He'd fought her silly notion of speaking for him at trial until finally she agreed to hold her silence. Tremayne would destroy her in a trice, and that inn had been part of her family for generations. He could not allow it.

Tremayne stepped up to the dock, his hand on a Bible. Gaelan forced himself to stay calm, hands clamped on the railing, biting his lip through the blackguard's lies until he tasted the salt of his own blood.

"The man deals in the black arts, was what my sweet Lil said to me as she lay dying from one of Erceldoune's special potions. Poisoned her, he did. Told her it was going to make her better. Well if dead is *better*, I suppose it's what he did." Tremayne laughed, a low growl. "He should be burnt, but we're too *civilized* for that nowadays. Well, I suppose the hangman's noose is just as effective!"

Able to stomach no more, Gaelan leapt from his chair. Two hands took hold of his arms, shoving him down hard onto the wooden bench.

"Perjurer!" he cried before his lawyer stopped him with a hand to his shoulder.

"You do yourself no favors, Mr. Erceldoune," he whispered. "Hush now, else—"

Every muscle in Gaelan's body twisted and clenched; he felt like a trussed pig. He glared at Tremayne as the man passed but inches away, walking from the dock back to his post near the door. The jury was dismissed, only to return a moment later, faces set and sour.

"Stand, Gaelan Erceldoune," pronounced the judge, the black silk cap fluttering on his head.

Gaelan stood coiled and silent. He would accord Tremayne no sort of victory, never let him witness the panic that pulsed through his veins.

"Mr. Gaelan Erceldoune, apothecary of Smithfield in London, you shall be returned to Newgate Prison, where you were last confined, and from there you shall be hanged by the neck until you are dead, and thereafter your body buried within the precincts of the prison. May the Lord—"

The hangman's knot would secure around his neck, and he would stand unafraid, unbowed, like his father. Would the gallows surgeon be apathetic, declaring him dead the moment he'd lost consciousness, or would he be clever and wait for a death that would never come? Gaelan prayed for the former. Onto a barrow he'd be thrown for transport to the prison graveyard. Night would fall, and he would make his escape into the woods, running hard, not stopping until he'd reached the shore—a corpse misplaced or stolen, one among the many. Who would notice?

But luck had not been with him of late. What if his body refused to surrender as he dangled, the heavy, coarse rope slicing, burning into his neck as he struggled for air, praying for a death that refused to take him? Led from the courtroom through the mob of spectators, Gaelan could not purge from his mind the vision of such a spectacle, nor its aftermath.

A clang of iron gates echoed behind Gaelan with ominous finality, the world receding with every shuffle of his bound feet. Deeper and deeper within the old fortress walls he trudged, turnkeys at each elbow, through a labyrinth of passageways and yards, gates and gratings, until they descended to his cell. Finally, he was alone.

A stingy ray of bleak light filtered through a single filthy barred window. Dimmer and dimmer it grew, until gray day turned to black night. Rats skittered through the straw, keeping him vigilant. They awaited his sleep with waning patience, for then they would feast— he would provide a better meal than spiders and cockroaches. But he would resist as long as he could.

The darkness mingled with his exhaustion to conjure menacing phantoms of straw and insects, yet he refused to submit. *Concentrate, Gaelan! Do not fall to sleep!*

A fixed point might settle his nerves. Imagining Stella Polaris, his mind's eye drew from it, the outline of the Starry Plough, neighboring groups of stars and their constellations. The entire night sky unfolded in the confines of his small cell. Reciting their familiar names aloud in Greek, then Latin, soothed him, but the sedate music of the languages became a lullaby, blotting out the yells of the condemned and the turnkeys, propelling him to float further and further from wakefulness. . . .

The morning light woke Gaelan to yet another day of despair. He scratched at his itching skin; the rats and insects had dined well. But the lesions had already faded to nothing but irritated prickles. The cell gate opened, and a guard hauled him from his pallet, thrusting Gaelan down a long row of cells and into the prison courtyard.

"Fresh air time, Erceldoune. Treasure it whilst you might. For in less than a week, you shall meet your Maker!"

The yard was nearly empty; the few prisoners huddled along an immense stone wall with battlements one hundred feet high.

"What are you doing here on this side of Newgate?"

Gaelan was startled by a small, wiry man standing at his shoulder. The man's face was vaguely familiar.

"Man like you, educated and all—an apothecary, *I've* heard tell—Smithfield, isn't it? Likely have some money set aside; so why are you here with the rabble when you might acquire for yourself a nice spot on the other side of our little village?"

A second man approached, and now he recognized them both: Tremayne's men. This one could barely speak for his raucous coughing; disease ate away at his arm.

"Aww, I see you remember us. Lovely. Well, word from our . . . boss . . . has it that you're some sort of magical healer, Erceldoune! So heal me!"

More men approached, and Gaelan searched the yard for guards—anyone who might forestall the likely outcome of this "welcome." There were no routes of escape, and no way to fight off the growing gang, which seemed to increase magically as men appeared from every corner, pulling closer and closer.

"I was talkin' to you, healer!" the prisoner persisted. The circle of men drew tighter still.

"What would you have me say? Had I my herbs, I would do my best to cure you, or at the very least give you laudanum to diminish your pain." He was unconvincing.

"Well, apothecary, you will soon enough pray that you had some for yourself!" A knife's blade flashed in the periphery of Gaelan's vision, trained on his left flank.

Ah, so that's what they've in mind—beat the executioner to the draw, here and now. Why take chances on a reprieve? The first blow was to his lower back—he was ready for it—but the second drove him hard into an iron grate. He licked away the pungent taste of salt and metal as blood poured from his lip. He moved to stand, but the blade of a rusty knife came down hard, slicing through his abdomen again and again, until there was nothing but silence and the stillness of unconsciousness.

CHAPTER 18

Gaelan awoke slowly. Night had come again. No, not night, he realized as coarse buckram bit into his face from brow to cheek. He'd been blindfolded!

The attack flooded back to him in vivid detail. But how long had he been . . . here? Was he back in his cell, or had he entered some new circle of hell? He moved, trying to sit upright, yanked back by the sharp pressure of metal around his neck and wrists. Why had he been chained to a wall? And when?

This is not my cell. The smell was different, mustier, more oppressive; the rank stink of congealed blood and vomit pervaded his nostrils. Then there was the complete silence: no shouting, no clanging of cell doors. No sight, no sound, no idea where the bloody hell he . . .

A man's voice fractured the silence. Close by . . . just above him. Gaelan jumped, and the irons pulled tighter. How long had the man been there, waiting?

"Mr. Erceldoune, you are awake. Welcome to Bethlem Royal Hospital."

Gaelan drew a sharp breath as the coarse band prickled at the tender skin of his temples. He knew of this place and shunned it, as did all Londoners. "Bedlam! What the devil am I doing in Bedlam—and shackled?"

"Better question: how in the blazes did you manage to survive so expert a knifing? Pierced straight through to kidney, spleen, stomach, liver. By rights, you should be quite dead, bled to death in the prison courtyard. And here you are but three days hence awake, coherent, and with barely a scratch upon you as evidence of injury. Might you enlighten me on how that might possibly be?"

The amiable even-temperedness of his visitor's voice unnerved Gaelan more than the shackles. A chill shuddered down his spine. "Why am I here?"

The pungent stink of his captor's breath drew nearer yet, beneath the suffocating aroma of his sweet, spicy cologne. The man's breath tickled the shell of Gaelan's ear through the blindfold. "A man who is able to sustain such severe injury yet, paradoxically, not be injured presents to society quite a danger, you must agree—as a medical practitioner yourself, that is?"

A line of cold sweat shivered down Gaelan's back as he struggled not to be sick. Bedlam was run by the worst sort of sadists, preying on the mentally unfit and impoverished; he'd heard the stories. "Who *are* you?" he demanded, unable to hide the tremble in his voice.

"I, sir, am Dr. Francis Handley, physician, anatomist, and qualified mad doctor. You have been given over to me, Mr. Erceldoune, so that I might study the phenomenon of your . . . unusual . . . physiology. It is a keen interest of mine to study rare species, of man in particular, just as Mr. Darwin examines the adaptability of his Galapagos finches. Your healing abilities are, to say the least, extraordinary, and I must wonder whether you are a harbinger of our own human future."

Gaelan struggled as futilely with his bonds as with his terror. What in God's nature did this madman have in store? "Am I not to hang, then? What of that scheme?" Beads of perspiration trickled from beneath the blindfold and down his face; his reserves were running thin as his imagination played out the terrible possibilities, not one a good outcome. He yanked again on the shackles, more instinct than hope.

"I am afraid, Mr. Erceldoune, that pulling on your binds will only serve to tighten them; they are designed that way, and it is quite an effective deterrent. So it is in your best interest not to struggle thus.

"No, you shall not hang, and for that you have me to thank. You ought to be grateful to have been spared that circus. And what a waste that would be! Besides, I suspect the noose would do little other than make you uncomfortable."

Gaelan spoke through gritted teeth, fighting to maintain the semblance of defiance. "I've no bloody idea what you mean!"

"I will explain, though I wager you know more than you say. That attack would have killed any man of ordinary constitution within hours, minutes! Yet the physician at Newgate witnessed quite an extraordinary marvel as you lay in the sick ward. It was he brought you to my attention, knowing of my interest in Mr. Darwin's work. And so here we are."

Gaelan tried to muster disdain, but fear and exhaustion muddled his thoughts. *Lasciate ogne speranza, voi ch'intrate.* Abandon all hope, indeed.

"Please, then, would you remove the blindfold, at least? I wish to view my surroundings—I grow dizzy and disorientated without the ability to see. . . . I need . . ." The sound of his own pathetic voice made him nauseous. But Gaelan could not get his bearings, clutching at the solid metal of his manacles as if they were a lifeline. He tried to calm himself, evening his breathing in the hope it would steady him, if only a little.

"Ah, yes. That could well be the sedating medicines we have fed to you. They can render one . . . slightly out of kilter, Mr. Erceldoune. They shall wear off in due course and, if you stay calm, will not be used again."

"The blindfold?"

"I've some questions for you." Wood scraped on wood, and Gaelan sensed Handley even closer by. "First, the obvious: how did you do it?"

"Apparently, my attackers were not as effective as they'd hoped."

Handley laughed heartily. "By Jove! *Apparently* is a good word for it. Appearances can be deceptive, can they not? And by the way, trying to be clever is not the way to earn the removal of that blindfold, which you so ardently desire."

Gaelan sucked moisture from his cheeks, trying to wet his parched tongue. "Then I shall tell you in all seriousness," he croaked, "I haven't a notion *at all*. Perhaps it is the water of Newgate's cisterns—or the food. Perhaps better clues lie there." Just the exertion of talking sapped Gaelan's remaining strength.

"Still too clever an answer, I am afraid. Is it possible, then, that you truly *not* know your abilities? Highly doubtful, yet . . . Perhaps it was fortuity spared your life? Again, you do not strike me a lucky sort of fellow. But you are an apothecary, a gifted apothecary, I hear tell. Have you some skill in alchemy as well, I wonder? And then, perchance, have you conjured in your laboratory the most elusive secret of life eternal? It is quite the shame your workroom was destroyed by fire, your library as well, I assume, since none of your possessions were found. Well, I say, it is of no matter; we shall know soon enough, and if indeed it was chance spared your life, we shall then not keep you a moment longer from the waiting arms of death the law has prescribed for you."

Without warning, the rough bandages were ripped away, and Gaelan was staring into a candle flame held so close that it singed the raw skin of his face. He squeezed his eyes tight against the brightness.

"I want to see them, Mr. Erceldoune; do open them for me." Handley's voice coiled around him. "We shall begin our study tonight, after you've had something to eat. You must be quite famished."

Gaelan was left alone in the cell.

At least the blindfold was gone, but it took only a moment to wish it was not. The oily-slick stone walls dripped foul moisture, and insects of several varieties—all well-fed and swift—darted from straw to wall and back again. But his surroundings were the least of his worries.

A tray was thrust beneath the bars. Maggots basked in the thin gruel. *Revolting. Let them have at it.* They were soon joined by a small host of creeping things. Gaelan kicked the tray away and tried to dispel the image.

The cell doors banged open; Handley had returned, a large leather pouch in his hand. "So, Mr. Erceldoune. Shall we become partners in this grand scientific adventure?" he asked, scrupulously avoiding the dinner tray as he pulled a chair before Gaelan.

Handley withdrew a scalprum of gleaming metal from the pouch. "A small cut, Mr. Erceldoune, on your forearm. That is all—a simple experiment. You shall barely feel it for the sharpness of the blade, though you should prepare yourself, for I shall go quite deep, but I promise to be swift and precise. And then . . . then, Mr. Erceldoune, we shall observe."

Gaelan withdrew his arms within the confines of his shackles as far as he could, feeling the irons tear at the skin of his wrists, but it was better than being touched by this lunatic.

Handley nodded, and two turnkeys appeared from the gloom beyond the cell. "Surely, sir, you are not disquieted by this small blade, and I *was* rather hoping for your cooperation. But if not—"

The men stood on either side of him, hauling his arms out into the open. Gaelan felt the tear of sinew as they twisted his wrists forward, exposing them to Handley's blade.

Handley took firm hold of Gaelan's arm as the blade slid easily through skin and vessels, stopping only when it hit bone. The scalprum was removed, and blood flowed in a claret river.

Gaelan watched, transfixed, as tender skin closed around the wound, and the bleeding stopped. Not in a long while had Gaelan observed the process of his skin knitting, tissue healing. "I—" He wanted to say... something. But the dim light further faded until awareness fled him and darkness enveloped him.

Awareness returned with a slap on the back and raucous laughter! "Jolly well done, Mr. Erceldoune. Jolly well done!"

How long had he been asleep? The wrist and hand were now washed free of blood, an expanse of pale skin amid the griminess of his right arm, with nary a mark upon it.

He shivered. So now Handley knew. Two hundred years Gaelan had managed to elude discovery, and here he sat, powerless, in the hands of a lunatic doctor bent on "studying" his anatomy. No reprieve, no chance of escape, even into the arms of death. Gaelan cursed the ouroboros book, his father, and the goddess Airmid for burdening him with this curse.

"Who knows I am here? Besides you." What of the men who attacked him: the gaolers and turnkeys, the doctors? What of his execution?

"To all but me and the physician who treated your injuries at Newgate—and the two guards you've just met—Gaelan Erceldoune died of wounds suffered during an unfortunate attack by a notorious gang. And henceforth you shall be known only as 'the patient,' a man with no name but to me."

CHICAGO'S NORTH SHORE, PRESENT DAY

CHAPTER 19

Gaelan drifted toward wakefulness, his surroundings unfamiliar. *Where is this?*

Panic whispered through his nerve endings as he tried to move his arms, finding them bound. *What the bloody hell...?*

Harsh phosphorescent yellow-white light seared his eyes. When he turned his head, the room seemed vaguely familiar: shining steel and drab green.

The clatter of metal upon metal—instruments in an aluminum pan—pummeled his shredded nerves. Behind him, a steady beep— oddly comforting. Around him, the astringent clean smell of alcohol and strong soap, iodine and starched linen... *Is this a hospital?*

Memory returned in quick bursts. He is falling, the bike a ball of fire, careening down the bluff.... More falling... flames. Landing hard, then... nothing. A siren... being carried, then wheeled... An ambulance... *Christ.* He had to get out of here before...

A muffled voice echoed from somewhere nearby. "Three broken ribs. Fracture of the left femur—two places, right tibia. Grade three splenic laceration... BP 96/59. Isolated third-degree burns: left arm, right thigh. We'll need to go in. Get the bleeding stopped. Let's prep him—"

The room collapsed into itself as instruments, masked people draped in green, machines, syringes swam in and out of focus like discotheque strobe lights while he watched from outside himself. He was floating, not unpleasantly. *Drugs. Very good drugs....*

Handley's face materialized above him, and the room came sharply into focus as the edge of a scalpel glinted ominously in the piercing white light. He wore a modern surgeon's mask, but the rheumy eyes, the wire spectacles were unmistakable, the voice a frighteningly familiar patter. . . .

"Gentlemen, we shall now expose the patient for what he is. What a remarkable specimen of human natural selection he represents, does he not?" Handley's voice was muffled behind the mask. And there were others in the room, but Gaelan could not see them for the light.

"Shall we anesthetize him?" an unfamiliar voice reverberated in Gaelan's ear.

Handley was adamant. "No. We must understand whether this man feels pain in the same way we do."

Gaelan struggled to move, but metal bands secured him to a narrow table. Pressure throbbed against his head; the band around his middle cut into his flesh like a knife with every beat of his heart. His hands and feet prickled and burned as feeling left them, held in a vise-like device, surely of Handley's own invention.

A new voice: "Where shall we make the cut, then, Dr. Handley?" He knew that voice . . . ! Gaelan shivered—he was freezing cold, so very cold. And wet. A blanket. Please, a blanket!

"It is you who funds my research, my lord. Where do you propose I make the incision?"

"I say cut off his member. Cut it off so he can never use it again."

"Here, here!" Lord Kinston's voice joined in agreement. "My dear Lord Braithwaite. Shall we cut off his presumptuous cock, so he shall know his place and never again endeavor to rise above his station!"

"Strip him!"

No!

Gaelan awoke, breathing hard. He managed a deep breath, holding it for a few seconds before letting it out again. In and out. Slowly, in and out. His heartbeat slowed along with his breathing, as he took in new surroundings: pleasant aqua walls. Sunlight pouring into the room. Flowers. He was surrounded by them: roses, daisies, chrysanthemum, and several varieties he'd never before seen—vases and baskets of them. *Where . . . ?* He sat up. Bad idea, he realized, lightheaded, as he fell back to the soft faux-down of the hospital pillows.

"Oh. You're awake! Hallo."

Simon? *What is he doing here?* More to the point, where was "here"? Simon's feet were propped on his bed as he reposed in an easy chair, doing a crossword puzzle.

"Simon . . . How—" Gaelan raked his shaky fingers through his hair. Fuck. If only the snare drum in his head would stop, he might swim his way through the fog and concentrate.

Simon looked up from the newspaper on his lap. "Morphine sulfate. You might be a bit muddled."

"Mmm. Morphine." *Ah. A bit?*

"Do you remember what happened? And why you were riding your motorbike up in my neck of the woods?"

"I don't—"

Simon passed the *Tribune* to Gaelan, pointing midway down the page. "Miracle Man Survives Fiery Motorcycle Crash in Highland Park."

As he scanned the article, the crash continued to replay in fractured, staccato jump cuts in the murky bog of his head. "Miracle Man . . . no one could have survived that . . . incredible ER story told by multiple witnesses . . . Is he even human?"

"Bloody hell." He shoved the newspaper out of sight. He'd read enough. *Fuck.*

"There's much more. They can't seem to settle on an appropriate title for you in the media: Superman . . . X-Man . . . Mutant Man . . . none particularly clever, but hashtag MiracleMan is trending on Twitter. There's a whole subreddit devoted to you as well. Number one on the front page. At least it was yesterday."

Gaelan ignored the attempt at humor. How could Simon be taking this all so lightly? "Can you ask for the morphine to be stopped? It's making my head explode, and I can't think at all." Gaelan clamped his hands to his head in a futile effort to subdue the assault.

"You're a star," declared Simon, affecting the exaggerated Midwestern drawl of a game show host. "No idea until I saw you on the telly . . . John Doe. Rather pedestrian." He gestured grandly around the room. "By the way, the flowers are 'speedy recovery' wishes from your legions of fans. You're practically a religious icon!"

Gaelan scowled. He had neither the stomach nor patience for Simon's amused sarcasm. *Bloody great. Can life get any fucking worse?* He had to get out of here—out of the hospital, out of Chicago. Now was not soon enough.

Simon's tone softened considerably. "I came immediately, soon as I realized . . . knowing there would be . . . trouble. There were at least six witnesses, four of whom swore you were dead at the base of that bluff, including one of the EMTs. And two bystanders caught the whole thing on their phones. Spectacular crash, but not really news beyond the local media. Miracle recovery? CNN and twenty-four seven coverage. Last I checked, one of those videos had gone viral. More than seven million views, and—"

"How bad was it? I mean . . . what happened to me, what was . . . seen . . . after—" How could Simon be so fucking calm? Sitting there, a smile on his fucking face, reciting the facts as if there were nothing at all to be fucking frantic about.

A knock on the door. "Mr. Erceldoune?" *The doctor.*

"Good morning, Mr. Erceldoune; you're awake. Great. I'm Dr. Samuelson."

Simon eyed him warily. "I thought his doctor was a woman —Smithson?"

"I'm a specialist. . . . Would you excuse us? I'd like to speak to Mr. Erceldoune in private." He pulled three stoppered test tubes from his lab coat pocket and placed them along with a clipboard on the tray table. Gaelan had a fairly certain idea of the likely topic.

"My friend can stay—"

Simon nodded and stood, piling the newspapers on the chair. "Certainly, Dr. Samuelson. Time for a coffee anyway."

The doctor pulled up a chair after the door closed. "It's good to see you awake. Do you remember what happened?"

"Not completely." An innocent first question. An honest answer. "I'm still a bit...hazy. I'd like the morphine stopped, if you don't mind."

The doctor glanced at the morphine pump and shook his head. "Not sure that's such a good idea. Not yet. It was lucky your friend recognized you from the news. He gave us a little information, but there are some gaps. So if you don't mind—"

Gaelan shrugged, waiting for the axe to fall. "I'm not sure what I can tell you that Simon hasn't, but—"

"I confess I've never seen anything like it in my twenty years in medicine. I'm pretty sure no one else has either!"

Gaelan forced a laugh. "I come from hearty Scottish stock, I suppose—" Gaelan eyed the monitors, watching his blood pressure and pulse accelerate, knowing the doctor could perceive his anxiety ratcheting up just from the rapidity of the beeping.

The doctor pulled back the sheet to expose Gaelan's leg, shaking his head. "Five days ago, there was a severe burn on your leg. Right there, on your thigh. I would swear to it in court if I had to, yet—"

Five days? He'd been out of it for five days?

The doctor palpated the area just above his right knee, and Gaelan winced dramatically. "Hey! That bloody hurt!" he protested, emphasizing how *not* healed he was.

"It looks like a barely peeling sunburn now." Samuelson shook his head in disbelief. "To be honest, I don't know how that's possible."

The door opened again, and a young doctor entered, handing Samuelson a folder. "Mr. Erceldoune, great to see you awake! I'm Dr. Smithson, your attending physician. You put on quite the show for us down in the ER. Has anything like that ever happened before?"

Did she mean the crash...or its aftermath?

Samuelson stared at her—a warning.

"Sorry for interrupting. Just wanted to check in on you; I will leave you in Dr. Samuelson's hands. He's on our genetics research team...."

She left quickly, eyes never leaving Gaelan.

Gaelan tried sitting up again, and Samuelson pushed a button on a gadget. The head of the bed rose slowly. The doctor placed the device in Gaelan's hand.

"Better?"

He nodded, letting out a deep breath, slightly more comfortable now. The beeping slowed. His eyes closed, but he opened them quickly, refusing to succumb to the sleepiness washing over him. *Concentrate, Erceldoune!* He really needed that bloody morphine pump stopped. Now.

"Use the cursors to raise and lower the bed. The rest operate the TV and the call button. I'm sure if you press it, at least five nurses will come running in here. Half the female staff has a crush on our mystery Miracle Man."

"Thank you, and I've long since stopped believing in miracles—"

"You mentioned your 'hearty Scottish stock.' Do you have any recollection of family members, you, yourself... anyone who recovered from injuries unusually quickly? Rapid tissue regeneration, we call it—"

Ah, here it comes. Gaelan concentrated on the yellow roses atop the windowsill, contemplating the practicality of fleeing through the window. "No.... I mean to say, I've been pretty healthy, yes. Never been in hospital before, so—"

"The rapidity of your tissue regeneration defies anything within the experience of anyone on the hospital staff. It could be related to an underlying disease, a genetic anomaly, even certain cancers, perhaps something triggered in your organ systems by the trauma itself. I'd like to keep you here a few more days, run some tests, try to get a handle—"

"No."

"Nothing invasive, just a tube or two of your blood. See what makes you the Miracle Man."

"No," he repeated with more emphasis. *Tests. Samuelson meant genetic tests. No bloody way.*

Samuelson's eyes widened in disbelief. "You're not at all curious?"

Curious? Yes, but not enough to let this genetics bloke go prodding about his chromosomes. Gaelan had often wondered whether, somehow, the elixir he'd taken—as well as the one meant for Sophie Bell—had triggered some sort of genetic mutation. He'd read every scientific paper he could find, every journal article, media report, anything on genetics and aging. Perhaps modern science could help him understand their condition well enough to reverse it, even in the absence of the ouroboros book. He owed it to Simon at least to try.

By now, Gaelan could have a PhD in molecular genetics if he'd an inclination for a formal education. Well, save for all the lab work. But he was not about to let this . . . genetics fellow run his DNA through a bloody gene sequencer. *No fucking way.*

It wasn't that the situation hadn't its appeal, risk of discovery be damned. What an opportunity it might be. A leap toward the truth, perhaps a way back to mere mortality? An end to this perpetual life of hiding and exile. Tempting . . . so very tempting. . . .

Gaelan tamped down on the impulse to agree, finding a shred of clarity in the drug-induced swamp of his thoughts. Curious? Yes, he was bloody curious. But what of the consequences? If it had been just him and Simon, that was one thing . . . but allowing a stranger with his own agenda into the mix . . . and the publicity, more unwanted publicity, would follow. Did he really want to subject himself to that sort of notoriety? And what of the risk that the key to immortality might fall into *anyone's* hands? The machine's beeping ratcheted up again.

"Mr. Erceldoune? Are you okay? I think you went down the rabbit hole there for a second."

"Yeah. I'm fine. What did you ask me?"

"Aren't you curious about . . . all this?"

"No. Not really," he said a bit too dismissively.

"Of course I understand your reluctance. But this is a chance of a lifetime for . . . medicine . . . and for you as well. Don't you want to know how this happened? Because I sure as hell can't explain it!

"This is my specialty, genetics. My life's work. I've missed four nights' sleep reading the literature, looking for anything that might explain . . . Nada! Look, Mr. Erceldoune, to be honest, right now the dean and the board are about to chalk up everything we saw as a combination of instrument failure, human error, and mass hysteria—"

Good. That was fine by him. In a day or two, a week, there would be a new story for the cable news people to chase. And everyone would leave him the hell alone. "Maybe they're right, then. Look, Dr. . . . Dr. Samuelson, I get it. You want to explain what you think you saw, and to be honest, I've no idea what condition I was in when I came here. But I've *no* bloody interest in being studied by you or anyone else. I just want to go home. . . . This is all a lot to process. . . . Never been in a wreck before. . . ." It was such an effort to talk; he was breathing hard with exertion. Gaelan's heart rate had now vaulted to 150 BPM, the numbers on the machine flashing red. *Oh fucking great!*

Samuelson glanced at the monitor. "Look, Mr. Erceldoune," he said quietly. "Of course, you're not obligated to anything. Just think about it. I didn't mean to upset you."

Good. He was backing off. Gaelan whispered thanks to the inventors of the wondrous heart rate monitor and its dramatic beeping. "You haven't. And I will, I promise. Consider all you've said."

The door opened again, and Gaelan breathed a sigh of relief. An interruption. *Just in the bloody nick of time.*

"Would you mind, Dr. Samuelson . . . the morphine—"

"Do you want it turned up? I know you said you wanted it off, but it will help you sleep."

"No. I still want it off, if you don't mind. Clouds my thinking." Something didn't add up to Gaelan. They already had plenty of his blood—he was sure of it. "Dr. Samuelson, wait a moment. I do have a question for you. I assume you've taken samples of my blood; why haven't you already run those tests?"

"Have you changed your mind? You've only to sign a simple consent form—"

"No. Sorry."

"We can't run your blood through a gene sequencer without your permission. . . . Something called informed consent."

Gaelan nodded. All he wanted to know. At least there was that, and as long as he refused, nothing could be done about it. "Thank you. And I do promise to consider your request," Gaelan managed with all sincerity.

CHAPTER 20

Simon Bell sat in the hospital café stirring his tea, absently contemplating the swirls of sugar and milk as they merged into the whirlpool of Earl Grey. He sighed, the years of running and evasion—the corrosion of Sophie's endless haranguing—weighing heavily upon him. How had he ended up in this place, years out of his time? A single event—a desperate attempt to help his wife—had careered out of control, its reverberations still echoing nearly two centuries later.

"Excuse me . . . ?"

A young man stood alongside Simon's table, a small wire-bound notebook in his hand. Simon stared down into the tea, pretending not to see him, but the lad seemed not to get the hint.

"Excuse me, but aren't you Anthony Danforth?"

Simon breathed out, relieved. A fan, of course, and not another blogger or reporter aiming to badger him about the Miracle Man. The young man likely recognized him from the book signing. He assumed his best auteur pose. "Yes. I am. And what can I do for you? And, by the way," he said, nodding toward the notebook, "I never do on-the-fly interviews."

"Mind if I sit?"

"I do, actually. Just finishing a cup of tea and then . . ." Simon looked up, and the kid was already gone. *Very well, then!*

Simon kept one eye on the lad as he took a seat at a crowded table nearby. *Oh, bloody hell.* They were animatedly gesturing toward him as they talked. Simon cringed as he caught bits of the conversation.

"He's that Holmes writer. . . . Saw him at Barnes and Noble the other day. . . . Danforth? . . . Friend of our Miracle Man. . . . A real X-File. . . . We need to get him!"

Taking his cue, Simon left his teacup half-full and escaped back to Gaelan's room.

When he arrived, a flock of nurses hovered over Gaelan. The monitors were issuing frenzied alarms, numbers flashing red as they fussed with tubes and dials. Not a good sign. What had happened in the short fifteen minutes he'd been gone? Finally, they were alone.

"Simon, we need to leave. Now. Where've they put my clothes?"

Simon sat on the bed. He knew that look; Gaelan was at the very thinnest edge of his composure. "They're a ruin. Why? What's going on? What did the doctor say to you?"

"They aim to *study* me, Simon, and I cannot abide that! I fear not only the endless poking and prodding, but what they'd do with the information from it. I'm trying to remain clearheaded about this. I truly am. But I'm near the end of my tether."

Simon nodded and placed a hand on Gaelan's arm. He understood that fear, which had deep roots for Gaelan beyond his own personal safety. How often had Gaelan wondered aloud—vehemently—about what the powerful and ambitious would undertake with the key to immortality? Simon could not disagree. "Are you fit even to stand on your own feet? I know your internal injuries are much worse than they might appear—"

"I've no bloody idea how fit I am, and it doesn't much matter, does it? I can't stay here. What if—"

"Steady yourself, man. Those monitor numbers start flashing again, and they'll send that army of nurses back in here posthaste."

Gaelan closed his eyes and exhaled shakily. "Might you lower the head of the bed? My head is swimming—" He handed the bed control to Simon.

One glance at Gaelan, and it was obvious there was no way he'd be leaving the hospital on his own feet. Yes, his injuries appeared to be healed, but Simon knew all too well that the process took its own physical toll. It might be days until Gaelan could walk well enough even to make it to the bathroom without assistance.

Simon tried to reason with him. "Look, as far as I can put together, most everyone is chalking it up to faulty equipment, misdiagnosis, whatever else they can manage to conjure without sounding either too incompetent or bloody off their nut. And with medical confidentiality, etc., the media have little to go on other than anecdotal reports by bystanders. The doctors and nurses won't say a word for fear of a lawsuit. Still, you're a bit of a sensation. Seven million views—impressive." He smirked.

"Fuck you." The trace of a grin cracked through the anxiety on Gaelan's face.

"Sorry. But at least I made you smile a little. Can you talk about what happened, or should I let you rest?"

Gaelan shook his head. "No. Stay. And why are you looking so bloody smug, anyway?"

A nurse interrupted, wheeling a computer cart. "Mr. Erceldoune, how are you feeling? Your recovery is so amazing! Everyone's talking about it, like you're some sort of . . . I don't know . . . Superman or something—"

"Indeed. Thank you." *Now go away.*

She glanced at the monitors and typed notes into a computer. "There are a couple of police officers from the Highland Park Police who want to have a word with you. Are you feeling up to it?"

Now what? "Not really," Gaelan responded, trying to sound as weak as he could muster. "I'm quite tired—"

"He just has a few questions about your accident. Reports and all."

Simon stepped in. "Really, could this not wait? My friend—"

"Don't, Simon. Look, I told the doctor already. I recall only fragments, brief flashes, and . . . mightn't we do it tomorrow?"

"Mr. Erceldoune?"

Two young uniformed officers, a male and female, stepped into the room. Gaelan sighed, rubbing his temples. "Look, I'd prefer if we might do this another time and—"

The female officer spoke, her tone sympathetic. "The doc said it was all right to ask you a few questions." She looked at the nurse and Simon. "Can you two give us a few minutes? Promise it won't be long."

Police could be a problem. Did Gaelan even have a driving license? Registration for his bike? Papers of any sort? *Damnation! Of course he did, didn't he?* "I . . . was just leaving," Simon said. "Anything you want from your flat?"

"Only a set of clothing, if you don't mind."

Simon left, listening for a moment at the door, hearing nothing but hushed voices.

The two officers sat. "Can you tell us what happened?" asked the male officer.

How many times had he been asked that in the last two hours? He had to be cautious with them. His papers would not stand intense scrutiny. He'd had this identity for the twenty years he'd been in Evanston, but that was before September 11, 2001, when the world became much more treacherous to navigate.

Could they deport him? He waved off visions of immigration officers taking him into custody, like in the movies. Where would they send him? On paper, he had no real identity, only the manufactured life of some poor sod who'd died somewhere in the UK years ago and fit his description well enough. Gaelan Erceldoune no longer existed except as a *nom de guerre*, suitable for a dealer in rare books. "I confess I don't recall much. The road down to the beach was icier than I thought—"

"Thing is, we can't find you in the DMV records—"

"DMV?" *What the fuck was DMV?* Was that where he got his driving license?

The female officer took over the questioning. Good. She seemed less intimidating at least. But maybe that was the plan. "People have all sorts of reasons for giving a false name to a hospital, but we have to get your real name—"

"Yes, well ... you see Erceldoune ... it's an old family name from long before I was born. I own Erceldoune's Rare Books and Antiquities on Foster in Evanston. The name seems to fit the shop right enough. My business papers and identification ... my driving license ... are all under my *actual* name ... Cameron Balfour, born Dumfries, Scotland, in the UK." Gaelan shrugged, hoping it would suffice. No one had been injured but him in the accident, and no damage was caused—he didn't think so, at least. With any luck . . .

Her partner interrupted, much less patient. "Mr. Erceldoune . . . Mr. Balfour—"

Gaelan managed a weak laugh; it sounded genuine enough to his ears. "I generally go by Gaelan Erceldoune . . . easier . . . the business, you know, less confusing—"

"The tox screen indicates residual THC in your blood. Were you driving impaired?"

Gaelan tried to sound indignant. "Not at all, Officers. I would never—" He winced; the pain was real, if fortuitous, as it flared from his abdomen to his lower back. "Forgive me, I had the morphine stopped. . . . I *hate* the thought of drugs in my system. Make me so very foggy," he managed between gasps. "I—"

"Would you like me to call the nurse for you?"

"Yes, thank you. Look, would you mind terribly if we did this tomorrow? The doctors tell me I've been unconscious for several days—"

The female officer glanced at her partner, and they stood. "We'll be back later this afternoon to get our report. You get some rest, okay?"

"Yes. Thank you, Officers." A sudden slicing pain left Gaelan nearly breathless. Perhaps disengaging the morphine was not quite so excellent an idea, after all.

First Samuelson and now the police; what was next? Gaelan shuddered at the thought. Was the game finally up after nearly four centuries? What *would* be so terrible about it all coming undone? Here in the twenty-first century with all its amazing technology and advanced science. Perhaps it was time. So what if he was "immortal"?

Research was drawing ever closer to the heart of it, anyway. Nobel prizes, multibillion-dollar corporations cloaked in veneers of scientific pursuit . . . when in truth all they sought was same holy grail pursued by kings and alchemists for millennia. He and Simon were the key to it all; why not finally resign themselves to the inevitable?

Because it is a terrible idea.

LONDON, PRESENT DAY

CHAPTER 21

Anne Shawe, MD, PhD, swore at the walls of the empty borrowed London flat. Tomorrow, she would be on the 7:00 a.m. flight to Southern California and a completely new life: a posting at the Jonas Salk Institute, and just far enough away from Paul Gilles. Ex-fiancé Paul Gilles . . . and his grisly new pet project. And his little blonde tart. The romance—the entire sham of it—was dead long before she'd caught the two of them in flagrante delicto in his flat—in *their* flat. She'd seen too much—knew too much about Paul's work with Transdiff Genomics not to end it anyway.

Anne shivered at the image of Paul scouring the cavernous bowels of the Imperial Museum, cataloging the preserved remains of Bedlam inmates two centuries gone and matching them with the ravings of a lunatic doctor. In the hopes of what? Finding some elusive key to immortality? *Hah!* Who did he think he was? Transdiff was supposedly a top-flight genetic research firm, and he wasn't bloody Indiana Jones.

"Let the poor wretches rest in peace," she told Director Lloyd Hammersmith. "It's akin to grave robbing, and I want no part of it." She'd been emphatic. But Paul wanted in from the start. *Well, let him have it.*

She recalled Shakespeare's epitaph: "Blessed be the man that spares these stones, and cursed be he that moves my bones." Gilles and Hammersmith were disturbing both stones and bones while salivating over accounts of some long-dead, tortured soul who had the misfortune to be locked away in Bedlam for four and a half years. *Why can't they let him be?*

She brushed her teeth, trying to avert her gaze from the red-blotched eyes that stared out from the mirror. *What is black and white and red all over?* How much concealer would it take to eradicate the black smudges, which would undoubtedly deepen from hours of travel and jet lag by the time she got to California? Heathrow to Chicago, a ten-hour layover, and then finally on to San Diego and the institute. Maybe she'd just stay there, basking in the Southern California sun and never return to Transdiff—or Paul Gilles.

Just what she needed and right in her wheelhouse. *Turritopsis nutricula.* Anne had never been more enthusiastic to snuggle up with jellyfish . . . a fascinatingly *immortal* jellyfish. And as far from Dr. Paul Gilles and Transdiff Genomics, Ltd. as possible. Screw that, screw him, and screw the bloody, fucking United Kingdom for spawning wankers like Paul Gilles.

Maybe by the time six months had passed, the Bedlam project would be a dismal failure, Paul would lose his job, and she could return to London triumphant with a new major credential on her CV. Stockholm, here we come! *Hey, a girl can dream.*

Anne yawned. She should try to sleep, knew it would be a lost cause; stopping her mind from racing was as unlikely as going back to Paul. She unrolled her sleeping bag and tried to get comfortable enough to respond to the several e-mails awaiting her reply. She opened her laptop just as her mobile chimed.

"Hallo?" Mum. Again.

"You're sure you don't need a lift to the airport, darling?"

"No, Mum. I've a taxi ordered for early tomorrow already." Anne opened the e-mail app.

"Cousin Agatha's book, are you taking it with you?"

"Of course. Why?"

"Did you ever crack it? You seemed quite taken with it, and I thought perhaps Paul, with all his curiosity about it—"

No more than her own, and she was far cleverer than Paul. It wasn't a priority; she'd tackle it once she settled in California—and without Paul Gilles's "expert" advice.

Four new e-mails. Three from Paul. One from a name she didn't recognize. "Mum, I'd love to talk, but I'm quite exhausted and my flight's at seven." She dragged Paul's e-mails to the trash folder.

"Maybe there's someone there who can help you—"

"Hmm?"

"The book. I must say, my own curiosity is quite piqued. I mean, what's a strange volume like that doing up in Agatha's attic gathering dust? Must be worth a fortune! You should have someone take a look at it. When you get to the States, I mean."

"Sure. I'll have some time whilst I'm there to dig into it more than I have. I won't bloody know anyone, so digging into Agatha's mystery book will be a fab diversion."

She opened the e-mail from the unknown sender. Dr. Andrew Samuelson, Evanston Hospital. Who was Dr. Andrew Samuelson, and where was Evanston Hospital? She'd never heard of either.

Call-waiting beeped. "Mum, I've got to run. Another call."

"Love you, darling. Text me when you land, will you?"

"I'll try. Bye. Love to you and Dad." She pressed the swap button. "Hallo?"

"Dr. Anne Shawe?"

"Yeah, that would be me—"

"Hi. My name is Dr. Andrew Samuelson—"

"Oh. The e-mail. I just saw it—didn't read it yet." A bit odd . . . e-mail and a phone call. Okay. He had her attention.

"Yeah. Um . . . No. Sorry. No problem. I . . ."

Anne smiled. *The doctor is a bit flustered. Hmm.* How many times had she made cold calls over the years? Nothing was more awkward. "So what might I do for you, Dr. Samuelson?"

"I read your paper in the *Annals of Genetic Research.* 'Telomeres and Rapid Tissue Regeneration in Human Subjects: A New Theory.'"

It had been a very small article. More of a research note. Two years, and it had come to quite a bit of nothing. It was far overshadowed that year by the Nobel-winning telomere research.

Much more interesting was her research on longevity; now that held some promise—and to her, the key to her own family history. Tissue regeneration was a science fiction better left to Paul and his slew of overfunded defense contracts. But she had published—and lectured—about it, and admittedly, creating a real-life superhero was much sexier than adding a few years—and more quality—to the lives of the elderly and infirm.

"Look, Dr. Shawe, I'll come right to the point. I have a patient. Crash victim . . . should have died in the ambulance. But it's only days later, and he's practically ready to be released. I can't explain how that's possible. I read your note and some of the research your firm is doing—"

These phone calls came four or five a year. Wild goose chases, all. Other explanations, more mundane, *and* much more plausible, always proved correct: underlying disease, environmental mutation. . . . "What does the sequencing show? Anything unusual at the telomeres?"

"He's not especially cooperative."

"Him or his DNA?"

"Him. Look, I think he's the real deal. My graduate work was in molecular genetics, and I'm not usually the kind of guy who jumps to conclusions without hard evidence, but—"

"And you can't do genetic testing without his consent. Look, I'm in the UK. Where are you?" She was moderately interested. He sounded sincere—at least *he* believed what he was reporting . . . and why not?

"Chicago. I don't suppose I might induce you to pay us a visit, look in on our reluctant patient? I guarantee a paper's in it, and it will be worth your while. We're trying to keep a lid on the whole thing, though."

"Why?"

"It's just *that* weird."

His incredulous laugh amused her.

"Lots of rumors and speculation among the masses and the media, but if it was confirmed to the press that we got a guy in here with the regenerative ability of a—"

"Jellyfish?" *That*, she would fly halfway across the globe to see.

"Problem is, we don't know how long we can keep him. He's *jittery* as a jellyfish, I'll give you that. Cops are interested in him too. Any way you can do this, and sooner rather than later? I have a feeling this guy is going to bolt as soon as he realizes we can't keep him against his will."

"You're in luck. I have a ten-hour layover in Chicago tomorrow. I'm on my way to a six-month stint at Salk in San Diego. Can someone pick me up at the airport? I won't have much time, but I can at least take a look at the records and pay your patient a visit."

"Absolutely. I'll e-mail you the details and his charts."

"Can you do that without his consent?"

"Welcome to his patient care team, Dr. Shawe."

Anne Googled Dr. Andrew Samuelson and clicked on his hospital staff bio: "Harvard Medical School, board certifications in surgery, internal medicine, and genetic disorders." *Not bad looking either.* Sounded just like the diversion she needed.

BETHLEM ROYAL HOSPITAL, LONDON, 1842

CHAPTER 22

*T*he dead and dying would be thrust into Airmid's healing well, and she would sing to them. Her understanding was a gift, her science, magic. All exposed to her healing prowess, they were restored—no matter their sickness—to full vigor through the protection of her great cloak.

But her father Dian Cecht, god of medicine, was greatly jealous, for she was a more powerful healer than he could ever be. And he scattered her knowledge to the four winds, the language of herbs and medicines garbled and made nonsensical in the chaos. Yet in her wisdom, Airmid had inscribed it all long before that day, in a book of wonders, an indecipherable mystery to any but those rare mortal men in whom she had put her trust.

The story lingered in the darkness as Gaelan rested his head on the cool stones of his cell. Handley was done with him for this day, and Gaelan cursed Airmid's name as he had every night for four and a half years, disparaged this most cruel book of "wonders" that robbed him of death and dignity. "Let me not wake on the morrow," he pleaded in futility, his mouth rusty with blood, his spirit broken, the air so heavy that his words melted into the stifling void.

But she alone would visit him, a comforter, companion—only a vision, a fever dream, he realized. She sang to him for hours and hours, told him stories of Tuatha de Danann, their wars, their travels. He knew it was his own memory chanting to him, stories told to him as a boy. But for a little while each night, Gaelan would find sweet respite in her voice, and on the morrow Handley would begin again.

Gaelan gripped his thigh, pressing upon the deep slash; it throbbed, and each pulse of his heart bled hot and sticky through his fingers. But the pressure blunted the brutal agony that had spread over his being. If he could only stay completely still, concentrate on other things, distracting things, he knew it would pass in an hour or two.

Gaelan jumped at a sound. Was that, too, imagined? Laughter. A whisper of memory from the afternoon's depravity . . .

"Have you ever cut clear through to the bone, Dr. Handley? What would happen to your patient then? How long to heal such a deep, deep slice?" Handley had only just received a large bag of gold coins from a certain Lord Braithwaite, a man of particular zeal. *"And I venture that sharpness of the blade might affect the pain your subject feels during the vivisection; what say you to that, my dear Dr. Handley?"*

"I do not know, my lord. I always try to use the sharpest blades; I do not wish to torture, but merely study this one's unique regenerative properties. I am, after all, a scientist, not a sadist."

"But are you not curious? Can you know for certain, for example, that a dull blade would not be more humane?"

Gaelan looked from Handley to Braithwaite in terror; the question was ridiculous, but he knew Handley would embrace the idea as soon as he heard the gold coins clink in his greedy fist.

Handley retrieved a knife from a cloth wrapper, and Gaelan flinched. It was old and rusted, filthy with blood and dried gore—probably his own. He sucked in a breath, waiting for the blade's disease-ridden teeth to bite into him. What would it be this time? His arm? The soft tissue of his neck? His leg—the challenge of tough muscle and sinew? He would not scream. He would not give them the satisfaction of hearing him keen and beg for mercy.

"Look at that, Lord Braithwaite! See?" Handley sniveled. *"The man barely flinches—truly astonishing."* No miracle there—the magic of Handley's special morphine preparation numbed him from all but the vaguest awareness.

Then even the dimmest recognition of his surroundings had mercifully dissipated into a sieve of nothingness, and long before the blade had sliced through his quadriceps muscle and down to the femur. And now he had only to live through the aftermath.

Gaelan removed his hand from the wound; the bleeding had stopped. However his physiology repaired itself—he'd never understood it—seemed quite backward to him. The wound was nearly closed, yet the pain in his leg would endure for days as the muscle and other tissues slowly regenerated.

If only he would go mad, lose his mind, then he would no longer possess the capacity to care. But his accursed mind remained sharp; there would be no reprieve. Each session, Handley stole a bit more of Gaelan's humanity, small nibbles of his soul, one bite at a time—the snake eating not its *own* tail, but consuming one humble apothecary. And as he stared ahead into the abyss that had become his home, Gaelan knew that somewhere, Simon Bell was laughing.

The midafternoon July sunshine flooded into the haze of Bailey's Pub. Simon Bell sat alone, contemplating the way the light sparkled like small stars in the amber of his ale. It was a diversion between pints number three and four. In November, it would be five years since Sophie's passing, and Bailey's was now home and hearth—away from the denunciation of ancestral portraits, the compassionate tongue-clucking of James, his mother's (and Mrs. McRory's) incessant doting.

Simon looked through the plate glass, shielding his eyes against the glare of the sun. He'd counted the months by progress on the railway trestle just across the street. Nearly done now, it was an apiary of activity, a Tower of Babel in the midst of London.

The steady clank of iron mallet upon iron spike, the dull thud of timber falling into place, the spit and spark as metal melted and melded into a filigree crisscross of iron and wood.

He felt it before he heard it: a deep rumble that shook the pub like an earthquake. His ale shivered in the confines of its glass. Then, an otherworldly shriek—a horrifying, thunderous keening like a thousand demons arising as one from the graveyard, the grinding of metal upon metal.

Hands on his ears to stifle the horrifying clamor, Simon gawked through the window as a cascade of metal and wood bent and twisted before him as it bowed to the cobblestones below. The trestle bobbed and swayed at an absurd angle just above the pavement—at once sickening and fantastical. Then the entire street seemed to freeze in place as onlookers took in the scene in stunned silence until all at once, everyone began moving again, descending upon the maelstrom.

His pint abandoned, Simon joined the gentlemen and workers, ruffians and merchants, boys and men racing to pull the injured from beneath the gargantuan iron structure before it collapsed entirely. He wandered toward the heart of the wreckage, wading through the dead and maimed. Limbs without bodies emerged from beneath the rubble, askew and unnatural.

He had just pulled to safety a third man, examining him for signs of life, when another low rumble moaned through Simon's bones as the trestle shuddered once again, an iron dragon spewing green and orange sparks. And then, just above him, the entire structure gave way. From somewhere in the distance came the terrible snap and crush of bone, the tearing of flesh, Simon only vaguely aware it was his.

Just as Simon uttered a final entreaty for a quick end, the universe complied and there was nothing but blackness—no pain, no feeling at all. Sophie's voice called out to him, seeking him in the darkness.

But he could not reach out to her. Frantic, he shouted for her as she faded into the distance.

No! Wait! I'm here, darling. I'm coming; wait for me!

But she was gone.

LONDON, 1842

CHAPTER 23

Light. The sensation warm on his skin, too bright, orange flares behind his eyelids. Simon squinted into the glare, daring himself to look, expectant, ready for the acknowledgement of his death. But before him stood neither angels nor his beloved Sophie, but James's anxious countenance. Inexplicably, Simon was not dead.

"Simon?"

Testy. James's voice was definitely testy, ready to pounce upon Simon's first word. He'd not the stomach for it, not yet.

James was saying something, and Simon strained to hear, but his voice was drowned out by the thundering tons of wooden beams he yet heard in his ears. Then sleep pulled him under again.

Lacerating pain finally woke him as that moment beneath the trestle returned, obscuring all else from his vision. Glass and metal and wood splinters, gargantuan matchsticks slicing through him like fresh-churned butter. The burn of sparks and the sweet, sticky odor of spilled creosote robbed him of breath. He gagged on it, forcing himself upright—not a good idea.

Simon glanced about him, seeing not the wreckage of the collapsed trestle, but his own bedroom and James standing over him.

"Simon! Thank God! We thought we'd lost you!"

Simon allowed himself to sink back into the pillows, a sigh escaping his lips. Nothing made a whit of sense.

"You might have been killed, you know."

Simon remained mute as his faculties returned. He was not especially inclined to hear James's inevitable discourse on self-destructiveness. "I was attempting to help. I—"

"The constable said you ran into danger recklessly over and over again, as if you cared not a fig for your own life."

Simon rallied; James's hectoring was adequate incentive. "To *some*, that might sound rather heroic. You make it sound as if it was a death wish—"

"Am I wrong, then? It would not be the first time these past four years you have tried to do yourself harm."

James sat heavily in the bedside rocking chair, his top hat placed on the table. Simon had no good retort, but he resented James's constant interference . . . had done since Sophie died.

James removed a handkerchief from his breast pocket, dabbing sweat from his bald pate. "Your mother—everyone, dear boy—was worried sick days on end. It is miraculous that you recovered. Beyond. You've nary a scratch left upon you. How is that possible?"

Simon shook his head slowly. "Bad luck, perchance," he replied sourly.

James glared, fingers nervously drumming his ample thighs. He leaned forward, his voice a menacing whisper. "Now, I'll have none of that! Careful, my dear cousin, or *you'll* end up one of Francis Handley's guinea pigs, eh!"

Still dazed, wrapped in a laudanum fog, Simon could not conjure a face to that name. "Who?"

"Handley . . . Bedlam's mad doctor, of course! Tell me you've never heard of him! Perhaps your head is yet addled. A regular sideshow he has going there, with his 'anatomic experimentation.' But all quite discreet, and only for the most affluent men of a certain character. Of course, I've no patience for that balderdash, and if I had a say, I'd put a stop to the entire thing. Gives medicine a bad name."

A flash of memory grazed the periphery of Simon's thoughts, so real, he flinched at the image: a rusty iron beam falling toward him. He blinked, and it vanished, leaving him pale and shaking. He sucked in a breath, letting it out slowly.

"Are you all right, Simon?"

"Yes. I . . ." The full weight of events began to bear down. He should be dead. "How many died, James?" Simon asked weakly.

James gazed at the floor a long while.

"*How* many?"

James looked up, and his eyes were red and moist, bearing the truth. "Twenty-seven were pulled from beneath the trestle. *All* but you, dead."

A long silence hung between them. Simon knew that no matter what he might say, James would assume it was intentional, that Simon meant more to do himself harm than to rescue men from a crumbling construction site. And that was a lie, wasn't it?

"It has been nearly five years, Simon! Five years! Six suicide attempts you've made, and I won't even mention that you've given up your medical practice entirely to drink yourself to an early grave. You do realize that you risk being sent again to the sanatorium?"

Simon sickened at the thought. Three times Lady Elizabeth had shipped him away to Peck's Seaside Sanatorium in Blackpool, where he spent weeks at a time to "regain his health," entombed in an opium cocoon.

"Well, you *have* mentioned it, and I aver, as always, it is none of your bloody business, nor my mother's. You are my cousin, not my keeper."

"I am your physician, and I've made a promise to Lady Elizabeth to look after you—"

"My God, James! Will you listen to yourself? I am five and thirty. I do not need you to *look after me*! Please go. My head throbs, and my body feels—"

"You've barely a scratch on you, cousin. And you are damned lucky. How you managed to escape with nary..." James shook his head, regarding him with confusion etched in his expression. "Quite astonishing."

"I ask you, please leave me be."

James started to go, but stopped, and, instead, dragged a heavy chair to Simon's bedside. "So, you've really not heard of Francis Handley and his amazing indestructible man?" James chuckled. "Perhaps the tale will improve your spirits with its outlandishness, especially where it concerns your buffoon of a brother-in-law. Really, my dear cousin! It's all the talk of London medical society. That puffed-up mad doctor believes himself to be some sort of Charles Darwin. Better than Darwin! The very idea . . . and with a human subject!"

"To speak true, James, I've no idea what you are talking about. Enlighten me, would you? Especially if it might brighten my mood." Simon sat up, and the room swam. He sank back into the down pillows.

"And what does my esteemed brother-in-law have to do with Bedlam? Braithwaite is a ridiculous coxcomb, marquess or not, and still I cannot believe my sister married him. I do not care how large his fortune, or how many tenants reside on his estate. Doubtless, whatever he's gotten himself involved with is without value to me or anyone else. But do go on. Amuse me, cousin!"

"Well, to hear Lord Braithwaite tell it, Handley has locked up in his chamber of horrors a man whose wounds magically disappear—in moments, mind you!" James laughed loudly. "No matter what is done to him—*no matter what*! Again, 'tis only a story, and you know with whom it originates, but apparently," James said, lowering his voice to a conspiratorial whisper, "this Bedlam inmate was transported from Newgate several years back. And . . . and that Lord Braithwaite has paid Handley a handsome fortune to discover the wretch's trick."

"Ha! An indestructible man! You have indeed lifted my spirits, cousin." Simon shook his head in disbelief, dissolving into peals of laughter.

"Mind you, don't laugh so hard you relapse into unconsciousness, Simon!" James shrugged. "Of course, I believe not a quarter of what he has to say about anything. But *your* recovery, Simon, never mind Handley's so-called discovery, is truly a medical phenomenon—and genuine, not the tale of an ignoramus with far too much gold to waste on trifles."

"Far too much gold to waste on my *sister*, who evidently quite likes trifles. She must, or she would never have married the fool!"

"Well, cousin, now I have seen you are finally back with the living, I must be off. I shall stop by tomorrow." James shook his head, regarding his cousin a last time from the threshold. "I daresay, you must not have been as badly injured as you appeared; the lacerations are healed, and however broken your body seemed to me, it must have been mere sprains and contusions. Quite amazing."

Simon paid heed to James's heavy footfalls on the stairs. He gasped as before him the memory again unfolded: the deafening crash of iron, the trestle hurtling toward him, an out-of-control coach. He shivered, wondering if ever he would be free of it.

CHAPTER 24

A week later and Simon felt right enough for a short stroll. He walked the path in Regent's Park, glimpsing with envy couples arm in arm, children at play—a world apart from his gloom. The flowers in full bloom would have five years ago brought a smile to his face as he listened to Sophie recite genus and species while waxing rhapsodic on color and perfume, but they now only served to further dishearten him.

Weary from the walk, he sat on a bench and took a long draught from the flask hidden beneath his frock coat. It failed to extinguish the depression, as did the second, and the third, but then she appeared, a vision. Dressed as she had been *then*, Boxing Day 1836, the last time he knew joy. . . .

Sophie's sapphire gown had cascaded behind her, velvet and satin butterfly wings lending her flight as she'd glided down the thick burgundy carpet of their winding staircase and into his embrace. Her hair done up, captured in a diamond tiara, she looked every bit the fairy queen. It was her birthday, and Simon had promised her the opera—*La Donna del Lago*.

"John will bring round the cabriolet in no more than fifteen minutes, Simon, so make haste and wash the hospital from your skin; you stink of it. Your clothes are laid out for you."

He leaned in to kiss her.

"No, Simon!" She laughed, slapping his hand away. "After you've changed! I shall not miss a moment of this night, and if I do, I shall never forgive you."

Simon brought his hand to his heart in feigned pain. "You wound me, you cruel, cruel lass."

"I will not soften. Now go!" She giggled.

He bounded down the stairs ten minutes later, letting Sophie perfect the knot of his cravat. "Better." She smiled, pecking him on the cheek and handing him his hat and cloak. "Lavender and rosewater are so much more pleasing than the scent of sickness and death, my love. Much better! You may now kiss me properly."

And later, drenched in the sweet romance of Sir Walter Scott and fine champagne, Simon undid the pins that held up Sophie's hair, allowing it to fall through his fingers and down her back in long, dark tendrils. "Brush it for me, Simon! You do such a fine job with your physician's hands."

"Your wish, my love, is mine to indulge." Every stroke of the soft bristles through her thick curls aroused within him the desire to take her immediately. His other hand followed its own course down the back of her neck, her shoulders, and lower still. Simon delighted as her pupils darkened with a need matching his own, until the brush was forgotten on the floor along with their clothing and they fell upon each other. It was many hours until they slept, quenched and content in each other's embrace.

Morning spilled light into the bedchamber. Simon awoke first, and propping up his head, he watched the sunbeams dance over her naked curves. He replayed the night and its ecstasies as he traced the beams with his finger—a game—hovering inches from her—not touching, but so very close. Would it awaken her? Would she sense his near touch by some preternatural connection that required no direct contact? He tested the theory . . . and his ebbing resolve not to touch her. He was riveted to the deft movement of his fingers so very close to her skin.

Sophie stirred, and he pulled back, waiting to see if she might yet be asleep; he was enjoying this far too much to wake her. If she awoke, she would certainly draw the bedcovers close about her.

"Simon? Whatever are you doing?"

He had the decency to be embarrassed. "Nothing, my love, go back to sleep," he whispered close into her ear. But now he was not so certain he wanted her back to slumber. Rather . . . he paused, flicking his tongue around the shell of her ear.

"Simon!" She was now fully awakened and turned into his arms. "You say you wish me to fall back asleep, yet you seduce me, you pirate!"

"Pirate?"

"You plunder from me my well-earned sleep, and you steal from me my maidenhead. If that not be a pirate, sir—!"

Ah, he thought. *She has her own game in mind.* "And what of you?" he protested. "You lie there, bedcovers askew, and not a thread of clothing to hide your curves. And, incidentally, you've not had possession of your maidenhead since I stole it from you ten years past. You, my love, are the seducer, not I!"

"Indeed? Then let me at my work, sir!" She climbed astride him— her lustiness, he'd long ago learned, matched her wit and intelligence. She rode him as she rode her white steed, not ladylike at all, but full astride and relentless. But he was ready for her and rampant as if he hadn't had her for weeks, not hours.

"My love, slow down, I beg of you. I shall not last—"

"Shush!" she called out, dipping her head to capture his mouth, his tongue, biting hard on his lower lip as she dissolved into wave after wave, gripping ever harder until he followed her over the brink, spent.

Sophie rolled to her side, tucking her head into the crook of Simon's neck, nipping at him still, surely leaving her mark just beneath his jaw. "I love you, my darling Sophia, with all my soul, as I have from the day I first beheld you."

"My darling . . ."

A whisper ruffled the hair behind Simon's ear, rousting him from the memory. He jumped, turning in the direction of her voice, finding himself alone on the bench.

"Shh. Simon. Do not despair. It has been too long, my love, and you

must live again." Sophie's bountiful lavender skirt nearly nudged his knee as she sat beside him, and he could almost feel the white feathers of her bonnet tickling his nose as she laid her head upon his shoulder.

A quick glance assured him that no one was about to notice him speaking to the air. "It is an ironical thing you say, my dear. It would appear that I cannot *but* live."

"Then do not squander this gift you are given—"

"It is no gift, my love, when I cannot be with you. I only wish to join you, to hold you—"

"I am with you always, as you know—but in the garden's bloom, in the song of my favorite birds. Here beside you in the park as you walk its paths. But I pray, do not weep on my grave and pine so—"

From the corner of his eye, Simon spotted his brother-in-law coming toward him. "Ah! Dr. Bell! It is indeed good to see you up and about—and so soon! Eleanor will be so incredibly pleased to hear of it."

Simon exhaled, the breath caught in his throat. Thankfully, Sophie had vanished. "Thank you, Lord Braithwaite," he huffed, recovering his composure. "You are very kind. I'd not known you were in London."

"I've business with my solicitor that could not be handled in Sussex. Might I sit a moment? It is quite hot today, do you not agree?"

Well, it is, after all, July. Simon resisted disdain, instead directing his gaze up through the quivering of oak leaves for any sign of Sophie. "Is my sister with you?" Simon asked. "It's been not often enough I have seen Eleanor since your nuptials."

"She will arrive on the morrow. The house is, as we speak, being opened."

Simon brightened. "Might she spend a day or two at my house, do you think? I so miss her."

"I see no reason why she cannot, especially as you are still recuperating from your injuries. It should do you some good, I think, and I am certain she would love it. Your gardens are so lovely, Dr. Bell, and she does enjoy them so."

"It is done, then. I shall make arrangements and have her room prepared." Simon followed the flight of a gull as it soared above them.

"Jolly good!" Braithwaite cleared his throat, his voice dropping to a low growl. "Forgive me, Dr. Bell, for broaching a delicate subject—"

Simon tensed; he lost the gull as it disappeared in the trees. Whatever "delicate" subject might his brother-in-law wish to discuss with *him*? "Do go on—"

"Forgive my bluntness, but from what your sister has told me, you should be quite dead, Dr. Bell, and yet here you are, I daresay, looking healthier than I."

There was an oiliness to Braithwaite's voice that matched his demeanor. Simon ignored the unease he sensed up and down his arms and back. "Looks are often deceiving, and I am yet recovering my strength, though I must confess that I, too, believed my injuries would be more severe."

"Remarkable constitution you must possess, then. That bodes well, I might suggest, for my future progeny." A loud laugh emerged from deep within Braithwaite's chest. "Although I must say, we've been married near a year and Eleanor is not yet with child."

"There are many reasons, Lord Braithwaite—"

"Yes, yes. Of course I know all that. But she is not young, and—" He seemed to consider it a moment. "But never mind that; Eleanor is a fine wife, and I am happy she would have me! But I would like to hear more about your miraculous recovery, Dr. Bell. I have made quite a study of such physical resilience. In point of fact—"

Ah, here it comes. Braithwaite's braggadocio about his indestructible lunatic.

He listened quietly as Braithwaite spun his unbelievable tale, thankful that James had prepared him for it.

"Quite the fascinating show he performs, and perhaps someday we shall even learn his secret. In fact, we are quite close," he said, drawing near to Simon's ear.

Braithwaite's glee was truly repulsive, more so than the ghastly details of these supposed "experiments," which could not be to any degree as horrendous as he described. *Good God!*

"Why have you not simply *asked* him?" Why indeed, when it was so much more entertaining to torture the poor wretch of a man?

"Ah, but we have. And it is quite amazing what he has already divulged—not much, to be sure, but we have taken his blood, samples of his skin, from his wounds as they inexplicably heal. Those are the things shall lead us to the grail, the glory of discovery all on our own, with or without his cooperation." He spoke with the enthusiasm of an explorer on safari.

Simon excused himself, certain that with the next image he would vomit. "Lord Braithwaite, please forgive me; I am still unwell, and should return home to rest. I shall look forward to Eleanor's visit tomorrow then?"

"Of course, Dr. Bell. Come noontime, she shall be at your doorstep."

A preposterous man. How could *have Eleanor married him?* But was there an element of truth in Braithwaite's bragging?

Simon flexed his arm, his leg as he rose from the park bench. Everything normal; nothing hurt. There was not even stiffness.

Why was he not dead? He *had* died. But then he had *not*. Other incidents swam through his memory, fleeting images: a minor riding injury, a bruise on his leg that vanished within an hour; a shaving laceration that healed within minutes, not days; a mishap with a knife that sliced his hand, one that should have taken stitching and many weeks of healing, yet required neither. Taken alone, they were oddities to brush off without further consideration. But taken together . . .

And then the matter of his incompetence at suicide. Five attempts with cyanide, two with arsenic, four with curare—differing formulations and dosages, each a dismal failure—eleven attempts in four and a half years, not counting the original attempt with the elixir, and here he was, yet alive. As unlikely a scenario as surviving the trestle collapse, all of it impossible to explain by any normal understanding of science and medicine. Did he possess a constitution similar to Braithwaite's "indestructible man"? If, that was, Braithwaite had not confabulated the entire business.

It would not hurt to meet Braithwaite's "brilliant discovery" and see for himself. He would not gawk, and certainly he did not condone the torture of a man. Yet perhaps they might talk a little while, man to man. To what end, who could know?

The opportunity to raise the subject presented itself over brandy and cigars, the last night of Eleanor's stay. "Another, Lord Braithwaite?"

His brother-in-law lifted his empty glass, and Simon filled the crystal snifter before joining Braithwaite on the settee.

"I admit it; you've got my curiosity up. Please understand, sir, I do not want a demonstration or a show; I wish to speak with this unique . . . specimen—alone, as a physician. Might that be arranged?"

Braithwaite smiled, a disgusting, victorious grin on his face, a hearty welcome to an exclusive club. "It would not be difficult, Dr. Bell. I am certain, especially given your prominence as a physician, that anything might be arranged—for the right contribution to Dr. Handley's research, that is."

"Money is no object." Simon tilted the glass, downing the brandy in one gulp.

"We have formed a consortium: Dr. Handley, myself, a few select others—financiers. I've only just joined the group myself, but finally after four years of . . . confinement he's begun to let slip more and more, some sort of 'magical' formulation, he says." Braithwaite laughed, setting down the empty glass as his wife entered. "Ah, Eleanor, there you are. Where have you been, my dear?"

She fluttered across the room, her full skirt brushing the floor, her cheeks pink from the night air. "Out in the garden, watching the stars as they come out. Venus is so very bright tonight—"

"Ah. Well, my dear, I must be going," Braithwaite interrupted, standing. "You shall return home on the morrow; please be ready to make your departure by noontime. And on Sunday we shall leave London until the season."

Eleanor nodded tightly.

"Thank you, Lord Braithwaite, for allowing my sister to stay here these past days. She has been a godsend to my recovery. I have missed her so." Simon patted the settee. Eleanor sat beside him. He did not wish to see this visit at an end so soon.

Braithwaite took his wife's hand, kissing it quickly. "Good night, my dear." He nodded toward Simon. "I will have news on that other matter when I see you on the morrow, Dr. Bell. Good night, and please thank your cook for the sumptuous meal."

After the front door closed behind her husband, Eleanor visibly relaxed. "What other matter, Simon?"

"It is a small request your husband has been kind enough to assist me with—nothing, really. I must ask you, Eleanor . . ." He hesitated, feeling no right to intrude.

"What?"

Simon sank deeper into the cushions, propping his legs up on a low table. Eleanor looked weary, her blue-green eyes dull and lifeless. Even her dark auburn hair, done up in a fashion he had never seen her favor, seemed not right. "How does it fare . . . with Lord Braithwaite, I mean? You have been married now a year, but I do not detect any degree of bliss between you. Are you not happy?"

"Happiness? If you mean have I got what you and Sophie had, then, sadly, no. But how might I even dream of . . . when—"

She sighed wistfully, looking so melancholy, Simon was afraid tears would fall should she utter another word.

Her gaze hardened. "He is a harsh man, my husband, for all his polite manners. Yes, he treats me well, allows me my own pursuits. But love . . . ?"

She smiled faintly and patted his hand, and when she spoke, she did not continue the thought. "Speaking of your dear Sophie, Simon, there is something I need to discuss with you, so do not be angry with me for saying it."

"You could never anger me, darling. What is it?" Again, she seemed verging on tears.

She clasped his hand tightly. "You have us all worried, my dear brother. Mama is beside herself, and has been ever since—"

Simon scowled. "Et tu, Eleanor? I make no secret of my misery. I am bereft without my darling Sophia—"

"Yet she shall be dead five years come autumn. Five years! I do not wish to grieve you further, but you must give up this notion of suicide. It is against God's laws, Simon, and it is not to you for deciding the manner and time of your death. Sophie shall attend you on the other side."

"Eleanor. Hear me. She haunts me—some sort of phantasm; sweet and beguiling, she calls to me night and noon, beseeches me from beyond the grave. I know it is but a conjuring of my mind, yet—" He lowered his voice, confessing it to her as he had so many times before, but only to himself. "It is the guilt, even more than emptiness. I killed her, and it is beyond bearing—"

"My dear brother, she was beyond saving, and if you would but see . . . Perhaps her 'haunting,' as you call it, is her prayer that you let her rest at last, that you move on with your life—not give up on it or drown it in drink, *not run headlong into disaster.*"

Eleanor stood, her hands wringing as she looked to the window. "I do not love Richard. Neither does he love me. But I will, if I can, give him an heir. It is what Mama wants. Expects. And I shall, in return, live my life as I please. He will allow me that, at least."

Relieved that the subject moved to safer terrain, he was disquieted by his sister's resolute sadness. He knew with every fiber of his soul that she was miserable. "Mama shall not live past another three years, if that long, and you have your whole life before you!"

The candlelight emphasized the deep shadows beneath her eyes. "What would you want me to do, Simon? I know now it was a mistake to wed him, a flight of fancy. And it is in my nature to be thus. But divorce is nearly impossible, even should I desire it. I am trapped, though in a jeweled cage. And I am not *unhappy*—only just not 'happy.' Do you understand?"

Simon shook his head and turned her face toward his, his voice urgent. "You know, Eleanor, you shall always have a home with me and want for nothing as long as you are living. Never forget that. Lord Braithwaite is a brute and fool, and nothing would make *me* happier than to see you rid of him!"

CHAPTER 25

Simon's carriage stopped at Bedlam's gate, the asylum's central black dome an ominous shadow looming over the grounds. The immense façade swallowed the main entry, the doors a small mouth into the abyss—a living, breathing gateway to hell.

Inmates stared as he progressed through the main hall: wild, manic eyes, glaring warily at anything moving; frightened, furtive eyes, half-closed, looking barely ahead; dead eyes with blank expressions so vacant, he wondered whether any life at all lay behind them.

Wraiths consumed by dull light and stale air, small islands of isolation. Some were attired in finery befitting an aristocrat; some in rags, torn and unlaundered for who knew how long. Others roosted, rooted to every flat surface, muttering apathetically to none any could see; or fulminating, their cries and shrieks of loves lost or suffering endured, a fugue to God that fell upon deaf ears.

All sound liquefied into a muted cacophony, discordant but somehow symphonic as it rose and fell in odd rhythm. Simon stood in its midst, trying to make sense of it, but the music defied interpretation.

A sudden tap on his shoulder. Pivoting abruptly, he nearly collided with a frail, elderly man, standing far too close. A soft-spoken voice, disconcerting and incongruous in this hall of strangers, asked, "Forgive me. Dr. Bell?"

Simon nodded.

"I did not mean to startle you, sir. I am Dr. Francis Handley, director of this hospital and mad doctor to the lunatics of the Bethlem Royal Hospital." The doctor's warm smile and proffered hand failed to put Simon at ease. "I am sorry I missed your arrival; all of this must be disturbing to you, as it would to any *gentleman, even a physician*."

"No, not at all, *Doctor*." Simon did nothing to mask his contempt. "If you will—"

"Yes, our inmate. I cannot give you his name, you see, to protect his privacy and that of his family, poor soul."

An elderly woman approached, her white hair a feathery cloud, her painted lips a ruby pout. "You're quite the lovely . . ." Her gnarled fingers uncurled as she reached out to caress Simon's hair. Handley brushed her aside, gesturing to a keeper; her shrieks echoed even as she disappeared down a dark corridor, dragged by two keepers.

"I beg your pardon, Dr. Bell. I shall see that she is properly restrained—"

Simon could only imagine what Handley meant; he shuddered at the thought. "You have, I take it, been informed of my request? I should like to speak with this inmate *in private.*"

"I really do not think it a good idea—"

Simon pitched his voice just a notch below threatening. "Did not Lord Braithwaite hand over to you sufficient funds to cover this expense . . . your indulgence on the matter? I was certain the amount was—"

Handley stopped Simon, raising a hand in retreat. A benign smile crept over his face. "As you wish, then. This way."

They walked, miles it seemed, through twisted corridors and great halls, a sea of somnambulists, their bodies crammed into every alcove and corner, looking everywhere but toward Simon, the presumptive latest recruit to this mouth of hell.

An iron gate reaching floor to ceiling granted Simon and Handley entry into a separate wing, empty, quiet—a different world than the one from which they emerged. Simon sighed, tension gathering in his neck as they walked on, finally reaching a large room sectioned off by black iron bars, its floor covered with straw.

A lone figure huddled in a far corner of one cage, shackled to the wall. "I shall leave you here. Be assured, there are keepers close by; shout if you need assistance." Handley warned Simon not to expect much in the way of company. "He says nothing—just stares ahead. I honestly do not know what's got into him this day. He was animated enough earlier in the week. But suddenly . . . Well, he is a singular one, I must say."

"Might I have a candle to examine him? It is quite dark in here."

The doctor paused as if to consider an odd request, then handed Simon his own. Simon waited until he heard the clanging of the gate, signaling that Handley had departed this desolate little corner of Bedlam.

"Forgive the intrusion, my dear sir." Simon held the candle up to the bars, but the man remained still, his face to the wall. *Might he be asleep?* Simon waited, observing for a few moments as a keeper entered. The inmate flinched at the creak of old metal as the bars slid open.

Simon took a tentative step into the cell, then another; still the prisoner did not move. Drawing near, Simon heard it: the harsh, shaky gasps of breath. And then the familiar reek of blood and vomit slithered into Simon's senses; he fought the nausea rising from deep within his stomach.

The glint of dark liquid caught Simon's eye, and he drew the candle closer: blood and tissue.

How was it that this man, so obviously injured, likely dying, remained here in the filth of a cage, untreated? The blood was fresh and flowing, although Simon had yet to ascertain from where. "Sir, can you tell me, please . . . I wish to help you, but I need to know the source of the bleeding. Might I examine you?" He tried to erase the fear from his voice.

Simon stepped to the inmate's side and crouched low, candle flame the only light. He was mouthing nonsense, like the rest of Bedlam's inmates. He seemed not to sense Simon at all; perhaps the lunatic was beyond caring, lost in his own world.

Suddenly, the caged man turned on Simon, wild eyes boring through him. Simon was wrong; it was not nonsense the madman spoke, but Ovid, and in Latin.

"*Opiferque per orbem dicor, et herbarum subiecta potentia nobis.*" This he repeated over and over sotto voce, a repetitive chant.

Yes. *Metamorphoses.* Simon knew this well: *Inventum medicina meum est, opiferque per orbem dicor, et herbarum subiecta potentia nobis. Hei mihi, quod nullis amor est medicabilis herbis; nec prosunt domino, quae prosunt omnibus, artes!*

Simon whispered the translation almost to himself, hoping the words would touch some chord of recognition deep inside the inmate. "Medicine is my invention, throughout the world, I am called the bringer of help, and the power of herbs is under my control; alas for me, love cannot be cured by herbs, and the skills which help everyone else do not benefit their master."

CHAPTER 26

*E*rceldoune! *How could it be?*

This was no indestructible, immortal figure shivering in the corner of a cell. Had he not been murdered at Newgate years ago?

Any thoughts of the inmate's super-human physiology, immortality, or indestructibility were shoved away as Simon considered how to help this wretch. Cleary, Braithwaite had been at the very least badly mistaken. Far from indestructible, this poor man was dying, growing weaker by the second.

Erceldoune was barely recognizable: rail thin, hair in greasy tangles reaching beyond his shoulders. There was no sign he recognized Simon at all. Clothing, what remained of it, hung from his skeletal body, as worn and filthy as the man himself. But it was this impenetrable stillness that shredded Simon's heart.

Kneeling carefully at his side, Simon addressed him gently. He must stem the bleeding, which pooled beside Erceldoune's knee. "Mr. Erceldoune," he ventured, trying to break through his chanting. "Do you know me?"

Erceldoune nodded almost imperceptibly, and the Ovid suddenly halted as his gaze darted from Simon to a point beyond the bars and back again. Simon raised a comforting hand, placing it firmly but unthreateningly on Erceldoune's arm—but the apothecary scuttled away, curling into himself protectively as if expecting a blow.

Dear God, what have they done to you?

Erceldoune slowly lifted his arm into Simon's view, saying nothing. The limb trembled with the effort, a branch in a harsh winter gust, before falling back to his knees. He hissed.

Simon sucked in a breath. Erceldoune's left hand was a bloody stump, a gaping, raw void where the last three fingers should have been.

Little wonder he could barely move, barely speak. "Mr. Erceldoune, listen to me. You are suffering wound shock. I . . . Sit tight whilst I—"

Simon threw off his frock coat, quickly ripping from it the inner lining and binding Erceldoune's hand best he could. Placing his coat about the injured man's shoulders, Simon could feel him quake beneath its light weight.

He must contrive the means to get Erceldoune from this place— and quickly. This man was no *immortal*—that much was obvious— and Simon feared that should he be left in Handley's care, Erceldoune would be dead by morning.

The doctor entered, keepers close at hand. Simon needed to keep his wits about him; he could not accuse, or Handley would never let him leave with Erceldoune. Swallowing back bile as disgusting as the words now forming on his lips, Simon put forward his proposition. "I would very much like, *Dr.* Handley, to borrow your . . . patient. Clean him up a bit and study his anatomy. I . . . I have a *keen* interest in your latest experiment." He waited, observing Handley's reaction, stifling his rage, his balled fists thrust deep in his trouser pockets.

Handley smiled. "Do go on."

"I see you have severed three digits from his hand." Simon raised his voice to quell its quiver. "I assume . . ." He cleared his throat, forcing back the remains of his lunch before they spilled forth from his mouth. "I assume, sir, you wish to observe whether he has the properties of a salamander and will regenerate them." Simon ignored the urge to look back at Erceldoune.

Handley crowed, cold, raucous. "*Very good*, Dr. Bell. Your observational skills are quite remarkable. Your brother-in-law's commendation was well deserved. But I cannot allow this man to depart Bedlam."

Simon knew not how much longer he could keep up the charade. "Dr. Handley, I have a proposition I believe you will find adequate."

"I am listening." Handley folded his arms across his chest, waiting.

"I shall give to you the sum of one thousand pounds . . . for your scientific endeavors." Simon had no idea by what amount his brother-in-law had enriched Handley for his "experiments," but it seemed an amount that would at least gain Handley's attention. "And of course, *whatever* my discoveries, sir, you shall have the lion's share of credit at the next Royal Society meeting."

"Lord Braithwaite pays me a sum twice that over the course of one year, for his participation in our grand enterprise."

Simon seethed, his face hot, arms tense as rope. He tamped down on the urge to send Handley flying across the cell. It would not do for him to join Erceldoune as an inmate in this perverted vision of hell. "But this ... *sir* ... is for a mere two weeks' time," he managed between clenched teeth.

Long before the two weeks had passed, Simon promised himself, Handley would be put out of business for good, and never again have opportunity to harm any of the poor souls under his supposed care, most especially Gaelan Erceldoune. Simon needed to end this negotiation soon; Erceldoune had already lost so much blood, Simon feared death was too close at hand for him to survive.

"You have no idea what he is—"

"Do we have a bargain?" Simon spat, his control slipping with each syllable. He stared the little man down, not waiting for a response. "I shall send forth the funds on the morrow. You have my word as a gentleman and brother ..." The word stuck in his throat. "As a *brother physician*."

"Very well, I shall release him to you—for *one* week."

Simon knew this game had to be played with delicacy if he had any hope of prevailing. "Very well ... a week, then."

"We have a bargain, sir! However, do not forget—any findings shall be accredited to me."

"I'd not have it any other way, sir." Simon watched as Handley nodded to the keepers, who undid the shackles. Handley disappeared through the doors.

Simon sagged, his back and hand hitting the greasy wall of Erceldoune's cell. Sickened, he lost the remains of his luncheon as he retched, adding to the foul fluids covering the straw. *How could anyone force another to live like this?*

Recovered, Simon turned to Erceldoune, who had been watching, curious. "Can you walk?"

Erceldoune nodded tentatively.

"I've my carriage outside the gates." Helping Erceldoune to his feet, Simon virtually carried him through the chaos of Bedlam, Handley meeting them in the main hall. *How could it be, such horror in our time? In London?*

Finally through the gate, Simon was grateful to breathe in the relatively fresher air of London, his chest heaving with exertion and disgust as he trundled Gaelan Erceldoune into his carriage. "Get us quickly to my house," Simon ordered his coachman. "There is no time to lose."

CHICAGO'S NORTH SHORE, PRESENT DAY

CHAPTER 27

Simon was incredulous as he listened to Gaelan. He paced the hospital room, swiping a long-stemmed rose from a bedside vase. "You can't be bloody serious! You really mean to reveal all?"

"I am, Simon, I'm tired. And what harm would it do? All they know is I heal quickly; the last thing on their minds is that they're dealing with a four-hundred-something-year-old patient. To tell the truth, I've no other ideas."

And it was an awful idea, a dreadful idea—especially hand in hand with the discovery of Handley's diaries in London. Simon snapped the stem in two before hurling the entire thing across the room. "How could you, of all people, be so bloody reckless? It would be bloody ironic if this little brush with fame brought your . . . condition . . . to the chaps investigating those Bedlam journals. We need to get you out of here. The media are still hanging about; I was accosted by two bloggers and a reporter from Fox News in the café. Saw me leaving your room earlier."

Evidently, Gaelan wasn't listening to the urgency in Simon's voice. "Haven't you ever wondered?"

Christ, he sounded wistful. Bad sign. Simon tapped his foot, arms crossed in front of him impatiently. "What?"

"I mean, haven't you ever wondered what it is makes us . . . us? What did those two particular elixirs actually *do*? Say I decide to cooperate, let them do their DNA testing—"

Simon pinched the bridge of his nose. "What are you saying?

You've suddenly changed your mind? How often have you quoted me from *E.T.*? From the *X-Men*? From every movie in which they pick apart the poor alien? *I've* nothing to fear. No one suspects me of exhibiting superhero traits. But I am certain you'll bloody regret it the moment you agree. So don't! You need to get off, as they say, the grid. Go underground . . . fucking *hide*, for Chrissakes."

"I've always been curious, more so in the past couple of years . . . genetics . . . I've been studying—"

"Ha! Great. Study all you like; earn a doctorate, for all I care, but *do not do this*. Do not open your life in a way that cannot be reversed. I know you too well, Gaelan, and it would be the most—"

"I'm tired, Simon."

"You've said that, and I understand. I do. I'm not concerned for myself; no one thinks I'm other than who I say I am. No one recorded my torture nearly two centuries ago; no one has seen my tissue regenerate magically, like a stop-motion film. There would be no going back from it, you know, once you allow them in."

He had to talk Gaelan out of this folly before he made a decision that could not be undone. "I fetched some clean clothes for you. And what the bloody hell happened to your flat? It looks like a tornado took a direct hit on it. And by the way, whatever happened to your dogged insistence never to allow our little secret into humanity's hands? Lest the 'powerful acquire the key to immortality and subjugate the world' . . . I believe was your last word on the subject." Simon remembered it well; VE-Day, 1945, London. And it was a bloody good last word. Hitler might be long gone—and Mengele—Gaelan had underscored, but he'd been far from the last of the megalomaniacal bastards out there.

Gaelan blinked, ignoring the remark. "Can I just walk out?"

Good. He was coming to his senses. "Well, you're not a prisoner . . . I think you may have to sign some sort of release, but they cannot hold you here. I think I saw something on a television program; it's called 'against medical advice' or some such thing, but—"

Simon considered his motivations, with Sophie lurking at his neck. *"Is this what's best for him?"* she purred into his ear. *"Or for you?"*

He shook it off as if dusting a mosquito from his shoulder. He refrained from replying, knowing that Gaelan would immediately know Sophie was about. He wanted nothing of that.

"Here, put these on." Simon tossed a wool cap and a pair of Ray Bans onto the bed along with jeans and a Northwestern hoodie.

"Fucking Hollywood, this. You sure I won't attract more attention in this getup? Besides, I really don't think it's necess—"

"It is."

"You don't want to be seen with him. Guilt by association?"

She was goading him. Gaelan was naïve about so many things, his veil of perpetual skepticism notwithstanding. They would consume him alive: the media, scientists close to uncovering the last mysteries of human physiology . . . They would never let Gaelan go until they'd learned all his secrets—and there was nothing left of him.

"Do you know there are entire blogs dedicated to you? You've become a cult figure."

"Bloody hell!" Gaelan grabbed the cap and Ray Bans.

"Look, I know you're in a bad way. Between the diaries and now this—and that's on top of everything else you're carrying. But this is right, to leave. If my contact comes through—about the book, I mean—well, we can both put this behind us."

"Again, the book. Simon! It doesn't bloody exist anymore. I've spent the better part of two centuries seeking it. I have more contacts in the rare-book world than you can imagine. It's what I do, what I have done, and I have had no success. I've built an entire library of antiquarian scientific texts. Nearly half my personal library has been restored, so I do bloody well know what I'm doing, and I'm telling you the ouroboros book does not exist. It's vanished; for all I know it's . . ." He lowered his voice to a whisper, requiring Simon to draw near. "It's gone back to the ones who created the accursed thing in the first place—"

"What are you talking about?" Simon leapt backward, confused. Hadn't it been created by one of Gaelan's ancestors? Or tutors?

Gaelan shook his head. "Nothing. Sorry. My head's still a muddle—"

No. That wasn't it. That wasn't it at all. "What aren't you telling me, even after all these years?"

"Like I said, nothing." Gaelan looked away, revealing nothing but a desire to change the subject. "Fine. Right. Whatever you say. Let's get out of here."

Simon decided to let the remark drop for now. An hour later, Simon wheeled Gaelan through the crowded atrium; few took notice of them.

Anne Shawe and Andrew Samuelson emerged from the elevator on the fourth floor. Anne looked at her mobile, judging the time. They'd managed to leave the airport and make the drive in half an hour. "I know you're in a hurry, Dr. Shawe, so we'll go right up to my patient's room." He led her through the nurses' station and down a long, bright beige corridor. "Here we are." He knocked on the door and went in.

The room was empty, made up with fresh sheets, and the ribbed coverlet was tucked neatly beneath the mattress. Andrew bolted from the room with Anne right behind him, confused.

He was at the unit desk, speaking frantically to one of the nurses by the time Anne caught up with him, hanging back, waiting. "What do you mean discharged AMA?"

Andrew threw up his hands, returning to Anne. "He's gone. I . . . I wasn't his attending . . ."

"Look, you've got my interest up, I'll give you that, and as long as I'm here, would you mind showing me what you've got? Films, labs, history—"

"No history. But the rest . . . I'm sorry; I didn't expect . . ." He pulled a computer cart into a consult room, closing the door.

"Any chance we'd catch him at home? I'd love to actually meet your miracle man—"

"Thought you had a connecting flight to paradise—"

Anne cocked her head. "San—"

"Diego. I know. Paradise. Ah, here we are."

Anne scrutinized the files up on the screen as Andrew pointed out specific injury sites on a series of photographs. "And the hospital is saying, publicly anyway, that it's all attributable to errors? All of it? How?"

"They're not making these files public, and with HIPAA, it's not too likely they ever will. I'm not sure I blame them, but I'm sure I'm not the only doc who's interested in the case of Mr. Gaelan R. Erceldoune."

"Erceldoune? Odd name—"

"I think he's from Scotland . . . or Ireland or something."

"Well, if these images are genuine, this is one very extraordinary man. Unbelievable. How many hours between these, did you say?"

"I didn't. Less than two." He scrolled to another set. "These are after ten hours. You'd hardly think he'd had a shaving laceration! The internal scans aren't quite as impressive, but still pretty unbelievable." Andrew brought up a set of X-rays and CT scans.

"Amazing. Truly amazing." Anne glanced at her watch and sighed. "Mind if I make a quick call?" Andrew nodded, and she stepped out into the patient care unit.

There was no way she was going to leave. Not when she was this close to a living, breathing human example of rapid wound regeneration. She'd long ago dismissed the idea as science fiction. Simply not part of our physiology. She absolutely needed to meet this man, whatever it took, and convince him to let them sequence his DNA.

She made a quick call to her new boss at Salk. "Right. Perfect. I'll see you next Monday, with something hopefully so extraordinary it might win us all a Nobel by the time we're finished!"

When she was done, she returned to Andrew. "Good news, Andrew. I can stay on for a week."

"If we can find him—"

"What?"

"Settled his bill in cash; cops think there's something a bit off about his records. But all they'll tell me is that Erceldoune's an assumed name. Possibly an illegal—overstayed his visa and scared to death of being deported. Immigration is on a rampage in this country. Someone thinks he may own a small bookstore near campus, so maybe not an illegal."

LONDON, 1842

CHAPTER 28

Gaelan had been at Bell's house for five days, arriving barely alive. Torpid awareness percolated slowly through the haze of Gaelan's memory as he canvassed his surroundings, tethering himself to the cool reality of silk bedsheets and down pillows. He blinked, trying to focus through the blur that rendered the room in gauze.

Sleep was yet hard to come by; each time he endeavored it, Gaelan was transported again to Bedlam and Dr. Handley, grotesque and gnomish, gripping his vivisectionist's scalprum. That moment dissolved into another, forcing him to relive the horror as he lost the first finger: the sting of the blade, the dull ache as it sliced through tendon and muscle, the blinding agony as the bone snapped, his impotence to act, to pull away, the morphine barely dulling the edges.

He would awaken from it, sometimes after the first finger, sometimes the third, soaked and shivering, gulping for air that could not come fast enough into his lungs as realization finally dawned that he was safe. He felt well enough to dress—the clothing left for him was a decided improvement over his rags. Leaving the frock coat and cravat on the bed, he tried on the too-large trousers and billowy linen shirt. Probably Bell's.

The long staircase was a greater challenge as he hesitated on each step, unsure of his gait, his grip on the banister the only thing keeping him upright. The eyes of Bell's ancestors—generations of haughty medical men, peers of the realm, military officers, all preserved on canvas for posterity—looked down upon him. In one way or another, they were all to blame.

Bell and a companion were having afternoon tea when he entered the dining room.

"Ah, you are looking decidedly better, Mr. Erceldoune, and you have managed the stairs. Progress, indeed! Come, sit, dine with us. Cook has a way with sandwiches and biscuits like none other. Might I introduce my cousin, Dr. James Bell?"

Gaelan nodded in the cousin's direction before sitting. James grunted a terse "Good afternoon, sir," before returning his attention to the *Times*.

Beyond the curtains, there was the green of the garden, the soft melody of birds, all so foreign now. Perhaps in time, these pleasant images, sounds, and aromas would obliterate the terror of his dreamscape.

Naught seemed at all real, yet the cool silver-plate spoon balanced in his right hand seemed solid enough, the tea piquant and sweet, the ham sandwich salty and rich. How long it had been since he'd tasted real meat! *But is any of this real?*

James Bell snapped Gaelan from his thoughts. "Imagine that under-sized popinjay Bean firing at Her Majesty! And with paper! Can you imagine? And why else but to aggrandize himself with notoriety? Shall be a pity if he does not swing for this outrage. I do not care what the prince recommends; *I* venture that hooligan shall not be commuted to transportation for his outrageous act!"

Gaelan had read the accounts in the morning *Times* left at his bedside. A homeless dwarf—an outcast, even from his own family—poor, unfortunate sod. "If you will forgive me, Dr. Bell, perhaps you judge him harshly since you do not have an acquaintance with the sort of life Mr. Bean endures—"

James's glare evinced nothing but disdain. "Mr. Erceldoune—"

"Mr. Erceldoune," interrupted Simon, changing the subject in an obvious attempt to quell an imminent argument. "I've most wonderful news for you. Knowledge of the cruelty you endured, along with letters from myself and others brought before the Crown, *and* James's most excellent intervention, exonerated you."

"I see. And you expect me to . . . what? Thank you?" Gratitude was the last thing he felt. Exonerated for murder he may well be, but the sentence meted out by Handley and his minions would torment him for lifetimes. "And what of Handley and his disciples, the esteemed foppery of London society?"

A satisfied grin materialized across James's face. "That barbarian? Rest assured *he* has lost his commission as director of *that* institution."

"And his financiers, most *especially* Lord Braithwaite?"

James folded his newspaper, passing it to Simon. "There is little can be done about Braithwaite. Besides, he is—"

Simon spoke over his cousin. "Oh, and you should know, Mr. Erceldoune, Mr. Tremayne no longer bullies the good folk of Smithfield."

"Aye?" Gaelan urged Simon to go on.

"Murdered. Two years ago. A man came to his establishment to procure a tart, whereupon he was shown to the room of his own daughter. Went after Tremayne with a kris knife. Died upon the spot, the newspapers said."

"Poetic justice, I grant," Gaelan remarked without emotion. "Dr. Bell—" He turned toward James. "You were about to say something regarding Lord Braithwaite. *Besides* . . . what?" Gaelan observed the wordless conversation between the cousins. "Besides . . . *what*?" he demanded, impatience flaring.

Simon held up a placating hand, his eyes darting everywhere but toward Gaelan. "What James means to say . . . I . . . The abhorrent Lord Richard Braithwaite is . . . I can barely get the words past my tongue, sir. . . . He is married to my own dear sister."

"Braithwaite is your brother-in-law?" *Holy mother of God, how is it possible?* Gaelan's breath caught in his throat. The room spun as his heart crashed against his ribs. Air. He needed air.

What incredulous bit of fate had entrapped him in this labyrinth so near the Minotaur? Gaelan stood shakily, groping along the table to steady himself, until he reached the French doors to the garden.

Erceldoune was sitting on a low bench deep within the garden when Simon found him. "I thought you might fancy a stick," he said, holding out a gold-tipped cane. Erceldoune waved it away, peering into the gravel path.

Simon sat. He well understood Erceldoune, far more than he cared to admit. "Braithwaite is an appalling, monstrous man. My sister despises him, for what it is worth." An exaggeration, perhaps, but what else might he say to ease Erceldoune's mind?

"Poor wretches like John William Bean go to prison, whilst the Handleys and Braithwaites suffer not at all." Erceldoune studied his injured left hand, the bandages no longer stained pink. "Peculiar. It is almost as if they are yet attached. I can feel them throb with every heart-beat, and when I look down, of course . . . One at a time, he severed them. For the last, he gave the knife to your brother-in-law, who was only too delighted to play at being Butcher of Bedlam. I cannot rid myself of that morning; it ever plays in my mind, an incessant cycle of images. I fear I will never be rid of it."

Simon couldn't fathom it; he'd never amputated anything. He envisioned Erceldoune: held down, unable to fight back . . . Braithwaite's wild physiognomy, his undisguised delight in the barbaric act. Simon clamped down hard on the nausea as it rose up through his gullet. Nothing he could say would be enough. "I am sorry little more can be done about him. I—" If only he had spoken up at Erceldoune's trial . . . Would it have made any difference at all? Might he have spared Erceldoune nearly five years of inhuman treatment? "You asked me the other day how I came to be at Bedlam that day, and more to the point, how I happened to chance upon *you*."

"I did."

Simon thrust the point of the stick into the soft dirt, tapping nervously as he regarded Erceldoune. "Do you recall the railway catastrophe a few weeks past here in London? All those people killed?"

"And *how*," Erceldoune snapped, brittle and bitter, "might *I* have any knowledge of *that*?"

Stupid question. Simon looked up into the branches as a large woodpecker landed awkwardly on a sturdy limb. He watched it edge toward the trunk. "Of course. Forgive me." He paused. "Twenty-seven men, me amongst them, were trapped beneath tons of iron. All died of their injuries. Excepting me."

As Erceldoune impatiently brushed his foot along the gravel, Simon wondered if he was really listening at all.

"It was then I began to recollect other times when injuries healed not in days, but in a matter of hours, illnesses that should have, but did not, befall me. I realized I'd had not so much as a sniffle in more than four years."

A furious rat-a-tat-tat came from above their heads; Erceldoune startled at the noise, anxiously scanning the tangle of branches, his face ashen.

"Are you all right, Mr. Erceldoune?"

Erceldoune nodded tightly, his hand trembling. "You were saying . . . ?"

"Around this time, it came to my attention that there lived a man within the gates of Bedlam who was reported to possess a remarkable ability to recover from even serious injury. Beyond remarkable."

"You did not, then, have an inkling it was me?"

"The source of this information was—"

"Your brother-in-law. Of course." Erceldoune glanced briefly at Simon, who nodded in affirmation. "Aye, they all loved to watch Handley's exhibit of human curiosities and experiments, as he called it, and none more so than Lord Braithwaite." Erceldoune stood unsteadily. "I might have need, after all, of that stick you so kindly offered."

Simon handed it over. "Better?"

Erceldoune nodded, leaning heavily on the polished staff. "Perhaps . . . in this . . . accident of which you speak, you were not so badly injured as you thought. It would not be the first time someone robbed death of its due!"

"*Hear* me!" When Simon stood, he caught Erceldoune's eye,

holding it in his own gaze, speaking each word as sincerely as he might to be understood unequivocally. "I was unconscious for *days*, yet when I awoke, there was little evidence that I had been injured at all! Not even a bloody scratch!"

"And what, pray tell, has *that* to do with me?"

There would be no better time to broach the subject. "I must ask you something about your elixir—"

Erceldoune glowered, remaining silent.

"It cured her, Erceldoune, even as . . . even as she . . . died. The tumors vanished within an hour of administration. Astonishing!" The image, even four and a half years later, seemed not possible. Simon observed Erceldoune's expression change, as the import of it dawned. "I've never spoken of it to anyone until now." There had been no point. So what if the tumors had receded? Sophie was still dead. But Erceldoune should know.

Simon sat again on the bench. "I regret that I'd not spoken on your behalf . . . back then. I . . . I was angry, furious, and torn by grief over my wife's death—"

"Four and a half years of torture I suffered at the hands of a madman whose cruelty and barbarity knows no bounds, and you were . . . *angry*," Erceldoune spat with quiet contempt.

"Believe me, I did not know. Had no idea—"

"What? That I was yet living?" Erceldoune hobbled back toward the house through the hedgerow maze.

Simon followed, stopping him with a hand on his shoulder. "As for my silence—"

Erceldoune turned, facing him. There was no glimmer of warmth or understanding in his eyes.

"A terrible injustice, unforgivable for what it did to you. I cannot even presume to beg your pardon for it." What more could he say than this plea for comprehension?

Erceldoune dropped his gaze to follow a small tree frog as it hopped along the path and into the hedge. His voice when he spoke was barely above a whisper, resigned and weary. "It likely would have done me little good in any event. You'd no real evidence to present, only an overheard conversation, with no authoritative way of knowing whether I had poisoned Lil or not."

Simon held his breath, considering whether to broach the subject of gravest concern. Erceldoune seemed less agitated; perhaps it was the best opportunity Simon might have. "There is more. Concerning Sophie's death, that is." They had come back to the bench. "Might we sit? You look as if you are about to keel over—"

"Yes." Erceldoune eased himself onto the bench, still in obvious pain. He looked up, shading his eyes against the sun. A hawk soared above their heads, scrutinizing its quarry.

"It opened. The bottle, I mean. I was in my laboratory and—"

Recognition dawned slowly on Erceldoune's face. "Did you not grasp the instructions? The writing was quite clear—"

"It was not intentional, I assure you. The glass bung came loose and shattered on the floor. Not a day goes by that I fail to consider it was something I'd done that killed her by exposing—"

"The oxidation of it would change it, yes. And if she was ill enough or . . . Yet I cannot know with absolute certainty. So much of medicine . . . is art, not science." Erceldoune looked away.

"In my head, with the perspective of now nearly five years, I know she was better for dying quickly. I do not blame you for Sophie's death. I have too often seen the ravages of cancer, and I would not have . . . Not to say I would have hastened her death." Simon exhaled. "I had, once she was gone, nothing else left to live for—"

Out with it, man! Simon strode several yards, coming to an abrupt halt, his back to the bench. "I drank it, Mr. Erceldoune. I drank it. All of what remained, and—"

"What! But why would you—"

Simon turned, staring at Erceldoune, waiting for him to come to the obvious conclusion, but the apothecary sat in silence, impassive.

"I'd seen what it did to her and desired only to follow her. Yet here I am, confounded at each futile turn, seemingly unable to end my life . . . I only broach the subject with you because of—"

Erceldoune nodded, comprehension dawning. "'Many have said of alchemy,'" he began softly, "'that it is for the making of gold and silver. For me such is not the aim, but to consider only what virtue and power may lie in medicines.' But the power of it is not always virtuous, and wrongly used—whether by intention or error—it can cause many ill or strange effects: some wondrous, others horrific."

"Paracelsus again. You are fond of him, Mr. Erceldoune, it would seem. This is not the first time you have quoted him to me."

"Paracelsus. Yes, his wisdom is well-known to me; it defies the turn of three centuries for its inherent good sense. An alchemist, an apothecary—a healer, he was, but uninterested in the Elixir of Life—immortality—or the transmutation of cheap metals into riches untold, as were many of that trade. And so it was with my own family, akin to the thinking of Paracelsus. My own grandfather, his valued correspondent."

"Your *grandfather*, did you say? But that would have been more than three hundred years ago!"

"Aye." Erceldoune waited, saying no more. The hawk had disappeared somewhere beyond the hedgerow.

Simon froze, emotions overwhelming him. *Is it possible? Is it then true? But how?*

"That book, the one with the ouroboros on it . . . The one in my shop . . . that night . . . Do you recall it?" Erceldoune asked.

The wretched manuscript's cover had long since burned itself into Simon's memory. "Yes."

"Mind, it is but legend . . . but that book is quite singular, I have been told, and not of our known world, but from a different place, a different time."

What was Erceldoune talking about? He made no sense. Simon could only shrug.

"Are you familiar, perchance, with the romances of a certain Lord Thomas Learmont? The Rhymer, he was called. It was said by some in his day he had the gifts of a Merlin—"

"I cannot say I do, but what has that to do—"

"He was my ancestor and had been bestowed a 'gift'—that book—

by one fairy born. A Celtic deity. Airmid was her name. The book is said to be from the land wherein she dwells, perhaps still now, but beyond a portal in another realm, an *other*world."

This was absurd. Utter madness. Fairies? Portals? If Erceldoune was trying to bedevil him, he was doing a first-rate job of it.

"To speak true, I know little else of its origins, but I was knowledgeable in some measure of its contents. The recipes described within its pages have differing effects, depending on how they are prepared, the dosage, and when, during the progress of the illness, they are administered. It is precise, and all set forth in the book's pages. When you—"

"When I drank it, the elixir changed me, did it not, like a magic potion of some sort?"

"*Magic!* Understand, sir, that this book has no *magic*. It is *science*. It is *medicine*—chemicals and herbs and that is all—at play in the human body, amongst its organs and cells, vessels and bones," Erceldoune barked.

Simon had clearly upset him. "I only meant, sir—"

But Erceldoune was not to be interrupted. "My own *father* was burnt as a sorcerer owing to that misbegotten understanding of the manuscript." He winced, cradling his left arm, taking a moment before going on, less agitated. "It is science, not magic, that has made it impossible for me—and apparently you—to succumb to injury or illness."

Hearing this truth spoken aloud was an unwelcome validation of all he'd feared these past weeks. Simon nearly crumbled beneath its weight. Erceldoune said no more, propelling himself from the bench and toward the house, leaving Simon staggered and in shock to numbly consider this incredible turn of events.

Simon pursued Erceldoune across the lawn, catching up easily with the hobbled man. "It is unbelievable, Mr. Erceldoune, what you confess to me—all of it. Beyond comprehension. I cannot fathom it, *if* what you say is true!"

"It is. My two hundred and fifty..." He paused, counting to himself. "Two hundred and fifty-six years of living is testament to that. To be honest, I've no clue about what caused your... condition, and without the book, I fear I never shall."

"But you must solve this puzzle. Then reverse it, and *posthaste*! Delay not another minute. I've a laboratory in the house, and you may make full use of it as you desire."

"I cannot."

"What do you mean you cannot?"

"Without the book—its formulas, recipes—it would be but a useless occupation, I'm afraid. And I have no idea where my book has gone, or whether it yet exists." Erceldoune glowered. "Last I saw it, I was being hauled to the Old Bailey, and I've not seen it since. Perhaps it is . . . in a safe place here in London, perhaps not. Had I only not been convicted of Lil's murder, I might yet be able to do something to help you, but I am afraid it is quite impossible."

CHICAGO'S NORTH SHORE, PRESENT DAY

CHAPTER 29

Gaelan Erceldoune wanted only to be left alone. And that was the problem. They knocked on the door, calling out his name at all times of day and evening, hoping to get a glimpse of the "Miracle Man" as if he were some sort of Promethean monster.

The Instagrams and YouTube videos multiplied like cockroaches in every corner of the Internet. Even CNN's site had a small piece, thankfully buried in the human-interest bits below the fold. He thanked the reliable idiocy of American politics for the latest dire warning of a government shutdown, which claimed the news in endless cycles, pushing the story of his miraculous recovery further and further down into the dregs of Google News.

Simon assured him it would all eventually pass and Gaelan Erceldoune would fade into the annals of unexplained medical recoveries. Until then, he was trapped, afraid to venture past his threshold, where religious groupies had now set up camp. A string of votive candles was lined up along his building, flowers, wreaths, sticky notes—a bloody shrine. What, for fuck's sake, did they want with him? He could hear them murmuring, chanting at all hours.

The universe wasn't totally bleak. Two weeks had passed since the article on the Bedlam diaries, and nothing more. Perhaps Simon had been right.

He removed the gold pocket watch from his waistcoat for the third time in an hour: half past two. Middle of the fucking night and he was still wired, restless—stalking from the shop up to his flat and back again. Prison. No combination of whisky and drugs seemed to knock him back more than a notch or two, and when sleep finally claimed him, he was back in Bedlam, his screams echoing through the decades, waking him. Rinse, repeat.

The chanting at his door seemed to have stopped for the night. Gaelan put his ear to the glass. Maybe they'd given up, gone home, and finally left him the bloody hell alone. Daring to lift the blind, he looked out onto the sidewalk. Empty. Even the votives and flowers had vanished.

He grabbed a wool cap from behind the counter and pulled his leather greatcoat around him, collar up. Maybe just a short walk down to the lakefront, where he might be calmed by the reassuring rhythm of the waves as they crashed into the breakwater. A tentative step beyond the threshold...

"Hallo." A muffled woman's voice. *British?*

Gaelan jumped at the unexpected sound, which originated from somewhere within the fur-trimmed hood of an oversized navy blue anorak. He sighed. *Even at fucking two in the morning?* He staggered backward, retreating into the shop, slamming the door behind him. *No fucking way.* He sank to the floor, back against the wall.

The door opened again. *Fuck!* He'd forgotten to lock it. "Go the bloody hell away! Give me a moment's peace—"

"I didn't think you'd mind... my clearing away the clutter in front of your shop? It's amazing how people are always looking for something... novel... to worship. I guessed you might not be too keen on the shrine.... Gave me something to do other than freeze out there on your sidewalk—"

"Leave. Now. Please?" Gaelan grumbled, not looking up, his head buried in his hands.

"I will. I promise. Just hear me out. Five minutes. Less, if I can manage it."

Gaelan said nothing. Defeated, he didn't know what else to do. "I bloody give up," he said finally, each word a dagger flung blindly into dim light. "What is it I might do for you this *fine* night . . . erm . . . morning?" he hissed.

"Look. I'm not a reporter, not paparazzi. I don't want to make a cable movie about you, feature you on my talk show, or start a bloody religion with you as the new messiah."

He waited for a follow-up sentence, which never came. Instead, she joined him on the floor, sitting cross-legged beside him.

"You've told me what you're not," he said quietly, finally looking up, struggling to remain vigilant against the threat. She had discarded the anorak, revealing faded jeans and Doc Martens. M. C. Escher T-shirt. Long, thick auburn hair hung down her back, her dark blue eyes warm and alert, even in the middle of the night. "Now if you don't mind, your five minutes are quickly vanishing."

"I'm Anne Shawe. Dr. Anne Shawe. I don't suppose you've gotten my e-mails or phone messages, have you? I've been trying to reach you for three days."

"As you might imagine, I'm not quite in the mood for checking in on my e-mail." Gaelan pointed to his watch. "Ticktock." He'd stopped reading his mail on the third day, slamming his laptop shut after the fiftieth request for an interview.

"Look. Andrew Samuelson called me in on your case."

The genetics doctor. *Figures.* Her five minutes had become what seemed like ten. "I've heard enough, and you can leave. Like I told him, I've no interest in bloody tests." The conversation was quickly sapping what little energy he possessed.

"Please. Let me finish, and then I'll go. I promise. I slipped Samuelson two days ago. He has no idea I'm here; he actually thinks I caught a flight to San Diego." She picked up her phone, glancing at the face. "Yesterday."

The sincerity in her expression began to undermine his resolve. Should he believe her? Hear her out or send away this interloper, cast her out into the night, bloody anorak and all? Gaelan shrugged the coat from his shoulders and snapped off the wool cap. "Go on," he said, leaning his head against the wall, curiosity piqued. Holding up his right hand, fingers spread, he mouthed, "Five."

Her smile creased the corners of her eyes, and a fleeting image from long ago snaked through his mind, vanishing too quickly to take hold. "Five minutes. Great! I read your hospital file; as I said, I'd been called into the case by your doctor—"

"Samuelson. Except he wasn't my . . . *official* physician. He had no right to—"

"I *disagreed* with Dr. Samuelson. He was far too comfortable skating around the rules of ethics. His intention was to either badger you into consent or do the DNA testing without it. I was disturbed enough that I mentioned it to his dean. I understood his interest; I certainly share it, but no matter how astonishing your case, it doesn't justify a breech—"

Gaelan mustered his last reserves of contempt. "Then why are you here? Do you think your confession of Samuelson's sins will render me more pliable a subject? Lay myself bare to your scrutiny because you came to the defense of my privacy?"

"No, I don't. But I did want to explain myself, and hope you might answer at least a question or two on that basis alone." She turned out her pockets. "See? No test tubes or syringes to steal your blood whilst I distract you. Look. I came all the way from London to meet you."

Gaelan's eyebrow quirked. "I'm flattered," he spat, unimpressed.

"I would be lying if I said I didn't want to run your blood through a gene sequencer. I'd be a fool as well, given my field, but my interest in you—"

Gaelan summoned every bit of the exasperation he'd accumulated the past few days. "Dr. Shawe, I don't know what you saw in my file, but my physiology is no more unique than Samuelson's—or yours." He forced a laugh, imagining the notes in his chart: instant recovery, rapid tissue regeneration. How many exclamation points followed each notation? "I can still barely stand for more than a few moments at a time; my head feels as if it's harboring angry bats, and my abdomen feels . . . Well, it's quite beyond description."

"But it seems there is more in what you *aren't* saying. I saw photographs of a man, charred, severe burns, broken—"

"It's quite amazing what Photoshop will do, if you've a mind to manipulate an image." It was a terrible argument. Someone would have to have been diabolical enough to alter . . . how many images? But under the circumstances, it was the best he could summon. "What exactly are you implying, Dr. Shawe? That I am some sort of super-human miracle? Where is your scientific disbelief, that you would—"

"Yes. You are."

Gaelan stood, keeping hold of the wall, and took an unsteady step, his blood pressure plummeting. Catching himself, his right hand planted on the wall, he sat again, waiting for the lightheadedness to pass. "As you can see, Dr. Shawe, I am not exactly recovered. . . ." He held up his left hand, a demonstration of an imperfect man. "Is this the hand of a miracle of a man?" It was a slightly more persuasive tack, although he suspected she already knew about his deformed hand and had a ready answer for it.

"Fingers—limbs—are more complex systems. Amputated, they'd never grow back. Yes, you're still injured, but the rate at which you've recovered is like nothing I've ever seen. No one's ever seen before . . . not in humans."

"Perhaps, then, I'm part salamander?" He needed to get rid of her. He was too exhausted, too vulnerable; his fortress walls were under too much stress from weariness and wear. "Might we continue this—"

"I got into genetics, Mr. Erceldoune," she continued, ignoring him, "for a very personal reason, one to which I've dedicated my career. My family thinks I'm obsessed; I've lost one fiancé over it and missed several other, shall we say, relationship opportunities over the years owing to it. When you came to my attention, I was intrigued enough—"

"To catch the next flight to the US?" he snapped.

"No. But to make a stopover that has lasted several days longer than I intended. I was actually on my way to join a project at the Salk Institute in California—"

Gaelan didn't know what to make of Dr. Shawe. Genuine as she seemed, she was no different than all the others who wanted bits and pieces of him. Yet he was curious.

"The women in my family have lived extraordinarily long lives, it seems," she continued. "Going back at least five generations, but only in a single genetic line. Little sickness, and legendary rapid recovery from childbirth, from injuries—for my family at any rate. But it seems only the women, and only from one origin point in my family tree . . . and only down one branch. So I'd always wondered if there had been some sort of genetic component—that is, after I took my first university genetics class!"

"I'm sorry if you believe your family are eligible for their own Marvel comic series, or whatever. But why tell this to *me*? You think I'm a long-lost relation? A missing link?"

"I have only a few questions—"

Her five minutes had long since passed. "Why do you not run *their* blood through a sequencer?"

"My relatives? I have. And with extraordinary results, which brings me to you. I *need* to know."

Gaelan made another attempt to stand, then thought better of it. He was too weary to do battle in the middle of the night with this woman, her indigo gaze piercing through him.

Dr. Shawe rose from her position with the grace of a dancer, helping Gaelan to his feet. He wanted to protest, wave her off, be rid of her altogether, but instead he allowed her to lead him to an overstuffed reading chair at the center of the shop. She sat in the other, crossing her legs beneath her, and turned on a table lamp.

"I cannot get over your collection, your books. There must be thousands. . . . Brilliant—"

"What?" Oh bloody hell; he was never going to rid himself of her at this rate! He rolled his eyes, sighing. "It *is* what I do. Erceldoune's Rare *Books* and Antiquities."

His tone was brusquer than he'd intended; she looked hurt. Good. Maybe she would leave now. "So you've explained your 'why'; it fails to impress. And I've granted you far more than the allotted five minutes."

But she was already up and perusing the collection, examining the spines. "I've recently developed an interest in antiquarian scientific manuscripts. This is incredible," she exclaimed, drawing out a large volume. "Culpeper? I have to look, please? And then I promise, I'll be out of your hair."

Dr. Shawe settled back into the chair with the large book on her lap. "*Culpeper's Herbal.*" She ran her hands across the grooved leather of the cover, her index finger gliding along the perfect gilded edging— a solid brick of gold, it seemed.

Gaelan fought the urge to be drawn in, but the way she handled the volume, almost caressing it, entranced him. She opened to the title page, and her fingers traced down the page as she squinted through the difficult ancient typeface. "*The English Physitian* by Nich. Culpeper, Gent. Student in Physik and Astrologie, 1651," she recited with the excitement of a child opening a gift box. "Don't you feel it, Mr. Erceldoune?"

She looked up, catching him as he stared at her.

"Sorry?"

"When you touch these pages—the deep engraving of the print— how can you not feel the history of science run through from your fingertips to every nerve? It is an extraordinary volume. It must be worth a small fortune!"

"It is. And it is not for sale. Now, if you don't mind . . ." *Focus on getting rid of her, Erceldoune! Bloody hell.* She was like a mouse insinuating itself beneath the stove in winter.

"Oh. Sorry. Of course." She blushed.

Gaelan pinched the bridge of his nose. The throbbing in his head, which had not abated since returning from the hospital, escalated now to deafening, and he gasped as a sharp pain lanced spear-like through his skull.

"Are you all right, Mr. Erceldoune?" Her mobile rang, relieving him of the need to respond. "My boss. I'll ring him back later," she said quickly. "I'm so sorry to have bothered you. I shall get out of your hair. And what sort of doctor am I, keeping you from much-needed rest."

She started to go, reaching the doorknob before turning back. "Look, would you mind taking a look at something I recently acquired?

Tomorrow, I mean. It's a book. Very, very old, and I've no idea what to make of it. I have it back in my hotel room. It's quite remarkable for its obvious age, and—"

Anything to steer her away from more dangerous topics. "Yes. Of course I'll take a look at it," he interrupted, "as long as we don't discuss the nature of my injuries, DNA, or anything else to do with my physiology; I would be . . . *honored*. But I warn you, most so-called ancient books are replicas, not authentic. But I shall give it my honest appraisal. *Tomorrow!*"

Finally, she was gone, and Gaelan fell to sleep in his chair; he dreamed of Eleanor.

LONDON, 1842

CHAPTER 30

Gaelan's mind whirled as he and Bell entered the drawing room through the garden doors. Could it be true, then, that Bell had become like him? He'd not used the same combination of ingredients at all in the elixir, yet somehow . . .

"We must, then Mr. Erceldoune, locate your book forthwith. Whatever it takes shall be at your disposal. And should it—"

"Simon!"

"Eleanor, darling!"

The young woman fled into Bell's arms, her full skirt and petticoats swishing loudly as she swept across the carpet. Gaelan considered the scene, wondering who she might be. A new wife, perhaps? With her hair piled high beneath a feathered bonnet and fine gown, she was a striking woman, if not conventionally pretty. And Gaelan could not tear his gaze from her.

"Mr. Erceldoune," said Bell, settling Eleanor at his side. "Might I present my sister, Lady . . . ? That is, Eleanor."

Gaelan backed toward the doors. Might *this* be the sister married to Braithwaite? *Dear God, what was she doing here?* Could Braithwaite himself be not far behind?

"Eleanor, darling, will you please excuse us a moment?" Bell pulled Gaelan aside and whispered in his ear. "Calm yourself, Mr. Erceldoune. She is innocent of Braithwaite's proclivities, I assure you. She dislikes him, as I told you. I doubt he is with her."

Gaelan was unconvinced, quickening his pace toward the garden doors.

"Please, at least stay a moment and make her acquaintance. I promise I shall not reveal you."

Gaelan nodded, not at all reassured. Yet he would not be rude, however monstrous her husband.

Eleanor drew near and extended her hand. "Mr. Erceldoune." She gazed at him, her scrutiny flushing his face hot with its intensity. She knew . . . something.

"Lady . . . Braithwaite." He could barely spit out the name past his revulsion of it. Gaelan bowed slightly from the waist, taking her proffered hand, the tremble in his own impossible to still. He noticed a profound sadness in her eyes as he straightened again. But something else too. Terror? He dismissed the notion. Braithwaite was *his* tormentor, not hers.

"To what do we owe this surprise visit, my dear, and why did you not send word you were coming? I would have made preparations. Is . . . Lord Braithwaite with you?" Bell asked a bit too breezily.

She shook her head tightly, eyes closed; when she opened them, tears had gathered in her eyelashes.

Bell looped his arm about her back, and her head fell to his chest. "My darling, what is it? You must tell me."

"I would really rather not talk about it. In fact, I would beg you to tell no one that I am here, most especially Richar . . . my *husband*." She stepped back, her expression beseeching. "I would ask the same of you, Mr. Erceldoune." Tears spilled in delicate tendrils down her nose, already streaked and red.

"Perhaps," Gaelan said, excusing himself, "I'd best take my leave so you may talk in private. Dr. Bell, we shall talk again later."

Eleanor held up a hand. "No, please. Do not leave on my account. It would grieve me to know I've interrupted your conversation, and I am quite exhausted from my travels. I shall retire to my rooms and leave the two of you in peace."

Bell ushered his sister to a settee, but she did not sit. "Sis, please end the mystery, and tell us what is the matter?"

"I . . . I shall in good time. I promise, but I've not slept, and would . . . Would you mind awfully if I went up now? I've no stomach at the moment for tea—or company."

"Of course not. We shall send for you when it is time to sup."

"I'm sorry to be so mysterious, but—"

Gaelan observed Eleanor as she disappeared through the doorway. There was something not quite right about the way she walked, an odd limp that suggested . . . He shook it off. If it was something wrong, surely her own brother would have made mention of it.

"She is quite upset, but it shall all sort itself out, I am certain, at least I hope so—and soon. But, Mr. Erceldoune, please, might we return to our earlier conversation? Please do sit."

"I admit, I find it a trifle disquieting to discuss this particular subject whilst Braithwaite's bride is about—"

"You've little to fear from her; that I warrant."

Gaelan cleared his throat and drew a long breath. He'd never said it aloud. Ever. Not in more than two centuries. He drew a long breath. "I was born in 1586, to speak true. In the Scottish Borderlands, though I look not much more than a man of forty.

"I would but guess, Dr. Bell, that when you administered yourself the elixir, it affected you in the same way it did me when I administered myself quite a different medicine created from that same book."

"Did you suffer cancer as did my Sophie?"

"Not cancer—it was plague. It cured me to be sure, but as you see, it had other . . . consequences."

"Plague!"

"Aye. I'd not realized anything was amiss for ten years after. By then, my contemporaries had grown old and shriveled, yet I remained unchanged. When I created that medicine for myself, I'd been delirious with fever. Certainly, I would have died by day's end. It was only later I discovered my grandfather's notes in a scroll hidden within the book's binding. But, I assure you, my faculties were quite intact when I prepared the elixir for you. My head was clear. It was you—"

Bell shot him a skeptical glare. "You'd been drinking when I came to see you—"

"Not so much as you'd think. No. The formula was correct." Gaelan paused a long moment, considering his words carefully. "All medicine is poison, Dr. Bell. As a physician, you well know this. Laudanum given in a proper dose will ease pain and more. But too much will slow the breathing enough to kill. The line is razor thin and murky as well between enough and too much, between manipulating the components not enough and far too much. The combinations of herbs and natural mineral elements endless and unknowable. For your wife, the result was tragic; for you and me . . . ?"

"I need for you to reverse it. I cannot any longer abide living in this world. I must go to my wife."

"I have told you. Without that book it is, I am afraid, impossible."

Bell placed his hands on his hips. "I cannot believe it to be true. There must . . . there must be a way, some recipe elsewhere. Another book in that immense library of yours. Surely—"

Ah, now the consequences of Bell's inaction five years past came to the fore. Gaelan did not feel avenged. "Surely, I've no idea what's become of my library in these nearly five years of my *imprisonment*. And that book—I assure you, there is none other of its like. And now, sir, I am weary, and beg your leave; I yet tire easily. Please be so good as to tell your cook not to expect me for supper."

CHAPTER 31

Simon dined alone; not even Sophie's ghost visited him. He burned with the need to continue the conversation with Erceldoune. It could not end here. It must not! There had to be a way, and Simon's well-outfitted laboratory was the perfect place to pursue it. He would take Erceldoune there come morning; perhaps together they might discover an antidote. An antidote to immortality.

Simon wandered the house and, without realizing it, arrived at the threshold of the laboratory. It had been four and a half years since he'd set foot inside, however often he'd been up the stairs, only to turn back, unwilling to confront that terrible afternoon again.

The light of a waxing gibbous moon, bright in the clear twilight, poured in through the arched windows, despite the years of accumulated dust and neglect. He lit candles, which wove the room into a washed-out fabric of cobwebs and grime. Simon scowled at the scene. Perhaps not so well-outfitted, after all. This place was to him now a foreign land, pushed far out of mind. Any fond memory of it had been blotted out with Sophie's death.

Simon ran a finger aimlessly along the top of the workbench, his white cuff blackening along with his hand. What did it mean, this new state of affairs? That he would walk through life, never—ever—able to die? Never to be at his eternal rest with Sophie? That he would see James, Eleanor, nieces, nephews . . . all grow old and die?

"Would it be so awful, Simon, to live forever?" Sophie, her voice a song at his ear. Just like her to appear at such a moment.

"Except for the torturing part. Did you not see what they did to him for it? To live in fear of discovery like that for an eternity? To see all around me wither and die? To—"

"So you believe it with a single word from him; how do you know that what he says is not a cruel joke—revenge for his years of imprisonment? For

it is you he blames, whether he denies it or not, and is it not the harshest of punishments to suggest to you, now, what you fear the most profoundly?" She was wearing the yellow silk gown—innocent and demure, sitting upon the laboratory bench. She sighed, bored.

Simon picked up a glass cylinder, blowing a layer of dust from it. "And worst, my love, I can never join you in eternity. I must exist in perpetual purgatory of grief, apart from you forever, except upon your whim to visit me in my loneliness."

"Simon, my darling. Hear me. You must go on; it is now nearly five years, and it is as if you have stopped time itself. Look at the condition of your laboratory. What would your uncle say to you?"

He would laugh, that was what he would do, call him the fool he was. Simon reached for Sophie, stopping short in frustration when he realized he could not hold her.

"Have I not gone on? What other choice do I have?"

"But you have stopped living! Your days are spent in Baileys and your nights in a drunken daze. Until your accident. Perhaps it was a blessing, that. Woke you up from this dreary somnambulant so-called life of yours."

"Why must you chide me, my love? Perhaps it would be better if you simply vanished and did not torment me thus."

"My darling Simon. You've only to wish me away—truly wish me away, and then . . ." She was gone, and Simon drew in a deep breath, relieved, yet missing her already.

There must be a way to reverse Erceldoune's elixir. Either he was lying or didn't care to help him, but somehow . . . A knock on the door.

"It is Eleanor, Simon. Might I have a word?"

"Yes, of course," he breathed, recovering. Simon opened the door, brushing the dust from his coat. She took account of the dusty benches and neglected glassware. Simon was grateful that she said nothing of its forsaken state.

She walked lightly through the room, her skirt billowing along the dirty floor and cabinetry. "Do you remember, Simon, when we used to play up here? We playacted at Mary Shelley—I was our modern Prometheus, and you my grand creation?"

"Yes, I recall it." Of all the games they played as children, why this one in particular must she bring up?

"You know, I'm still envious of this house. It was always my favorite of all the family properties, this laboratory a magical alchemist's lair. Such sorcery to fuel the imagination amongst the odd-shaped glassware jars of powders, prisms that cast rainbows upon candlelight." She picked up a swan-necked flask, blowing from it a cloud of dust, examining its delicate bends, holding it up to a candle flame.

"So, my dear, are you ready to confess why you returned to London, and me, so soon? Have you finally fled that idiotic swine of a husband? I am not totally oblivious, and it is clear you arrived by train and with no trunk. Not even a satchel, Mrs. McRory proclaims." He immediately regretted the sharpness in his tone.

Eleanor glowered; Simon could nearly taste the bitterness. "I despise him."

"At least you've come to your senses about that! I have always thought him a poor match." Simon wondered if she suspected anything untoward about Braithwaite.

She sat on a high stool next to her brother. "Yet you never said a thing?"

Simon placed a comforting hand on her arm. "It was your own choice, and not mine, the mate you selected. Would you have listened, even had I interfered? I *am* grieved to have been right in my thinking about him, however. I cannot countenance the man, even more so now that—"

Simon was caught in Eleanor's gaze; he broke from it, turning away. She pulled him around to face her. "That *what*?"

"Never mind." He must change the subject. "Had I spoken a word back then, sis, how might that have changed your mind? I think not at all. You were quite steadfast in your decision. What is it about him you find so unpleasant now that was not apparent months ago? Have you found him penniless—and a fool?"

Eleanor gasped at the rebuke. She slapped him hard. "Simon! Do you think I care one whit whether I am rich or poor? Have I ever cared?"

"Forgive me, Eleanor. I do not know what possessed me to say such a horrible thing to you. But you've certainly no desire to be poor, else why marry a man like Braithwaite: estates, a peerage, servants to your heart's delight . . . ?" He could think of no other reason for her to cast her lot with him.

"I am nearly two and thirty years, and was until my betrothal, as Mama daily reminded me, a spinster. It grieved me sore that she worried so about my welfare. Father's entire estate will go to our brother Ben when Mama passes, as Uncle Samuel's has gone to you. I desired independence, and it was the only way."

"You call yourself independent? Married to Braithwaite? Ha! And it wounds me to know you believe I would allow you to grow old, penniless, and uncared for—"

"She wants me to have a home and children of my own. Lord Braithwaite loved me, and he was sweet and charming and kind . . . at first. I thought I was in love with him—I *was* in love with him!" She was near tears, hysterical.

Simon drew Eleanor into his embrace, holding her gently. "I am sorry to have harangued you. But what has changed now to make you flee him?"

"That, I am not ready to speak of. Perhaps in a day or two, if you will indulge me the time to consider what to say and how—"

"You speak in mysteries, Eleanor, but all right then."

She picked up a small glass tube, fingering it absently, the darkness receding slightly from her countenance. "Let's not talk of my worries. What are you doing up here? It is sore neglected, and I'm surprised you've not removed the roof and replaced it with more windows. It would make a beautiful solarium."

Simon shrugged. "Come, let us leave this dusty place. Would you join me for a brandy before retiring for the night?"

"I am indeed restless, but quite fatigued as well. Perhaps I should go to my room, try to sleep."

Eleanor stopped on the stair, pausing before the Cluny. "*Mon seul desir . . .*" she said wistfully, running her fingertips across the rich red of the tapestry. "I've always loved that tapestry. The meanings hidden within it are as many as the mysteries of the universe."

"So you will not tell me, then? Why you've left your husband?"

Eleanor slapped his arm, not quite playfully. "I told you, in due time. Besides, I've not said I've *left* him at all."

CHAPTER 32

Sleep was Gaelan's enemy, each blink of a heavy eyelid another step on a journey back to the nightmare of Bedlam. And this night dragged by interminably, made worse by the presence of Lady Braithwaite in the next room.

The forlorn silence was broken only by the plaintive whoop of an owl, its yearning cry growing fainter before dying on the breeze. So. What to make of Simon Bell? Was he truly destined for immortality, poor wretch? Gaelan supposed it was possible, but what was it then about medicines conjured from the ouroboros book that caused such an unnatural concomitant effect? Were others walking this earth like the two of them? Gaelan had wondered about such circumstance over the years, but . . .

Bell seemed oddly bound to reverse it. Yes, it was shocking to find oneself unable to die, and yes, Gaelan well understood the desire to join one's beloved in the afterlife, but why hasten death, especially when surrounded by such luxury as Bell found himself? Gaelan had wanted to die at times, more so of late, and only since Handley had made life so much worse than death. But had the opportunity presented itself, would he do it? Undoubtedly yes, whilst he'd been Handley's prisoner. He'd prayed for it, and nightly. But now . . . now that he'd been redeemed from captivity?

The clock ticked by the lonely minutes; he counted aloud, switching language every ten beats, a futile effort to push back against sleep. It would come, and he would be thrust through the gates of hell.

In the distance, the sounds of London: the bay of a stray dog roaming the street outside Regent's Park, the distant clip-clop of a horse carrying a weary traveler home or away, an infant's cry borne upon the wings of the warm July air and through the open window. Forestalling sleep the entire night would be all vain effort; exhaustion would soon overpower fear. He was too tired, too weak from his injuries.

What would it be this night? The blade slicing true and deep through muscle and bone until there was nothing left of his hand but a bloody stump? Poison? Rats? A rabid cur, its mouth frothing, teeth sharp and at the ready? Handley had tried them all—variety for his show. A scream startled Gaelan from the shadowland between wakefulness and sleep. Was it his own voice or the tenuous echo of a nightmare?

Droplets of cold sweat sprang out along his back, and he shivered, but at least he had awoken. Perhaps a brandy, or something stronger, was in order. He maneuvered down the stairs quietly as he could manage to the drawing room, and poured a large tumbler of Scotch whisky, savoring the burn as it coursed its way through his gullet.

The soft cushions of the settee and the alcohol-soaked lullaby of citrus fruit and ginger on his tongue released the tension gripping every muscle. Gaelan set the empty glass on the side table and drifted, calmer now. Perhaps enough . . .

A rusty scalprum appeared, suspended above him, wafting slowly as an autumn leaf. He sat up, once again alert, tense, his breathing too rapid and too shallow. *Damnation. Will I never be allowed to rest for even one moment?*

Restlessness drew Gaelan to the garden doors, and he gazed up into the night sky, the stars and planets, asterisms. The constellations. Their constancy the one thing in all his years at Bedlam to keep him tethered. How many times had he conjured them in his mind's eye, reciting their names from memory?

What might he observe of them this July night over London? There were times, so long ago, when it was so clear you could almost touch the stars. These days the heavens were choked with steam and coal dust. Peering through the garden doors and up, he was surprised to find the skies unblemished by the usual brown cloak of haze. *Ah, stella polaris.* He found, then, the Bear, down and to the left—the outlines of the Ursa Major, and the seven stars of the Plough. Off to the right . . .

"What on earth are you gazing at, Mr. Erceldoune?"

Gaelan spun around, staggering into a table. He exhaled shakily, heart fluttering. "Lady Braithwaite—"

"Forgive me, Mr. Erceldoune, I did not wish to startle you by stealing in here so quietly. I should have been more conscious of—"

Gaelan held up his right hand, halting the apology as he reclaimed his composure. "I . . . No need, my lady. On the contrary, you must forgive me; I am quite a bit on edge these days. . . . I've not . . . I've not been well—"

She'd lit the room with several large candles, one of which she yet held.

"No need to explain, Mr. Erceldoune." She looked over his shoulder through the window. "What is it out there to so mesmerize you that you did not hear me enter?"

The quiet warmth of her voice stilled the thrashing in his chest. Yet he must be on his guard; she was Braithwaite's wife, after all. "I . . . I have always been drawn by them . . . the stars, and—" He glanced away, toward the window, motioning up at the sky.

The candlelight rendered her melancholy eyes luminous, captured in the window glass. "Ah, then, you could not sleep, either?" Her wan smile beckoned a camaraderie he did not desire.

"I . . ."

"Please, let us sit, Mr. Erceldoune."

Gaelan nodded. He refused to allow this woman . . . Braithwaite's wife . . . to be his comforter. Yet he could not deny that he felt much calmer now.

"Forgive me. I know it must grieve you to be resident in the same house as I."

He looked away.

"I confess I know but a little of your terrible ordeal," she said with a sigh, nodding toward his bandaged hand, "and I am sore grieved by your suffering at Lord Br . . . at my *husband's* barbarous hands. I am aware," she said emphatically, gazing down at the carpet, "that apologies are insufficient by far. But please understand, it was only a day ago I learned of . . . and—" She dabbed the corner of her eye with a delicate hand. "He—"

True enough, she was not responsible for her husband's behavior, yet her very presence could bring Braithwaite—and Handley—down on him at any moment. He would not confide in this woman, of *all* people, no matter how much remorse, how much pain he beheld in her visage. "And what brings you from *your* bed at this late hour?"

"My room is near yours upstairs." Gaelan shook his head, confused. "You cried out . . . I was concerned that you might be unwell—"

He was mortified. "Please forgive me, Lady Braithwaite. I—"

"No! No! You do not comprehend me. I, too, could not sleep, but your shouts . . . they cut me to the core, knowing my husband was the likely cause of your extreme distress." She stared at her hands, clenched into tight fists in her lap.

Had he called out Braithwaite by name? He could not recall. "I . . . I . . . thought perhaps a whisky might calm me enough to return to my bed; then the starlight caught my eye just as you surprised me." He returned to the window, trying to wrest himself from her kind, sorrowful eyes.

"I have always been intrigued by the heavens, and had I been born a man, I might have been by now a famous astronomer. Our family tree is stuffed with *men* of science. I was quite interested in it as a student."

Opportunity denied for the conventions of society was something Gaelan well understood. "I know them all from memory," he said finally. "Asterisms and constellations, planets . . . The skies are the one thing unchangeable, yet ever changing. As a lad, I would sit at the edge of Glomach Falls on the west coast of Scotland, waters thundering below me whilst I gazed into the heavens, stars so close I could almost touch them. My father would come looking for me at dawn, only to find me asleep at the highest perch and admonish me roundly . . . until the next time." The memory was keen for its pleasantness. He'd not thought of it since his youth, and what conjured it now was beyond his understanding.

"Show me . . . the stars, I mean. I have forgotten so much. My pursuits have changed since childhood and—"

"You can see but little from indoors. The windows are too narrow, and the mullions . . . I was about to go outside, before you . . . interrupted me." Her company revived him, he had to admit.

"Might I accompany you? I wish to see."

Gaelan stammered excuses as to why it would not be a good idea. She rebuffed each one.

The night was cool, despite the earlier warmth of the July day. The steady hiss of nocturnal life animated the silhouetted trees; nightingales called one to the other, and the hoot of owls answered in counterpoint. A perfume of closed blossoms, new-mown lawn, and summer fecundity seeped into Gaelan's withered soul. He'd missed this peaceful solitude perhaps more than anything.

He did not mind the company, even as he recognized his fortress foundations begin to crack and crumble, falling away into the glistening blades of grass. Even as he felt the cold granite surrounding his heart erode into sandstone. So long he'd been denied the kindness of companionship, he savored this moment as if it were the sweetest of wines.

Eleanor shivered beneath her light boudoir robe, causing the tiny jewels in her necklace to shimmer in the moonlight. Miniature stars illuminated her face. Again, he caught himself staring. He had been too long without female companionship. Too long, when all he could summon was the will to withstand another day of torture. The idea of standing beneath a real blanket of stars with a kindly woman was so far from reality that . . . *No! This must be at an end.*

"You shall catch a chill, Lady Braithwaite. It is quite cold and damp out here—"

"I am far hardier than you give me credit for, Mr. Erceldoune. And . . . you promised to show me."

"Very well, then." Gaelan stood to her side, pointing upward into the sky. "You see, there is Orion." He indicated down and to the right.

"Yes. The three stars of his sword—I see it," she said. "The sky is exceptionally clear tonight, as if for our benefit alone. For who else would be awake at this hour? Ah, and there, do you see it? Mars."

"Yes. The red planet with Venus just beneath it and to the left—"

"Indeed!" Her face in the starlight was no longer gloomy, but beatific.

Somehow, she had drawn very near, and he could see the goose-flesh beneath her diaphanous sleeve. "I have no doubt you would make a fine astronomer, my lady. However, we should go in before you catch your death." An incandescent heat flared in his loins, a counterpoint to the chill as the delicate fabric of her gown fluttered against his shoulder. The blessed return of desire, so long absent from his life, sent a thrill through Gaelan. Yet, this particular woman—it must not be. It could not be. He chased away all argument to the contrary.

She nodded, rubbing her arms. "We should go in. You are quite right. And I could probably do with a brandy."

The drawing room was a welcome relief from the damp night air—and the beautiful, dangerous intimacy of the night sky. Gaelan poured a brandy for Eleanor, another whisky for himself. Her attention drifted to the settee, inviting him to sit beside her. After handing her the brandy, he took a seat, instead, in Simon's wingback chair. He had already allowed her far too close.

An air of tranquility had replaced her earlier disquiet, and she nipped at the brandy—tiny sips, each followed by a delicate sigh; she was no longer shivering. Their nearness and two tumblers of Simon's fine Scotch had worn away his caution. "Forgive me for saying, Lady Braithwaite, you seemed quite distressed this afternoon . . . when you arrived. And with your sleeplessness . . . I don't presume to know you, but even I could perceive—"

She said nothing; instead she pulled at a loose thread in the settee's brocade. Another approach, perhaps. Gaelan rose from the chair and crossed to the far side of the room, his back to her. "It helps, my lady, to talk of what pains us, and better still . . . easier still . . . if I may be so bold . . . with a stranger, than one whom we hold dear."

There was little he had not heard over the course of decades in the way of cruelty endured by wives and children, when they would pour out their troubles to him in the shop's back room as he tended their battered bodies and broken spirits. And he more than suspected Braith-waite was behind Eleanor's burden.

Her voice quivered as she finally spoke. "Lord Braithwaite ... my husband ... he is ... I fear, not what he seemed upon our betrothal. We were married a year ago and ... I'm sorry. I cannot—" The glass fell from her hand as she fled the room, faltering every few deliberate steps, steadying herself against the wall.

And he knew.

CHICAGO'S NORTH SHORE, PRESENT DAY

CHAPTER 33

Anne Shawe lay back into the "luxury sleep" hotel mattress as she reread her notes. At least she no longer had to camp out on the pavement like a university student waiting in line for concert tickets.

Who are you, Gaelan Erceldoune? Besides being bloody attractive. She sighed. He wasn't *handsome*. Not exactly, but that hippie renegade from the '70s thing quite fit him: unshaven, too-long, too-straight, floppy hair, leather waistcoat, billowy shirt. There was something out of step about him; a formal politeness seeped through his considerable ire and brought to mind BBC costume dramas and Charlotte Bronte. Yeah, so he was fucking attractive—for a middle-aged bloke.

Anne returned her attention to the *patient* Gaelan Erceldoune— equally fascinating. She opened her old-school lab notebook to the first page, reading over her neat script. "Triage reports serious injuries upon admission to the trauma unit, including third-degree burns. Doubts he'll survive long enough to enter the surgical suite, but by the time they're ready for him in the operating theatre, burns do not appear serious, and the internal injuries, although present, do not match the scans. Concerns all round at first about whether they've got the right patient at all."

The hospital must be thanking the stars above that patient records were immune to—what did they call it?—"freedom of information," because disclosing anything close to the truth, to the media or anyone else, would make them all look like blithering idiots. Even admissions of instrument failure and high-level human error provided a more politic explanation. Samuelson thought it was all "a crock of shit," and she suspected so did the trauma team, the ER doctors, and everyone else who saw what they saw. And all were bound to silence. Ah, but how long would it take for "anonymous hospital sources" to be quoted in the mainstream press? So far as she could tell, the media was quoting "citizen journalist" tweets and YouTube posts. Everyone "wants to believe" the unbelievable, but if it's true, chalk it up to mass hysteria, loads of error—and move on.

But the unbelievable was true—or so it appeared. But what was it about Mr. Erceldoune's genetics that defied the laws of human physiology? Something to do with fibroblast growth? Infinitely regenerative telomeres? Mitochondrial anomalies? Something with the immune system? *What do you know, Mr. Erceldoune, that makes you so adamantly refuse to let us test your DNA? What are you hiding?*

On the other hand, there were lots of reasons people didn't consent to genetic testing. Good ones, too, especially in America where a genetic condition could screw you out of health insurance one way or another. Perhaps Erceldoune refused to avoid being identified. Immigration woes? Was he an illegal? Or a criminal? One with a DNA profile he'd rather not make public? She laughed. She had to stop reading crime novels. Seriously.

She tried to push Gaelan Erceldoune from her mind, realizing she'd avoided her e-mail for nearly two days. *Fuck.* Sighing as she opened her laptop, she confronted reality: three e-mails from Lloyd Hammersmith, two from Salk, five from Samuelson, and one from Paul Gilles, his labeled with red exclamation marks and three heart emojis. Brilliant.

She opened the most recent from Lloyd. "Why are you not at Salk? And why are you not answering your mobile? And what's this I hear about you consulting on a medical case in *Chicago*? It isn't that crazy story about that so-called Miracle Man, is it? It's all over the tabloids here!! If it is, bloody brilliant on you. If not, and you're still in Chicago, would you mind checking it out, and let me know if there's anything there to help our work?"

Oh yes, Lloyd, there is a very big *something to it. But what would you do to Mr. Erceldoune should you get your greedy little hands upon him?* She wasn't ready to hand Gaelan Erceldoune over to Lloyd Hammersmith or anyone at Transdiff; they'd pick apart the poor man, right down to his chromosomes.

She continued reading: "By the way, you will not believe what we're finding in those Bedlam diaries. You'll be quite envious of Paul and regret not taking the lead on the project when I offered it to you first. Admittedly, the Bedlam doctor was some sort of proto-Mengele, but his notes are amazingly detailed. Five years' worth of dated journals! It appears that this unnamed inmate, if it is to be believed, could be broken, sliced, and diced. A few hours' downtime and he was ready for more. Fascinating read. We're scanning the whole works. I can send it to you as soon as we're through. I'd love your take on it."

No! She wanted nothing to do with those diaries. Ever since Transdiff Genomics, Ltd. had gotten five pages into the first journal, they'd become obsessed. Some sort of holy grail. But what ill-conceived holy grail would come to light by way of torture? She shoved the thought from her mind. Whoever wrote those diaries was likely deranged himself; who knew if any of it was more than fabrication? Or confabulation, at the very least?

And Paul, of all people...Dr. Paul Gilles heading the effort. "Darling," he'd rationalized, "the man was already tortured; I'm merely giving what he went through some meaning." It was morbid. And obscene. A sort of mental grave robbing in her humble opinion, whether he'd asked for it or not. And he hadn't. She hated Paul for a callousness she'd never known he possessed. But she was far from innocent. How many times had she looked the other way at a notation in a human research project file, not stopping to ask the questions she well knew ethics demanded? How different was that poor sod's torture a century and a half ago than what Transdiff... And where did silence end and complicity begin? Yeah. She was guilty, and it ate away at her.

Her mobile buzzed from somewhere beneath the bedcovers. She unlocked it on the fourth buzz, immediately wishing she'd let it go to voicemail.

"Hallo, Paul."

"Darling, where are you? I thought you'd be sunning yourself beneath the palm trees of La Jolla by now."

"I'm taking some time, seeing the sights of Chicago." She ratcheted up her iciest Dr. Shawe voice. "What might I do for you?"

"Did he tell you what we're finding?"

She responded with silence, her finger poised on the end button, until finally giving in to curiosity. "What do you want, Paul? I'm bloody tired."

"Sorry. Time difference, I suppose. Besides, it is a well-known fact, my darling, that you never sleep. I've a guy who's interested in that weird book of yours."

"Yes?" And *she* had no interest in hearing about this "guy."

"He's really quite keen on it. Willing to pay quite a fortune for it and—"

"No. And what the fuck are you doing—"

"I know you've no interest in selling, but I thought he might be useful . . . you know, in helping you decipher it. I saw his advert and thought of you. . . . Consider it a parting gift to aid you on this quest of yours. I figured if he was interested enough to advertise for it, he must know something about it. If it's the same book, at any rate."

Bloody hell. What was this about? Was Paul trying to endear himself, worm his way back into her good graces? *Not gonna happen.* Especially when he was at his most ingratiatingly smarmy. *Oh, Christ!* Why had Lloyd told him where she was?

"I sort of promised him I would send him scans from it so he might verify it's what he's looking for. Sought it for eons, he said. Name's Anthony Danforth, the author. So, I was wondering if you might . . . scan a few pages. Fax them to him. You've got the book and—"

"No. I have zero interest in selling it. You bloody well know that."

Anne hurled her mobile to the floor. She'd had enough of Paul, of Lloyd, Transdiff Genomics, Ltd., and the whole lot of them. *Wankers!* As soon as he'd seen the double helices engraved on the book's cover, he'd been hot for it. Yeah. Just before he proposed.

The book. It had baffled and consumed her since she'd rescued it from Cousin Agatha's attic six months ago, beneath a stack of old 78 RPM records, a yellowed fancy dress costume, a hideous ratty old wig, and three neglected photo albums. "Take what you fancy," the elderly woman had told her. "The rest will be going to charity."

And then there was the letter, tucked inside, sealed with wax. In the six months she'd had the book, she'd never dared to break that seal. She never would.

CHAPTER 34

S imon stared at his phone. Another bloody dead end. And this chap had seemed so certain of it when he'd answered the advert.

"I had no right to offer you the book. It belongs to my fiancée," he'd said on the phone. "She's not especially keen on letting it go, and I cannot say I really blame her. It's quite an interesting find. Found it rummaging around in some relative's attic or some such thing. Although I have to say, it is quite the strange manuscript. You say you may know something about it—perhaps you might be able to help us crack it? Once her curiosity is satisfied, perhaps she'll sell it to you, and we'll all be happy."

It was worth pursuing—*if* Gaelan was willing. And right at this moment, he was unlikely . . . But what if this was *it*? Finally, the bloody book? How could he let it slip through his fingers? "I might be able to help you," Simon responded. "Not myself, mind you, but an . . . associate . . . acquaintance of mine. A rare books dealer, an expert, particularly in antiquarian scientific manuscripts—"

"I see. Would he—"

"We would need the book itself. I do not believe he would be willing otherwise. . . . But if you fax me scans from it, I will show them to him and we shall see."

Simon held his breath. All Gaelan needed to do was read. Just as easy with scans. If he could be convinced to do it. And *if* it was the right book and if . . .

Might it finally—finally—be over? Might it now be possible to end it, to wrest himself from his lonely purgatory and let himself—and Sophie—finally be at rest? How many times had he been led down this path before over the years: an answer to an advert, a random phone call, a chance meeting at a book conference? Rarer and rarer had been the leads over the past few years, but now the e-mail from this Gilles chap . . . and his phone call.

But for all Gilles's promises, it seemed he was no closer to getting his hands on it. Scans and faxes. Gaelan would never agree to help him without the book in hand, and this would be yet another drawn-out exercise in futility. Patience. He needed patience. He could feel it in his bones. This chap was the real deal.

"You, my dear, are ever the Pollyanna when it comes to that bloody book."

"Can you not leave me alone in my misery? The way he described it . . . how could I not be optimistic?"

"Described it? How would you even know if his description was remotely related to that book? You've laid eyes on it exactly once! And, even then, only the cover. Just bloody get on with it, Simon. Live, for heaven's sake! Forget me. Let me go finally to my eternal rest. So what if you live forever? You can keep on writing those best sellers ad infinitum. Just think of the riches to be had."

"I am not interested in writing another word. I want this just to be over with. For both of us, my darling. So we might both rest in peace."

He'd tried to rid himself of her: mediums, ghost hunters, and the lot. Anyone who wouldn't think him completely delusional, that was. They'd all told him the same thing. "Give her what she desires: her freedom." They would go in circles. Just what the hell was that supposed to mean?

"If you're willing to free her, she will go, but not until." Willing? If only that were true. But, no. He was trapped with a keening, screeching ghost of his own bloody conjuring.

"You really do not wish me to leave. I could wail in your ear all day, and all night howl, and still you weep if I leave you alone."

Aye, there's the rub.

She screamed in his ear, sending the sensitive hairs at the back of his neck on edge with her shrill, keening shrieks. She was frustrated. So was he.

Simon turned back to his computer. The new book was coming slowly; each new title had required greater and greater effort. He'd known even before Gaelan pointed it out that his last three had been but retreads of the first three. Names and locations changed, and the victim as well. But . . . *Case of the Errant Influenza.* Simon had thought to put Dr. John Watson in the spotlight, alter the formula—perhaps then it wouldn't be such a bore to write. But the research had been more than a chore.

Simon knew only a little about modern pharmacology research—and an influenza vaccine to cover a murder required more than a bit of digging. But what to Google? He typed "vaccine" and "unethical" into the search box and clicked on the first article, a blog dated two years ago:

An ethics investigation of Transdiff Genomics, Ltd., a multinational pharmaceutical company based in London, was dropped suddenly last month under highly suspicious circumstances. All files pertaining to the case, which alleged that the firm engaged in unethical medical practices during clinical testing of a new vaccine, were sealed under the patient privacy rules. However, we at BeyondThe-News.net have learned from reliable sources inside the company that Transdiff, a major player in European genetic-based pharmaceuticals, had been using an experimental anthrax vaccine on children in a small Asian-Pacific island nation. No permission for clinical trials had been granted to Transdiff, and all twenty-six subjects died after being administered the vaccine, according to our sources."

Hmm. Yes! Now that would give his novel an interesting twist: a victim unwittingly set up by her husband to be part of a medical experiment with the intent to do away with her! Perfect. Simon's face grew hot, as he suddenly felt the pang of embarrassment. Twenty-six children dead, and all he could think was "plot device."

LONDON, 1842

CHAPTER 35

Gaelan was sipping tea in the dining room when Bell arrived for breakfast.

"Is Eleanor about yet?" he asked.

"No, Dr. Bell, I've not seen her since . . . yesterday," he lied, "when we were all together."

"You must eat at least a portion of Cook's hearty porridge; you are yet skin and bones, sir, and she prepared it specially for you."

Gaelan shrugged. "To speak true, I've little appetite—" He scowled as he pushed away the steaming bowl Bell had placed before him.

"You do seem, however, much improved since you left . . . rather, come to stay with me. And I wonder if you might be up to venturing out today? To the place you mentioned, where you stashed your library?"

Gaelan held up his hand in protest. He regretted telling Bell about the slim possibility that his books, including the ouroboros book, were yet in London. "You must understand, Dr. Bell, it has been nearly five years, and I very much doubt—"

"It is, at the least, worth a try, do you not think? And if it should not be there, we shall scour the whole of Britain—the world if need be. Money is no object, and I've solicitors aplenty to make inquiries!"

Gaelan had little desire to return to Smithfield. Dead, Tremayne may well be, but Gaelan had little doubt that his gang yet operated unabated all about the place. "Look, Dr. Bell, perhaps it would do better if you went yourself. There is a woman, Sally Mills, she is called, and I will write for you a letter of introduction. If anyone might have knowledge of my belongings, *she* would."

"Why would you not go yourself?"

Gaelan considered how much to reveal of his plans for the future. "My intention is to slip away to America as I had planned—before my arrest. I've little desire to be seen in Smithfield. To the good people of Smithfield Market, I am dead—murdered at Newgate Prison. And I am quite happy to leave it thus."

"So this Mrs. Mills has your books?"

"Most of my library, I left in an underground room beneath my shop. I doubt there is anything left of it." Gaelan drew a map. "The book in question was in my possession when I was arrested; I gave it to my assistant, but I've no idea what he might have done with it. If it is anywhere to be found around London, Sally would know. That is, if she is yet living."

"Perhaps it might be better to locate your assistant?"

"Obviously, though where he is I do not even venture a guess. I have already written to his father and await a reply. But now excuse me whilst I jot a note to Mrs. Mills."

Half an hour later and Bell had his introduction and was on his way out of Bell's hair—at least for a time.

As the sound of Bell's carriage grew distant, Gaelan mounted the stairs to his room. Great sobs pealing through Eleanor's bedroom door and through to the corridor stopped him short of his destination. She seemed barely able to catch her breath. He knocked softly, and her wailing slowed into hiccoughs. "Lady Braithwaite, are you all right?"

"Go away. I am fine."

Clearly she was not. "I thought perhaps ... your brother has gone out and ... we ... we might continue our ... our conversation of last—" The door opened abruptly, and he nearly lost his balance.

"What do you want of me?"

He had no answer, for he truly did not know what had drawn him impulsively to her door, and not to his own. Her pain, her weeping had nothing to do with him. Yet ... A long moment passed before he replied. "To speak true, Lady Braithwaite, I see you are yet distressed in the extreme. I would only offer my ear to you, as I did last night. Perhaps now that it is day, might you stroll with me through the gardens? The sunlight might do us both some good."

"Very well." She took Gaelan's offered arm.

The late-morning sky was the sort of deep blue that seemed only possible on a cloudless day at the height of summer. Gaelan led them to a low iron bench beneath a heather tree.

"Forgive me, Lady Braithwaite, for my forthrightness, but there is little time whilst your brother is out and we might speak alone. Is it your husband that so torments you? I only ask because evidence suggests ... And knowing ... if I may be so bold ... knowing what sort of man he is—"

Eleanor froze, and her hands curled into tight fists, which she pounded against the bench. Anxiety poured off her in waves.

"Forgive me if I have spoken out of turn, Lady Braithwaite." Gaelan rose, bowing slightly as he moved off, creating distance between them.

"Please, sir, do *not* call me by that name. By *his* name. I detest the very sound of it for what he has done!"

This, Gaelan was not expecting. Was such powerful anger on his account—for what had been done to him? Or had Braithwaite truly turned his violent nature upon his own wife as he imagined? "What do you mean?" He turned to watch her face crumple as tears once again threatened.

"Perhaps later. It is still too painful to discuss—even, I might add," she said with a melancholy smile, "with a kind stranger."

Gaelan sat beside her again, allowing the aroma of lush English roses to envelop him. He waited, content to have his thoughts diverted from his own troubles. Bell should be round the White Owl by now. Was Sally already chatting his ear off, quizzing him for medical advice about her sciatica?

Eleanor's gaze wandered from the rose garden to her hands to the large trellis across the gravel path—everywhere but toward Gaelan. She drew a long breath. "Please. I implore you: do not say any of what I tell to you to my brother. If he should learn ... if he should know ... he shall murder Lord Braithwaite without hesitation. Of this I am certain!"

"You have my word." *My solemn vow.* He urged her on, suspecting the source of her turmoil.

"I feel somehow, Mr. Erceldoune, *you*, of all people, would understand me . . . this . . . in a way Simon cannot. But I cannot venture a guess as to why you would offer to be my confessor . . ."

Gaelan waited for her to go on; silence surrounded them, save for the distant calls of two bickering blackbirds. "I have, my lady, seen much suffering, heard tales of distress and mistreatment in my . . . in my apothecary that . . . your brother mightn't have seen amongst his patients. Even ladies of your station might sooner come to . . . one like me . . . anonymously than to a physician amongst their own society if . . ." He politely declined to say it aloud. But he'd offered, he hoped, a tether.

She sighed, watching a bird as it fussed among the branches of a nearby tree. "My husband's temperament . . . his interests, shall we say . . . extend beyond . . . beyond the . . . voyeuristic proclivities of which you might be personally aware."

Gaelan felt the blood drain from his face. He was not sure he was ready to hear this lady's confession, but he could not retreat.

"His tendencies, Mr. Erceldoune, did not become known to me until the several weeks just past. For the first many months of our marriage, he was the epitome of generosity. Our home life could not have been more to my liking. And despite the fact I was skeptical of the match, I was more content than I dreamed—"

"But something changed?"

"It did." She rose to stand before a large bed of roses. She skirted her finger along the edge of a full-open bloom. "They are beautiful, the roses, are they not? My sister-in-law's gentle touch," she said. "These were her prize possession—her delight. Besides Simon, these gardens were all she lived for, especially after . . . She'd become quite ill several years ago, yet she would spend hours out here, admiring them, tending them. No gardener was allowed to touch them."

Eleanor plucked a flower, coming back to sit beside Gaelan.

"I observe a rose and see petals, pistil, and stamen," she said wistfully. "Thorns and pollen, the veins that redden the green leaf as if blood courses through it. I wonder what magnificent alchemy creates the scent and color: yellow distinct from red, distinct from white. Of course I appreciate the beauty of it, yet there is no beauty greater than comprehending the truly amazing parts to the whole."

Fascinated, he could not help taking it a step further. "Have you ever observed a leaf through a microscope's lens, seeing within it the symmetry of cells, the chlorophyll, what makes it green?"

She brought the rose to her face, inhaling the fragrance. "No, I have not. Few men in our exalted little society, it seems, care for a wife who is their intellectual equal, if not better. And I refused to conceal my nature or my curiosity, and there you have it! I married Richard, Lord Braithwaite, and as I said, he seemed a good enough match. He shared my love of nature, of science, allowed me to pursue my own interests, at least for a time. But then he revealed himself to me for what he was—a brutal, angry man with much power and little restraint. I saw it in the way he treated our servants and in the boasting of his grand and vile experiments."

Gaelan flinched.

"Forgive me, Mr. Erceldoune. I know this must grieve you, but you have asked, and now I fear I cannot conceal anything of it."

He nodded. "Please go on; it is I who invited you to speak freely. Do not concern yourself with my sensitivities." The conversation was verging toward a dangerous territory, but his curiosity was too profound. He wanted to hear all of it.

"He'd found, he said, the key to eternal anatomical regeneration— immortality. All that was required was a bit of experimentation before he would become world-famous for his 'discovery.'"

The air was suddenly too close, even as a breeze rifled the leaves above their heads. "And that discovery was . . . me."

"You." The compassion in her eyes was almost too much to bear.

"How did you know . . . ? That it was me . . . I mean to say." He'd meant to deny it, to deflect suspicion away from himself, but the words emerged almost of their own volition. As if he'd had no choice in the matter to reveal himself to . . . this stranger. The wife of his tormenter. This fragile young woman.

"Richard flaunted a daguerreotype one night upon his return from London. He went often to attend the House of Lords, and returned home telling his tales, most of which I assumed were drunken exaggerations. But this daguerreotype, he told me, would prove his veracity to me. The image was of you . . . his 'discovery.' That is how I recognized you from the first, although you are barely the same man as in the photograph. He was furious that you had been snatched from . . . them, just as he was to prove his point." She shrugged. "It had been a flutter. He wagered you would regenerate the fingers severed; others did not believe it and wagered against. He blamed Simon for . . . ruining it. I was not certain until I saw your bandaged hand. I am so very sorry, Mr. Erceldoune, for my husband's terrible . . ."

She was sobbing now.

"Well, apparently . . . *Richard* . . . was wrong. As you see, my fingers are far from regenerated. But hush now. Please do go on." Gaelan knew this was not to be the end of it.

"Richard was terrified of discovery, especially now that Simon and James had intervened in the matter on your behalf. And he regretted showing me the daguerreotype. Two nights ago, he threatened me in a drunken frenzy.

"He had a dagger, you see, a horrid, jagged blade. He warned me that if I said a word to anyone, and most especially my brother or my cousin James, I too would find myself with a severed limb, and not a mere finger. Then he . . . Oh my God, I've said too much. . . . What if he . . . ?"

She skirted the edge of hysteria. Gaelan ventured to place a reassuring hand on her arm, which trembled beneath his fingers. "Please know that I have no reason to speak of this, and certainly not to Braithwaite. Your confidence could not be safer."

She nodded and opened the high neck of her blouse, revealing a long scabbed-over cut near her ear. "My God, Lady Braithwaite—"

"He forced me . . . He held that dagger to my . . . I . . ." She was shaking so violently by now, Gaelan thought she would take ill, perhaps swoon, at any moment.

Unsure of what else might be done to calm her, Gaelan carefully placed his arm around her shoulder. "Hush now; you needn't say another word—"

"Please," she pleaded through her sobs, tears flowing down her face and onto her dress, "you mustn't tell any of this to Simon. You have promised me to keep still about it."

This promise he could not keep. It was too much, too monstrous for Braithwaite to walk away from it unscathed. Bell should know what his sister had suffered and why. "How can I not? Please do not hold me to an impossible vow—"

"You promised!"

"Aye, I did, but—"

Still shaking, she wept into his chest, her tears soaking through the soft cloth of his shirt. Encircling his other arm about her, Gaelan held her close, lightly stroking her hair.

He could only imagine the indignities she had suffered at Braithwaite's hands. "Lady Braithwaite," he ventured, gently as he could manage. "I noticed that first afternoon when you arrived, you walked . . . I . . . Forgive my . . . Your gait seemed . . . I have seen before . . . in women when—"

He had not the words to broach the subject with the required delicacy. Would anyone? "My lady, when a man performs certain . . . I mean to say . . ." He stopped, bewildered, unable to ask what he must. She was not, by far, the first woman with whom he had spoken of such things, but they always had come to *him*, seeking *his* help. With her . . . now . . . he was abashed and awkward. The question was irrelevant; he knew the answer without her saying a word.

"It is important that you tell . . . someone of this . . . violation. And I do not mean the scratch on your neck. If not your brother . . . any practitioner who might examine you. Do you understand me?"

She nodded uncertainly.

"There are . . . diseases that might take hold and—"

"I believe I am unharmed . . . in the way you mean," she said, taking his good hand, her voice steadier. "It is painful to be sure, to sit, especially. But I've not noticed bleeding nor evidence of serious injury. Is that what you mean to ask?" Her cheeks flushed, but she seemed calmer, almost dispassionate speaking of it.

"This man must be stopped! And your brother is one of only a few with the power to do it."

"And he'll do what? Richard is my husband, and as *such* I am his property to do with as he pleases. And who would believe ill of Lord Richard Braithwaite, good friend of the prince consort? I wish to speak of this not a moment longer."

She was adamant, and to be silent was against his better judgment. "As you wish, madam; I shall be still on the matter."

Gaelan regretted his promise as they sat quietly, knowing she would say not a word to Bell. She continued to rest against him, yet she seemed better, and the shaking had stopped. Eleanor brushed her fingers against the damp patch on Gaelan's shirt where her tears had fallen. It was the most intimate gesture he had experienced in years.

"We should go in," he said reluctantly. "I . . . do not think . . . I mean to say . . . Dr. Bell should be back at home presently and—"

Eleanor nodded. "Thank you, Mr. Erceldoune, for your ear, for your shoulder to sob upon."

"It's of no matter." Her face was too close; Gaelan stood, knowing he must break this moment before it escalated into something that might lead to disaster beyond imagination. She was vulnerable, and she saw in him a kindred spirit . . . a willing ear, and that was all. Her wounded spirit reached out to his. "Perhaps we should return to the house. . . ."

She took his right hand in both of hers, lacing their fingers together. He broke the contact, wresting his hand away as if burned. "I think, my lady, I hear your brother's carriage. We'd best go in."

"I believe I shall first take a walk; the air shall do me much good."

CHAPTER 36

"**D**id you find Sally Mills well?"

Bell nodded absently, coming into the drawing room where Gaelan sat alone, awaiting his return.

"Where is Eleanor?"

"She is in the garden having a stroll. And what of Mrs. Mills?" Gaelan rose from the chair and paced, more impatient for news than he might have thought.

"She is a fine, grand old lady, I must say. Clever, and a bit old for you, perhaps. But talk of *you* made her blush." Bell laughed.

"More mum than lover."

"Hardly. You are what? Two centuries her senior?"

Gaelan was surprised Bell had returned in such high spirits. Was it possible he had recovered the book?

"Well, in any event, quite a eulogy she gave you. I'd no idea you'd been such a popular figure in Smithfield Market."

"And . . . ?" Gaelan fidgeted with a letter opener.

Bell's voice darkened. "She does not trust me at all; she will only speak with you directly, if, as she said, 'He is in fact still living!' She was quite adamant about it. She understands that you've no wish to be seen round the market, and proposes you stop there late, after the pub quiets down for the night."

Gaelan nodded. It was as he'd expected, if not hoped for. "That is quite Sally, I'm afraid. Empiricist to the core. She'd never believe that I was alive, much less exonerated, unless she saw it with her own eyes. I only thought that a letter written by mine own hand would suffice. I'm sorry to have sent you on a fool's errand."

He'd have to risk a venture to Smithfield himself. "I shall go see her this night. I can promise nothing, and do not take her reluctance to speak with you as evidence that she has my belongings.

"I've not yet received a response from my apprentice's father, and I hold out little hope that he will be of any help in any event; it is unlikely that the lad yet resides on this side of the sea. He'd often spoken to me of America."

"Then all is lost?" Bell drew up close to Gaelan, pointing an accusing finger in his face. "I find it impossible to believe that with your vast experience and great knowledge there is nothing you might concoct to reverse this curse you've put me under."

Gaelan retreated to a corner of the room, ignoring the accusation. "I've revealed what little I know, and, I confess, I recall very little of that book but its splendid images. To speak true, I spent much effort these past four and a half years to quash as much knowledge of it as I was able. I well understood Handley's aim, and the very thought of him extracting from me, under such extreme duress, anything that might assist . . ." It was too soon, the wounds too raw. He could not yet speak of Handley or Bedlam without releasing the demons that pursued him like a shadow. He blinked in vain effort to forestall the vivid images that even now lurked in the periphery of his vision, and sent him staggering to the settee. "Might I trouble you, Dr. Bell, for a drink?"

Bell gestured to the sideboard.

"Would you mind, sir? I fear that arguing has rendered me . . . I am not yet myself."

Bell obliged. Gaelan finished the whisky in one swallow. "Dr. Bell," he said after shakily placing the empty tumbler on the table, "even should I recall the precise method by which I created the elixir for you, most of the ingredients were labeled with symbols, not names, and those ingredients themselves derived from still other elements and herbs. It is the way of alchemy to be obtuse, I am afraid. And with that particular book, it would not do, as you quite know, to improvise."

Bell was frustrated, that much was obvious, but what was there to do? Gaelan had done all he could, and the only hope was that Sally might know something—anything to provide a clue.

"Shall we go out to the garden, then, and keep my sister company?"

"Wait." Gaelan tugged on Bell's elbow, staying his hand on the garden door. "You need to speak with her—privately—about Lord Braithwaite," he said quietly.

"Why do you say that?"

"I promised not to break her confidence. But I can at least implore you to press her on it. I am not breaking my promise, however, to report that Braithwaite's brutality has not been confined to convicted felons and residents of Bedlam. You *must* speak to her, and do it soon 'ere her husband comes back to fetch her home, which undoubtedly he shall do."

"Sir, you alarm me!"

"Good. Then I have said quite enough."

Gaelan returned from his visit to the White Owl long past midnight. He'd not realized how hard it would be to walk through the marketplace again. So many reminders of a good life—and the worst that life had to offer him. He passed in front of the spot where his apothecary shop had once thrived. A sheep merchant's stall now stood in its place. Even in the dark, it was plain that the entrance to his cellar had long since been built over. If his books had been left there, by now they would be a ruin.

Seeing the astonishment on Sally's face when he removed the hooded cloak he'd worn brought a smile to his. She had for him one letter, kept despite the knowledge Gaelan was dead, from Tim, dated three years ago—from Tennessee in the United States. The letter burst with anticipation of his new life in America and the hope for Gaelan's eventual release from Newgate. Perhaps, Tim had imagined, Gaelan would join him across the Atlantic.

So, Tim had fled England immediately . . . gone by the time of Gaelan's supposed death in prison.

He was delighted that Tim had made his way to America, a land of opportunity where class made less difference than intelligence and ambition. He'd taken the entire library, he said, hoping that his mentor would understand and not be angered, promising to take care and use the recipes and notes to help people in the New World. "And," he'd said, "keep all of it safe for you, especially the unusual book with its many strange pictures, hopeful that someday I might restore the whole of it to the rightful owner."

Gaelan wondered if Tim yet resided there, in Tennessee. Perhaps that would be Gaelan's first stop upon leaving England.

Weary as he was, and with three pints of Sally's best ale in his belly, Gaelan thought perhaps this night, for once, he might drift off to a good night's rest, no terrifying dreams of Bedlam. But the crackle of the dying fire, the pop and snap of an old house settling, even the crickets and birds, all conspired to keep him from slumber. Restive, he thrashed among the bedcovers in the dead night air until fitful sleep claimed him. . . .

"Mr. Erceldoune! Mr. Erceldoune! Do wake up!"

Shaking. Violent shaking. Handley vanished, his red-hot brazier disintegrating into grains of sand, the searing bite as it melted his flesh fading as he awoke disoriented in the semi-darkness. But who was shaking him? Or was it his own body quaking with fear as . . . ?

A voice calling out to him—he followed its gentle murmur, not at all murderous, as it called his name through the fog of his dream. Not Handley. Not Braithwaite. Soft, strong hands gripped his arms, but not harshly, as the anxious whisper fluttered just beyond his ear. "Mr. Erceldoune, please! Do awaken, I beg of you!"

He blinked, vision slowly clearing into the dull ochre glow of a single candle. Eleanor Braithwaite sat upon the edge of the mattress, her cool hands upon his forearms.

"Mr. Erceldoune, you were howling something awful as if you were being ripped apart, and I could not bear it to hear anyone in such agony. Forgive me for entering your room, but—"

"No, please do not . . ." He sat up too swiftly, and his head began to throb in time with his racing heart, the now-familiar aftermath of these nightly episodes. He was unable to still the shuddering waves coursing through him. Beads of cold sweat prickled his arms and back, soaking through the cotton of his nightshirt.

The nightmare dissipated slowly as he came to full wakefulness, embarrassed at having woken Eleanor. "Do not apologize; it is I who should . . . I am sorry to have awakened you; the walls must indeed be paper-thin and— A bad dream's all. Please do not trouble yourself—"

"Do you recall any of it?"

"No," he lied. Quite to the contrary, he remembered every vivid detail. And even now the images hovered, shadows in the candlelight. "'Twas a nightmare, which has already faded from memory. I am sorry to have brought you from your warm bed." His heart still pounded, his head echoing each pulse.

"You have nothing to apologize for. You were more than kind to me this morning—"

The candle flame was too bright. "The light . . . would you mind?"

Eleanor extinguished the candle, but did not move.

"I am quite recovered now, in any event. Please, I beg you, return to your room. I have no wish for you to lose a moment's more rest on my account." In truth, he had little desire for her to witness him cowering in fear of shadowy demons that lived only in his mind.

He sensed her drawing closer, the mattress giving way ever so slightly above the down of the comforter. "My lady, what are you—"

"Mr. Erceldoune, please let me help. Something I learned . . . something that Richard . . ."

Gaelan tensed at the name, but then her small hands slipped through the fine strands of his hair to settle between his neck and shoulders. Gentle kneading and small circular motions released the knots that strung from the base of his head through to his shoulder blades. Such ministrations he had not experienced in so many years. Perhaps never at all. Relaxing into her touch, he knew full well his grave error of judgment. She should go, and now. Should Bell come round to the guest wing . . . The bounds of consciousness loosened, and he began to drift. "Thank you, Lady Braithwaite. You *have* helped. . . . Now you should go," he cautioned firmly, halfway to sleep.

"I fear that, should I leave, you shall once again find yourself in a state. I shall stay, if only a while, until I am convinced you are quite asleep." She slipped farther into the bed, adjusting the coverings so she was atop them. Her hands continued the steady kneading of muscle and tendon, so innocent, so very relaxing. The thin leaf of separation between them was unseemly, yet he did not really wish for her to stop. She was soft and warm and inviting, lying so close by him, and when she wrapped him into an embrace, all tension fled; he was in heaven itself.

A single kiss, soft and chaste, her lips against his temple. Sighing, he savored the sweetness of her as she breathed life into his withered and weary soul. He desired with all his heart to draw her nearer, yet propriety halted him, his senses returning. He ripped himself from her touch, once again fully awake.

"Oh my God, Mr. Erceldoune. I . . . I am so sorry. I don't know what . . . The lateness of the hour must have robbed me of my good sense. I—"

"I should have insisted you return to your room the moment I regained my equanimity. It is not . . . I . . . I am so very sorry, Lady Braithwaite," he said, adding the distance of her formal name. "I thank you for waking me from what has come to be a very frequent nightmare, but you should go."

"Would it be all right, do you think, if I stayed here, like this? It's silly, but given . . . I feel a kinship with you. It does help me to be near someone—"

Alarm bells pealed in his head. "Yes, we are indeed both victims of your husband, but I cannot allow you . . . Surely you must know that it is not right. . . . You must return to your room. You cannot be seen here when morning comes."

"Respectability has little to demand of me these days."

"You cannot believe that. You bear no blame for his vile actions." His resolve was slipping; he would miss her warmth the moment she set a foot on the floor. "Lady Braithwaite, I've an affection for you that I can neither explain nor deny, so strong it wrenches me beyond all reason. It bewilders me, I confess, and I fear with all my heart . . . that you offer . . . that *I* misconstrue your kindness and your closeness. And even if I did not thus misapprehend you . . . I could not take advantage of . . . Please, go now. . . ."

Eleanor nodded tightly and touched his cheek, her long, loose hair tickling his neck. She needed to leave before his last reserves of will fled. She stood.

Gaelan sat up, drawing the bedcovers close around him. "Wait." He had to ask. "Have you yet spoken with your brother? Told him?"

"I have not yet had the courage—"

"You *must* tell him." Gaelan closed his hand over hers, gripping it tightly. "If you cannot tell him, then free me so I may—"

"You promised!" She was trembling, sniffing back tears.

Running his thumb along the hollow beneath her eye—first one and then the other—he wiped back the wetness caught there, before cupping her cheek with his uninjured hand.

"*Listen* to me!" he whispered harshly. "This man must be stopped! Who knows what Lord Braithwaite will do to you if you return to him? He must by now know that I am in residence with your brother, who is already in a tenuous position because of it. Your husband is a powerful man, as well you know, and can destroy both Drs. Bell—James and your brother—with but a single word. He must be made aware, even only for his own sake."

"I am in terror of what Simon might do should he find out what Richard did . . . did to me. I entreat you—do not . . ." She was near hysterical now as she beseeched him again and again. Gaelan sighed, resigned, as he pulled Eleanor toward him, allowing her head to sink into his chest.

"Richard Braithwaite must be stopped," he growled softly into her hair.

"Please, Mr. Erceldoune. Might we just rest together here tonight? Do not send me back to my room. I confess that I sleep no more peaceably than you. It has been days since I've slept more than two or three hours. The terror of that night disquiets my rest and invades my dreams. Please just hold me?"

Eleanor planted her head in the crook of his neck, settling herself there, her long auburn hair a pillow to his cheek as he looped his arm about her. She whispered in his ear the simplest of tunes, and he was undone.

CHAPTER 37

There was now little point in waiting for Erceldoune's book to turn up. It might never. Simon turned to his own library for clues to his unfathomable situation. Erceldoune's could not be the sole work of its kind. Indeed, given the Bell family's illustrious history in the sciences, there must be something of use within his own vast collection. He only just needed to locate it.

He pulled a volume from a low shelf, a yellowed handwritten journal, and sat at his uncle's ancient desk. *On the Lapis Philosophorum: A Sceptical Perspective.* It was as good a place to start as any. But Uncle Samuel's notes were pages and pages debunking the very idea of any sort of Elixir of Life. "The alchemists have debased themselves in their primitive quest, irrelevant in the face of what we know of chemistry and medicine today. It is little wonder they have all but disappeared in shame."

Simon pinched the bridge of his nose.

"You'll not find what you seek in the books of rationalists like your uncle, my love," Sophie cooed into his ear.

"Ah, my darling. Where then might you suggest—"

"Dr. Bell! Dr. Bell!" Mrs. McRory ran panting into Simon's upstairs library without knocking, her face ashen.

"Good Lord! What is it, Mrs. McRory? Is it Eleanor? What's happened?" He jumped from the chair, slamming shut his book.

"It is Lord Braithwaite come to call, sir, and he is in a fit of rage. Did you not hear the shouts? For surely they split the very foundation stones of your house!"

Damnation! "Tell him to await me in the drawing room, and I will be there presently." Breathing deeply, Simon steeled himself for the inevitable confrontation.

Eleanor had been damnably frustrating since she'd arrived. He'd never known her to be skittish, but she was being restive as a humming-bird. But reticent—she'd barely spoken to him over the past three days, and when she did, it went round in endless circles. . . .

"I will not go back to him," she'd insisted when he'd at last con-fronted her about it. "And if I cannot stay here with you, I shall find another more welcoming abode."

"Of course you will always find a home with me, should you desire it! But how might I help you with your troubles, sister, if you will not confide in me? I am aware—more than aware, I might add—that you made a poor choice for a husband, and I aver he is more fit for prison than his hilltop estate. Leave him if you must, stay with me a lifetime, but you cannot hide from him forever."

"Simon, you do not understand!" she shouted, stomping across the floor to the other side of the room. "You cannot understand!"

"Enlighten me; I entreat you. Has he hurt you? If he has done something so horrible as to lay one finger . . . do me the justice, at least, of confiding it in me, so I may understand you and act upon it as any brother must."

And on it would go—Eleanor with her opaque expression and unyielding stance day after night after day. Simon had wearied of the entire business. Barbarous though Braithwaite had been to Erceldoune, he could not imagine what that had to do with her. Simon froze, con-templating a terrifying possibility. Might Braithwaite be persecuting Eleanor for his own intervention on Erceldoune's behalf? *Dear God!* He'd never considered it. No. Braithwaite was too cunning; he'd never dare reveal his disgraceful appetites to his own wife, for it could mean his ruination. But if Eleanor did not wish to return to her husband, he would do everything in his power to help her.

Stopping at the entry to the drawing room, Simon composed himself, checking his cravat, straightening his waistcoat—another second to ready himself for the imminent confrontation. "Lord Braith-waite." Simon forced himself to smile and extended his hand.

Braithwaite examined the proffered hand, declining it before pacing the room like a nervous bridegroom. "I shall get right to the point, Dr. Bell. My wife is to accompany me from this place and to our home where she belongs. If you fetch her, I'll not take up any more of your time. She has been days now from me, and to speak frankly, it is an embarrassment. I had to make my excuses for her whilst at court last night to dine with the prince and Her Majesty the queen, who were keen on meeting my new bride, of whom I have spoken so glowingly over the past many months. Perhaps she feels stifled in the country, so far from you and society. But I am willing... Tell her, if you would, I am even willing to open the London house permanently so that she might more easily come visit here as often—and for as long—as she wishes. It will take but a day or two to arrange it. However, I must see her first. Talk with her. Alone."

Simon did not much care for Braithwaite's condescending tone, resolving in the instant not to give up his sister unless it was her own choice. "My sister is her own woman, always has been. I've no idea what has transpired between the two of you, but she is always welcome here. If she has no desire to return to your home, whether in town or up north, I am not inclined to force her into something she has no wish to do."

"I am aware, sir, that you also harbor a murderer in your house—as a guest!" The insinuation concealed a sinister threat.

"If you are, my dear sir, aware of this, I certainly am not. Of whom might you speak?"

"One Gaelan Erceldoune, lately of Bethlem Royal Hospital and under the care of Dr. Handley, mad doctor and quite an expert in the treatment of criminally violent lunatics. However you managed to extract him from Bedlam is beyond me, and certainly none of my affair, but—"

"Mr. Erceldoune was acquitted of the charges, as you well know, and yes, he is resident in my home. What of it? He was wrongly imprisoned for an act he did not commit and was subjected to cruel punishment at the hands of your so-called *mad* doctor!"

Braithwaite fumed and sputtered unintelligible curses, turning his back to Simon for a moment. When he spoke again, his manner had shifted to a genteel calm, an actor swapping masks. Head in hands he sat—suddenly sorrowful, a husband beside himself with worry. "Look here, my dear brother-in-law, I have not come into your abode to argue about Erceldoune. Have at him, if it is what you desire; it is of no matter to me. Now if you please, sir, my wife. Where might I find her? I do sore miss her gentle presence and would endeavor to have her return with me to our home forthwith."

As Braithwaite pleaded his case, remorse forced itself across his features. "We had an awful spat—my fault, entirely, a misunderstanding of affection when I arrived home late one night last week. I'd had perhaps one too many whiskies at the club, and I disturbed her sleep. She fled 'ere I rose the next morning. The servants said she ran from the house with naught but the clothes on her back, and I was worried in the extreme for her safety, of course. Realizing her agitation, I did not know what she might do. Nor how I might make it right by her."

Simon's sneer disparaged Braithwaite's confession. "Yet it has taken you so many days to track her down *here*?"

"She left for me a note, eventually found, saying she needed some days alone—away from our home. I do believe six days is adequate time for my wife to have come to her sens . . . to forgive me. We are still quite newly wed, and I am no expert at matters of the heart. But do understand, Dr. Bell, I love your sister with all my soul and am much distressed to not have her beside me."

Simon did not believe one word.

"I shall speak to her, if you will give me a moment, Lord Braithwaite. I am not optimistic, however. Shall I have tea and biscuits sent in to you?" Simon had already begun forming in his head how to prevail upon James to use his connections at court to sever the marriage.

"Of course. Tea and biscuits sound lovely, especially if freshly baked by your marvelous cook."

"I do believe, Lord Braithwaite, that she has had some in the oven, if my nose does not lie."

"I thank you, sir, from the very bottom of my heart."

Simon exited the drawing room and started up the stairs toward the guest wing.

"A word, Dr. Bell?" Erceldoune tapped him on the shoulder, startling him.

"Might it wait, sir? I need to find Eleanor; I believe she is still in her room. And be aware. Lord Braithwaite is in the drawing room. I am certain you do not wish to cross his path—"

"If I but had a gun, I would slay him before he caught the first glimpse of me. But never mind that. It is your sister we must discuss. I could not help but overhear your argument, and you must *not* allow her to return with him under any circumstances." Erceldoune gestured up the stairway. "Let us remove this conversation to another place, shall we?"

Simon nodded. "I have no intention of doing so if my sister does not desire it, but how can I—"

Eleanor awaited them at the top of the stairs, her hands gripped on the gallery railing. "Forgive me, I was reading in the gallery and heard your voices. And, Simon, who could not have heard your argument with my Richard? Your roaring rattled the poor chandelier prisms something awful!"

A look passed from Erceldoune to Eleanor and back again, a tête-à-tête in furtive glances, questions and responses Simon did not even begin to comprehend.

"Lady Braithwaite." Erceldoune's voice dropped to a husky whisper. "I implore you, please tell him."

Simon interrupted the exchange; he'd had enough. Erceldoune obviously knew something, and it nettled him to be so in the dark. "Tell me what? Forgive my confusion, but, Eleanor dear, what the devil is going on?"

She finally spoke. "It is but a trifle, Simon," she said lightly, her expression fixed on Erceldoune. "Whatever Mr. Erceldoune may think, or may have said to you on the matter of my husband, it is *undoubtedly* an exaggeration." She laughed gaily. "Simon, my dear brother, you know me well. It is as much my own nature as Richard's fault that we rowed."

Her expression said something quite different, yet he could not refute her own avowal, no matter his inclination.

"And now I shall *go*. He awaits me in the drawing room?"

Simon huffed out a breath, exasperated by her sudden change of heart. "He does." Indeed, Eleanor could be the most mercurial of women, but there was something else afoot. He stopped her as she crossed the gallery. "Wait. Eleanor, dear sister, you must confess to me what is going on here." He looked toward Erceldoune, silently imploring his assistance.

But Erceldoune only stared at the floor, until Eleanor turned down the corridor and toward her rooms.

"Tell him I shall be down presently," she called out to Simon. "I've only to get a few things from my room and make myself presentable."

CHAPTER 38

Gaelan followed Eleanor to her room. "A word, if I may, Lady Braithwaite?"

She stopped, pivoting toward him, until she stood near enough he could smell the citrus of her perfume.

"Wait a moment." He held up a finger, listening for the faint click of the drawing room door as it closed, assured that neither Bell nor Braithwaite was in earshot.

"Forgive me, Mr. Erceldoune, I've a mere fifteen minutes to make ready to greet my prince; if you will excuse me—"

"There is something deeply amiss here. How can you return to him after what you confessed to me?"

Eleanor sniffed, addressing him with the disdain she might show a disrespectful servant. "I have rethought my position, Mr. Erceldoune, and am convinced that Lord Braithwaite's advances were no more vigorous than that of an amorous lover." She busied herself about the bureau, gathering a few things into a small handbag.

Her words were a dagger struck sharp and true. "What?" Gaelan tried to capture her eyes, but she resisted, refusing to engage him. "I . . ." Staggered, words failed him as he swallowed back anger over this mercurial shift. Yet he believed not a word of it.

"And the knife to your neck. Was that ardor? Was that passion? Do you think me so simple I cannot comprehend you?" He stalked the room, furious with her, with Braithwaite, the whole bloody lot of them. He struggled to keep his voice a whisper. "Tell me this again, but to my face, not hidden, with your back to me. You think I cannot perceive beyond your words, but you know me not at all. Even your hands belie your claims. I see them tremble as you endeavor to speak falsely." He stepped very near, her scent invading his nostrils. He must step back from this brink.

225

"I must be *mistaken* about the knife; 'twas his teeth must've grazed me on my neck, that is all! Admittedly, it was unfair of me to use you so when you were only trying to be kind. I was angry is all ... at Richard ... at Mama, at Simon ... at the world. And you ... you with your gentle manner despite the suffering you have endured—" She was fighting tears, and he wished them to fall—to reveal a truth she was trying so hard to deny. She turned away again. "For that I so humbly apologize, Mr. Erceldoune."

"You mean to go back to him?" he murmured.

"I do." She turned toward him, resting a delicate hand upon his arm. He grasped it, entwining his fingers in hers.

"Please reconsider." He watched her struggle as resolve receded from her expression. But he knew already she would not change her mind.

"What choice have I? To live solely by my brother's generosity, which shall never do? Go home to Mama, who will send me back to Richard in a trice? Cast my lot with you? A penniless ex-convict?"

He ignored the sting of her wounding words. "To be with me? I could never ask that of you. Ever. Why would you even think—"

The grip on his hand tightened as the other went to his face, tucking a long lock of his hair behind his ear—an intimate gesture that stole his breath. "No. I must go back to my lord, who will undoubtedly shower me with rubies and ermine. Who would not desire such adoration?"

"Please look at me, into my eyes, and repeat the claim that you wish to return to ... him, and I will know you speak truly from your heart."

"I owe you no explanation, Mr. Erceldoune, and certainly no more than I have given you. Your impertinence is an affront to me!" She pulled her hand from his, leaving him standing in her bedchamber.

He could not leave this alone, despite the rebuff. He followed her into the corridor, stilling her with a gentle hand on her back before she reached the end of the long hallway. "Eleanor ... Lady Braithwaite ... I cannot allow myself to believe that what passed between us was false, what you confessed to me of his ... was a lie."

She whipped around to face him, her features hard and cold as granite. "It matters little what you *believe*. I have the situation well in hand, I assure you." But the tremor in her voice troubled him.

She pivoted back toward the gallery, nearly knocking Gaelan off balance with the sweep of her skirt. He could do little more to mount a challenge without grabbing her about the wrist and physically stopping her. He let her go, irritated and smarting, observing her from the gallery balcony as she made her way down the stairs and into Braithwaite's waiting embrace.

He descended to the foyer as soon as he heard the horses pull away. "Dr. Bell, there is something not quite right in all this."

"I agree, but what on earth might I do about it? She is a married woman, and does as she pleases to do. Had I a choice I would have insisted, but you heard her—"

Gaelan sucked in a breath. To hell with his damnable promise of silence. "Dr. Bell, if I might speak frankly?"

"Go on, but do not speak to me in riddles and obscurities. I have had quite enough of that from both Eleanor and you these past days. If you've something to say that I should know, out with it, and clearly!"

"Your sister elicited from me a vow not to tell you, yet I feel compelled—"

"Out with it, man!"

Gaelan picked up a small cobalt blue bowl, weighing it in his hand as if to judge the import of his confession. "He forced her at knifepoint to . . ." He paused. Even now it was difficult to say the words without hurling the bowl across the room in a rage. "She showed to me a long scratch from jaw to collarbone as evidence that he threatened her—at knifepoint, you see—"

Gaelan waited a moment, watching Bell's face turn ashen. He gripped the bowl so tightly it might have broken had it not been so heavy.

"Threatened. But why? To what end?"

"Did you not see it, Bell?" Gaelan thundered, disheartened and angry at Bell's thickheadedness with regard to his sister. "Did you not witness it, plain on her face this very morning? The pain that flared with every hobbled step she took on the day she first arrived? Are you so absorbed with your own unending despair you failed to see it?" He brandished the heavy bowl, sore tempted to hurl it at Bell, setting it down instead. "I have seen it too many times in my day—the women I have attended: whores or wives, lovers, workers in terror of losing their employment, so many! Have you ever seen one of them, near ripped apart, bleeding, their eyes averted in shame as if 'twere their own bloody fault for it? Always with that same walk, like Lil that . . . that morning before . . . Her face yet haunts me at times."

Gaelan paused, his composure disintegrating. A breath, and he was able to continue, calmer now, if only slightly. "Perhaps it is the difference between us, Bell. Those you usually attend are too genteel to mention it—the horror of rape, of sodomy. They come to the likes of me instead, yes, even the oh-so-bloody proper ladies of your station."

"I *have* seen it, Erceldoune," Bell said, sagging against the wall, realization finally dawning on his face. He continued, rallying suddenly. "More than you might suspect. You are right; many fear the shame of discovery and would rather risk seeking help . . . elsewhere. But I have attended the aftermath a time too often of the butchery done by one of your brother apothecaries—"

Gaelan let the remark pass; Bell was right. Too many apothecaries, he had to admit, had no business treating a bloody nose, much less the carnage of rape, and he, too, had witnessed the damage they wrought. And if Bell wished to redirect his anger, then . . .

"But why would she return to him, and so readily? Would she not fear him? She seemed so determined to go back to him—to reconcile . . ." Bell stopped midsentence, his eyes darting up toward the second story, and then back to Gaelan, as if struck by a revelation. "Dear God. . . ." Bell fled up the stairs; Gaelan followed.

They entered a small study just off the gallery. "My uncle's pistols. He left them to me, and Eleanor would know where I . . ." Bell opened the case, dropping the lid when he saw an empty space where one of the small pistols had been.

CHAPTER 39

Simon bolted from the house, bellowing for his horse. He was upon it and off to Braithwaite's London house at full gallop, hoping they'd gone there and not to the estate in Sussex. If they had . . . He barely acknowledged the cursing pedestrians as they shouted at him, darting out of his way. He cared little but for his sister's safety, praying he was not too late.

Braithwaite's front door was unlocked when he got there. Simon breathed a sigh of relief that his guess had been correct and they had stayed in London. But bursting through to the foyer, he wished to God they *had* gone south, for then there would yet be time to catch them before the unthinkable had happened. He was too late.

The grand foyer of the Braithwaite London house had metamorphosed into a wholly new circle of hell. Blood painted the walls and pooled on the foyer floor. Eleanor cowered in a corner sobbing, her face, her gown painted sickly red, Simon's pistol still in her hand. At first, he thought her injured—that her blackguard of a husband had shot her. But the picture became clear as he drew near her.

Simon approached with cautious, quiet steps; he did not want to startle her—not with the weapon still curled in her fingers. "Dear God, Eleanor, what have you done?"

"Is it not obvious?" Eleanor said flatly through her tears. "I have murdered my husband in cold blood, and I shall hang for it." She stared straight ahead, her expression stony cold. She continued, resolute, defiant, despite her trembling hands. "And I would do it again in an instant."

"Eleanor . . . darling . . . Please give me the pistol." Several scenarios ripped through Simon's mind as he imagined the scene. Braithwaite had forced her, threatened her, held a knife to her a second time and . . . No, this was calculated. He approached Braithwaite's body; she'd shot him through the back of the head. There was little left of it, like a jack-o'-lantern smashed the day after Hallowe'en. Eleanor was covered in his blood and tissue; she dripped in it bodice to hem. She seemed not even to notice, or be sickened by it, as she stared straight ahead.

"It is done, Simon. I—"

"Did he—"

She looked up at him, tears still streaming down her face. "Did he what? Try to force me—again? I would suppose that your houseguest confessed what I confided to him the other day ... what I asked him not to share?"

He gathered her in his arms. The blood would need explaining to the servants once he got her home. But they would be quiet about it, he was certain; they were loyal. It would be the least of his worries. *What's to be done with her, with . . . this?* Simon took in the horrific scene. "Yes. Erceldoune confessed it, but why did you not tell me yourself?"

"I was afraid you would—"

"Would do what? Murder him? Like *you* have done? My God, Eleanor what shall we do?" He must get her from this place and safely back to his house. Who knew what passerby might have heard gunshots? They needed to move swiftly.

"There is nothing to be done. Simon, what he did to me—I could not go on. I would rather die in the hangman's knot than live in constant fear." She broke down entirely in her brother's arms.

"Shh. We'll think of something. Obviously, there are no servants about with the house closed." It was a question.

"He brought me here straightaway from your house. We are alone. To be sure, Simon, I believed with all my heart that he meant to do me in right here, and—"

"Self-defense, then? Hardly likely, since you stole my pistol. That alone signifies intent. Has this been your plan all along—to murder him first chance?"

"Self-defense only in the loosest sense, I fear. Besides, even *if* it was, do you really believe I would stand a chance in the halls of English justice, given Richard's position? At best they would lock me up at

Bedlam as a madwoman. At worst...well, we shall find out soon enough."

"My carriage should be outside in a moment. I rode here like a madman on horseback, knowing that you'd stolen my pistol from its case. Let us go back home, and we will think it through; we shall call the authorities after you've cleaned up—and we rid ourselves of that weapon. And its mate." Eleanor looked ready to swoon from her ordeal.

"You cannot be serious, Simon. I shall not let my brother become an accomplice to this crime."

"Hush. Say nothing more of it." The carriage had arrived. "We must move quickly."

Simon wrapped her in a blanket found in the library and trundled her into the carriage. "My sister is very ill," he instructed his coachman, whose horrified expression begged further explanation. "She is vomiting blood...and more. Make haste and get her away to my house as quickly as you can. I shall meet you there." Simon mounted his own horse and sped through streets, barely aware that he, like Eleanor, was covered in the remains of Lord Richard Braithwaite.

※

Gaelan's boots echoed through the three-story foyer as he paced like an expectant father, growing more anxious with each moment. No good would come of this, and he could not thrust from his mind the vivid image of Eleanor in Braithwaite's brutal hands. How had he let it happen? Allow a tether to so firmly attach itself from her heart to his? And now he was in agony as he awaited her fate.

Simon erupted through the door, covered in blood. He was shaking, appearing to be in shock, as if he had emerged from a battlefield, not a London house. His words emerged in short gasps punctuated with deep draughts of air. "Erceldoune," he managed, "there is little time before my carriage arrives with Eleanor. Braithwaite is dead!"

Gaelan froze, absorbing the blow. Had Simon, then, murdered

him? He could imagine the scene, Simon interrupting God knew what and shooting Braithwaite dead.

"How is *she*?"

"How the bloody hell do you think she is? She just bloody murdered her own husband!"

"*Eleanor* did? My God." There were a thousand things he wanted to say, but the words refused to form.

"Erceldoune! Do not simply stand there agape! Braithwaite shall be missed soon enough, I assure you, and we must—"

"Then you mean to do nothing, not tell the police?" Gaelan's eyes widened in surprise. Yet, what might they say that would keep Eleanor from the noose?

"No. As I said, they will discover him soon enough. And I must use the time to figure out a course of action, although what it may be escapes me." Simon poured himself a whisky, steadying himself on the sideboard, quickly draining the glass before then pouring another in its wake.

"But where is Eleanor?" Both men turned to the sound of the front door opening. Eleanor entered, wrapped in a blanket, dazed, and disoriented as she swayed. Gaelan captured the faintest gleam of life in her eyes, holding to it like a beacon. She took a small step toward him, but faltered, swooning into his arms.

"Bell, if the police should come by and see the two of you covered in blood—"

He nodded. "I shall bathe and dispose of these clothes; then I—"

"Allow me this one occupation, I beg you; I shall attend Eleanor."

Simon raised an eyebrow before nodding slightly. "You will find towels and blankets in the linen closet upstairs. Clothing, you will find in the armoire in her dressing room." He mounted the first stair before turning back toward Gaelan. "Erceldoune. Should any of the servants inquire—anyone *at all* inquire—Eleanor suffers from the bloody flux . . . and they must stay far, far from her!"

With difficulty, Gaelan removed his coat and draped it across the drawing room settee. He carefully laid Eleanor upon it. *It should do for the moment.* He was grieved to leave her even for the few moments needed to locate clean clothing and blankets.

Yes. Dysentery. It was as good an explanation of the blood and the state of the woman as any—for the moment. A keen eye, however, would recognize the lie in an instant.

Even in her sleep, Eleanor twitched and stirred restively, her whimpers cutting to Gaelan's core. He smoothed back her hair, trying to calm her as he cleaned her face and hands. The dress was a ruin, and must be burned. His left hand still useless, he struggled removing the gown one-handed. Finally, it was off her, and he smiled at the small victory. The heavy fabric of her gown had managed to absorb nearly all the carnage. Her petticoats could be left in place at least.

By the time Simon came into the drawing room, Eleanor was wrapped comfortably on the settee, a pillow beneath her head, still asleep. Together, the two men kept vigil, waiting in silence, watchful. Gaelan stood finally, going to the garden doors, looking out into the incongruous peacefulness of summer, its colors incomprehensible in the dull gray lifelessness of the room. He massaged the painful remains of his left hand, no longer bandaged, the scars healed, replaced by smooth skin, as if there had never been three fingers there at all. Even healed, it was now a pointless appendage. "I should have been the one, Bell. It should not have been Eleanor. I . . . I should have done it."

"What are you saying?"

Gaelan shook his head, ignoring Simon. "I should have—" He pounded his fist against the doorframe over and over in frustration, welcoming the blood as it trickled down his wrist, more with every blow. Had he only known of Simon's pistols, he would have done it. No, that wasn't it at all; he'd been petrified to see Braithwaite standing not fifty yards away in the foyer. He'd not the courage to confront his tormentor, so Eleanor did it. He knew she'd done it for her own reasons, but she'd taken control of her misery and delivered Braithwaite into the hands of justice that the scoundrel otherwise would never know. And now, unless he acted, she would hang for it.

"They'll suspect me anyway—the police, will they not?" Gaelan had not intended to say it aloud.

"What? What the devil are you saying?"

"Eleanor would not be a suspect, at least not at first. Why would she be? I am so much more likely, and in residence here? Given my history with the man? It is perfect. I stole your weapon, confronted him in his own castle, and slew the sadistic monster."

"That is insane!"

"Would that I'd had her courage, it would have been my bullet in his head, not hers, for what I suffered at his hands." He hoped Simon would see the sense in it—it was the only way out of this calamity.

"It is madness, what you suggest. Eleanor can easily plead self-defense—driven mad by a brutal husband. No court will convict her, and she will be put safely away in a private asylum for a period of time. . . . God knows she will be a wreck in any event! She is not the first, nor the last, gentlewoman to have killed a husband or lover for—"

"Are you mad, Bell?" Infuriated, Gaelan hurled a goblet into the fireplace, watching it shatter on the stones. "You cannot seriously desire her to be committed to an asylum, private or not. Of course, she would not be committed to Bedlam, yet any asylum would mean at the very least the death of her vibrant spirit. I will not see this befall her for executing a monster. No! I've a much better plan."

CHAPTER 40

"This is beyond insane," Eleanor exclaimed, finally awake, sitting on the sofa in a nest of blankets. "I will *not* have you do this, Mr. Erceldoune. Not for me nor for yourself. Please leave it be! I have made my peace, and I regret it not a whit! I would murder— yes, murder—him again in a trice. To have . . . have him walk free . . . to do as he pleases with impunity? I cannot fathom it. Could not fathom it. Surely he would have killed me himself and . . ."

Finally, she broke down into shuddering sobs—wave upon wave. First Simon, then Gaelan approached, but she waved them both away, forcing their helpless retreat.

The authorities could be at the door any moment; it was only a matter of time. Simon implored her to listen to reason. "We have been through this, Eleanor. Please go upstairs to your rooms. You should not be down here when the police arrive."

"If I might have a moment with your sister alone, Bell?" Gaelan knew he would need to tell her all of it, the whole bloody truth, if there was hope she might agree to the plot. But would she believe him, or instead think him noble, willing to sacrifice his life for her? He waited until Simon closed the drawing room doors behind him.

He knelt at Eleanor's feet, taking her hands in his, self-conscious when she ran her thumb along the crest of his mutilated hand. "Your husband was correct about *one* thing, Eleanor," he began haltingly. He'd never told anyone besides Simon, and it was more difficult telling her than he imagined. "There is a reason I offer myself in your stead—a practical reason."

How to say this and make her believe it? "Four and a half years, try as they might: vivisection, rats, rabid bats, fire, the flail, the blade, bullets . . . they could not kill me. Your brother, a physician, *knows* it to be true." He stopped. Gaelan saw no need to expose Simon as well. "Knows it to be true of *me*."

Gaelan had wondered time to time about the guillotine. What then? Would his head come loose from his body and stay alive? Or would it writhe on the planks, refusing to wither and die, like Irving's headless horseman? It was something Handley, for all his devilry, had not endeavored to demonstrate.

Eleanor tried to stand, but fell back to the cushions. "Do you think me a fool, Mr. Erceldoune?" she said. "I know what you are up to. You think your life is worthless after the horror you experienced . . . and at *his* hands. And you wish to end your life, and Richard's murder makes for a convenient vehicle. Suicide by execution!"

Gaelan struggled not to be stung by the implication.

"No . . . I know that isn't true, my dear Mr. Erceldoune." She touched her warm hand to his cheek, lifting his gaze to hers. "But I cannot let you die in my place; I could never live with myself. I—"

They had no time to go to and fro like this. "Hear me, Lady Braithwaite . . . my darling Eleanor. The police shall soon be knocking at the door. You *must* believe me. Yes, this is a chance for me, but not what you think. Never before, Eleanor, have I thought to use my . . . my condition . . . to exploit it to such excellent advantage. How can I not, now when your own innocent life is at stake? What use is it, this curse under which I have lived for two and a half centuries—so many, many lifetimes I have been granted . . . endured? Can I not surrender even one for this? And *know* it is not for you solely I do this, but for my own self as well."

His face grew hot as she searched every inch of his countenance, which he laid open for her to see into his heart and soul.

"Even should I believe your incredible story, how can you know this potion, this 'bit of magic' as you call it, won't kill you . . . really kill you?"

"Please. I ask you to trust me, as I have trusted you with this most profound secret of mine. There is none who knows it for certain but your brother . . . and now you. After this is over, and I walk back into this house quite alive, you will have at your disposal the means to ruin me should you ever desire it. Discovery is the one thing in this life I fear most. My sanity will not withstand another ordeal as I have only just been through—"

Eleanor chewed on her lower lip. She was considering it. *Good.* She leaned into Gaelan, pressing her forehead onto his.

He waited, feeling the frisson of her assent transmit through to him. "Yes," she whispered.

He sat beside her on the settee; Simon would return any moment. Taking her hand in his, he lifted it to his lips. "Thank you. I promise, it will be all right." She was so close. His hands tangled in the chaos of her hair as he drew her in, gently capturing her upper lip, then the fullness of her mouth. Fire roared within him despite the situation, but there was no time, and with regret, he left her, and joined Simon in his laboratory.

The plan was simple enough. A poison—one that would kill a normal man instantly, and well match the effect of a hanging: breathing stopped, heartbeat halted long enough, he hoped, for the scaffold doctor to confirm he was, indeed, dead. An injection through a vein in his wrist at just the right moment. Timing was everything.

"And after?" she asked once they'd returned to the drawing room. "Once you come back to us?"

He bowed his head, unable to meet her eyes. "I shall leave these shores, never to return. I will be off to America and reinvent myself as I have so many, many times before, and shall do again and again. And you shall be free of this albatross, to marry and grow old and fat with many grandchildren, my sweet Eleanor. Now, retire to your room, whilst your brother and I await the inevitable."

"But, I want to stay!"

It would not do for her to be about when the police called. She was no actress; her guilt . . . and her attachment to Gaelan would be written too clearly upon her countenance. "No, my lady. You cannot be here."

Her tears fell, and she seemed to comprehend. Gaelan swept his thumb across the arch of her cheek to wipe them away. "Now, go."

The trial was swift, and Eleanor gripped Simon's hand when the black cap was placed atop the judge's wig. Gaelan looked up toward the gallery, a reassuring smile crossing his features. "My death," he had told her in the letter he'd left for her, "shall transform to opportunity. I shall arise like the Phoenix, reborn and anonymous in a vast and glorious new land. But should all go well, I hope to see you one last time before I depart Britain forever."

Five days later, at ten in the morning, Eleanor and Simon stood at the front of the gathered mob, joining with the crowd in tossing rotted vegetables and worse as the wagon bearing the condemned man drew close. Eleanor's eyes never left him, and she couldn't help but notice when Gaelan caught the tomato hurled at him by Simon, pocketing it quickly, a silent nod exchanged.

And when the knot was tied about his neck, Simon held her close. She cheered as was expected, but could not stand to see it, refusing to witness the strangulation of the brave man who stood upon the scaffold in her place.

"Courage, sis. You must watch the show, for that is *only* what it is—"

"You do not think he suffers? I do. I know he does. And I cannot bear to watch it."

"Hush now. You must shout your hurrahs, heartily like the mob. You do not know who may be watching."

Gaelan swung, struggling for breath, mouth agape as the crowd around her roared—bread and circuses. She wanted to vomit. Suppressing a sob that rose from deep within, she uttered a silent prayer of thanksgiving to Gaelan, fervent and with desperate hope that she would be afforded the opportunity to throw her arms about him soon.

"There, d'you see, Eleanor?" Simon gestured very slightly with his head toward Gaelan's hand, clenched in a fist as he injected the poison. Cheers went up throughout the prison courtyard as the limp body was taken down and thrown onto a barrow. A doctor hovered nearby, checked for a heartbeat. Finding none, he declared Gaelan Erceldoune deceased. "So much," he shouted with glee, "for the man who cannot die!" The crowd roared; raucous laughter filled the courtyard.

Simon explained the second half of the plan to his sister as they rode home from the hanging. "Eleanor, my dear, I have arranged through the Royal Academy, and using a few well-placed connections, to procure Erceldoune's rather unusual body for further study, something done to 'honor' your late husband's heroic scientific efforts."

"But what if he really is dead? He looked so lifeless lying there. So very still, Simon. I would not be able to bear it if—"

"Trust me, will you not? He will be right and fine in a few days at the most; this I know. This poison he concocted, yes, it is fatal, but only to an ordinary man, which Gaelan Erceldoune most assuredly is not. Shall you come back to my house, or will you go stay with Mama in Cheshire?"

"How can I face her now? I would likely blurt the entire thing out to her in a fit, and then we are all done for. No I shall stay with you until I know he is safely in your hands and well. Only then do I believe I can begin to place this nightmare behind me. Besides, I do want to see him, if only to thank him one last time before he vanishes from our lives."

Late in the afternoon, Gaelan's lifeless body, wrapped in rough brown hopsacking, was brought through the back of the house and up the stairs. Eleanor joined Simon in the laboratory as soon as she heard the porters leave, locking the door behind them.

Simon was already struggling to remove the coarse bag from Gaelan's face. "Here, Eleanor, give me a hand, would you? We need to move him from the floor; it may be some hours before he revives, and I want him comfortable when he does. Between the effects of the hanging and the poison—I do not know; it could be hours or days . . . or . . . ."

"Was it necessary to take the poison injection if the hanging . . . ? He never explained—"

"He wasn't certain the hanging would actually *kill* him, even if only temporarily, and he wished to take no chances. Imagine if his body refused to die? No. He needed an assurance—immediate and fatal—as you witnessed."

"Would that I'd have had some of that! 'Twould have been far less a mess to rid myself of that monster of a husband, I daresay."

Simon's face registered surprise. "That is rather coldhearted."

"The world is a far better place without Lord Richard Braithwaite."

Eleanor sat beside Gaelan's bed tirelessly, terrified he would never awaken. She ate nothing nor slept but for an hour or two, keeping her vigil. He was cold to the touch, his lips blue.

She entwined their fingers, fighting revulsion from contact with the lifeless body. Her tears fell hour upon hour, soaking the white muslin sheet—his shroud—as she prayed for his recovery, believing with all of her soul that he and Simon had been wrong—he would never awaken, not from this.

Two days, and suddenly, a rumble vibrated through her where she'd laid her head against Gaelan's body. There was an intake of air deep from within his chest, and she leapt from her chair in surprise.

He blinked. "Eleanor," he whispered, his voice parched and hoarse. "Water . . ." She held a cup to his lips as he propped his elbows on the mattress.

"Do not drink so fast," she whispered in his ear, unable to suppress a smile.

He nodded weakly, gesturing for her to put aside the cup as he grasped her other hand, holding onto it as he brushed his lips across her fingers with his last ounce of energy before falling back to sleep.

CHICAGO'S NORTH SHORE, PRESENT DAY

CHAPTER 41

Anne walked the several blocks from her hotel to Gaelan Erceldoune's shop. Hammersmith's e-mail was still on her mind, and the more she thought about it, the more adamant she became. She would reveal none of what she knew about the Miracle Man. Anyway, she was bound by the rules of patient confidentiality.

Mr. Erceldoune had agreed to have a peek at her book, and she wasn't about to betray him, especially not to Transdiff Genomics, Ltd. and Lloyd Hammersmith.

She looked to the west, noticing that the late-afternoon sun had painted the glass and brick of the buildings a surreal amber-pink as the light reflected bright off the mirrored windowpanes. She was captivated by the fusion of art and architecture. Erceldoune's shop, ancient and dwarfed by the glittering skyscrapers, was barely visible beneath the elevated tracks, and she wondered if it was an intentional choice for the reticent man. The street outside was quieter than it had been the day before; the miniature shrine she'd swept away had not yet been replaced. She smiled, satisfied that she'd done something nice for him.

"Dr. Shawe. Please come in." Gaelan surprised her with the warmth of his greeting. The reading table at the center of the shop was set with fresh fruit: grapes and small tangerines. The kettle was steaming at the center, and the room smelled of oranges and ginger, not the mustiness of the night before.

"I see your fan club has finally abandoned you—"

"And the media vans as well. It seems my fifteen minutes of fame are at an end. Thank you, by the way, for clearing the flowers and candles. It helped, I'd venture, and had much to do with this welcome return to anonymity."

His mood was much improved; maybe he'd finally gotten some sleep. He poured out two mugs of tea. "I love Constant Comment. Thank you," she said.

"It's not. I blend my own teas, something I've . . . I learned to do long ago, back home. But you're close. It's fresh orange peel and clove, a bit of ginger and cinnamon bark, and black tea. A touch of cayenne. I suppose it's similar to traditional chai. Do you take milk and sugar?"

She nodded, breathing in the fragrant aroma before taking a sip. "Where *is* home?" His face darkened; he didn't like the question. Clearly.

"London?"

The lilt in his voice made his reply more question than answer. "You don't sound like you're from London."

"By way of Scotland, then. I've lived most . . . much of my life in London. I've been here, however, for several years." He rubbed his hands together—a pirate about to plunder a treasure. "Now, this book you've got for me. I am *quite* curious."

"I unearthed it six months ago, and I've tried deciphering it with the help of a colleague, but he's as clueless as I am. As are a couple of old classmates, researchers in Oxford's classics department, experts in this very sort of manuscript. They believe it extremely old, and genuine. *Not a replica.* It's got them flummoxed too.

"It's written in so many languages—although I'm told that's not uncommon, but they've never seen anything this complex. I even thought of scanning some of the pages and running them through translation algorithms, but they tell me that it would confound any currently available software. It's not just the symbols and icons, but you'll see, the text is embedded within drawings within drawings and—"

"Let me have a look then, see if I can make some sense of it. I'm no Oxford don, but I seem to have acquired a way with perplexing manuscripts."

Anne hoisted her messenger bag to the table. "I think it's some sort of alchemy manuscript or something. A lot of pagan imagery in it ... all quite mysterious. Perhaps it's the secret to Stonehenge at last! At any rate, it's possible that the manuscript's value will eventually turn out to be purely sentimental. But it would be brilliant if I've stumbled upon a genuine historical find!"

She struggled with the heavy volume, a tight fit in the leather messenger bag. "Apparently, the thing has been in my family for generations. I was told—"

Anne fell silent as Gaelan held up a hand when the volume finally dropped to the table. He held his breath and stared, first at the cover, then at Anne. He gripped the tabletop, as if to steady himself, and Anne wondered if he was about to collapse.

"I ..."

"*Dian Cecht murdered his son Miach, jealous of his surgical skills. And three hundred sixty-five herbs sprouted upon his grave—the number of joints and sinews. Miach's sister Airmid spread the herbs upon her cloak, organized by properties—a cure for every illness and disease known and unknown as yet to humankind. But Dian scattered the herbs and destroyed her cloak, so that mortal humans would never share in the power and immortality of the otherworldly creatures—the fairy gods.*

"*But it was little known that the recipes had been preserved and placed in a book, given to a man who'd ventured through a portal in Scotland and into Airmid's world, the place to which she had fled in the wake of Dian's wrath. That man, my son, was your ancestor Lord Thomas Learmont of Erceldoune. It is your legacy to pass on to your own sons. Do not neglect it. . . .*"

Gaelan's heart missed a beat, then another, and the room began to spin; the tabletop became his tenuous anchor. He should say ... something, but his ability to speak had vanished, his tongue as immobile as the rest of him. Standing only made the room spin faster, and he lost his balance, regaining it only as he backed into a counter. He slid down, settling finally on the floor, dumbfounded.

Generations, she'd said, it had been in her family—*his* book! But how was that possible? Was this some sort of delusion? A new and terrifying dimension of the PTSD triggered by the week's events? A break from reality so perfect, it seemed . . . tangible . . . tactile . . . real?

And what of Dr. Anne Shawe? Was she also not real? If he went to the window, would the media circus, the fanatics and their shrine, still be at his doorstep?

He lifted his head to see her sitting quietly at the table and gawking at him as if he were completely insane. That was no delusion. "Please, Dr. Shawe. A moment if you will."

"Are you all right, Mr. Erceldoune?" She was beside him now, taking up his left wrist, finding the throb of his pulse. One hundred five beats per minute—he'd already counted.

He shook her off, still deep within himself. She was talking, but he could barely discern his *own* thoughts, let alone hers.

He must touch it, feel it in his hands, know it was real. Know for certain that *this* was not—what was it called?—a psychotic break with reality. Gaelan leapt in one motion to his seat at the table.

Dr. Shawe sat opposite him. He knew that look too well after his stay in the hospital. He could only think to describe it as doctorly concern. She was likely five seconds from dialing 911, but he didn't really care. Closing his eyes for a moment, he spread his hands across the book's cover, feeling the deep engraving of the embossed hawthorn tree. Its gleaming jeweled hues had not faded with time. It was just as he remembered it.

Gaelan had yet to utter a word, and had no clue of what he might say to this young woman. None.

"Mr. Erceldoune. Please." She held the mug to his lips. "Drink."

He nodded, taking a small sip of the tea before waving her away. "Thank you. I . . . I don't know what came over me. . . . I must not yet be . . . quite myself. The week has been . . ." Not especially convincing, even to his own ears, but he hoped it was enough. "Your book is . . . This cover, it is beyond amazing. I have no words. . . . I haven't seen its like . . . Forgive my stammering, but to be honest, I am quite staggered." That much was true, at least. "The volume is pristine—the cover, at any rate. It seems time has not worn its beauty at all. I mean, it appears to be hundreds of years old. I've not seen many . . . any, in fact in . . . in . . . such perfect condition." He had to stop the prattling. "Where did you say you found it?"

"It's brilliant, isn't it? My cousin's attic, of all places! Six months ago."

"Indeed!" *All these years in a bloody attic. Un-fucking-believable.*

She was smiling like a child on Christmas morning. Good. At least she wouldn't be harassing him about his medical history. For now.

Decades of searching, buying and selling, trading and acquiring, trying to reassemble his library book by book with never even a valid clue to the whereabouts of the only book that really mattered. And now here it was, returned to him through luck or fate. He now knew Simon's lead was another false alarm!

The earthy aroma of old leather and yellowed vellum made the volume come alive as he opened it in his lap. Tracing the images on a random page, his fingers soaked up the textures, solid and real: the coarse paper, the embossing of quill and ink, and the fluid patina of the ornamentations.

"Yes . . . brilliant." He tried to force a professional distance, but it disintegrated even before the first word. "I . . . Will you excuse me? I shall be only a moment. I need to . . . find something in my office that should be of some help," he lied.

Gaelan set the book on his chair before backing into his small office, his eyes never leaving the volume until he closed the door. Every remaining bit of reserve uncoiled as he locked himself inside. After spotting the crystal decanter on the credenza behind his desk, he poured a large glass of whisky, hands shaking. Gaelan savored it as it slithered over his tongue and down his esophagus, washing over him. One more to steel his nerves and face Anne Shawe—and the book . . . *his* book.

He returned to the table, calmer. "Sorry—"

"Are you all right, Mr. Erceldoune?"

"Aye. No, I am. Fine. Fine." His hands roamed the cover again, the smooth edges of the hawthorn tree worn and soft, more like silk than leather. *Professional distance* . . . his new mantra. Anne was observing him, assessing him, waiting for his analysis. He was an academic with a rare find. *Professional interest.*

He opened to the first page, running his index finger over the text. "An elaborate hand, its texture is like fine engraving. Every page would have been inscribed by hand, of course. It is far too old to have been printed on a press."

The script was so very familiar. Old Gaelic—a name, his ancestor's. Below that, a further inscription: "*tiodhlac*" (gift), "*iochdmhorachd*" (compassion), and another name, "Airmid."

He had forgotten so much about the book over the decades. But now, with the manuscript restored to him, finally, memory flooded back with the suddenness of an earthquake.

The inscription was in Gaidhlig—Scots Gaelic, not Irish. But that made no sense. Airmid's people had been in Ireland a long time before Gaidhlig had become a language of its own. And his family had not been of the Highlands, where the language had been spoken, but of the Borderlands, as far as he'd known. Confusing, but not the least of it.

Latin and Greek, Old Norse, even Hebrew covered nearly every inch of this first page. He'd been tutored in all these languages, but too long ago. . . . Their history and nuances . . . would he even possess the ability to deconstruct a single page, much less hundreds? The Greek and Latin, even Gaidhlig and Gaelic he could parse—with enough time, but Norse? Hebrew?

An ouroboros bordered the title page in a multitude of metallic colors, deeply embedded into the paper—colors still vibrant and rich as the stained glass in Westminster Abbey.

"Mr. Erceldoune?"

Oh, fuck. Dr. Shawe. He'd forgotten her entirely. She drew his attention to an outer border just above the snake. "As you might imagine, as a geneticist, I found this in particular completely astonishing. The helices, I mean. They are everywhere, even on the cover."

He cleared his throat, trying to force the words past his tongue. "Sorry?" He'd barely been listening.

"Molecular genetics. Sounds weird, I know, but somewhere in my fantasies, this book holds some sort of genetic secret. Please do not laugh at me, but there's something deliciously mysterious and ancient about it. How can those not be depictions of DNA molecules? And then, all through the volume, the numbers twenty-three and forty-six in designs, in texts. Forty-six chromosomes, twenty-three pairs. You'll see it as you peruse . . . and the ouroboroses. At first, I thought they were only unusual design elements, and then I did some research on the Internet. The ouroboros has always been a symbol of eternal life. But I shall stop talking a mile a minute and let you get a word in. I'm sorry. It's just so . . ."

Gaelan stared at her as if they resided on two different planes of existence—she in a different, faster reality, while his had slowed to a quiet creep. He'd zoned out again, but he'd heard enough to understand what she was more than implying.

He could not disagree. There was in the design more than the mere suggestion of modern genetics. Brilliant, but impossible. Confounding. He'd never put it together before. How would he? He'd lost the book more than a hundred years before Watson and Crick discovered the double helix of DNA. He forced himself to concentrate on what Dr. Shawe was saying.

"It's completely ironic, me being a geneticist, finding that book, hmm? My research is built upon the molecular genetics work of Blackburn, Greider, and Szostak, winners of the 2009 Nobel Prize. But I'm babbling, being a total genetics nerd. Sorry. But who knows?" She laughed. "Perhaps this book is the secret to the Elixir of Life, and I shall visit Stockholm myself someday! Or better still, a commissioned television series: *Forgotten Secrets of the Alchemists: A BBC Documentary Series*! It is a book of alchemy, isn't it?"

He prayed she was merely lost in the euphoria of her find. The fact that she was a geneticist, *and* in possession of this book, chilled him to his core. It was a mix dangerous for him—and the entire world. He'd experienced firsthand the consequences of the mad quest for immortality. But it did not end with Handley and Braithwaite, nor with the Elixir of Life. Gaelan had read so many accounts of cruelty in the name

of medicine: ruthless madmen—purported scientists and doctors all—
who would rip the last shreds of dignity from their victims, even in the
twenty-first century. For fame, for money, for power. And at times, just
because they could.

Mengele fit that last category. He'd read a book on Hitler's Angel
of Death years ago, curious about what would drive men to such utter
cruelty, and it had plagued him for weeks. The hollow, pleading eyes of
the victims haunted him, reflecting back his own face pleading, his life
in the butcher Handley's hands. There were always Mengeles waiting
to be born, hiding beneath their scholars' hoods, experimenting on the
poor and unsuspecting.

Gaelan's attempt to muster a semblance of detachment was met
with failure. "I'm sorry, Dr. Shawe. This book. I—" He had to say something, but what? *It's mine! You can't have it; hand it over and leave*? That
would go over well.

He could not afford to frighten her off, and he knew he'd already
gone more than half that distance. She was studying him as if he'd gone
completely barmy.

Gaelan cleared his throat. "Dr. Shawe, what you must think of
me." He forced a laugh. "You must think I'm a bit daft. I'm sorry. This
book . . . You've no idea how long I've sought . . . I've sought one like it—"

"That much is obvious! One like it? Then this manuscript is not
unique?" She looked disappointed. "Are there others, perhaps even in
your collection? I'd love to see—"

"No. No. It is . . . it *is* unique. Completely. Others might have
existed at one time, but not for centuries, I think." Adequate by way
of explanation, but no, there had never been a book like this one.
"Volumes of its kind would have been burned long ago . . . errone-
ously considered the work of witchcraft. But this is not a grimoire—a
magician's conjuring book . . . at least I do not think so . . . from examining but one page," he quickly added. "But I must say, that in its day,
one might have justifiably thought it sorcery. Or from the gods." He
pointed to the name Airmid, skipping the inscription to his ancestor.

"Airmid was the Celtic goddess of healing. She was of a people

... fairy folk, according to legend anyway, called the Tuatha de Danann, 'people of the god of Danu.' Some historians speculate they were of the Hebrew tribe Dan ... Danu."

"Not a myth, then?"

"Who knows for certain? After Christianity took hold, myth and oral history fused and fractured several times over.... It is said that the Tuatha de Danann were an advanced culture: literature, science, technology. Generally in Irish legend, but they also appear elsewhere in Celtic lore." The world solidified beneath Gaelan's feet as he found himself on firmer ground.

"You seem expert in your knowledge of Celtic mythology!" Her smile disarmed him, warmed her eyes to sapphire in the shop's lighting.

Gaelan shrugged. "Part of being an antiquities dealer—and a sometime professor. I teach occasionally at the university.... And, well, I am Scottish." He managed a shy smile, hoping he'd managed to be at least a little convincing. "Historical memory, perhaps."

Pulling his chair closer, he guided Anne through the first several pages of the book. "Fascinating," he said, opening to another page. "See here? The several languages?"

"I recognize the Greek lettering, and the Latin text, of course."

Gaelan beamed, impressed. "Can you make it out, then?" Yes, much firmer ground.

Anne shrugged. "A word here and there. An Oxford education finally put to use? Is that Hebrew?"

"It is. Or Aramaic, more likely, I think. Alchemy texts often used kabbalistic symbology and language, hence the Aramaic." But if the manuscript originated with Airmid, then was it an alchemy manuscript at all—or something quite other, made to resemble one?

"Ah, here..." he continued, running his fingers across a different page, this one decorated with symbols and notes radiating from a central ouroboros design. "This, I believe, is Romani."

"But why so many languages?"

"These texts were meant *not* to illuminate and explicate; they were meant to be decipherable only by other adepts—colleagues, associates, apprentices, family, if they were so inclined, as it were, to follow in the family trade. To be an able alchemist—a gifted alchemist—would have been to wield a certain power. So why, as it were, 'spread the wealth'? Of course, alchemy was discredited centuries ago and replaced by chemistry." But would any alchemist have been able to parse these pages? Gaelan doubted it.

He returned to the first recipe: a page decorated by a barren hawthorn tree, its thorns slim as needles, its branches thick and rendered in bright white-blue metallic ink extending across the page. The writing, uniquely all in Latin, was scripted in a tiny, neat hand, crammed into the spaces between the tree's sprawl.

"Ah," remarked Gaelan, nodding. "You see, this is *Arbor Dianae*, Diana's tree. It is also called *Arbor Philosophorum*, the philosopher's tree." He could almost hear his own father describing the page to him as he was now to Dr. Shawe. It was akin to suddenly discovering a favorite book of fairy stories hidden long ago in a forgotten cedar chest.

Everything was new to him again; he grasped meaning now through the prism of twenty-first-century eyes as he plunged into the intricate workings of the book. But just the same, he enjoyed playing the wise tutor, absorbing the freshening delight of an enchanted pupil . . . honey direct from the hive.

"But the writing . . . here, and here," Gaelan pointed out, his finger moving deftly, symbol to symbol, guiding Dr. Shawe's eye. "Here is the formulation for it. Diana's tree. Are you familiar with it from your studies?"

"Sorry, no, I'm afraid not."

Slightly disappointed that she wasn't, he explained. "It doesn't matter. You see? Mercury, dissolved in silver nitrate, crystallized into an amalgam. Hence the arborescence of it—the tree. Diana's hunting bow—"

Anne shook her head. "I'm sorry, but I don't . . ." Then her eyes lit with recognition. "Diana? *Oh!* From mythology? Wasn't she a Greek goddess of . . . something? I do recall the bow of—"

"Silver. And you see here, in the corner of the page . . . there is Diana, her bow gleaming in a metallic ink of some sort, probably saturated with silver or a silver compound."

He took in the remainder of the page, vaguely aware he almost seemed too expert at a manuscript he'd supposedly never before seen. He brushed off the feeling. "I wonder . . ." he said almost to himself. "An ounce of pure silver in *aqua fortis*—that would be nitric acid in our terminology—then diluted with distilled water. Add to that, two ounces of mercury. From this solution, it says, will grow a living tree, thus proving that life itself originates in the minerals." He shrugged. "I suppose that is true in a sense, since everything is composed of minerals at some elemental level, and . . . ?"

Wait a minute! What if the illuminations weren't *only* decorative? What if they were actual ingredients embedded within the page's design? It was a completely mad idea, but what else would explain the precise layout of the page—and the particular colors chosen for the design? Of course, there existed illuminated manuscripts using metallic inks, but not to this extent, at least not in his experience. He'd never heard any such claim about alchemy texts, but this book was unique—in the extreme. Fucking brilliant—a complete apothecary, or an alchemist's laboratory—completely portable. And completely invisible to all but the few who held its key.

Then what had been the point of his father's apothecary box, all those jars with the odd symbols? Now, Gaelan's mind nearly exploded with the possibilities. Might they have been concentrates or raw materials to create new inks as they depleted from the page with use? He'd never considered it. Of course not; the very idea he was considering was completely absurd. But if true . . . He needed to stop the speculation and return to earth. Immediately.

He closed the book gently. "Dr. Shawe," he said calmly as he could, "you said, did you not, that you discovered this book in an attic? Discarded and forgotten? You know nothing, then, of the book's origins? How your family happened to acquire it?"

"I—" Her phone rang. "Please excuse me."

"The signal is better outside, so—"

She nodded as she opened the door, leaving the book with Gaelan.

CHAPTER 42

There was a chill in the early April air, and Anne wished she'd brought her jacket. Fucking Paul. Again. She affected her best "piss off" voice possible. "What do you want now?"

"What've you learned about our Miracle Man?"

Our Miracle Man? Just who the hell was pulling the strings? She hadn't said anything to Lloyd, in fact, been completely noncommittal about even looking him up.

"Nothing at all. Why?"

"Hammersmith wants to know."

"Who appointed you his bloody surrogate?"

"Don't evade the question."

"I never said I was going to find out a bloody thing about him. I've no interest in your project, Paul, in case you didn't already know. If you're so interested, you track him down." She stopped herself before letting slip her intention to resign from Transdiff altogether. *Once I've put the bloody lot of you out of business!*

"Then why have you not shown up in La Jolla—"

"I'm hanging up, Paul. You're not my boss, and what I do on my own time is of no interest to *you*, most particularly." She thought a moment. "I'm seeing an old boyfriend. A professor at University of Chicago. There. Satisfied? My. Own. Business. Now piss off."

"Look. Fine. That bloke who's interested in your book? In Chicago. How's that for coincidence? At least you should look him up whilst you're in town. Maybe he knows something and can help you with it— even if you're not interested in selling." She wasn't about to tell him that she'd found someone perfectly capable of deciphering her manuscript, much less that it was the Miracle Man Paul Gilles and Lloyd Hammersmith had been pursuing. She needed not one bit of assistance from Paul—or anyone else.

But she had to throw him some sort of bone, if only so he'd bugger off and leave her the fuck alone. "Fine. Send me his e-mail address and phone number. If I've a chance, I'll ring him up, but I'm leaving for California day after tomorrow."

There was a silence on the line.

"Anne. Don't hang up yet. We've found something. In those Bedlam diaries. A pretty good description of the patient. It appears the man was missing three fingers on his left hand. I'm telling you, luv . . . you should locate him. . . . Fame and fortune await us all."

"The book person?"

"No, the Miracle Man, darling. Don't purposely misinterpret what I'm saying. I've seen his photo. Like our Bedlam inmate, he too, happens to be missing three fingers. From his left hand."

What was Paul suggesting, that Gaelan Erceldoune was somehow connected to his nineteenth-century lunatic? That he *was* that man? "You can't seriously be thinking those diaries have some connection to that poor sod who crashed his motorbike."

"I didn't say he *is* our guy. I'm only just saying, luv. Find him. Talk to him. Please. Maybe there's some sort of genetic defect. Maybe he's a descendent. Maybe along with the regenerative ability comes a genetic deformation of the left hand. Just find him!"

"You can't be bloody serious, Paul!" A genetic mutation that causes both a congenital malformation and rapid wound recovery? "It's science fiction."

"Who the hell knows? It's an odd coincidence, and don't deny it. And we've seen weirder stuff. Much. That's all I'm saying. And what if there is a connection? Aren't you at all curious about what Mr. Gaelan Erceldoune's telomeres tell us?"

Anne couldn't tell if Paul was being at all serious. She hoped not, but knew his—and Transdiff's—latest obsession. She wished she'd never heard the word *telomere*, nor proposed the idea that infinite cell regeneration was *theoretically* possible in humans. No cell death. No death. Live forever. Infinite tissue repair. Immortality—unless of course you got decapitated. Or bled out before the cells could regenerate. Ridiculous. Bollocks. Humans were not jellyfish, and her research had no human application. That, if ever, would be years away. But how, then, to explain Gaelan Erceldoune? Paul wasn't wrong about that. She was more curious than she'd dare let on to him.

"Good-bye, Paul." She knew him well enough to understand that if he really thought he was onto something, he would soon be on his way to Chicago to investigate for himself. She shuddered, feeling unexpectedly protective of the man on the other side of the shop door, so guarded and wary of her, yet when he opened that book, he'd changed completely. She couldn't let Paul near him. The poor man would be consumed whole.

Anne clicked "End" and opened her e-mail app to write a preemptive note to Hammersmith. That should stall them for a day or two at least. "Dear Lloyd, Investigating Miracle Man. Very difficult to locate, despite hospital records. Have read his file. Extraordinary tissue regenerative abilities. Never seen anything like in a human. Refuses consent for DNA testing. Will let you know if I can find and convince. Give me a few days. Annie." She opened the door and returned to Gaelan Erceldoune.

"Dr. Shawe." Gaelan ushered Anne back to her seat with a sweep of his hand and the most charming smile he could muster. The interruption had been welcome, a chance to gather his wits—and rehearse his best pitch. It was worth a shot, although he doubted she would part with the thing. "I very much would like to buy this book from you." He did not wait for her response before continuing. "For my personal library. I'd never sell nor trade it. Not ever. I have longed . . . longed for one of its sort—for years. I have examined it whilst you've been on the phone. Although it appears at first glance to be an alchemist's bible, I believe it is more than that.

"It is . . . the sort of work . . . a . . . collector . . . an aficionado of medical antiquities, as I am, seeks his whole lifetime. I would love to take a stab at it . . . analyze . . . deconstruct . . . rudimentary, I'm certain, but . . ." He gazed at the volume, now open between them, hoping he would not give away his desperate longing for it.

"I hope you might entertain an offer to sell it. Price is no object, and I am willing to pay you much more, I am certain, than you would receive from any other buyer." He would sell his entire library—worth millions—to have it, if that was what it took.

"It is not for sale. At any price."

"Be assured, I will translate it for you, every page, annotate it in readable English, so you, given your own interests and background, might also benefit immensely from its contents. It is a fair trade. Just name your price." It was too much; he'd pushed too hard. She would suspect something.

But she did not react, simply reiterated her refusal to part with it. "It's not for sale. I am sorry if you misunderstood my intention. I would, however, greatly appreciate your assistance both in deciphering the pages and helping me to understand its origins—if that is even possible. I would pay you, of course, as a consultant—whatever your going rate is. Name *your* fee for helping me. Beyond purely academic interest, I have a feeling that this manuscript might be a clue, however slight, to my own family's history. So I offer you a collaboration; we shall *both* benefit from it. But, I'm afraid, it's not for sale."

Gaelan was mute. He rose from his seat, struggling against quickly gathering resentment. Dr. Shawe was right in her decision. Who would part willingly with such a prize? He felt it slipping through his fingers. The book had literally fallen into his lap, yet would now be lost to him forever? Inconceivable. There must be a way. . . . He stepped behind the counter so she could not observe the depth of his disappointment.

"Here, Mr. Erceldoune," Dr. Shawe said finally, breaking the silence, beckoning him back to the table. "What do you think this means?" She pointed to an image of a crow with an olive branch in its beak.

"I have no bloody idea!" he snapped petulantly. He refused to be treated as some sort of interloper. *Consultant? Indeed not!* "I would have to have more time to study it." *Calm yourself, Erceldoune.* It would do no good if she walked out now, with that book. He'd never see it again if she did that. But if he was, indeed, the only one who could help her, why would she bolt? No, she was as determined to untangle the manuscript as he was to possess it.

"That olive branch. Does it not look to you like a strand of DNA? They're everywhere if you look closely enough!"

Gaelan could not help himself, and he returned, looking over her shoulder at the image. "Surely you must be aware, Dr. Shawe, that you are projecting your own modern scientific training onto a work hundreds of years old."

"But the question remains. Why that shape?"

"I rather more think," he said, still annoyed, but unable to contain his interest, "it is an infinity symbol, and far more likely that the author was in some way seeking, as did most of his brethren, the answer to life itself. Did it lie in minerals—a philosopher's stone, as some would call it? Some alchemists, even apothecaries, spent their lives in search of it. Even Sir Isaac Newton was obsessed with the idea of solving the mystery of eternal life within the minerals found in plain sight on this earth. Why *not* an infinity symbol?"

Gaelan grinned, recalling the heated debates he'd had with Sir Isaac back home in the Apothecaries' Hall over the healing properties of one herb over another shortly before the man's scholarly pursuit turned to matters of mathematics and physics. But it had been Newton's insistence on contextualizing alchemy with the spiritual world— the occult—that rankled, causing a rift between them. Gaelan knew all too well that the physical ramifications of "life eternal" had little to do with God or the afterlife.

"But it is interesting," Anne continued, pressing the issue, "that the symbol for 'infinity' here so resembles what we now know to be the double helix of DNA. What a coincidence, given my research! Like it was somehow meant to be." She blushed. "Forgive me. It's silly, I know. But somehow at this moment I can't help but feel that it was somehow my destiny to unearth this book."

The passion with which she spoke and the inquisitiveness in her eyes kindled a spark he'd thought long dead. It both warmed and terrified him.

"And then there is you. A man who by all accounts has an inexplicable ability for wound repair, unheard of . . ."

Ah, there you are. Reality. What she's really after. The book was a tangent. He was the prize. *Do not forget this simple fact.* Exactly what was needed to remind him of his mantra: professional distance. *Do not allow yourself to be sucked in.* "Just what are you suggesting?"

She scowled. "More coincidence . . . more destiny, that's all. You don't feel it?"

"Not at all, but point taken," he said, coolly, hoping to redirect the arc of their debate. He dismissed her argument with feigned disinterest. "Getting back to the matter at hand, I think that connecting a medieval manuscript with a field that would not be discovered for centuries to come is more than a bit of a stretch."

How could a text credited to Airmid—to mythology—incorporate sophisticated, modern, science? It was as impossible as . . . as what? An immortality formula? A recipe to cure plague?

Her cloak, before her father scattered it to the wind, contained upon it the secret to healing through herbs and minerals all of the ailments known and unknown to humankind.

What if this book was, for lack of a better term, Airmid's "backup copy," and Lord Thomas of Erceldoune the convenient repository? Given to him to conceal from her father—to preserve it for all time?

Gaelan nervously raked a hand through his hair, contemplating his options, coming up nil. "I tell you what, Dr. Shawe. I will help you. But I would need it—need to borrow it—for some time. Perhaps two weeks, perhaps two months." Perhaps forever. Gaelan was far from certain whether, once back in his possession, he could let anyone wrest it from him without violence.

"Why do I feel I would be doing you as much, if not more, a favor by letting you have at it?"

"I would be lying to tell you that I don't covet the thing—"

"After that admission, I insist we do this together or not at all.

There is no way I shall let this book out of my sight. Surely you'd vanish with it, and I'd never see you *or* the book again!"

Perhaps it would not be so dreadful, after all, to have her nearby. Her expertise would be far from a hindrance, but he'd need to redouble his guard.

"The entire way!" she insisted. "I want to know what you are doing as you interpret the manuscript and your reasoning. I want to understand this legacy of mine—destiny or not—nearly as much as I am interested in your unusual regenerative abilities. I've not forgotten *that*, of course."

Of course not. And he would do well to never forget it.

Her face was flushed with excitement and mirth. It would be a challenge not to be disarmed by her eagerness or the warmth of her smile, which had already eaten away the edges of his guard.

He would give nothing away, rebuff all questions, be ever vigilant. *Professional distance. Academic interest. Repeat on the hour. Every hour*—as long as Dr. Anne Shawe was around. Gaelan nodded, his lips drawn tight. "Understood. But if I might have it overnight to get a head start, keep it in my possession whilst we work on it, I might make faster strides in deciphering it, do you not agree? I promise to keep not one fact, one idea, from you. I tend to work at odd hours. Even tonight. I . . . I seldom sleep, and I've a mind to get through this book quick as I can. And mind, I intend to move on from this area, and soon. I hate publicity, and I've had more than my share these past days. Soon as I've sold this property, I'm gone, so I'd best get to my task, do you not agree? Feel free to sleep upstairs in my flat if you'd like."

She seemed to hesitate, consider the proposition. Gaelan hoped she would simply take him at his word and return to her hotel. "I am exhausted. I've not slept either . . . and my jet lag . . . I give up. Very well, but I shall be back tomorrow morning nine sharp. And you must promise to be ready for a day's work—together." She glanced at her wristwatch. "Good Lord. Look at the time! Okay, nine. Sharp. I'll bring coffee."

Gaelan ushered her to the door and watched as she disappeared from sight. Finally alone with the book, he leapt upon it, heart pounding. He hugged it to his chest—a long-lost love. And he wept.

I do not know, my dear ancestors, what trick of fate has brought this manuscript back into my hands, but at long last I have the means to right a wrong and end my friend's life. It is all he desires in the world. And what of me? Shall I disappear and begin again, reborn? Or is it finally time to put an end to my own nightmares? It struck Gaelan, harder than he thought possible, that with Simon gone, he would be truly and finally alone. And it terrified him.

LONDON, 1842

CHAPTER 43

"Well, Erceldoune, tomorrow is an eventful day for you," Simon declared as he took his leave for the night. More than a week had passed, and Gaelan was finally fit for his voyage across the sea. As much as he knew he needed to vanish, part of him longed to stay here, with Eleanor. But with every passing day, the risk of discovery increased.

The murder of Lord Richard Braithwaite was a notorious crime, and it would not do for the executed murderer to turn up living. There was little choice *but* to leave. He presented no viable future for Eleanor. She should remarry, forget the horror of Lord Braithwaite, enjoy the inheritance of his riches, and never give another thought to the apothecary Gaelan Erceldoune.

"I have booked you first-class passage to New York, and you head for those exciting shores with a full bank account and our deepest gratitude. I am heading up to my rooms, so I will bid you both a good night."

"The money, Bell, is wholly unnecessary; I did this for myself, as much as for your sister, as you are aware. I should have killed him when he first walked into your home—"

"But it is necessary." He pulled Gaelan out of Eleanor's hearing. "I full well expect that you will use at least some of those funds to locate that book. I hold you to it, and to restoring me to my more mortal self. Do not, therefore, think of it as either a gift or charity."

"Then you have my thanks—and my word. If I find the book, you shall be the first to know of it."

Simon embraced his sister and left the two of them alone in the drawing room. A peaceable silence surrounded them as they now sat alone opposite each other. "We really must say good-bye so soon? You cannot stay, even for one more—"

"We have spoken of this already, Eleanor. Would it be any easier if it was next week? Next month?"

She shook her head. "I cannot tell you, Gaelan . . . Your bravery . . . There are no words can be found in any lexicon that—"

"Hush, don't let us waste what little time we have on trivialities. Come sit with me in the garden? It is a beautiful night, and the sky is lit only with a crescent; the stars will be out in spectacular display. And it shall be the last time I see the skies from these shores." Gaelan rose from the settee and extended his good hand, bowing deeply.

A breeze cooled the unusually balmy August night, sending a shiver through Eleanor. Gaelan stood behind her, hands on her shoulders, directing her gaze upward into the heavens.

"Mars is out tonight, do you see it, Gaelan?"

"Aye, the red planet, and do you see there . . . ?" He held her arm, caressing it as he oriented her. "Do you see, there, nearly straight above our heads? That is the Corona Borealis, Ariadne's Crown. If you keep looking, you will see the points of it. You, my dear, dear Eleanor, are so like her, the courageous Ariadne. Do you know the story?" He turned her in his arms so he might behold the stars captured in her eyes.

She nodded, reciting, a schoolgirl before her tutor. "Ariadne aided Theseus in slaying the Minotaur, and they fled to Naxos, where he left her only later to be found by Dionysus, who wed her. But Theseus was cruel to Ariadne; you have not been—just the opposite—although it is true you have slain the Minotaur."

"Well, to speak true, it was you that slayed the Minotaur. But like Theseus, I must abandon you, and for that I am sorry. But I swear you shall find your Dionysus, who shall treat you with tenderness and love and cause you to forget both Braithwaite and me for all the children and grandchildren that shall surround you all your days. With me, there would be only sadness and regret. You *know* what I am."

Eleanor pulled back slightly, regarding him, emotion overflowing.

"I know." She brushed aside a lock of his hair, reaching up to kiss his temple.

Gaelan sighed, overwhelmed. He captured her mouth, devouring it before moving to her jawline and down to her breast as his hands followed, caressing, touching. He could not get enough of the taste of her. He grasped her hand in both of his, kissing each of her fingers, desire and emotion engulfing him like a tidal wave. There was nothing to do but give in to it, savor every moment he had remaining with her and engrave them all in his memory for eternity.

Eleanor tugged at his hand, leading him into the house. "Come, my love, let us go upstairs."

Morning broke, and light poured in through the window, bathing Eleanor's bed in warmth and sun. She awoke, wrapped in Gaelan's arms, the ecstasy of the past night still enveloping her. She turned, facing him as he slept beside her peacefully. A single sunbeam illuminated his hair, painting it red-gold. She kissed the spot just in front of his ear, her breath a whisper. "Good morning, my darling."

He awoke, stretching, and his arm curled tighter around Eleanor as he drew her closer. The drowsy warmth of his smile did not conceal his melancholy. "Morning, love. What time is it?"

"Just past six."

He frowned, nodding tightly, the reality of his leaving dawning upon his angular features. "I must arise soon, my love; I've a journey ahead, you know." He looked away, not quite able to conceal his regret from her.

"We have a little time, do we not?" She put to use her best coquette's smile. The events of the past weeks had faded to an ache, except for Gaelan's departure. She did not want to say her fare-thee-well, not yet. Not ever. But she had no choice. Yes, she could follow him to New York, but what then? He was right; there was nothing to be done but let him go. But not quite yet.

She ran her toe along his flank, eliciting a low purr.

"So you aim to give me a proper good-bye then, lass?" He quirked an eyebrow, dipping his head to kiss her, a frenzy of sensation pooling across every inch of her skin.

Gooseflesh arose along her arms and legs as he tasted her, his tongue darting along her collarbone to her breast and lower still until she thought she might swoon from it. He grew hard along her thigh, and she only wanted to feel him inside her again. She needed him in that spot, which last night had sent her into spasms of delight and left her boneless and spent. She had never known that feeling, and she would die should he not bring her to it before he was gone for good.

"Ah, my love, there, yes . . . " she hissed as he entered her, showering her again with kisses light as butterfly wings, driving her mad with desire until she shattered into fragments of light and color, holding onto him as he followed her, breathless and bathed in sweat.

Gaelan rolled away slightly, tucking Eleanor in the crook of his shoulder. He touched the jeweled pendant resting on her collarbone. "Ariadne," he said quietly.

Eleanor shook her head, confused.

"Your necklace. I admired it that first night in the garden, but I could not see it clearly in the dark. It is a labyrinth."

"Yes. A gift from my father's father. I'd always thought it an odd piece, and I'm now embarrassed to say I'd never connected it to the labyrinth in Ariadne's tale. But of course. Where she first met Theseus."

He ran his thumb across the diamonds set deeply into the tiny maze. "It is a sign, if we are to believe in such things. So, then, it is settled. You shall stay here in Naxos and await your Dionysus, and as for me, I must be off to Liverpool; I've a ship to board, and you, my beloved seductress, shall make me tardy."

Gaelan nearly relented as she tried a final time, appealing directly to his heart. "I implore you, do not leave me here alone, widowed again. Please take me with you!"

"Would that it was possible, my love. But I cannot. . . . It would not be fair to you. It is a rough life I am bound for, despite what you might hear of the place, and despite the fortune you and Simon have insisted to burden me with. And as I said last night, I could not bear to see the resentment in your expression as you grow old, and my own heart shattering when I lose you, as I have lost everything and everyone time and again. It is better—for us both."

She imagined herself: old and tired of living, wrinkled and stooped, her husband a vigorous man of only forty years tied to a woman old enough to be his grandmother. He would resent her, and she him. Gaelan was right, of course. Reluctantly, she nodded. He sat up, kissing her a last time as she tried to memorize every plane of his face, the tickle of his shaggy mane, the dark, soulful eyes, now so overflowing with emotion she had to look away.

By the time Gaelan had washed and dressed, Eleanor awaited him in the drawing room with Simon.

"I am off to be born anew as soon as I alight in New York. I shall send word of my whereabouts when I can. Good luck to you, Bell."

"And you. I don't know how to thank you for what you've done for Eleanor. You did not have to do it."

"I did, and I am glad for it." He regarded Eleanor, who sat quietly with no word of farewell to him. "I should have told you sooner, Bell, about Braithwaite; then perhaps something might have been done to put a halt to the entire thing. As for you, Lady Braithwaite . . ." He took a tentative step toward her. "I only hope that time will put asunder that terrible act you were forced to commit. I—"

She leapt from the chair embracing him, not caring what Simon did or did not suspect. Gaelan blushed as she kissed him. "You shall forget me, Eleanor. You must, and find happiness, my love."

With a tight, silent nod toward Simon, Gaelan disentangled himself from Eleanor, leaving the house as he heard the carriage come around to the kitchen door. Eleanor fell to the settee and wept, a terrible pain in her chest as if a cord pulled tight had been ripped from her heart, leaving in its wake a chasm.

CHICAGO'S NORTH SHORE, PRESENT DAY

CHAPTER 44

Gaelan locked the door and removed the ouroboros book to his tiny office, sweeping aside the glues and cleaners, rags and solvent cans littering his desk. He opened again to the first recipe, wondering if he should test his theory immediately. Was he right? Was it possible that every ingredient was embedded into the illumination inks? *Fucking bloody brilliant, that.* It was a wild idea, wholly implausible. *But what if?*

He resisted the urge to tinker impulsively, not when there was too much he did not yet understand or had forgotten over the centuries. That had been his mistake in the first place, and it cost him, Simon, and Sophie Bell. There was a missing piece, something his father never had time to explain, omitted from his notes. He needed to find it before he dared experiment. He regarded the book with new eyes, feeling the weight of history, of family. This was his legacy, and he meant to fathom it as his ancestors intended him to do.

He'd a sudden urge to write his notes longhand; Microsoft Word didn't seem quite the proper vehicle for this endeavor. After tearing the plastic from a fresh legal pad, he sat with pen in hand and set to work.

The text was infinitesimally tiny in places, and his oversized magnifying light helped immensely, as he wondered how he had ever managed it by mere candlelight. The navigation was difficult, and he struggled through the varying languages, which often switched direction midsentence or halfway down the page and back again by the end. The text twisted and wound within and between, around and under the illustrations, never crossing the boundary into the illuminations themselves.

Memory seeped through the decades, along with his translation skills—aided, he admitted, by the god of Google—at first a trickle, and then a tsunami, as he began to make sense of the languages and symbols. Impulsively, he would stroke his hands over the images and words, hoping the rough surface of the writing, the radiant color and texture of the designs would somehow percolate through to his soul and bring about an epiphany.

Hours later, he pinched the bridge of his nose, bringing the light closer as the letters blurred and pricked at the edges of his vision. He must keep going, he knew, get as much done as quickly—and accurately—as possible, he reminded himself, before Anne Shawe returned in the morning. By the time he pushed his chair away from the desk, it was after three a.m. And he'd only managed six pages. He desperately needed a break.

Picking up his mobile, Gaelan hit number one on the speed dial.

"I have it." He didn't wait for the "hello" on the other end.

"What?" A groggy voice. "Who the bloody hell is this? Have you any fucking idea of the time?"

"Aye." He looked at his pocket watch, energized. "Half three. Practically morning. I *have* it . . . the *book*. Did you not hear me?" Gaelan fought the urge to howl his excitement. He needed to stay measured. Calm. In control of his faculties and grounded in reality. This wouldn't have been the first time he'd called Simon, frantic, in the middle of the night. And it would not do for Simon to believe Gaelan had become completely delusional. It wasn't as if Gaelan hadn't considered the option himself at least twice already.

"How?" Simon was more alert. "And why could this not wait until morning?"

"Says the man who has been obsessing over it for nearly two hundred years. Don't be annoyed, Simon. I couldn't sleep."

"So you thought I shouldn't either?"

"Look. I don't want to speak about this over the phone. . . ." Gaelan listened through the silence.

"You're sure you're not just confused? Because, coincidentally, I've also got a line on the book, or have you forgotten? Have you taken something? Or is it just one too many Lagavulins? Because it's bloody unlikely that—"

"Of course I'm bloody sure. And it isn't a *line* on the book or some elusive little clue or 'perhaps.' I have it, looking at it right now, touching it, in actual fact. Unless I've finally flipped, in which case . . . Look, *I* may be immortal, but my mobile battery, sadly, is not. If you want to continue this conversation, we need to meet in person."

"There's an all-night IHOP near the Wilmette train station. Do you know it?"

Gaelan considered. He knew the place, mostly haunted by cops on break at this hour. He didn't much fancy running into his friends from the hospital, unlikely as it was in Wilmette. "I do, but I'm not sure. . . . Should we be discussing . . . our condition . . . in so public a place? Maybe you might drive down here?"

"At three in the morning, do you really think anyone would be listening, and if they are, would they really care? And I hate coming to your flat in the middle of the night . . . the train tracks, you know."

Simon and train trestles; his phobias ran nearly as deep as Gaelan's. "You have a point. And thank you for reminding me you're every bit as much a nutter as I am. I shall meet you there in twenty minutes."

Was it possible? The ever-skeptical Gaelan Erceldoune insisting he had the elusive book, not only a lead, but in his actual hands! Unless he didn't, and it was all in Gaelan's head—equally likely. Just how stoned was his old friend tonight, given all that had befallen him these past weeks?

Simon wandered through the house and out into the garden, the motion-sensor lighting creating a path through the rough-hewn stone. He skirted beyond the path, down to the tip of the promontory wall, and stared out into the dark stillness of the lake. He listened for a few minutes more to the gentle thrust and parry of the waves lapping at the rocks below. His imagination took flight contemplating the finality of death—his own.

Dying had been only a theory for so long that it had lost all practical meaning. He could leap over the wall without a second thought, lie on the rocks for days, his tissues regenerating while he lived on morphine and biscuits. Each time he'd tried it, hoping for death, he'd been denied. He realized he'd been simply luckier than Gaelan never to have been found down at the water's edge like that, after a plummet that would have killed any mortal being. What if he had? Then he'd be the bloody Miracle Man. *There but for the grace of God* . . .

"*So, my dear. Is it over, finally?*"

Sophie! Simon caught himself as he nearly tripped on the root of an old oak tree, startled by her voice, too loud in the quiet of night. "Gaelan says he has the book. And I shall die, and you shall be set free, and we can be together." All the years she had haunted him: shrew or lover, banshee or sweet seductress, she never looked as she did now— dressed in simple, white muslin. A harbinger, perhaps?

"*How many times have you promised this to me? And even should it be true, how do you know that what you seek lies in a book you've seen but once?*" She floated specter-like beyond the garden wall, opalescent white above the black of the lake.

"I hope—"

"*But you do not know!*" Her voice was a screech, hawklike, close to his ear—*chilling. "All these years, you have held me here, tied me to a world in which I do not belong. Do you think I want to be with you now? For an eternity? The very thought depresses me. If you have not had it in yourself to sacrifice your desire to be with me after so many decades . . .*" She harrumphed. "*Now, your Mr. Erceldoune. He knows what it is to sacrifice for love!*"

Simon sighed. Not again. He hated it when she did that. "I cannot control what is in my heart; I have tried, believe me, I have, and . . ." But she had vanished just as his mobile ringtone echoed off the rocks and into the night. *What now?*

"I'm on my way. I shall be there in—"

"Mr. Danforth? This is Paul Gilles."

Simon took a step backward, nearly losing his footing on an out-cropping of rocks. "Don't you know it is the middle of the night here?"

"Sorry. Look, I wanted to let you know, I'm coming to the States tomorrow. Oddly enough, the woman I spoke of, the one with that book you're—"

"Yes?"

"She's reluctant to sell, and to be honest I can't really say I blame her. But she happens to be in Chicago on business. Perhaps we can all meet, so you might at least see this manuscript you're so keen on?"

"You'll be in Chicago? When?"

"Likely day after tomorrow, given the time difference—"

"Of course." What the devil was going on? Was there, impossibly, a second book? Or was Gilles simply leading him on? But to what purpose? Or was this Gaelan's fragile grip on reality warping into a whisky- and weed-fueled delusion? He sighed, not knowing what he would find beyond the boysenberry syrup at the IHOP.

CHAPTER 45

Gaelan waited in a booth, mindful of the door as Simon arrived and sat down. He'd produced a miniature mountain of shredded napkin, blowing it to the side of the table as a bleary-eyed server approached. "What can I get for you gentlemen this fine spring morning?"

"Just coffee if you wouldn't mind," said Gaelan. "Milk and sugar, please."

"Pecan pancakes please. And coffee. Black."

They watched her sashay off to the kitchen, not speaking until the pot had been placed on the table along with Simon's pancakes. "Don't worry, we'll pour for ourselves. Thank you so much," said Simon. He slathered on half a carafe of maple syrup and did not speak again until he saw her sit in a booth at the front of the empty restaurant. "So we already have it? How?"

"Quite bizarre, in actual fact. Very, very odd." Gaelan explained Anne as best he could, still not quite believing it himself. "And I don't believe there is a 'we' in this. If I recall, it *is* my book." He grimaced. "Unfortunately, this Dr. Shawe insists on being my shadow, gazing, as it were, over my shoulder as I work."

Gaelan leaned into Simon. "It shall take me *weeks* until I finish with it, I think, unless I hit upon some sort of key encrypted in the text to guide me. It's a huge volume, and I am not sure for how long I'll have it."

Simon raised an eyebrow. "Where is it? You said it was in your possession and—"

"Of course it is, and it's back in my shop. I'm not imagining it, Simon, if that's what you're thinking. Do you really think I'd bring it . . . here?" he whispered. "What I mean to say is that it's been lent to me . . . sort of. But it is, I suppose, not *technically* mine. I am certain *Gaelan Erceldoune's* legal claim to that book, if ever there was one, expired many decades ago. Of course, I shall continue trying to convince her to sell it, but so far . . ." He shrugged.

"But why do you need it all, when you've only to look up one bloody page?"

"Two—including the recipe I conjured for myself. But do you seriously have to ask that? It was by not fully appreciating both context and consequence that . . . Who knows what might happen should I try to . . . ? It is all I need . . . all *we* need is for something to go awry . . ." This was not a new debate for them. What if a mistake had more global implications, something neither of them would have considered in the nineteenth century? "Suffice to say it'll be a long process, and I cannot rush through it. I am only on the sixth page after hours at it. It should go faster as I begin to perceive patterns, if any are there to perceive, but as yet . . ." Gaelan swept his hair from his eyes, and poured another cup of coffee. He was still uneasy about being in so public a place— exposed—discussing the book.

"But how did this woman come by it? And how the bloody hell has she found you? And why? And why now? And at the same time I've also gotten a lead? It is all a bit convenient. Although I must admit, there seems to be some sort of hitch—"

"What are you saying? You don't believe me?" Simon had that patronizing look about him. *Bloody hell, here it comes.*

"You must admit you've been under quite a bit of duress of late, yes? Are you entirely certain your mind hasn't conjured the entire thing? Somehow conflated—"

Gaelan sniffed, trying to ignore the accusation, as one piece of the puzzle began to make sense. "You get a bloody lead on the book approximately every six months. But if you *have*, in fact, come across the real thing, perhaps *Dr. Anne Shawe* is the hitch you mentioned. She said that she'd had some help trying to interpret the manuscript, and perhaps—"

Simon shrugged. "This Dr. Gilles mentioned—"

"Dr. Gilles. Paul Gilles. She had a phone call from someone called Paul whilst she was at the shop. I heard her say the name. So if that does, in fact, explain at least one mystery, it leaves, what, four hundred others? And I've answers to none of them."

Gaelan sat back in the booth cushions, watching Simon devour the last of his pancakes. "How can you eat like that in the middle of the night?"

"Like you said, it's nearly morning!"

"Look, Simon, I shall endeavor to undo ... your condition ... best I can, as soon as I can, but I cannot drive this woman away, risk her just picking up and leaving—with the book." Gaelan reflected a moment, the confluence of unlikely events striking him again, and after so many years of nothing. "I cannot begin to tell you, Simon, how it makes me feel a sense of wholeness and peace for the first time in—"

"I can see that already, and it worries me."

"You can? And why would it worry—"

"This Dr. Shawe. All of a sudden, she shows up, just after you've been nearly exposed? A geneticist, of all things? And in possession of your book? Do you really believe her story? You don't think ... ?"

Gaelan did his best to reject Simon's concern. Yes, Anne had come to him because of the accident. Yes, she was connected with those hospital ghouls who coveted his DNA, but the book was unrelated—a happenstance occurrence, the sort of which happened all the time. A fortuitous coincidence, that was all.

"I don't know, but don't let your guard down with her, Erceldoune, for both our sakes. You're more than a bit fragile now—more vulnerable than usual. The diaries, the accident, now this? I know you. How you get when—"

Gaelan shook off the remark. He was *not* fragile, and certainly no more than Simon, who, after all had his very own ghost. He tapped a teaspoon testily on the tabletop. "You know, there is a saying, 'Whose house is of glass, must not throw stones at another.' Do you wish to hear my theory or not ... about the book, I mean?"

Simon nodded. "Go on."

"It's quite brilliant actually, and I've wondered about it for years, but of course I couldn't test it. When I created the elixir for you, I matched the symbols in the book to powders and desiccated herbs in my father's old apothecary box. But it wasn't necessary. In fact, I think contents of those bottles may have been the fixings for concentrates, sort of replacement cartridges, if you will, like on a printer. The proper formulations emulsified into inks are embedded within each page diluted to perfect concentrations. And perhaps by using the original material, I rendered the elixir too rich, hence—"

"Was this not something you might have known?"

Gaelan shrugged, noting the indictment in Simon's tone. "My father was arrested and executed by King James before he'd finished tutoring me on the book. There were notes at one time—a scroll my father's father had hastily affixed into the spine of the book—before he, too, was arrested. It had been lost . . . somewhere, sometime. I have no idea when, but long before I'd ever contemplated putting any of it into practical application. I'd never considered . . . But you see, the inks themselves are crafted of metals and their compounds. Each rendering *illuminates* the recipe on the page. *Illuminates*," Gaelan repeated, emphasizing the brilliance of wordplay. "You only need to interpret it properly. Match symbols to colors to shapes to substance: from text to image to text to crucible. I believe that everything we need is embedded in the very illustrations that illuminate the book itself."

"You're sure?" Simon grumbled, clearly unconvinced.

"No, I confess I am not. Not yet. As I said, I've only managed to plow through six pages, so I confess, this is all a bit of a leap."

"A *bit*?"

Gaelan continued, undeterred. "Unlike the matching substances in the apothecary box, the illustrations are not coded, or at least not obviously. This book was never meant to be understood by just anybody; its very structure is an elaborate lock with an exotic combination. Look, even if I am wrong, perhaps with our current understanding of chemistry, medicine, and pharmacology—even computer algorithms—the manuscript might well lead us to the correct formulations nonetheless."

"Incredible," Simon said flatly, drumming his fingers on the table.

"Indeed. But you seem rather underwhelmed. You might finally have your death wish fulfilled; it's all you ever talk about, so I would think you would look happier than you do now."

"Sorry. There are an awful lot of ifs in your theory." He paused. "No. That's not it. It is Sophie. She tells me now that we shall never be together, even after I . . . if I . . . How can I let her go? What if she is not waiting for me? What if—"

Gaelan rolled his eyes. "Having second thoughts, are we? You mean, then, to live on, keeping her trapped in eternity? That's a bit selfish, don't you think?" He was really too exhausted—and too delighted with himself—to snipe. "Look. Right now, it is *all* a big 'if.' And even if all the variables are resolved, and *if* I can create an antidote, it might kill you immediately or simply reverse the original effect. Or do nothing at all. We shall have to wait and see."

CHAPTER 46

Gaelan spotted Anne as he pulled up in front of the shop. She was pacing, her face pinched in anger—or agony. He wasn't certain which. What the devil was she doing here? She'd said nine, not seven. He parked, catching her attention as he shut the car door.

"Dr. Shawe? What—"

"Mr. Erceldoune, I've been ringing you for hours—"

He could hear panic in her voice. "My battery..." He pulled his dead iPhone from his pocket. "What is it?"

"We must talk. I've not slept... I—"

"Is it about the book?"

"No, not the book. Something... Might we go in?"

Gaelan nodded, unlocking the shop door. She was trembling. They sat, and Gaelan waited for her to speak. He was not up to any new twists.

"Mr. Erceldoune, I've not been completely open with you about my work." She paused, taking a long breath and a sip from her Starbucks cup. "I work for a pharmaceutical concern in the UK called Transdiff Genomics, Ltd. Perhaps you've heard of it?"

He tensed, feeling the prickle of dread in his neck and down his back. The company rang a distant bell, but he'd read a lot about genetics these past years. "Perhaps, but—"

"They are working on a project. And I say 'they' rather than 'we' because I have gotten myself posted to the Salk Institute in order to avoid them—entirely. It is my intention to resign my position at Transdiff as soon as I'm able. You see, I am opposed to what... I mean to say that I recently discovered... and then... you understand, on ethical grounds. You must believe I wanted nothing to do with it from the start—"

She was very agitated and was making no sense. Gaelan tried to understand what she was trying to explain despite the rise of his own anxiety. "Please, Dr. Shawe. Do slow down. I've no idea what you're talking about. What project? I don't—"

"Last month, workers in London unearthed something beneath the Imperial War Museum during a renovation."

The Bedlam diaries. Gaelan froze. He struggled to maintain his composure, but already he felt the blood drain from his face. *No*, he nearly screamed. He struggled to listen through the clammy fog of fear.

"Transdiff won the contract to study the find. They were diaries, very old diaries, from nineteenth-century Bedlam. You see, the site had at one time—"

"Yes," he managed noncommittally, "I have . . . read about that." But why was *she* so upset? Why come to *him*? And why now? Had they made a connection of some sort? Speculation that somehow led back to him—to the Miracle Man? Gaelan held his breath, hoping that the terror surely in his eyes would not give him away.

"I need you to know that what they are doing is more than disturbing to me—has been since they first made the discovery. There's no consideration of the ethics involved, not in anything they do, and . . ."

Gaelan thrust his hands in his pockets to hide their shaking. He knew where this was leading, and it was increasingly difficult not to react. "I am sorry, I still don't—"

"There are . . . descriptions." She hesitated briefly. "They seem to fit you: your coloring, your height, features . . ." She gestured with her head toward his left side, her cheeks red, as if embarrassed to call attention to his ruined hand. "The deformity. Of course all of that could be . . . likely is . . . coincidental, but then there was your accident and the incredible miracle of your recovery, and my colleagues now believe you might be—"

She was clever, and there was little chance she had not begun to put the pieces into place one by one. Her denial of it represented the last vestiges of her scientific skepticism. And soon, those too would disintegrate, and his world would collapse beneath the weight of the facts and evidence. He summoned the remains of his composure in an effort to disparage what she and her colleagues were suggesting. "You cannot seriously believe that I . . . that I am that man." Gaelan desperately hoped his body language did not telegraph exactly that.

"No. No, of course not! But that you are perhaps connected— genetically. Somehow. A distant relative. A descendent of the man in the diaries."

The tension gripping Gaelan's every muscle loosened ever so slightly. Perhaps this was going in a different direction altogether.

"Transdiff are quite obsessed with this project, throwing loads of money everywhere to make sure they are in complete control of it. They've only just committed to fund a new wing of Royal London Hospital, just for the exclusive right to pick apart this poor wretch's past. The things that had been done to him in the name of science! By any definition—torture. And how much better are Transdiff . . . my own colleagues—what they do with . . . ?" She paused, her mouth drawn into a tight line. "I mean to say . . . how could anyone salivate over the torture of that poor soul like that? As if they'd found the bloody holy grail!"

"But it is only a diary, is it not? Words written long ago, perhaps by an inmate himself. Or herself. Not real evidence of anything, is it?"

"The diary seems to be authentic. The doctor in whose hand it is written was the director of the place. And it bears his official seal. And, no, there is no hard evidence. As you say, only written records. But does it really matter? It's ghoulish, what they're doing. They're mining the place for tissue samples as we speak. Let it be, I say. Let that be the man's burial vault. Lord knows he must've died there. This was a human *being*, and they are pecking over his remains like . . ." She was now shaking with rage. "They'd offered me the project, but what little I was willing to hear made me ashamed to . . . I withdrew my name from consideration. They agreed and assigned a 'more appropriate' researcher."

"I see." Gaelan was stunned by the revelation. How much had she revealed about him, now that he'd let her in? His heart thrashed in his chest, and he was certain she could see it even through his shirt. Gaelan tasted blood, realizing he had bitten through his lower lip. How much longer he could maintain this charade of disinterested calm, he did not know. Turmoil ravaged his esophagus, making him regret, only an hour before, consuming an entire pot of strong IHOP coffee.

"I still don't understand why you were upset enough to be wearing out my sidewalk at such an early hour."

"My colleagues believe they are onto something. Nobel Prize material, if not more. A human specimen with a specific genetic anomaly— an ability to regenerate injured tissue with a rapidity heretofore unheard of in our own species. And to do so infinitely, and with no permanent damage. They believe—"

Gaelan needed a cigarette. Desperately. "Excuse me a moment." He needed time to regroup and get his wits about him again. But there was nowhere to run, nowhere to hide. He slipped through his office door, wishing it were a wormhole, a black hole, a rip in the space-time continuum—anything to transport him from this moment, this place, the inevitability that his long-held secret would very soon become public spectacle.

Gaelan studied Anne as he emerged from his office a moment later with his tobacco pouch. What to make of this woman, sitting in his shop, head in her hands, sniffling back sobs. Obviously, she agreed with her colleagues' assessment, and made the leap right to him. Otherwise, why confess any of it, and to him in particular? But he would give her nothing. Gaelan fumbled with the tobacco and papers, then gave up on the endeavor, returning to his seat. His hands were far too shaky to manage rolling the thin tissue. He searched his waistcoat pocket, finding a fag. He lit it, inhaling the smoke deep into his lungs before trying to speak. "What has *any* of this to do with me?"

"My colleagues at Transdiff wish to interview you. Perform a few basic blood tests. And have asked me to inquire. That is all. I realize that you've refused genetic testing, and I respect that, but at least . . ."

He regarded her, the battle raging in her eyes. Curiosity, defensiveness, defiance—and shame—all fought for dominance. He took another drag, watching the cinders fall from the tip. He needed her allegiance . . . or at least her silence. If only while he worked on the book. Would she turn him over or keep quiet? He wasn't entirely sure.

Time, which had expanded for centuries, now seemed suffocating and compressed. So many years and he'd eluded exposure. More than four hundred, with the exception of the four and half under Handley's "care." And now? Gaelan knew all about the Transdiffs of the world—"big pharma." He'd read more than enough about the way they pursued research, things that would make Francis Handley blanch.

Flight was out of the question. No matter where he might venture, and in this day of TSA, TIA, and immigration clampdowns, how far *could* he actually get on forged papers and his wits? He was trapped, cornered; he'd be picked apart and studied, a twenty-first century scientific sideshow. And that would only be the start. He could not suppress his anguish as he imagined what the future might hold. A horror-movie scene unfolded in his mind's eye in slow motion: a small child, held down, strapped to a table. Large-bore needle digging into his spine, a piercing scream as the boy is infused with Gaelan's own DNA while he watches, helpless, from another gurney. The boy writhes in agony, only to seize and die, and then be discarded into a waiting incinerator. "No!"

"Mr. Erceldoune?"

Gaelan jumped at the sound of Anne Shawe's voice, the image disintegrating to dust. He could not allow it to happen. He'd always been hard on Simon for his single-minded desire to die. Now death seemed the only recourse possible, and for that he needed Dr. Shawe.

"Mr. Erceldoune, are you all right?"

Calm yourself now. They can prove nothing, but if she leaves, she takes your book. He sucked in his lower lip, biting down hard. *You must be indifferent or she'll know . . .*

"Sorry. I . . . I am still unwell from the accident. . . . I . . . I thank you for your . . . for your honesty. Of course, the very idea . . . " He forced a laugh. He knew how to do this—be the actor. He'd had years' experience at playing this part. "Completely absurd. Science fiction." *Change the subject, fast.* "Shall we get back to work on the book, then?"

He worked through the day as Anne sat nearby, reading. She'd promised not to disturb him, and she kept by her word and her distance. By the time he'd interpreted several more pages, he'd pushed Transdiff, and even

Anne, from his mind as merely theoretical threats. A few hours later and Gaelan finally detected a rhythm to the manuscript—not a code, really, but patterns in the illuminations and in the text.

The work went easier from there as barely remembered bits of knowledge were restored to memory, a new lock unfastened at every page, leading to the next and the next. Breathlessly, Gaelan navigated page to page toward some unknown horizon, feeling the breeze at his back. Each turn revealed a new discovery. Through a twenty-first century prism, the sophistication of the science in this ancient tome was breathtaking.

Viruses, bacterial infections, immunological disorders, cancers . . . impossibly described in detail within metaphorical images by now plainly readable to him, each accompanied by recommended treatments. Every bit of practical knowledge and understanding Gaelan had acquired over several lifetimes of study had become clues to the puzzle, from his earliest childhood tutoring sessions with his father and grandfather, to online coursework so extensive he could have by now earned at least two or three PhDs. Exhilarating. Intoxicating.

Then there were the references to chromosomes and genes: configurations of twenty-threes and forty-sixes in images hiding in plain sight among double helices that could only have been read as artistic motifs, alchemical markings—perhaps magic.

More peculiar still were the numerous references to Airmid and the Tuatha de Danann, images and heroic tales scattered throughout, antithetical to what was obviously a scientific text. But what if the legends and early histories were correct, and the Tuatha de Danann really were a far more advanced civilization than any other on earth at the time? Had they been exiled long ago, their knowledge deemed witchcraft in the tumult of the Dark Ages? Their enlightened understanding a gift refused . . . then rebuked?

Gaelan rubbed his weary eyes, stealing a glance at his watch. It was late, nearly five. He'd been at it for ten hours already. He looked up to see Anne sitting nearby, her iPad out, reading. He vaguely recalled sandwiches and coffee placed near his hand. And did not recall eating or drinking, though only crumbs remained in the dish and the cup was empty. He smiled at her thoughtfulness. Perhaps she wasn't the dire threat he'd imagined.

Remarkably, he'd made it nearly through the entire manuscript, and in one sitting. It was time to go back to Diana's tree and test his theory. He was ready.

And then he saw it as his eyes settled on an elaborate heather tree wound with infinite knots. Text braided itself in and out, twisting between the turns and loops. He placed a finger gently on what he believed to be the origin letter, and followed it, only to be directed five pages ahead. There he found another instruction, this one sending him ten pages backward, and then another. Back and forth through the pages as though he himself were weaving the words together. Finally, a fragment that led to a page toward the end of the book: "*Ag teastáil i ngach oideas de an mheascadh ar rud breise—eilimint enhancer.*"

Bloody hell. "A catalyst!"

"What?" Anne called from her perch.

"Nothing. I think . . . no, best not to say. Not yet. Give me some time." Fuck. He didn't need her hanging about his shoulder. Not now, not when he was so close. He watched as she went back to her reading. But she was no longer in repose. She would be waiting now for him to speak again. He brushed off concern and returned to the work. Deciphering this new business about a catalyst.

Of course. There was nothing straightforward about the book, so why would the recipes themselves be explicit? Each required a unique catalyst in order to work exactly right. But where? And how were they concealed?

He continued his scrutiny, squinting through parched eyes. Yes. *Yes!* There it was. Keyed not to this page, but to another—a multiple of five: two plus three. Another twenty-three reference. The enhancer—the catalyst—was, like all other necessary elements, embedded in the illuminations, but never on the same page as the recipe. But without the correct catalyst, the book warned, the resulting medication would be too potent, entirely ineffective, or unstable.

So that was what he had missed, what he'd never realized, and why in his case—and Simon's—the elixir had gone wrong. Was that what his grandfather had written into that scroll? Or what his father hadn't the opportunity to teach him before he'd been executed? Gaelan shook his head. "Bloody hell! It's brilliant."

"Let me in on the discovery?" In an instant, she was at his side.

Fuck. "Sorry. I . . ." What could he tell Anne that would not give him away? "It is a recipe book—"

Anne shook her head. "A what?"

"A pharmacopeia—a medical book, but much older than that Culpeper edition you had in your hands the other night. The inks, those within the illuminations . . ." He again explained his theory about the embedded inks.

"But would they still work? I mean this book is hundreds of years old—"

"I don't know. But I think, yes . . . I mean, why not? The book looks to be in fine enough condition—"

"And you got that all from the manuscript?"

Gaelan paused, breathless with the discovery. "Yes. It is all there. And not at all easy to get to. Each page is an enigma, and the key to the enigma is another enigma, but wrapped in a paradox, wrapped in another secret." He was grateful she had no bloody idea at all that, yes, it might well be all there in the text and illuminations, but it was incomprehensible without the essential body of knowledge he possessed in his head: ancient medicine, chemistry, alchemy, language, mythology.

"It's genius," Anne said, her eyes sparkling with excitement. "And you, sir, are brilliant! I cannot believe this book is mine, even if I might never completely understand it. Incredible!"

"Yours." He'd almost forgotten. Of course it was bloody hers. And there was nothing he could do to alter that. She would leave and take it with her, and again it would be lost to him, and now, when he finally understood. And what if she gave it to her colleagues at Transdiff? What would they do with its knowledge? *If* they could get to it. And that was one very big "if"—without him. And that was never going to happen. *Never.*

What good this book and its medicines might have done in its day had the world not been mired in fear and intimidation, inquisition and burnings. Had the Dark Ages not destroyed all sense of wonder and the fairy folk—the Tuatha de Danann and their kindred in all parts of the isles—might the Black Death never have plagued Europe, might all the great pandemics have been avoided? Enlightenment had been in humanity's hands, and humanity refused it, tossed it onto the pyre and lit the flame.

"I believe," he said finally, solemnly, "that the knowledge contained in this book—a millennium old if I am right—reflects a scientific wisdom long ago lost and only just now being reclaimed, bit by bit, by modern science."

"Whose wisdom?"

Gaelan laughed. "You'd be hard-pressed to think me sane if you . . . heard my theory. But trust my experience as an expert in my field; the value of this manuscript is beyond price. It is . . ." He hesitated, certain he would trip on his own excitement and confess it all if he didn't stop now.

"Are you okay?"

"I am. Yes. Fine. But for now, it is all slightly wild speculation. I need to confirm that I can properly read at least one of these recipes well enough to gauge the amounts, mix the right reagents, and create the intended formulation."

Gaelan opened to a page near the front of the manuscript. "This one appears less complicated than most. The required ingredients are fairly simple, and I believe I have all the needed solvents in my workroom, and the chemicals . . . in case I'm not correct about the inks or they are past their . . . shelf life."

Anne looked at him dubiously. "You're a bookseller, not a chemist—"

"Antiquities dealer, you forget." He smiled. "My dear Dr. Shawe, I have an entire chemist's arsenal. Never know when you might need a spot of nitric acid." He sprang from his chair, swept aside a curtain, and opened the door to his backroom, where he brought her to his workbench. His gaze swept the room, scanning it for anything potentially incriminating. "I also blend custom teas here . . . that spice tea you so enjoyed the other day." Could it have been only *yesterday*? He hoped she'd miss the crop of small marijuana plants sprouting beneath a growing lamp in the corner.

"I'm impressed, Mr. Erceldoune. This bench would fit nicely in any scientist's lab."

"Ah, here we are," he said, turning her attention to the work at hand: nitric acid, distilled water. "And if I am correct, the mercury and silver are embedded into the page. The classical method of creating a Diana's tree takes days, perhaps a week, but the text implies only a few minutes, so . . . you never know." He pointed out a passage in the middle of the page.

She shrugged.

Of course she'd have no clue. *She cannot see it.* He would make certain to keep it that way.

He mixed the solutions and carefully scraped away small amounts of the inks, placing them into a beaker. "Now," he said, taking a small scraping from a purplish ink on a different page, "the catalyst, or as they called it, the enhancing element."

They waited, perhaps only a minute or two before a tree materialized from the bottom of the beaker. Gaelan held his breath, quite spellbound, as the crystals formed and created the fragile and exquisite arborescent structure. Gaelan relished the unabashed delight in Anne's eyes as she observed the experiment. She reminded him in that instant of Eleanor that night so long ago, gazing at the stars—if only a little. She caught him staring and blushed, but did not turn away; instead she smiled with such radiance, he nearly forgot himself—and who she was—as he stood there transfixed, robbed of all ability to think or speak.

Simon's warning tugged at him. But this . . . this was like a chemical reaction, churning in a crucible as it raced toward equilibrium. It astonished him, even as he tried to ignore it, even as he warned himself that she meant only danger to him, perhaps his ruin. *The mantra. Remember that bloody mantra: professional distance.* He muttered it under his breath, hopefully too quiet for her to hear.

They needed a real test of the book. Not the simple magic trick of a Diana's tree, but a genuine medical recipe. He showed her a complex drawing, another ouroboros design. "This is to create a pain medication, on its face, a simple formulation by today's standards, yet here it is, in a book hundreds of years old. But here"—he pointed to another part of the page, a text boxed in blue ink—"here, it refers back to an image on an earlier page, a flower, something I would have missed had I not already translated that page. The specific elements I need to create the painkiller are on a different page. And the catalyst on yet another. But it is not consistent. That is why it is so important to follow it through step-by-step in proper sequence."

"Show me." Anne tried to follow his reasoning as he translated on the fly, asking questions about everything. "Salicylic acid!" she said, finally. "The properties of this formulation, taken together . . . aspirin! But how?" She shook her head, looking completely flummoxed and amazed.

The book proved something to Gaelan he had long believed about the alchemists in the family and why they always worked their trade as apothecaries. This was less a text on the alchemists' dream of making gold from lead or discovering some holy grail of life eternal, and much more about healing sickness. It was as Paracelsus said. *"Many have said of alchemy, that it is for the making of gold and silver. For me such is not the aim, but to consider only what virtue and power may lie in medicines."*

The next page described what seemed to be the symptoms of a Streptococcus infection. Anne, peering over Gaelan's shoulder, pointed to a series of small brightly colored circles within an elaborate rendering of fairies and gryphons. "Have I been so transported by all this that I can only conclude that those small circles represent cocci-shaped bacteria? Yet, it isn't possible for a centuries-old book to contain such images, not when microbiology was literally unknown until van Leeuwenhoek in the seventeenth century? I must be imagining it, yes?"

"Honestly, I don't know any more." Gaelan rubbed at his eyes and absently reached for a mostly empty beaker of solvent and missed, nearly tipping it over. Anne grabbed it before it fell to the floor. "I must be bloody exhausted. I could've sworn that was my coffee mug. And I could do with some caffeine, to be honest."

"Oh dear, we *have* been working at this for hours—*you* have been at this for hours; I have been a spectator in the cheap seats."

"No. You have been a help. My knowledge of medicine is limited at best—"

"Still, the tireless translations; you *are* exhausted. I can see it. Your hands are shaking. I must let you get some rest. Look. It is half five now; let's stop for the day. We can resume in the morning—"

"No. Please. I feel an urgency to do this right now . . . that I am close to—" He stopped himself.

"To what that can't wait until you've rested? Look. I'll take the book and your notes and type them into the computer—"

"No. Please. Do not take it from me." Gaelan had not meant to plead. "I'm sorry. I . . . I could not sleep even if I wanted to. The idea that I am so close—" He'd been good so far, not revealing much, despite his exhaustion and the thrill of rediscovery.

"Fine. Then I have a proposition for you. I shall stay here whilst you rest. Your flat is upstairs?"

"It is."

"Then let's go up there, and you can nap. I shall order us some dinner and type up the notes. I have my laptop right here. And then we can resume once you've had some rest—whether that's later this evening or tomorrow. You, sir, are on the verge of collapse, and that is my opinion as a physician."

"Very well." He stood too quickly, and the room spun. Too much coffee, not enough to eat, and no alcohol for two days had driven him right to the edge. Anne helped him catch his balance as he led the way to the stairs.

Finally, in the flat, Anne settled Gaelan onto the sofa. "What happened here?" she asked.

"I suppose it wouldn't do to tell you it's meant to be like that—organized chaos? An experiment in entropy?" She didn't look convinced. Or amused. He shrugged.

He'd had neither the time nor energy to tidy the mess from that horrible night. Papers and folders, books and electronics still lay scattered all over the living room floor: small piles, large hills . . . a disaster.

He had no inclination to explain the outburst that caused it. "You might find my library interesting," he said, trying to divert her attention. "And I could use some coffee."

"Coffee is the last thing you need."

He watched her peruse the bookshelves. *Good.* "My personal collection. None of these are ever for sale." He stood, stretching his arms, before going into the kitchen. "I have an excellent selection of small batch beans from a local roasters," he called from behind the pass-through counter as he rummaged in the cabinet above it. "What do you like? Guatemala Fair Trade? Perhaps Sumatra—the beans are already ground." *Sumatra it is.* He tapped several spoonsful of the grounds into a large capsule and set the pot on in place. *Five cups, I think.* He pushed the brew button and waited for the machine to do its magic as he watched Dr. Shawe continue to ogle his collection.

"Bloody hell!" she said finally, turning around and joining him at the counter. "Newton, Galen, Boyle, Huxley, H. G. Wells, Paracelsus! What an incredible . . . Where on earth . . . ?" She beamed excitement at the discovery. "I had no idea that H. G. Wells wrote anything other than science fiction."

"Wells wrote several biology texts. I have three of them—two of them unpublished manuscripts."

"How did you acquire this incredible collection? It must be worth a fortune!"

"One at a time. Can't remember, not really. I suppose over a period of years," he said evasively. How could he admit that each of the volumes had been a gift, a few autographed to him personally? Perhaps this was not such a keen idea, after all.

Gaelan poured two mugs of the aromatic brew, offering one to Dr. Shawe. She waved him off.

"And you definitely do not need any more caffeine, Mr. Erceldoune."

Ignoring her, Gaelan took two sips and thought better of the idea, leaving the mugs on the counter. She was probably right.

He propped himself on one elbow as he lay on the sofa, vowing not to sleep as he watched Anne discover his collection. He'd never had a woman up in the flat—or any flat, for that matter. Not since Caitrin. Decades upon decades living like a monk. Too complicated to get involved, too easy to fall in love and . . . what then? Much better to remain aloof. Keep his distance. *Yes, keep your bloody distance, Erceldoune! Do not let her get under your skin.* It was Simon's voice in his ear. God, he was tired.

"I find it incredibly hard to believe you're single," she said, again refocusing the direction of their conversation.

"I'm . . . I'm a widower." He hadn't meant to disclose that bit of information. *Fuck.* He was drifting, growing too comfortable with her up here.

"Oh. Sorry. I mean . . ." She looked stricken.

"Don't worry. It was . . . She's been gone for many years now."

Anne looked completely bewildered but didn't, fortunately, press the issue. "I should order dinner. But you should try to rest awhile, until the food arrives at any rate."

"Pizza place . . . number's on the fridge." He was nearly asleep when he heard the distant ringing of a phone.

CHAPTER 47

It was Paul Gilles.

"It's him, Annie. It's that Miracle Man bloke. From the accident. I have proof. Did you ever find him?" His voice was a sickening sing-song; she could visualize the Cheshire Cat grin plastered across his face.

"What are you talking about, 'It's him'?" Her heart sank.

"There's a daguerreotype, luv. Stuffed into one of the diaries."

"A what?"

"One of those old-fashioned sepia rotogravure things. And I'm holding it up right next to his photograph—Miracle Man's photograph. It's the same person; I'd swear to it in court."

"Paul, whatever are you talking about?"

"You bloody well know what. And you're hiding something. I know you; I know that voice. You've met him, haven't you? But the question is, why haven't you told us?"

"You're mad. I haven't . . . and I haven't found him. To be honest I never looked very hard. I managed to look at his charts—and don't ask me how—but that's the end of it. And you are aware I can't disclose anything from them without his permission. And until—"

"Bollocks. What is it? You want the discovery for yourself? Well, never mind. Doesn't matter. We've got him. That photo is a dead ringer for the Miracle Man. Mr. Gaelan Erceldoune of Evanston, Illinois. And if you're holding back from us—"

"Paul. I wouldn't; it's just that . . . you know, American legal bollocks. I cannot—"

"And his hand? The one with the missing fingers? Severed. It was the final experiment done by the physician at Bedlam on the 'the patient,' as the mad doctor calls him. Our Mr. Erceldoune, AKA Miracle Man. There was only one more entry beyond that. Some sort of screed on the injustice of gentlemen in medicine not wanting to get their hands dirty with lunatics and such. Methinks the mad doctor was a *mad* doctor."

"Don't be daft. Erceldoune would have to be at least two hundred years old, if this man was an adult when he was tortured. It's a reckless leap, and you know it. Have you discarded your scientific good sense along with your ethics?" But was it really such a stretch, given the latest research? If a human could regenerate tissue infinitely, was infinite life possible? She thought of her T. nutricula research—her immortal jellyfish. But tissue regeneration did not ordinarily suggest any sort of immortality. Salamanders die, despite their physical capabilities. Extrapolation to humans . . . well, could it be? She shook off the thought as fanciful, and Paul's wishful thinking for untold riches.

"I don't happen to think it's such a leap," he said. "And, even if it is, there's plenty of evidence to suggest further exploration."

"The photo cannot be very good if it's genuine and that old. Likely faded, easy to mistake. Don't jump the gun, Paul. I know you're good at it . . . being quick on the trigger," she added to emphasize the dig. "But I'd hesitate if you value your professional career. Does Lloyd know where you're going with this?"

"He does, and I'm on a flight to Chicago tomorrow night. Mr. Erceldoune has won a trip back home to the UK. He is coming to London. With me."

Oh God. She glanced at Gaelan's sleeping form. More peaceful than she'd seen him these last few days. But she needed to wake him up and warn him.

"You're making some awfully big assumptions, Paul. First, you have to find him, and then what if he doesn't want to go to the UK? Will you kidnap him? Would he even have a passport?"

"We'll figure it out when I get there. By the way, make any progress on getting hold of the contact I gave you—on that book of yours?"

"I don't need him. If you must know, I've found quite a brilliant scholar. And Mr. Er . . ." *Bloody hell.* Anne couldn't believe she'd nearly said his name. She tried to think of every possible other letter combination to make Er... "Sorry, not mister," she stammered. "*Dr.* Eric Luther." *Oh holy fucking mother of God.* Paul prided himself on knowing her so well. She hoped he was as wrong about that as he was right about everything else. The silence on the other end of the phone line dangled for endless seconds.

"Ah, so you have met him. And collaborating with him. Excellent. I knew you were hiding something. You were always a terrible liar, my love."

And then she heard it. At first, it was a low whimper, a cry, like a child trying to avoid a beating, getting louder. She clicked "End" on her mobile.

Then pleas, begging whoever it was to stop. "No. Not again. Please!" A low wail. Anne watched Gaelan thrash on the sofa, wondering briefly if he was having a seizure, but then she realized. Not a seizure, but some sort of waking nightmare—his eyes were wide open in terror.

Kneeling beside Gaelan, Anne softly called out his name, trying to engage him, whispering at first, then raising her voice very slightly. Nothing.

His forehead creased with tension, his mouth drawn into a tight line between his screams. The nails of his right hand bit into his palm, drawing a small trickle of blood.

The thrashing stopped, but now he was trembling. She wanted to pull the blanket up around his shoulders, but knew she shouldn't—it could make matters worse if she alarmed him. He must come out of this. Slowly and on his own.

An idea: perhaps she might sing to him, a low, lulling wordless tune, ancient, its twists and winds, lilts and trills almost harp-like, from the fairy folk themselves. It had always calmed her as a child when her grandmother would coo it into her ear.

Gaelan blinked, and slowly, slowly the tension receded first from his forehead, then his jaw; his grip loosened enough to let her apply pressure to the wounds on his hand, but when she looked, the wounds had vanished, leaving only incongruous streaks of dried blood running from the middle of his palm to the wrist. She shook her head in disbelief. *Bloody hell!* Rapid tissue regeneration—in a human? Had she really witnessed it? Proof seemed to stare her in the face, yet her scientist's mind wondered if she had only imagined it, and the dark streaks were simply inks from a very old book that had left their mark on his arm.

"Gaelan?"

His eyes focused on Anne's face, widening in horror as his gaze shifted to his arm and realization dawned. He threw off the blanket, staggering to the bathroom without a word.

"Please leave," he called out from behind the door.

"Gaelan. Listen to me!" She heard the water go on full force in the bathroom sink. She let him be, realizing this had not been the first such episode.

She heard the shower turn on, then off. More waiting. It had grown dark outside.

Finally the bathroom door opened and he emerged, hair wet but combed through. Vintage leather blazer, black faded jeans, dark blue dress shirt with aqua cuffs, as if he was off for an evening of clubbing.

He barely noticed her as he crossed the living room, or if he did, he ignored her completely, leaving without a word, slamming the door behind him. Anne stood alone amid the mess of his flat, feeling foolish and bewildered.

CHAPTER 48

Gaelan needed to walk. Find some peace from memories that seemed to be pursuing him with more vigor of late—since the discovery of the Bedlam diaries. And get away from Dr. Anne Shawe. He headed east toward the lake. Perhaps he would find comfort in the rhythm of the waves as they lapped onto the shore. At least this time he was on foot, and the likelihood of another catastrophic accident was minimal. The walking path above the lake was deserted—too cold, he guessed. Perfect for him, though. Bracing. Reviving.

An empty bench. He sat, grabbing a rock that caught his eye as it glinted in the starlight, its crystalline planes reflecting pink and blue. Some sort of calcite, he thought. He blew off the accumulated wet sand, cleaning the remains with his shirttail, examining it, wondering if it was more than just a simple rock. All rocks were more than they seemed. *What's hidden inside you? A geode, perhaps? Quartzite? Calcite? Either would be a rare find here on Lake Michigan, but not unheard of.*

He opened the heart rate app on his watch. One hundred eight. Better than it had been back at the flat, but not great. The hot shower had put an end to this latest episode. And Handley had faded from his vision. But the inevitable killer headache had been left in its wake. Fair trade. For now. But in his haste to escape the humiliation of facing Anne Shawe, Gaelan had neglected to take something for it. *Fuck.* He hurled the rock against a nearby tree, watching it shatter, its crystals disintegrate into tiny slivers. *Calcite.*

How could he go back and face her? What must she think? Fact was, he liked her. After more than a century avoiding entanglements, he had to be attracted to *this* woman. *All the gin joints in the world . . .* Despite the fact she worked for a company that would destroy him, despite the fact she'd ventured dangerously close to too many truths, these past two days had been . . . good. Welcome amid the chaos his life had become over the years. Exciting. The brilliant discovery, sharing it with someone who possessed the curiosity to still be amazed. And now? She must think he was completely unhinged. And now that he'd explained the book to her—or enough of it—she'd take it and disappear, and he'd never see it again. Or her. *Fucking Handley always wins.* He sighed, defeated.

Gaelan gazed up from the horizon; the twilight sky was breathtaking. Clear, with only a small sliver of moon to obscure the stars, their steadfastness a tether. Removing his iPhone to open his favorite astronomy app, he realized the battery was still dead.

He didn't really need an app to map the night sky, so long ago etched into his memory. Looking up and to the south, he squinted Vega into focus, so very bright, and then the Lyre. Then the bright orange-yellow of Boötes, and he knew he would find *it* just to the right. Ariadne's Crown.

His thoughts drifted to Eleanor—the Corona Borealis, their nexus into perpetuity, the skies never changing, his constant in the algebra of the universe.

That tune Anne had hummed to him—he knew that lullaby, and well. It had played in his mind so often over the years when he was at his most dispirited, always helping him to go on, put one foot in front of the other. Eleanor had murmured it so near his ear that night she'd comforted him just as he floated between wakefulness and sleep. She'd died never knowing what it had meant to him. A common enough English melody, he supposed, as he avoided projecting significance on it.

"Gaelan."

He turned, startled, as Anne sat beside him on the bench. The last person he wanted to see.

He shrugged, trying to ignore her, turning his attention to locating Venus. Or Jupiter. Or anything but her nearness.

"Thank you, by the way. For awakening me." His voice was a soft lilt barely above a whisper as he continued to scan the sky. *Ah, there's Venus.*

"I don't suppose you might want to talk about what happ—"

"No. I do *not* want to talk about it," he snapped, his concentration broken. She looked hurt; he'd not meant to snipe. She'd done nothing to deserve it.

Gaelan scooped up another stone from the pavement and propelled himself from the bench. He walked toward the water's edge, and she followed, standing at his shoulder saying nothing, so close he could smell the jasmine of her perfume as it mingled with the fertile, moist aroma of sand and algae, fish and chilled air. More intoxicating than any three tumblers of Lagavulin and twice as deadly. He sighed, drinking her in, every sensation magnified by her closeness. And she was so very close, her hand resting lightly on his arm. It had been meant to steady him, but instead breathed wildfire through his veins.

"Are you doing any better, Mr. Ercel . . . Gaelan?"

"Yes. All better now." He feigned a weak smile, noticing her use of his given name. He turned toward her, considering what to say. He wanted to trust her. "A long time ago . . . something terrible happened to me. It's nothing I can talk about, but sometimes . . . PTSD, I suppose."

Anne nodded, as if considering his words. She would soon probe him for more if he didn't veer away from what would soon become treacherous waters. He looked out toward the horizon again, watching the stars reflect on the black glassiness surface of the lake, so placid in the windless night air.

"If we stand here, at the water's edge, and look up and to the right slightly . . . Do you see that star, the one that's very bright and has an orange cast to it?" She nodded. "And then just to the south—"

"I'm not sure I see where you mean. . . . Can you . . . ?" Anne positioned herself in front of Gaelan. "Maybe if you might direct my gaze from a better angle." She barely kept her balance in her stiletto-heeled boots.

It had been a long time since Gaelan had been so physically near a woman. He grinned, reminded suddenly of Simon's perpetual teasing about his "monk's" existence. But it wasn't far from the truth. Easier to live without than yearn for something that would only cause more pain.

"Here." He took her right hand in his and moved it in the direction of Ariadne's Crown.

"What are we looking at? I can barely see anything!"

"It is called Corona Borealis, Ariadne's Crown. I was only just looking at it. It comforts me when my . . . PTSD turns especially ugly. Tethers me. Reminds me of someone . . . I once knew." She eased herself deeper within his arms, and he was transported to Simon's garden on that first night with Eleanor so very long ago, distantly aware he was conflating past with the present. And Anne, with her indigo eyes . . .

"Oh!" She giggled, losing her balance and catching Gaelan off guard as they both tumbled to the sand. "Ariadne's Crown?"

"You know the story from Greek mythology?"

She was practically sitting in his lap, making no attempt to move. Anne shook her head, her hair tickling his cheek. "Sorry, no. I slept through most of my classics courses." Keeping hold of his hand, she stood shakily, leading him back to the bench.

She reached over, gently turning his face toward her. A kiss would only bring disaster. He needed to break the intimacy that had enveloped them before he was completely lost. But nearly two centuries of resolve began to slip through his fingers as fine as the sand beneath his feet.

A bag of half-eaten French fries sat at Gaelan's left foot. He scooped it up and tossed one of the fries to a small rodent scavenging the beach. He was joined by a second. They fought over it, chattering noisily. He threw the entire bag their way, watching them do battle.

Anne slapped his hand playfully. "They'll get heart disease, and it will be all your fault!"

Feigning horror, Gaelan brought his hand to his chest.

She surprised him by entwining their fingers, a sensation so familiar, yet so new. *So much for professional distance.* Emboldened, Gaelan lifted her hand and brushed his lips along her fingers. But Anne replaced her hand with her lips, kissing him openmouthed, trying to deepen it. He hesitated, shyly pulling away, but only slightly.

Oh, get a fucking grip on yourself. She is the enemy.

But everything that had transpired between them contradicted the argument. It simply could not be true. Gaelan ran his tongue along her lower lip, savoring the taste.

Common sense fought its way back through the fog of desire. He could not let it happen. Must not. He broke contact, regretting it immediately.

"I'm sorry, I . . . What's the matter?" she asked dreamily.

"Say I am a bit old-fashioned." It was the weakest of excuses.

"Oh. I see. Well, I am not." Anne threaded her fingers through his hair, stopping to caress a particularly sensitive spot at the back of his neck, which shivered down his spine and right to his groin.

The battle was lost. Giving in to the sensations, he drew her into an embrace as her lips continued their relentless barrage on his mouth, his jaw, his neck. He moaned a low growl into her ear as he responded.

Do not get close enough to get involved had been his guiding principle since Eleanor. And those nearly two hundred years of avoidance mounted a final, futile assault on Gaelan's usual good sense. But the parched, arid land in which Gaelan had kept his heart for those many years began to quake and the ground tremble. He allowed Anne to lead him down the street, into the shop, and up to the flat.

"Look, Anne, I'm sorry," he protested without much bite as they entered his flat. "This is a bad idea. It has been—"

He reached for her other hand, holding them both in his, trying to stand his ground. She ignored the gesture, reaching past his barriers to brush her lips against his, soft and sweet.

The room spun; he was dizzy from emotions and desires, long denied. He gasped as she deepened the kiss, the flare of arousal assailing every nerve ending.

"Anne . . ." Decades of restraint, of refusal, evaporated in the white heat that flared between them. Grappling with clothing, they left a trail from the living room through the kitchen and into the small bedroom. It had been so very long, yet nature compensated for Gaelan's inexperience, thirst for her—for this—his guide as Anne's relentless fingers and lips plundered his vulnerabilities, and it was nearly enough.

Exhaustion, weakness from injuries still healing, the too-recent

PTSD episode, and the emotional toll of the last two weeks conspired against the pure flame of passion. Flushed and panting, Gaelan could not sustain the rhythm needed to complete the act.

It was over, leaving them both, he assumed, frustrated. A dismal failure. What could he expect? He was a wreck of a man, and very much out of practice—far too many years of celibacy. "I'm sorry, Anne." He sat up, facing away from her, his legs resting on the floor. "You can go now." There was no point to her staying, no point to trying to conceal the defeat and bitterness in his voice.

She reached out to him; he recoiled. Her cool, gentle hand at his back, her fingers tracing the lines of sweat as they traversed his spine were a keen reminder of his humiliation. Twice now in the span of hours she had seen him for what he was: a poor, deluded ruin of a man.

"Gaelan—"

He held up a hand, stopping her. "Please. I'd like to sleep. Alone, if you don't mind. I believe I've endured quite enough abasement for one day, don't you?"

"Okay . . . okay. You rest, and I will finish typing up the notes from today. Later—"

"No. There is no later," he said sharply. "Not today, anyway," he added, the edge gone from his voice. "Come back tomorrow, and we'll continue work on the book. Please. *Please.* Just leave me be."

"Okay, but let me finish the notes. You won't even know I'm here. Then I'll leave and see you tomorrow morning. Do try to sleep at least?" Anne's feet padded barefoot across the wood floor; the door closed quietly, and he listened for her footsteps on the tile, hoping she'd left him alone in his misery.

He held his breath, wondering if she would take the book and just leave. The coffee machine engaged, and he heard the comforting click of her laptop keys as exhaustion began to nibble at the edges of awareness. He sighed, reaching for the glass pipe on the nightstand. In the distance, he heard the sound of a mobile ringtone.

CHAPTER 49

Anne grabbed her phone on the second ring. Paul Gilles. *Bloody hell.* He purred with smarmy delight. "Hello, darling."

"Paul." She hated that self-satisfied voice of his. *What was it this time? What had the diaries revealed?* She shuddered. "To what do I owe this call? You do realize it's half two?"

"Not here, it isn't. We found it. The bloody fucking holy grail. A tissue sample."

"You're joking. A tissue sample almost two hundred years old? Is it even usable? I doubt it's the least bit reliable. And how can you be certain it is from—"

"It is a finger. Likely left-hand ring finger. And guess what?" There was a sinister, gleeful tone to Paul's voice that sent a shiver through Anne's spine. "We're running it through the gene sequencer. Now. We've got him."

Not again. She laced her tone with as much exasperated disdain as she could muster. "Paul, leave the poor man be. He's just been through a terrible ordeal and—"

"And walking around as if he'd skinned his knee? Indeed. We need him, and if you can't deliver one small—"

"What then? Kidnap? I do not want to hear this. It's why I left London in the first place—that and you. What are you doing? I don't even know you anymore. What you are planning goes beyond the bounds of *legitimate, ethical* scientific research."

She bloody well knew they'd already gone way beyond it, time and again. She knew considerably more . . . had seen considerably more than Paul could imagine she had. And if it came to it, she would leverage her knowledge to protect Gaelan.

"I'm hardly Mengele . . . and I know that's what you're thinking. *That* honor would go to the chap who chopped off—and very nicely preserved—a man's finger in the mid-1800s. I just want to know if it is your friend's missing finger in the jar. All I need is one small sample. Anything will do of course. Blood would be best, and don't tell me, Dr. Anne Shawe, PhD, MD, expert in telomeres, that you don't itch to know his genetic makeup."

"Of course I do, but I won't have anything to do with your bloody project. I know what Hammersmith—and you—have been up to, and if the authorities ever learned . . . If these last months have taught me anything, it is that I no longer wish to associate my name and reputation with Transdiff." Anne was shaking with fury. It was everything she could do to hold onto her mobile.

Paul's voice dropped to a whisper, the sneer gone, replaced by something far more sinister. "What do you mean? What do you *think* you know?"

Shite. "Nothing. Only that I know it was the worst mistake of my life hooking up with a wanker like you. I am only the worse for it."

"I'm on a midafternoon flight. I cannot wait to meet your Mr. Erceldoune and verify how he lost three fingers from his left hand."

"How much does Hammersmith know of what you told me?"

"Why, all of it, of course, my darling. You don't think *I* would hold back any important information from our employer, do you?" The dig hit its mark.

"Look," she said, quietly opening the door to Gaelan's bedroom, hoping he was still asleep. He looked restless, but not awake. "That book he's been helping me with? You've no idea what he's discovered in it. It's incredible—beyond amazing. We need him on our side. His value is far beyond any anomalous physiology he may or may not possess. And if you harass him or try to force him into something he wants no part of, he'll bolt, and there will go any chance of—"

"That's great about the book, but it changes nothing. He *will* be coming back to London with us, and I guarantee you, it is in his best interests to do it. I'll see you in . . . twenty hours, give or take. Look, darling"—Paul's tone turned ingratiating and sweet—"don't suppose you'd be keen to pick me up at the airport?"

"Not bloody likely." She clicked off.

Paul and Hammersmith had tossed aside any sort of ethical compass long ago, and she could only imagine what they had in mind for Gaelan Erceldoune. They'd not rip him apart like that sadist in Bedlam. They were far too civilized for that. But if they genuinely believed that Gaelan Erceldoune was the real deal, a man who had lived for centuries . . .

Science had not progressed so far that the greedy could not dream of the philosopher's stone of ancient alchemy and the guarantee of limitless wealth and life eternal. She shuddered to think of the Pandora's box that would open if Transdiff really were that close to having an Elixir of Life.

There would be time enough in the morning to warn Gaelan. For now, he needed to rest, without her intrusion. Anne was anxious; there was no way she would sleep. She needed something to occupy her hands and the hours until dawn. Although she'd never been very excited about housework, she had to admit, Gaelan's flat was a disaster that needed serious tending.

She'd known him only a few days, yet she was more drawn to him than she'd been toward Paul Gilles or anyone she'd ever known. Anne picked her way through the mess on his floor, trying to create neat piles, placing them on his desk, without trying to read anything. More papers. An iPad. A photograph . . . a very *old* photograph. A rotogravure image, perhaps from the nineteenth century, she thought. Sepia, barely visible beneath the faded, cracked, and yellowed surface.

Except for the face. That was clear enough. A Victorian-era woman standing in a garden, not young, not really beautiful, yet her smile was so genuine, her eyes so warm, almost liquid. Her long hair, dark in the image, hung loosely down to her shoulders; she was clad in a simple dress that seemed to billow away from her, perhaps in a breeze. She wore a bonnet and carried a bouquet of daisies. There was something very familiar about her, as if she'd seen that face somewhere. . . . Of course, everyone had those photos stashed in albums and hanging in frames. Victorian grandmamas or spinster aunts from a long-ago era.

And they all had the same pose—always carrying a basket of flowers. *De rigueur*. Still . . .

She needed better light. Under the bright fluorescence of Gaelan's magnifying lamp, the image became clearer. Yes. The face was familiar. But impossibly familiar. It could not be. Staggered, Anne lost her footing, falling backward into a high-back wing chair, the photograph clutched to her chest.

It would be morning back home, and her mother would be having coffee with her cousin Diana, who knew everything about everyone in the family tree. Perfect. She opened Skype on her phone and clicked her mother's icon, waiting as the app reached across the Atlantic.

"Mum!"

"Annie! Is everything all right? Good heavens! What time is it in America? It must be middle of the night!"

"Yes, I'm fine. Fine. Erm . . . Look. I've come across an old photograph . . . at . . . a friend's house. And I could use a quick sanity check."

"Why? Whatever is going on, luv? You sound quite strange."

"It's been a rather strange few days indeed, and I'll tell you all about it when I can talk longer, but do me a favor and have a look at this photograph, would you? Does this person look familiar to you? I think it looks awfully like Gran." Anne held the image up to her phone, hoping it would transmit clearly enough.

"Well, it might be, but firstly, the clothes are all wrong. That woman is dressed very definitely nineteenth century—early nineteenth century, I should think. Gran was born in the 1930s. So it cannot be her, unless they're all in fancy dress, but I admit, it looks quite a bit like her. Hang on, I'll ask Di. We're having coffee, as always this time of day, but she's out in the garden admiring my Norfolk tulips. Perhaps I can wrest her from them."

Anne waited, feeling suddenly foolish. The woman in this photo was probably Gaelan's great-great-grandmother or other ancestor, fallen out of some photo album and into the chaos on the floor. It was sweet, in any event, she thought, he would keep an old photograph like that. *Hmm.*

"Annie, I've got Di here."

"Hallo, Annie. How is Chicago, luv?"

"Fab. Di, would you mind having a look at this old photo I've found? I'll hold it to the phone. I could swear it looks like my grandmother, but obviously it is not, as my mum just pointed out. It's probably nothing to do with us, but—"

"Well, let's have at it, then. You never know where the family tree spreads, and—" Once again, Anne held the photograph up to her phone and waited.

Silence for a long moment. Anne removed the photo to see Di, whose eyes were wide in astonishment, a hand over her mouth. She had never known her gregarious cousin ever to be struck dumb about anything—or anyone. Until that moment.

"Di?"

"Call you back. Wait. No. Have you . . . I will e-mail you something in about five minutes. Stay right where you are. I know *exactly* who that is. But how on earth . . . ?"

Anne wandered the room, carefully avoiding the remaining piles of papers on the floor, suddenly in no mood to tidy. She checked her wristwatch. Ten minutes had passed. Why hadn't she heard back from Di?

Her gaze drifted to Gaelan's bookshelves, as neatly organized as the floor was an entropic mess. She scanned the spines, fascinated by the elaborate gilded engravings on some of them, each a work of art.

She removed a volume: Arthur Conan Doyle. *The Return of Sherlock Holmes*. She loved Holmes.

She opened it, finding on the inside cover an inscription in a flowery hand. She read it and read it again, and a third time. "To my sceptical friend and favourite apothecary-alchemist, Mr Gaelan Erceldoune. Some day you shall know me to have spoken true—mark here my words." At the bottom of a longer passage, the initials "ACD." *Arthur Conan Doyle.*

Each bit of circumstantial evidence clicked into place, from Paul's damnable finds to this photograph . . . and then there was the matter of his recovery, which she'd seen evidence of with her own eyes. And now this. Still she tried to convince herself that the inscription was meant for Gaelan's grandfather. Yes, that would make some sense, would it not? But the truth of it hit her like a lightning bolt. Any of these alone could be refuted, but all together . . . She was torn. She had the fucking holy grail of genetics in the palm of her hand . . . and in the next room, a man who would be destroyed with public revelation of the discovery.

Anne blinked back surprise just as a text came through followed by her phone's signal, startling her in quick succession.

"Annie! Did the photo come through? It is quite old, I grant you that, but I daresay it is the same woman."

Anne squinted into the screen of her phone, suddenly thrilled she'd opted for a large screen. "Who is she?"

"Her name was Lady Eleanor Douglass, and she was born in the early nineteenth century. Tragic story. Some miscreant murdered her first husband, an earl, out for revenge, it is said. It's all rather hazy and part of the family skeletons, you know. But it all turned out right for her in the end, or so says the family legend. She would be your great-grandmother's great-grandmother's grandmother . . . or something like that. She had four children: three girls and a boy." Di stopped, as if just then realizing the strangeness of Anne having a photograph of this woman. "But Annie, dear! How on earth did a photograph of Eleanor Douglass come into your possession, and in America of all places? Good heavens!"

"That, my dear cousin, is an excellent question, and one for which I've no answer—at least not yet." Anne's hand trembled as she held the phone, shaking her head in disbelief at this latest revelation. "Thank you, Di. Would you put Mum on the phone?"

"Annie, darling, what is going on?"

"I've no bloody idea, Mum. None whatsoever! I need to go. I'll ring you later. I promise." She continued to stare at the texted photograph as she sat on the sofa, shaken to the core.

CHAPTER 50

Anne padded quietly into Gaelan's bedroom, noting the faint aroma of hashish; no wonder he was sleeping soundly. She studied him, still coming to terms with the fact she was staring at a man possibly two centuries old.

On the other hand, it would certainly explain some things, including "rare books and antiquities." A perfect cover for a man not of this century. His old-fashioned courtliness, the occasional formal manner of his speech, the books—the signed Conan Doyle. She shook off the idea as bollocks fueled by Paul's morbid zeal. But she knew there was far too much coincidence for it to be coincidence.

But the photograph was much more difficult to explain away. Who was this Eleanor Douglass to Gaelan Erceldoune? Perhaps she was a distant relation many times removed, and nobody special. If Di had an aged photograph of this woman, why not Gaelan? So she and Gaelan were related somehow. A little strange, perhaps. A small world. And that could explain why she felt drawn to him—a sort of shared genetic history, and a far more likely proposition than the possibility he was a two-hundred-year-old immortal being.

Her mind drifted to Paul's phone call. She wondered what Trans-diff might do to coerce Gaelan's cooperation. Would they go to the press with it, knowing he'd be hounded by the media until a trip to London, all expenses paid, would be a welcome escape into some sort of protective, gilded cage?

Paul would do it, threaten to reveal it all to the tabloids, or slip it anonymously, photos and all, expose decades of a hidden life, then offer protection, privacy. Money. Guarantees that would all be genuine . . . to a point.

If Gaelan was really that man from the diaries, he'd likely agree to almost anything once backed into a corner. What an awful constellation of possibilities Gaelan Erceldoune had before him. Trapped in an intricate labyrinth with no means of escape.

Gaelan shivered in his sleep, almost a flinch. *What dreams do you dream, Gaelan Erceldoune? What horrors you must have endured. Is that what you see when you close your eyes, even decades and decades later?*

Slipping in beside him, she tried not to awaken him or get close enough to startle him. But she wanted to be near when he awoke.

Why would morning not come?

Then there was the book. This extraordinary manuscript Gaelan Erceldoune alone seemed able to understand, his mind flying through its acrobatics when none of the scholars—not one—she'd consulted could make heads or tails of it. And he'd been so keen on it that first moment he'd seen it. She'd thought it a bit peculiar then, for him to be so immediately . . . enraptured. Was that the word? What was his connection to the book, which was—of course—also connected to her family?

Gaelan moved, awakening, finally with a catlike, languorous stretch, rolling to his side, facing her now, his long hair a veil across his eyes. Another stretch, followed by a yawn. He blinked and switched on a bedside lamp.

"Hey," he whispered, yawning again, looking puzzled, but not annoyed, a sleepy smile crossing his face. "You're still here? What time is it?"

"Half five," she responded softly. "Hope you don't mind. I was lonely, and your sitting room is a bloody mess. Thought it might use a woman's touch." She smiled down at him. "I wanted to be here when you awakened. Much, much has happened since you fell to sleep."

"Not quite awakened." He yawned. "*Too* bloody early." He pulled the duvet over his shoulder. "Nearly four hours without waking, though, a new record for me, I think. Thank you."

"What for?"

"You must be the reason." His voice was soft, still floating between sleep and wakefulness. The smile turned playful. And still more than a little stoned, she guessed.

"I—"

He lifted an arm, inviting her in.

"Gaelan, we have much to talk about—"

"Can it not wait?"

She *had*, after all, planned on giving him until dawn to sleep, and he was quite persuasive. Anne could think of far worse things than to snuggle beneath the blankets. And he seemed in no mood to discuss much of anything. *Fine.* Settling in closer, she allowed Gaelan to draw her near; he was warm, cozy, and it felt spectacularly comfortable and right. *No more than half an hour!*

"You seem to be doing better."

"I am. No monsters in the closet this time. Perhaps I *do* have you to thank—"

"And whatever it was you smoked in that bowl." She gestured to his nightstand.

He shrugged sheepishly. "I do what I have to do. But it is rather good hash."

"Do you have them often? The dreams?"

He gently kissed the corner of her eye—the first of a pattern, a trail that led down her jawline to her neck and shoulder. His hand followed, deft, delicate—she wondered if he was not actually touching her, but transmitting pure sensation as his fingertips floated above her skin. All other thought was being pushed from her mind by the feathery tingle of Gaelan's hands and lips.

"Gaelan—"

"Shh. Can you not see, lass, I'm quite occupied?" His voice was dreamy; it flared through her every nerve ending.

Her brain protested that this was not a good idea, but her body refused to listen, seduced by Gaelan's tender, slow, insistent ministrations. They had no time for it. What if he was unable to . . . and it made matters worse? What if . . . ? Her questions went unanswered as he popped the buttons of her blouse, punctuating each pop with his devastating mouth, each kiss sending a kick of pleasure through her core.

He paused suddenly, confronted with her brassiere, as if uncertain how to free her from it. Abandoning any thought of resistance, she assisted, demonstrating the art of unclasping the garment while on her back.

"Ah!" He smiled, observing, taking it from her, examining it as if it were a novel plaything, before tossing it aside to wrestle with her jeans and panties.

Had he never seen a bra before? Another clue in the puzzle that was Gaelan Erceldoune. She shook off the idea as Gaelan continued his exploration of her body. She surrendered all rational thought as his tongue found every sensitive spot.

She danced on the edge of ecstasy, aching and pulsing with desire. He hesitated a moment, sitting back on his knees, looking at her. He was beautiful as he sat poised between her knees, aroused, his pupils black, and dilated with desire. Yet he seemed to falter. He was unquestionably ready, but there was clearly something on his mind.

"Are you okay?"

He nodded. "Sorry. It has been a long time for me, not counting . . . earlier, and I don't know that I can—"

"Here, let me." She reached for him, and he inhaled deeply as he let her guide him, as if he were a virgin. She gasped as he filled her, and she felt whole in a way she'd never felt with Paul. Their rhythm built to a crescendo as he took her to the edge, then pulled her back and left her in delighted frustration until finally they fell together, not into a black void, but into the warmth of light buoyed by each other.

They were both panting, drenched in sweat and each other as he rolled to his side, propping himself on an elbow. He curled his hand through her hair, drawing her into a last, deep kiss. "Good morning," he said finally.

Anne sat up. She ran her thumb down his face, temple to cheek, cupping his jaw. A final kiss. "That was . . ." From the corner of her eye she could see the faintest light begin to seep through the blinds into the room. "We have to talk." She sat up cross-legged, running her fingers through her hair shakily. "A very lot happened, my darling, whilst you were sleeping."

He pulled on his T-shirt, his gaze no longer dreamy, attention focused on Anne.

What to say first? She wanted desperately to know about the photograph, but she needed to warn him about Paul. Maybe he could get away, go somewhere . . . something. Even if Paul's—now very much plausible—theory was wrong, it didn't matter. Gaelan's regenerative abilities were so unusual that he would never be allowed to escape examination. If he was right . . . "Two things, one urgent, the other, a coincidence so strange you will never believe it." She located their clothing tangled beneath the blanket at the foot of the bed. She tossed his clothes to him, and dressed quickly.

"Urgent. What is it?" She watched the blood drain from his face, as if he had some inkling. He was about to stand; she stilled him.

"First the urgent. My ex. Paul Gilles—"

"Yes. The chap with the diaries."

"He's to arrive from Heathrow in only a few hours."

"Why? And what does that have to do with me? Do you think he'll challenge me to a duel?" Gaelan reached for her, but she batted his hand away.

"My darling, this is more serious than anything you might imagine." It was clear from his worried expression that he quite understood. Probably more than he intended to let on. "He has a photograph—an old photograph found with those Bedlam diaries, and the man appeared to be . . . Well, according to Paul, it appeared to be . . . you." She said it quickly, as if to do so would make it easier. It did not.

"I see."

His mouth opened into an O, as if he intended to say something more. He looked away.

"There's more."

No reaction at all. He sat on the edge of the bed, staring at the wall. There was no easy way to do this. Out with it—for all its ghoulishness. "He also discovered tissue samples. Preserved, apparently quite expertly for the time." She rose and moved, crouching in front of him so he could not avoid her gaze. "One finger, left hand. The samples match a journal entry made . . . the final clinical entry by the doctor of record. . . ."

Gaelan closed his eyes for a moment, his face ashen. He stood, steadying himself on the bedpost, and silently finished dressing. Ignoring Anne, he went wordlessly into the bathroom, closing the door quietly, as if to slam it would break the silence now surrounding them.

"You have to leave before he lands." No response. "I know this is a shit hand. Even if you are not the man in the diaries, the simple fact of . . . your recovery from the accident . . ." She went to the bathroom door and knocked shouting his name. No response. She tried the knob; the door was unlocked.

He was sitting cross-legged on the floor, back against the claw-foot tub, elbows propped on his knees, head in his hands. He seemed unaware she'd come into the room. After putting down the lid on the toilet, she sat close to him.

"I saw in your library a book autographed by Arthur Conan Doyle. 'For strange effects and extraordinary combinations we must go to life itself, which is always far more daring than any effort of the imagination,' it said. Are you the improbable truth that remains after I have eliminated all else? Can you possibly be that man described in the Bedlam diaries? Did Conan Doyle inscribe that to you? With you in mind?"

No response. He simply stared ahead, withdrawn into someplace deep inside himself.

Anne slid to the tile and lifted his chin, looking deep into his eyes.

He nodded slowly and sighed; her heart broke as she saw the defeat in his expression. The game was no longer afoot; it was up. And he believed he'd lost, running out of places to hide. "Handley," he said simply.

Anne shook her head, not understanding.

"His name was Handley. Francis Handley, mad doctor of Bedlam." He was speaking as if to himself.

"You must get out of here—"

"Wait. You mentioned there was something else?" His voice was unsteady, as if processing that there was something, perhaps even more unimaginable, she'd not yet said.

She took his hand, and he allowed her to lead him back to the bedroom. "There's something I need to ask you."

His eyebrows arched as he shook his head. "More?"

Anne wondered how much more he could handle. He looked shell-shocked, like a bombing victim trying desperately to make sense of his surroundings. "You'll see." Would it be too much to show him the photograph of Eleanor Douglass? Her medical training—and her heart—told her he was teetering upon a razor-thin cliff, but would the connection draw him away from that dangerous place or push him over the edge? She wasn't sure.

Anne left and came back into the room with the two photographs of Eleanor Douglass. Sitting on the bed, she grasped his right hand, carefully entwining their fingers. "Who is she?"

He glanced at the daguerreotype before him, quickly looking away. He answered simply, as if from a dream. "Someone from another lifetime."

Anne held her breath, taking the other image from her lap and placing it on his. "Is this the same woman?"

CHAPTER 51

In the photograph, Eleanor Bell Braithwaite stood between Simon and a man Gaelan did not recognize. She wore an exquisite wedding gown; her eyes, so sad and beautiful, seemed distant for so happy an occasion. She held in her arms an infant, draped in white lace.

Gaelan blinked back tears as he touched the screen of Anne's phone, caressing the image of Eleanor. He walked away, out of the room, after taking the phone from her hand, his gaze never leaving the screen. Opening the glass doors, he went out on his terrace, staring into the dawn sky, overwhelmed. He knew he had to say something, but had not a clue where to begin.

He heard Anne step out onto the small balcony. He cast a backward glance to see her standing on the threshold observing him with solemn eyes, such a beautiful deep, dark blue. He turned back, gazing east toward the lake, at the low-hanging clouds, ominous, yet magnificent in the early-morning light: dark purples and greens, pinks and reds.

"Who are you?" she asked quietly, now at his shoulder, her hand resting upon his arm. There was no accusation in her voice, only compassion.

He had answered that question only twice before, once to Simon and the other to Eleanor. The world was more sophisticated than it had been in 1625, when people merely ran away frightened. Or threw you on the pyre to burn. But now, as then, the urge to pick apart and study anyone who was "different" overpowered men's good judgment and nobility, no matter that the object of curiosity was a flesh-and-blood human being.

Some would call his condition—and Simon's condition—a gift from God. And some would yet risk all, would steal or murder—or torture—to obtain the faintest clue. The holy grail. The philosopher's stone. The Elixir of Life. It had so many, many names. To him, to Simon, it was a curse—an existence in limbo.

For Gaelan, the curse was to live without love, without family. His compensation, though meager at best, was to experience the joy and delight of discovering in each successive generation the evolution of science and technology: electricity, flight, space exploration, movies, computers, etc. The incredible advances he'd witnessed had been enough to lighten the burden of a life lived too long. But it had not filled the void of a heart empty for well over a century. Since the day Eleanor died. . . .

She had been ninety, and Galan had not seen her in sixty years. Simon was angry he'd shown up then—1902—when there had been no word from him in all those years, not even a note. Had Simon not realized, even then, that Gaelan was in a hell that not even Dante might have imagined? Cut off, isolated, apart from everything and everyone he cared about, even his own daughter? He was supposed to be dead, and he needed to stay that way. What else might he have done?

"Do you think this has been easy?" He'd argued bitterly with Simon upon his arrival. "Look at me! I look the age of her grandchildren. How would that have gone with her, I ask you, hmm? I need to see her!"

Simon grasped Gaelan by both his arms gently, imploring, "Leave her be, Gaelan. Leave her to die in peace."

Gaelan swallowed hard, looking up into Simon's cold eyes. "You think I've not had regrets?" He held up a hand, calmer now, and Simon released him. "How many times," he confessed, tears gathering, "how many times I booked passage . . . only to turn back at the last moment. But I could not let her go to her rest without seeing her *one last time*. I need to tell her . . . How can I let her die without telling her not a day has gone by when I've not thought of her, gone to sleep with her face in my dreams?"

Simon nodded. He sat next to Gaelan, placing a comforting hand on his back. "She's upstairs in her old room."

He returned to the drawing room an hour later shaken, as if his heart had been ripped to shreds. "She's gone," he said finally, voice hoarse and choked. "She's gone," he repeated, falling into the arms of the sofa, his body shaking with sobs, inconsolable.

"I know you loved her, Erceldoune," Simon had acknowledged finally. "And I suspect that, though she has never confessed it to me, her eldest child—Ariadne—might well be yours. I know the two of you . . . At any rate, she was born in March the year following your departure."

The sweet, sad memory faded to a blur of dull grief as Gaelan noted Anne now standing by his side, her hands on the railing. "The sky is beautiful at this time of day, Gaelan. Remarkable, the clouds, the sun just breaking the horizon. What an amazing view to greet you every morning."

"How is it you came by this photograph, Anne?" He tried his best to keep the chaos raging inside him from seeping into his voice.

Anne quirked an eyebrow. "Why don't we go in and sit a minute? But we've not much time."

He nodded, again allowing her to take his hand.

"This photograph," she began, "is of my great-grandmother's great-grandmother's grandmother Lady Eleanor Douglass."

Anne's ancestor, Eleanor? But how?

"But why do *you* have her photograph?" she asked.

"It is a very long story, Anne, and I am not certain we have time." He was still riveted to the image, so clear—much clearer than his battered old photo, stolen from Simon's study the morning he'd left for America. "Suffice to say, I loved her, and I had a daughter with her, born in 1843." There. He'd said it. Honestly as he knew how. "Had I told you a week ago, you'd have thought me quite delusional. Bloody hell, you might yet."

A horrifying thought crossed Gaelan's mind as he paced from the settee to the window and back, refusing to look at Anne. Finally, he came to a halt in front of her. Horrified.

"No! No, no, no. This cannot be. I understand that you are *her* descendent, but is it possible you are mine as well? My God!" *What a cruel, cruel irony that would be!* After nearly two hundred years in the desert, to be falling in love with a woman quite possibly his great-great . . . however many greats-granddaughter? He scrubbed the heels of his hands into his eyes, trying to comprehend it all. It was impossible.

"Gaelan. Come back to me. Focus. The book. Is that connected to all of this, somehow, do you think? Is that why it's been in my family—because of this strange connection? Paul believes there is mention of it in those diaries. A magic book of some sort."

Finally, he laughed harshly, shaking his head. The final piece of the puzzle had set in place for her at last. "Ah, the book. I am certain that somewhere in the diaries there is mention of it. But so much of everything that happened during those five years is a blur."

He blinked away an image of Handley's face as it slithered into his vision. "Yes, the book is, in fact, mine; it went missing immediately not long before my . . . my captivity. It was 1837. But I cannot say how it ended up in your cousin's attic. I have been seeking it myself for nearly two centuries, both here in North America and in the UK, but never found it. It is why I became a rare books dealer in the first place. I'd always held out a hope, but never, ever a clue, a valid lead . . . to the one manuscript in the world that really means anything to me."

"A moment." Anne grabbed her messenger bag, taking from it a sealed envelope. "This was tucked into the book when I first discovered it. It was sealed, and I felt . . . I had no right to open it. But my heart tells me you are the intended recipient."

Gaelan took the envelope with trembling hands, his heart racing. He ran his thumb over the words "To Papa," but he couldn't manage opening it. He was shaking too badly. *Ariadne.* "Would you . . . ?"

She opened the envelope, handing it back to him before turning toward the bedroom.

"Anne, stay. You've every right to know what is in this letter." He scanned the page, his eyes too filled with longing and emotion to make out the words. "Would you . . . ?"

Anne took the paper, stained with age and tears. "Of course." She read, stopping several times, the words choked in her throat:

"My dearest Papa, I do not know if this book shall ever find its way into your hands. I came upon it three years after my mother's death. She had long ago told me who you are, and what you did for her. For us. But she refused to divulge how I might find you—not even your name. Mama told me that you must dwell in secret.

"Recently, I learned of a half brother, here in my old age. Your son, he told me. Iain he is called. Lord Iain Kinston. And it is from him I acquired this manuscript, your book. He said it was given him by a man you knew who wished only to return it to you from his safekeeping. I tried to explain to Lord Iain that I did not know you. But he told me how his family had badly wronged you, and that he did not deserve to keep so precious a gift. And so I hold fast to this book, and although I am now past seventy, and a great-grandmother, I cannot help but wonder at times if you are nearby or if I only dream it.

"I leave this letter for you in hopes that, should this book someday find you, you shall understand you were cherished and loved—and sore missed. With love and affection, Your Ariadne."

"My son, Iain . . . but he died. I was told . . . I was certain of it. But how is it possible?"

Gaelan remembered the day he'd returned to Kinston's estate. He'd found Caitrin's grave easily enough, but never Iain's. Then Kinston's lackeys came, and the arrest and all else happened in such quick succession he'd never given it any more thought. He'd assumed the worst, of course, that Iain had been disowned and thrown into a pauper's grave, never thinking that Kinston would raise him as his heir. Then it came back to him in a flash of memory. The family watching him being led off the Kinston estate. He'd thought it odd they'd include a servant to enjoy the spectacle, but there she'd been, and holding a baby in her arms. Might that have been his Iain?

His son . . . an earl? This was unbelievable. And Iain and Ariadne had met. It warmed him to know that. But of course they were now long, long in their graves. He closed his eyes, trying to shut out the grief of sons and daughters, grandchildren, great-grandchildren all dead. None of whom he'd ever known. He wept for them all.

Anne interrupted his thoughts. "Gaelan, we must go, and soon."

He nodded slightly, allowing her to brush away his tears.

"You say the book is yours," she said, "and I gladly return it to you. But I must ask the question, given what we've discovered about it. Is there a connection between the book . . . and your condition?"

Gaelan explained how he'd used the book—and how it had changed him, never mentioning Simon. No need to involve him in this mess.

The telephone interrupted, and Gaelan jumped, startled by the jarring sound. He fell upon it to answer before it rang a second time.

"It's Simon." There was something not right about his voice. "We have to talk. Now."

"I'm not alone," Gaelan whispered. "Hang on." He placed his hand over the mouthpiece of the portable phone. "Anne, I have to take this call in private."

She nodded and went back out to the veranda, closing the glass doors behind her. Gaelan went into his room, his eyes on the bedroom door. "What is it?"

"Transdiff Genomics."

"The firm researching the diaries. Anne . . . Dr. Shawe, she—"

"Yeah. Her. She bloody works for them. Have you any idea what they're up to?" Gaelan noted a rising panic in Simon's voice he had never before heard.

"I do. I was going to ring you up as soon as the hour was decent and I was sure you weren't going to throttle me for waking you."

"I've been researching my new novel, and I came across something disturbing enough, but I've only just come across another . . . This firm . . . they're actively engaged in medical experimentation on humans. Without consent. Children stolen from their beds, purchased from desperate parents trapped in distressed countries. Injected with infectious cocktails . . . I am sending you a link to the site now. Check your e-mail. And you must get as far away from this Anne Shawe as you can. . . ."

Gaelan hung up and padded into the sitting room. He opened

Simon's link, eyes widening as he read a blog, dated three years ago. Had Anne known the sorts of atrocities committed by her firm in the name of science? He refused to believe it.

But it made no difference if Transdiff was on its way to Chicago. *Fuck it all!* The connections all clicked into place. He pushed open the veranda doors, a decision made.

Anne turned. "Are you all right? Who was on the phone?"

"Anne, the ouroboros book cannot fall into Transdiff's hands— under any circumstances, given what you've told me of them, especially. It should not fall into anyone's hands. It must, in fact, be destroyed."

"Destroyed? Who was that on the phone?" she asked again, and a frisson of suspicion swept up Gaelan's spine.

"It doesn't matter. A friend . . . an associate." He sucked in a breath. "What do you know of Transdiff dabbling in human medical experimentation?" Gaelan sought her eyes for the truth.

She sighed, turning her back to him. "I learnt of a project, supposedly defunded three years ago, a year before I joined the firm. Two months ago, I was copied on something I shouldn't have been. Saw files not meant for my eyes. No one at Transdiff knows I had any inkling. I tried to tell you. . . . It was why I asked to be detailed to the Salk Institute. I—"

Rage and revulsion grabbed Gaelan by his stomach and twisted. He was nauseous. "But you said *nothing*?" he managed to sputter. "Do you not know that inaction is as much—" He punctuated each word with all the outrage he could muster. "That silence is complicity? Have you any idea what those children . . . those parents . . . ? Dear God, the suffering." Any tender feelings he had for Anne evaporated into scorn. She had stood by and allowed it to continue. Looked the other way when she had the power to stop it!

She looked beaten. *Good.* "Gaelan, you must go! Before Paul arrives."

"Leave. Now. Before I—"

"Listen to me. There is so little time. But I cannot allow you to think that I would perpetuate . . . If they find out, my life is over. Destroyed. They will kill me, quite literally."

"What are you talking about?"

"I have been leaking information to Physicians for Humanity for weeks. I've not been allowed to tell anyone—for my own safety as well as to protect the information. The posting at Salk was my way out, so I would be away before their report was issued."

She clasped his hand; he yanked it from her. "You can verify my story. I'll give you my contacts with the organization. But only after you are safe from Transdiff. Until then, you don't have to trust me, but please believe that you are in grave danger. But not from me."

Gaelan wanted so much to believe her . . . to trust her, but . . . Suddenly, she was close by his side. He searched her eyes, and saw himself reflected back. He nodded, the anger dissipated. She was right about the danger.

"I need to destroy that book. They cannot be allowed to get their hands on it—or me. There is too much at stake. Too much they can exploit."

"But the science in that manuscript . . . the medicine. Who knows what else is in it? Cures for cancer? Diabetes? For new diseases, even those yet to be discovered? It is an incredible find, a discovery that could do so much good in the world—in the right hands. What beyond our knowledge of medicine—of genetics, perhaps—lies within it?"

"Good, yes. It could do that. But in Transdiff's hands? Or any others of their sort with an agenda less beneficent than greedy? This book bestows humans the ability to become immortal—or to create an immortal being, impervious to physical injury. Can you imagine the price some would pay for the merest slice of tissue? Much less, the formula to create endless variations? Imagine an army of soldiers who could be sent into battle again and again, never mind the incalculable injuries to their minds and spirits—a fate so much worse than death.

"What havoc could be wreaked on the world by an unscrupulous government with the key to creating an entire race of such beings? How long would it be before the entire planet devolved into a war-torn wasteland?"

Gaelan realized he was ranting, but this scenario was one he had feared for centuries. "I have seen the sort of cruelty over my lifetime that no one should. We are not ready as a society for this book to see the light of day, no matter how much good it might do humankind." He was spent and breathless, his rage fueled by exhaustion and the now very real possibility he might become party to this . . . grotesque and brutal game.

"Then what? You'll destroy it, this book you've sought for all these years? Now that it's finally restored to you?"

"Do you think I want to destroy it? Destroy myself, now that finally I have found . . . you? But what choice have I? You tell me your colleague is en route now, and he means to learn whatever secrets my physiology possesses. If they are as ruthless as you suggest, the book, the knowledge, the secret to what I am are all in danger of the most despicable exploitation. I will not be part of it!"

Gaelan kneeled before her, imploring her to understand. She looked stricken. He realized she'd not yet considered the necessity that he, like the book, must be destroyed. "You know I cannot go on living, my darling. And this book, finally and most providentially, provides me the means to end it. It was never something I'd intended to do, for despite it all, I've rather enjoyed this century. And then meeting you . . ."

He cradled her face with his good hand, his thumb caressing the edge of her cheekbone. "It is ironic, but I really have little choice, and just when I again feel so much like living. There is something I must do first before I put an end to this. I have to create a toxin . . . an irreversible antidote to immortality." There were clues in the book that would guide his hand. A centuries-old burden began to lift from his shoulders.

"Is there a formulation in your magical book that perhaps only reverses the effects?"

"You see, my dear Anne, this is the problem; it is not magic. The immortality, if that is what you want to call it, is a side effect. The recipes—the medicines—work in a very specific manner. In all cases, whatever happens does so at the cellular level, and if done with absolute precision, just enough. But vary it one way or the other, it could either kill or make a person immortal."

"How would you even know which one to use to—"

"I have found hidden bits and pieces that point me towards what I seek, fragments scattered throughout the manuscript; I haven't yet pieced together anything remotely complete. Another day or two, I think."

He raised her hand to his lips, his eyes locked into hers, brushing his lips across her fingers one at a time. "I'm sorry. I truly am. I have not been drawn to a single soul as I have been to you since Eleanor. I didn't understand why; now I suppose I do. So many generations removed, and you yet have enough of her in you that my very spirit perceives it—"

"We should go. Get you checked into a hotel under an assumed name—at least until you can finish work on the book—find the pois . . . the antidote."

Tears had gathered on her eyelashes. Gaelan forced himself not to be distracted. He realized in that moment how impossible it would be to leave her, even as the germ of an idea flitted through his brain.

The buzz of the intercom jarred Gaelan from his thoughts. "Is it . . . ? Did you tell your ex how—"

"It cannot be Paul. He doesn't even know where to find you."

But who would be coming round at sunrise? He pressed "listen," saying nothing.

"Buzz me in. I've no desire to stand a moment longer under your bloody elevated tracks!"

What the devil was Simon doing outside his building? "No, I'll come down. I can do with some air."

CHAPTER 52

Simon eyed Anne suspiciously, motioning Gaelan to a distant spot in the alleyway. "That man I spoke of . . . about the book . . . And who is *she*, by the way? I thought you never—erm . . ."

Gaelan glared at him.

"It's her?"

He nodded. "Leave it be, Simon. And yes, I know. He's on a plane." Gaelan glanced at his watch, looking back toward where he had left Anne standing.

"How do you—"

"It is a bit of a story, but I haven't the time right now to explain—"

"I couldn't reach you. I thought—"

"I am quite fine." He turned. "Anne, there's someone I'd like you to meet." She joined them. "Dr. Anne Shawe. This is my friend . . . the author Anthony Danforth."

"Those Holmes novels, of course," she said flatly. "I've heard of you. Sorry, I tend to read only the Conan Doyles. Bit of a purist, I guess."

Simon shrugged. "I—"

"*Anthony*," Gaelan interrupted testily. "What's so urgent?"

Simon cocked an eyebrow toward Anne. "I would really rather not—"

Anne placed her hand on Gaelan's sleeve. "I should get back to my hotel, luv. I'll be back in what? An hour?" She started off, but Gaelan stopped her, taking her hand.

"It'll be all right. I promise," he whispered into her hair before kissing her. "Now you can go." Gaelan reluctantly let go of her hand and returned his attention to a stunned Simon, whose mouth hung agape.

"Look," Gaelan said finally, "we've much to do. *I've* much to do, and very little time. Walk with me. I could use an espresso." They ducked into the corner Starbucks.

Gaelan was silent until they were on their way back to his shop. "I have discovered, Simon, what I believe will be an antidote to the elixir."

He was clearly not listening. "You do realize she works for what might possibly be your worst nightmare. And that is saying quite a lot. Are you completely mad?"

Gaelan shook off the remark. "I've no time to explain Dr. Shawe. Look. Are you interested in this, or would you rather question my ... relationships?"

"Go on. Of course I'm bloody interested."

"I realized, finally, all of it came down to the manipulation of catalysts embedded within the manuscript text. It's hard to explain, but if we have time ... later ... I'll show you. Puzzles within puzzles."

"And the antidote is somewhere within these ... puzzles?"

"Deeply hidden, and you have to know where to look, build one bit of knowledge on the next. I guess the author—or authors—of the manuscript understood that poisons should not be easy to conjure."

"What about the woman? How much does she know?"

"Anne knows ... about *me*. I've told her nothing about you at all."

Simon looked horrified nonetheless. He pounded his hand into a lamp pole. "Bloody hell, Gaelan, you *are* insane!" he said sotto voce.

"Perhaps. It's all a bit weird, and, to be honest, I've not entirely wrapped my brain around it all yet. There will be time, I hope, later, to explain, and you will find it quite interesting, to say the very least. But for now, I can only tell you, I've a ..." Gaelan took out his key, but the shop door was unlocked. "Did you unlock ... ?"

Simon shrugged. "I never tried it; it's early, and I know you've not reopened since the accident. I assumed you were upstairs in the flat. You must've forgot to lock up. Wouldn't be the first time."

Gaelan shook his head. "I don't think I ..."

They entered the shop; a man was sitting in an easy chair, an iPad on his lap.

"We've tried getting hold of you for days, Mr. Erceldoune, but you've not answered your e-mails."

"So you thought it was fine to break into my place of business? And you are ... ?"

"My name is Dr. Paul Gilles. I work with Anne Shawe. I hoped you wouldn't mind."

Gilles didn't strike Gaelan as Anne's type at all. He reeked of corporate ambition, PhD geneticist or not. Bespoke suit, wingtips. *Manicured nails?* "I thought your flight wasn't due to arrive until this afternoon."

"I caught an earlier flight. Lucky break."

Or a lie to catch them unawares and unprepared. Or Anne had lied. Gaelan pushed that thought from his mind, refusing to allow that she would be a part of this.

"This is—"

"Danforth. Anthony. And so we meet in person."

"Mr. Danforth, you've probably worked this out already, since it is clear you know each other, but Mr. Erceldoune is now in possession of that item you seek," Gilles said.

"Dr. Gilles, would you like some tea?" Gaelan asked, sitting in the other chair.

"No, thank you."

"I would. Simon, might you do us a favor and put the kettle on in my office? I believe Dr. Gilles has some questions for me." Gaelan sat, resolute and calm. "I'm afraid you've broken into my shop needlessly. I am perfectly willing to come back with you to London. You've caught me; you know what I am. I suppose there is no particular value in fighting a game that is lost. The question is, what do I get out of it?"

Simon emerged from the back room, and set down the tea service. "Might we have a word, please?" Gaelan ignored the urgency in Simon's request.

"In a moment. Please. Join us."

"Mr. Erceldoune, I believe we can arrange quite a nice contract for you—as a consultant, if you will. You know, your new friend, Dr. Shawe, is under the impression you'd not want to be found, much less . . . collaborate with us. She did you a disservice."

"Did she, now? There's something else—a problem, I suppose, not difficult to fix."

"I'm listening."

"A passport. I don't have one, and as you might imagine, I've no papers of citizenship that would stand any sort of a security or immigration check. You'll need to provide that for me."

"I am certain it can be arranged. I'll call London this morning. Contract, passport, airline ticket. One way."

"I'm not done. I insist that the contract stipulates I can never be named, never suffer indignities the nature of which I've been subjected to previously. No publicity, no connection to any Miracle Man. Complete, total anonymity. Can you promise that? Contractually, I mean."

The door opened, and Anne walked in. She blanched as she looked from Paul to Gaelan. "Paul!" she stammered. "I thought you were on a much later flight—"

Gaelan observed the ex-lovers. He saw nothing between them but bitterness and decay. "Got lucky. Your Mr. Erceldoune and I were just having a very productive chat. He's not at all reticent to join our endeavor; I can't imagine why you thought otherwise. He quite sees the opportunity in it.

"Are you sure, Anne, you won't reconsider and re-up with the team? Forget Salk. Your knowledge of telomeres will be invaluable to us. Think of the good you'll do. Curing cancer? Lupus? Scourges and plagues of all sorts? Finding a way to prolong life and increase its quality for all? In answer to your question, Mr. Erceldoune, yes. I think we can put language of that sort into the contract. We want to please you. A collaborator, not an experimental subject. A partner in this endeavor."

The very idea brought the taste of bile to Gaelan's mouth. He chased a horrific image from his mind: battalions of warriors equipped with his DNA, precisely tuned, commanded by one immortal megalomaniac or another, able to stay in power lifetimes beyond lifetimes.

Anne glared at Paul, then turned her attention toward Gaelan. Her hurt, stupefied expression distressed him. He ignored her as best he could. There was nothing to be done about it, at any rate.

Paul Gilles removed a large envelope from his briefcase. "Just a few formalities to verify you are the person we're seeking." He was staring at Gaelan's left hand. "How did that happen?"

"Severed by a sadistic doctor called Handley. At Bedlam, July 1842. As you are well aware." He was satisfied that he'd managed to say it with any sort of calm detachment. But the effort cost him; it was all he could do not to retch. He struggled to focus the entirety of his attention on Gilles—and away from the baffled looks Anne Shawe and Simon Bell shared between them.

Paul placed a battered daguerreotype in Gaelan's hand. He flinched, recognizing himself: skeletal, hair a tangled mane; he was filthy to his bare feet, his clothes caked with his own blood. Shoving away the photograph, he swallowed hard. "It is me. Taken sometime in 1841 or '42, I think." There were few photographs taken.

"Might we get a sample of your blood to run through a DNA sequencing device?" A request, not a demand.

"No, not yet. In London. You get nothing until I'm back in the UK, the contract seen by my solicitor, approved and signed."

Gilles smiled. "Very well."

Anne crouched at the arm of his chair. "Gaelan, what are you doing?" she whispered, breaking his concentration.

He paid no mind to the thousand questions lurking in her eyes, which even now searched his for reasons far beyond his ability to express. "It's as you said, luv," he replied lightly, "the greater good. So many can be helped; it would be simply selfish of me to deny the world my presumably extraordinary DNA. Besides that, what's the point of fighting it anymore, with such damning proof staring me right in the face? I've made a decision, and I'm not unhappy with it. One more thing, Dr. Gilles. I'd like to fly back to London with Dr. Shawe. I've never flown on an airplane before, as you might imagine. I came over to America by ship long ago. It would make me a trifle less nervous about all of this if I could travel with a companion. And since I am acquainted with your colleague . . ."

Gaelan turned to Anne. "I know it's an imposition, Dr. Shawe, but would you mind delaying your trip to California just a few days more?"

She hesitated only a second before responding. "Of course not, Mr. Erceldoune. Paul?"

She agreed. Good. She was playing along with him a game that right now must seem to her utter madness. She was trusting him without knowing what with. *Patience, my love. I know what I'm doing here.*

"Lovely," added Paul. "And maybe on the flight, Mr. Erceldoune might convince you not to return to the States at all once you've arrived back home. So it is settled. I shall fly back tonight and oversee the contract personally. Meantime, I'll see about getting Mr. Erceldoune a passport and have it overnighted. Expect the contract in your e-mail within the next forty-eight hours. I'll need a place of birth and birthdate for the passport."

Gaelan couldn't help but laugh before considering what to say. "Er . . ." He coughed. "Edinburgh. But I'm not sure you'll want to use my actual birthdate."

"Obviously. I am curious, however."

"Twenty-four March 1586."

Gaelan watched as the door to the shop closed and Dr. Paul Gilles exited. He held up a hand, saying nothing, and nodded toward the door. "Has he gone?"

Simon went to the blinds, opening them slightly to look out. "He's gone." He turned back into the room, fuming as he paced. "What the bloody hell was that?"

Anne continued to stare at Gaelan, hands on her hips, eyes blazing. "*Exactly* what he said. What the devil were you thinking? Join the team? Collaborate? You can't be serious."

"Oh, I'm quite fucking serious. Just not about giving free samples of me to the likes of your ex-fiancé."

"Then what—"

"I've an idea."

CHAPTER 53

They decamped to Simon's larger, more comfortable home after stopping at a scientific supply store near the Northwestern campus. Simon had helped Gaelan set up an improvised laboratory in his luxurious second-floor bathroom. "This idea of yours; it's quite the double cross," Simon noted, setting out an array of beakers. "It calls to mind another double cross—one that ended in disaster."

"But only for Richard Braithwaite. Yes. Eleanor," Gaelan replied, nodding slightly, surprised that Simon had made the connection so quickly. "I felt her near to me, as if she spoke to me through time, affording me the courage—the courage she displayed—back then."

He thought for a moment. Simon needed to know about Anne. There was no time for the entire bizarre tale, but at least the man might go to his grave knowing Eleanor's descendant. What he did with that knowledge was up to him.

The Magic Flute floated up through the grand foyer, interrupted by a knock at the door. Anne. "Gaelan."

"A moment, luv."

"Your passport has arrived, I think."

Perfect. The toxins were finished. He carefully placed a glass stopper into one amber bottle. Then into two smaller cobalt vials he placed stoppers, which he'd wrapped in soft wax. Holding the bottles up to the bathroom light, he was satisfied the wax was evenly distributed around the neck. Soon it would harden to a secure seal, perfect for travel.

He pocketed all three and turned to the final page of the manuscript—a beautiful rendering of sky and sea on a starry night, the place a high rocky cliff planted with a single hawthorn tree, its branches barren. Beneath it slept a man, beside him a woman, more light than flesh—not quite human . . . other. Airmid? The outlines of the illumination, scripted in black, a fine copper hand in Latin and Gaelic.

"Tempore quamquam abest ut crescant et labatur si venistis ad hunc locum istum egregium locum semper et invenies me. Justus dormientes et expecta."

"Though time may grow distant and we fade from this place if ye come to this goodly land, ever shall you find me there. Just fall to sleep and wait.

"Airmid's medicine . . . herbs of every variety, she had spread upon her cloak. But they were scattered to the four winds by her father, jealous of her healing power. But Thomas Learmont of Erceldoune in Scotland, before the time her people had sojourned to Eire, had shown her a kindness in her grief at the loss of her brother, the anger of her father. And the fairy Airmid gifted Thomas a book, one that held the secrets of the minerals and herbs and healing and medicine. And Thomas promised to preserve it and perhaps someday return it to her."

There were numbers beneath the script—coordinates, he speculated. Gaelan put them into a GPS app on his iPad and came up with a dot on the northern coast of Scotland in the Highlands. It made some sense, from what he recalled about the Tuatha de Danann, of Denmark, some said. But from the *north*. He emerged from the makeshift laboratory and into Anne's arms.

She cupped Gaelan's cheek, moving a lock of his hair behind an ear, looking gravely into his eyes. "I know you can't tell me where you're going with my . . . your . . . book, but . . . I'll never see it again, will I? Or you?"

"I have traveled such a long distance; I am weary and ensnared in a labyrinth with the minotaur chomping at my heels."

"Sorry?"

Ah, yes. She didn't know Greek mythology. He'd forgotten. "Nothing. Just an obscure metaphor." He shrugged.

"You would really throw away the possibility that your book—that you—might achieve some greater good living, and not dead?"

He placed a finger against her lips, stilling further protest. "Tomorrow you will get on the plane, and when you arrive in London, you will tell Paul I ditched you at O'Hare and you had no choice but to board, given the nature of immigration and international travel these days. You will give him a letter from me and say nothing else. I can tell you no more than that. Please trust me. Yes?"

"There's more you're not telling me."

"Anne, let's not waste our last night arguing. This is all settled, and there is nothing you can do to undo it." Gaelan embraced her, still not believing that he had found love again, and again would abandon it. He backed away as his body responded to the gentle prodding of her thigh.

"What is it? Why—"

"To have fallen in love with my own descendent. It's rather Oedipal, to say the least, despite the span of generations between you and my daughter Ariadne. I cannot put myself—"

"Listen to me. Eleanor had many children. What I tried to tell you the other day. It is my cousin's family that are long-lived, and not my direct ancestors. No one in my immediate line: grandparents, aunts . . . no one has lived extraordinarily long, I assure you. Both my grandmother and great-grandmother died of cancer. I am *not* Ariadne's descendent. Yes, I'm very likely Eleanor's descendant, but not yours."

These past few days had been, equally, the most peaceful and most turbulent in his life. But now Gaelan felt the peace that can only come from wholeness. That Hebrew word he'd encountered in places throughout the manuscript. Shalom: peace, but more—completeness. The void within him had been suddenly filled to overflowing; he'd been reunited with his book, found purpose—and found family in Anne. And love, albeit brief. Since that horrible afternoon when Anne woke him, the dreams, the flashbacks had retreated to a distant corner of his mind, if only temporarily. Gaelan had no illusions that they would return, but perhaps he would be . . . gone . . . long before then.

"Come, my love, let's go upstairs," Anne whispered.

He nodded, letting her lead him up the stairs to her bedroom.

The first rays of sunlight spilled over them, and Gaelan awoke. He looked down at Anne, knowing they would soon be on their way, down divergent paths—she, back to her life, and he to finally meet death.

A month ago, he'd never have believed it, to choose death, given the choice. But there was no choice. Not anymore. Life had run its course.

He removed the e-ticket from his passport folder and glanced at the departure time: 2:00 p.m., Virgin Air to Heathrow and then straightaway to Inverness.

"Morning." Anne was awake. "What are you doing?"

"Making certain of my flight time. What time is yours?"

"It's at four; you know that."

Gaelan rolled a cigarette and lit it. "Sorry. A bit nervous. I've never been in an airport, much less flown."

"That's what you're nervous about?" She smiled, trying to pull him down into the sheets.

"Hey, I shall set the bed afire; Simon wouldn't like that much."

"Much rather you set me afire. And we've *plenty* of time."

"Aye." Gaelan put out the cigarette and lowered himself, drawing Anne beneath him. She was wet and already aroused. The awkwardness of their first time had transformed into an easy comfort as he found a rhythm that elicited from Anne the most abandoned moans he'd ever heard. If he'd been a sorcerer, he would cast a spell and freeze them in time, right here, right now.

Anne gasped as the wild contractions of her orgasm shook her, sending him careering over the edge of ecstasy as he followed her. Afterward, they lay together in silence.

"You're worried," Anne said finally.

"Aye. Yes. Anything—everything—could go wrong. My flight could be delayed, and I might run smack into your Transdiff friends at Heathrow."

"You won't. Trust *me*."

"I do, my darling. I am entrusting you with far more than my life. But, Anne…what if…what if the people…Airmid, her kin… whomever this book belongs to…? What if they're gone? I mean really gone and—"

"No guarantees. I suppose, then, you will do what you must. Destroy the book…before you…before you drink the contents of that vial."

It was the first time she'd acknowledged it aloud, the inevitability of this, his final journey. "I have something for you." Gaelan produced a test tube packed in dry ice. "I didn't know if it had to be refrigerated, but—"

"I don't understand—"

It was a single tube of blood—the ultimate token of his trust in her. "It's mine. My gift to you. You've my notes from the ouroboros book and now a vial of my blood. Perhaps it might do you some good—or the world. Who knows?"

"But, Gaelan, the risk. You're giving your life . . . our life together to make certain it's all . . . all destroyed forever. I don't know if I can assume such a burden. I—"

"I trust, my love, that you will keep this safe and not let it into Transdiff's hands. Use it to . . . study, to understand. Perhaps someday you shall win a Nobel Prize with it, cure cancer with it. I only ask that you use it well and wisely."

He had one more gift for her. The autographed copy of Conan Doyle.

"Always, my love, remember me when you read the inscription. Now you must go before I lose my resolve—"

"But—"

He halted her protest with a final kiss, drinking her in to sustain him for the long days ahead. "Know that I do this, Anne, only because there is no other way. If there was a way to alter my genetic makeup, to reverse the process—and do it in time—I would. With all my heart, I would. But we both know as long as I am living, Transdiff will not stop, and to find an antidote to reverse my condition could take lifetimes more than I can afford."

She nodded, tears running freely down her cheeks.

Gaelan watched from the gallery as Anne said her good-bye to Simon, taking from him a large accordion envelope. *Forget about me, my love, and be happy.*

CHAPTER 54

Anne was off, and with any luck, she would be at Heathrow breaking the news to Paul Gilles in approximately ten hours. The front door closed, and Simon breathed a sigh of relief as Gaelan came down the stairs.

"So, Gaelan. This is finally the end for us. We must drink a toast to old friends."

Simon poured two large tumblers, each filled to brimming with Lagavulin.

"To our beloved Eleanor," Gaelan offered.

"To Arthur and Joseph. And to Sophie; banshee or not, she did not deserve this unrestful rest."

Gaelan nodded. "Perhaps you will see her soon enough." They touched glasses. "Slàinte!"

"Do dheagh shlàinte. However, you do realize, my old friend, that we've just drunk to each other's health and we intend quite the opposite."

Gaelan smiled easily. "Force of habit, I suppose." Resolve had lifted a four-hundred-year-old burden from his shoulders. "Well, my friend, I shall be off shortly. I suppose 'See you on the other side' might have been a more practical toast.

"Mind, Simon, I made this to exact proportions. As I did with my own, but a slightly different formulation—specific to the elixir I'd made to cure plague. Take all of it if you wish to die. This will not reverse the elixir; it will kill. It is a potent poison, but it will do it fast. There should be no pain in it. The Tuatha de Danann were healers, and even their deadliest poisons were not meant to prolong suffering, but to be quick and effective."

"All medicine is poison?"

"Not in this case. This recipe is explicitly a toxin, no medicine to it at all. There is no good in it, I can see, save the murder of an enemy. Or a suicide. Have you told Sophie?"

"I've not seen her for days, come to think of it. She's left me in peace. She's not been round since we've been occupied with your accursed book."

"Perhaps, as I have long said, my friend, she only wants you to go on living and let her be dead. Do not pine for her on her grave, and she will vanish. You've had little time for pining these last days. Perhaps she has truly left you after all this time! Are you certain you do not desire to stay a bit longer on this earth? Haven't you a new novel coming out shortly?" Gaelan could not suppress a laugh.

"You'll be gone, and she will return, I am certain. But with you gone as well, I shall be truly alone in the world. No. I must end it; it is long past time."

Gaelan sighed. "Then I give you this vial and hope it brings you the peace you have so long craved, my friend. It is likely for the best, in any event. I thought I was safe from discovery, and had been for what? How many years? And then a simple accident in this age of electronic wizardry, sorcery beyond anything my ancestors might have foreseen in their age—"

"I'm well aware. So, my old friend, it is a death pact we sign here, yes?"

"I suppose it is."

"And Anne?"

"Anne will write about what she learned from me and the book—it will give her a lifetime's work. She has my notes, and my library, and now—"

"And now that you've told me of her tie to Eleanor, she shall have my fortune as well. It seems I owe you a debt of gratitude once again, to have connected me with . . . my niece, is it? Somehow it is comforting to know that I go to my grave having known her. It is a gift beyond measure."

"You told her, then . . . about yourself?"

Simon shook his head. "That I couldn't bring myself to do, at least not . . . But it is all there in a thick packet of papers I insisted she take with her. She will know soon enough. She is, after all, my closest known relation, my own sister's descendent, unbelievable as it is. It will be a story to tell her children someday—"

Gaelan flinched. That was not something he wished to think about. They heard the taxi as it pulled up to Simon's door.

The two men embraced, wishing each other success as Gaelan hoisted his messenger bag over his shoulder, patting it to make certain the book was inside.

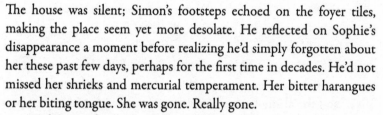

The house was silent; Simon's footsteps echoed on the foyer tiles, making the place seem yet more desolate. He reflected on Sophie's disappearance a moment before realizing he'd simply forgotten about her these past few days, perhaps for the first time in decades. He'd not missed her shrieks and mercurial temperament. Her bitter harangues or her biting tongue. She was gone. Really gone.

Had Simon finally done what she'd wanted all along? All that was required to let her go and send her back to her eternal rest? What was that ballad she'd always wailed, her cries and shrieks punctuating each and every verse? That was it: "The Unquiet Grave."

> *Cold blows the wind to my true love,*
> *And gently drops the rain,*
> *I never had but one sweetheart,*
> *And in greenwood she lies slain.*
> *I'll do as much for my sweetheart*
> *As any young man may;*
> *I'll sit and mourn all on her grave*
> *For a twelvemonth and a day.*
> *When the twelvemonth and one day was past,*
> *The ghost began to speak:*
> *"Why sittest thou here all day on my grave,*
> *And will not let me sleep?"*

Simon wanted to believe that Sophie had finally broken free of him; he'd never wanted to hold her against her will. But his heart had mourned her, had felt guilty about her death—perhaps he had held her, but unwillingly so. And now she was gone, let go. At peace. There was only one thing for Simon to do. He uttered a fervent prayer as he took in hand the cobalt blue vial Gaelan had prepared for him: that Sophie would be waiting for him, not the banshee she had become, but the soul mate she had been back then.

"Simon, my love."

Sophie.

"I thought you'd gone—"

"I have, my love. I am free, and I return to you of my own will. I know what it is you aim to do and shall be awaiting you when the time comes."

"Soon, love, soon." It would be all right.

He held up the amber bottle to the light, studying the liquid as it swirled in the glass. He put it to his lips and drank as if it were his only sustenance and not a poison. He tasted the tang of metal, like fine silver, and the alcohol solvent; the scent of almonds and orange peel surrounded him as he felt himself falling into a vast white sea of light.

Sophie awaited him, her hand extended, dressed in sapphire velvet, a diamond tiara in her black hair, radiant.

He was home.

NORTHERN HIGHLANDS, SCOTLAND, PRESENT DAY

CHAPTER 55

Thurso was on the northernmost tip of the Scottish mainland, overlooking the Orkneys. It was a wild area of stark beauty, the very feel of it otherworldly. Gaelan landed in Inverness and hired a car, taking his time to drive north and west through the Highlands. The road wasn't easy, and the car awkward to drive, with everything reversed. There was little traffic, but more than once, he had to remind himself to drive on the left, not the right as a car traveling the opposite direction would surprise him coming over a hill or round a curve. It wouldn't do to crash—again. It would be all he needed.

He'd been to this area as a boy, he'd thought, though much had changed. Feeling freer than he had in centuries, he knew he would be released from his burden soon enough—and then what? He felt for the small vial in his pocket. Medicine, he'd told the TSA agent at O'Hare, needed for seizures when in flight.

The book had never been his to give away or to keep. Lord Thomas Learmont of Erceldoune had been but a steward, keeping Airmid's powerful book of healing until such a time came when it might be used—with wisdom. A time that never would come in all the ages thenceforth.

Perhaps there had been a time once when true enlightenment might have come to pass, when a nexus was possible, formed of knowledge tempered by understanding, technology bounded by empathy. Gaelan wondered if that had been Airmid's idealistic hope when she handed the book to his ancestor so long ago—an antidote calculated to heal the world of its darkest ages. To bring about a new Camelot that could never be.

Yes, there were the Anne Shawes of the world, but far too many Handleys and Braithwaites—and the Transdiffs who would with this knowledge transform the world into something toxic and vile. "And Lyle Tremayne," he said to no one. The name still tasted bitter on his tongue as he thought of the man who'd condemned him to hell in the first place.

Gaelan's GPS instructed him in a female British accent to turn left as his watch tapped him gently on the wrist. He smiled. Magic. A wristwatch with the ability to guide him halfway around the world. He would miss these little amazements.

"Your destination is in five hundred feet." Gaelan stopped the car at the base of a small grassy hill and looked up to see the hawthorn tree of the book's cover. It was unmistakable. He trudged to the top and gazed along the coastline; puffins skittered across the water, leaving small whitecaps in their wake.

Setting up his campsite, he built a small fire and unrolled a down sleeping bag before relaxing beneath the tree. The light was fading now, and Gaelan watched the stars emerge one by one, and the planets. In the distance he thought he saw the glow of distant, fading glaciers, their white-blue adorning the water in an eerie haze.

He lay back on his sleeping bag, shoving a pillow of his clothing beneath his neck, and looked up. The Aurora Borealis lit the sky like he had never seen before: magenta, phosphorescent blue, tangerine, every color imaginable. The book lay at his side. He patted it gently, noticing Polaris gleaming bright so far to the north as the electromagnetic display faded. The stars were close enough to touch up here, pockmarking the black sky. Ah, there it was, Ariadne's Crown.

Perhaps he should drink the toxin now. Did it matter? Would the goddess Airmid—who, for all Gaelan knew, never really existed outside of legend and ballad—appear through some invisible portal to reclaim her book?

No. He must see this through to the final act. There would be time ... after ... *After what? After the fairies visit you and steal back their book?* He laughed, thinking of Sir Arthur Conan Doyle and his steadfast and quite paradoxical belief in their world.

Finally, exhaustion overtook Gaelan, and he fell into a restless sleep, his dreamscape a towering maze, grotesque images of Anne's Transdiff colleagues at every turn. They chased him with syringes and scalpels until they caught him, strapping him then to a silver gurney. He could not move; he could not breathe. "The medical find of the twenty-first century!" The proclamation echoed everywhere as Gaelan fought with the restraints, awaking in the dark to find himself wrestling with his sleeping bag.

Panting and bathed in sweat, he sat up, elbows on his knees, as he tried to settle his breathing. *It will be over soon. No more nightmares, no more torture relived in an infinite loop for all eternity.*

Gaelan had given up on going back to sleep when a breeze rustled through the leaves above him. And from somewhere nearby a sweet melody called out to him—an old folk tune, enfolding him, clearing his thoughts of trouble, as it drew him into a dreamless, peaceful rest.

"Gaelan—"

The voice was gentle as a breeze whispering through tall grass, close enough it tickled at the shell of his ear. This was different, more insistent than the murmuring song that had lulled him to sleep. His eyes fluttered open, and he squinted into the morning light as it washed over him. He patted the ground to his right—the book was gone. His first thought was that Gilles had somehow found him—found out his scheme. Had Anne been coerced, or had she betrayed him ... ? No! Unthinkable. It must be here ... somewhere ...

"Gaelan."

Shielding his eyes from the glare, he recognized her sitting there, swathed in a corona of sunlight. He blinked several times, and her face came into sharper relief. No explanation sufficed but that he was yet asleep, and in the midst of an improbable dream.

But then a delicate hand reached out, cupping his jaw, real as the dew that had gathered on the grass overnight. "Hallo."

"Anne," he breathed, trying to sit up. There was something amiss with his left hand, but his confusion over this . . . vision momentarily pushed it from his thoughts. "Anne, what are you doing here?" he inquired, not yet entirely certain whether this was real. But not even his most real delusion would have tasted so sweet as Anne's gentle kiss.

"He *told* you!" Gaelan wanted to be angry. "He'd *no* right. . . ."

"A note stuck to some papers he insisted I take. Coordinates: no destination, no name. I hazarded a guess and trusted in the Google."

He should never have shared those particulars with Simon. But he'd been so fucking amazed by the manuscript's final bit of brilliance, and after all, they'd both be dead within a day.

A thread of suspicion wended its way through Gaelan's mind. "Just how did you escape Paul Gilles?"

"I never boarded my flight. It took off without me. I got a flight to Copenhagen, and from there to Wick. I drove the rest of the way. Cash transaction—thanks to my long-lost cousin *Simon*. The papers he left me . . . deeds, a will, and a very long letter. I've not read it all, but enough that I think I understand at least some of it—and his connection to you."

Gaelan frowned as he wondered if his dear friend, Eleanor's brother, Anne's . . . uncle . . . had finally found peace.

"I'm sure when I didn't show up at Heathrow . . . I'm not fooling myself. They'll be after me. I daren't show up in the UK—at least not until my report about their activities is published three days from now. They offered to push the deadline."

Gaelan had not at all planned on this turn of events. He could not begin to imagine taking the toxin in Anne's presence. How could he put her through that ordeal? He had to get rid of her. Or something. But how could he when she gazed at him with eyes so luminous in the bright sunshine that . . . ?

"I could not imagine your last hours spent alone, my love. Do—"
Her eyes widened to saucers.

"What is it?"

"Your hand! Did you not notice?"

"My . . . ?" That was it—his hand; it was leaden, as if asleep—numb. Indeed he was occasionally plagued by the phantom of his lost fingers, even decades later. He'd brushed off the sensation.

Gaelan sat up fully, and his hand fell into his lap. Where there had been three stumps, there were now fingers—perfectly formed. He could not tear his eyes from the sight. Even after all these years, he wasn't quite sure what to make of it. But how . . . ?

Airmid and her brother Miach had healed the warrior Nuada, replacing the silver hand created by Dian Cecht, with one of flesh and bone, making him whole.

Gaelan flexed his fingers slowly, stiffly, feeling the strangeness, noticing, then, a small wrought-silver necklace, encrusted with glittering stones, draped across his palm—a labyrinth. A small scroll lay at his side in an ornate Gaelic script:

> *Bone to bone*
> *Vein to vein*
> *Balm to Balm;*
> *Sap to Sap*
> *Skin to skin*
> *Tissue to tissue;*
> *Blood to blood*
> *Flesh to flesh*
> *Sinew to sinew;*
> *Marrow to marrow*
> *Pith to pith*
> *Fat to fat;*
> *Membrane to membrane*
> *Fibre to fibre*
> *Moisture to moisture.*

He knew this poem—Airmid's poem—the incantation she'd chant as she healed the sick and wounded.

Gaelan placed the delicate necklace in Anne's hand. "For you, my dear Anne."

She fastened it around her neck, where it shimmered with prismatic light.

"I shall wear it always, but where did it come from?"

Shrugging, Gaelan explained that he had no idea. "It was here, in my hand, when I woke just now . . . The book is . . . gone." He hesitated, reluctant, now that Anne was here by his side, to say it. "It is a sign, perhaps, that my long journey is, at last, coming to an end. . . ."

Gaelan choked back his emotions as he gazed at the labyrinth resting against Anne's breast. It looked so much like Eleanor's—and so right around her descendant's neck. What did it signify? He could speculate—if only there was time. Which there was not. What time he did have, he would spend in the company of Dr. Anne Shawe. Until he would shoo her away to do what he must do.

Gaelan's thoughts drifted back to his hand. What if he was wrong, and this "sign" was not to end his life, but . . . ? What if something else had changed of his anatomy, besides the acquisition of three new fingers? What else had been altered, and what if the antidote—the poison formulated to exactly counteract the plague elixir—would not now work as intended? Or was he only trying to justify a reason to stay . . . to be with Anne, if only for a little while longer?

He knew *that* was impossible. His escape was a brief diversion, and Transdiff was likely days, if not hours, from finding him. And once they'd gotten their claws into him . . . No his death would be far preferable for both of them. He could only imagine Anne's suffering in the knowledge that he had become Transdiff's pawn—their lab rat. A third way. There had to be a third way. A moment of panic, and then an idea settled in its place.

"Are you all right? You look . . . strange . . . distracted."

"Aye. I'm fine. Fine. It is nothing—" But Gaelan knew Anne would not release her concern until he explained. "I've a plan." Gaelan sighed, assuring himself it *would* be all right. *If* . . . it worked.

The Falls of Glomach were the second highest in the UK, and only a four-hour drive from Thurso. It was nearly one o'clock when they arrived; the mists had lifted. To the west, Anne could see the Isle of Skye and all around them, the early spring bloom of the Highlands.

"It is beautiful, Gaelan, extraordinary. I've read about this place, but it's so far from London. I've never been here before." She breathed in the unearthly magnificence of the falls, yet could not keep the tremble of fear from her voice.

Gaelan took her hand, directing her gaze. "I've not been here for hundreds of years, yet it, like the stars, never changes—and ever changes." She could barely hear him above the thundering of the falls, a short walk away.

The notion that this man to whom she'd bound herself so closely might have been . . . no, *was* . . . her ancestor's soul mate was impossible to comprehend. And now the thought that she might lose him . . .

Gaelan interrupted her thoughts. "I spent so many summers here as a wee boy, scrabbling up these very rocks and hills, even down the cataract a time or two on a dare. Come, let me show you the gorge." He and tugged her toward the crevasse.

The water's roar blotted out all other sound as he reached into his pocket, withdrawing a sealed vial, offering it to her. She took it and held it as a talisman, grateful he'd not taken it.

Gaelan had been right; the site was packed with tourists, hiking, taking pictures of the astonishing scenery. Perfect. An audience. It would all be rather pointless, Gaelan had explained, without one.

"Trust me," he whispered into her ear as he drew her into a tight embrace. His warmth surrounded her on this chilly precipice. He kissed her ear, her hair, each closed eye until finally he captured her mouth. And too quickly, he pulled away.

No. Please not yet. She grabbed his sleeve, trying to forestall the inevitable.

"Trust me. It *will* be all right. I promise. It must be this way."

And she believed him, though in her heart she cried out for him not to go, not so soon. Not ever.

Anne watched Gaelan trek across the small field to the edge of the cataract before he turned toward her a final time, his eyes fixed on hers. "Trust me," he mouthed before disappearing down the gorge.

She gasped, clutching the vial until her knuckles turned white. A moment passed, then two. She was almost oblivious to the blur of activity about her.

She fingered the fragile labyrinth pendant at her neck. She'd Googled the myth of Ariadne, curious about it since Gaelan had pointed out her crown of stars in the night sky the other night. And now she needed to help her Theseus slay Minotaur, and he would abandon her to face the world alone. She did not know in that moment when . . . or if Gaelan, now reborn as her Dionysus, would return to her. "Trust me," he'd said.

All around her, people ran toward the gorge, shouting, nearly knocking her to the ground, as they gathered at the edge of the cliff. "He's fallen!" "Someone call 999!" "Help!" Anne barely heard their cries through her sobs.

She opened her phone, waiting. An hour passed, perhaps two as she sat in the scrubby grass. The ambulance had gone, and all but a few park police had vanished. The news vans had abandoned the scene as well. For who could have survived such a plummet into the crevasse? Stories would be filed about an anonymous man who jumped from Glomach.

Finally, her phone vibrated twice. A text message. "The Empty House." Anne smiled through the tears still blurring her vision. Standing, she dusted off her jeans and approached the uniformed officer writing notes on his clipboard.

"I knew him—the man who jumped. His name was Gaelan Erceldoune."

ACKNOWLEDGMENTS

Writing a novel can at times be a solitary pursuit—hours and hours at a sitting, spent alone, inside the heads of flawed (and sometimes very nasty) characters. But the process of creating a viable manuscript and a great, well-told story takes more than one person's imagination and a good word processing program. I have many people to thank for their encouragement, support, critiques, and so much more.

First, to Rene Sears, editorial director at Pyr, for acquiring *The Apothecary's Curse* and the rest of the team at Prometheus, especially copyeditor Jeff Curry, publicist Jake Bonar, and editorial assistant Hanna Etu. Thank you so much to gifted fantasy artist Galen Dara for the gorgeous and inviting artwork that graces the cover of the novel and Jacqueline Nasso Cooke, whose cover design completes the perfect package for *The Apothecary's Curse*.

Thank you to all those who gave me feedback during the early days of the writing process, especially Erika Mailman and my fellow scribes in Mediabistro's Novel Writing workshop and Jody Allen of Rings True who read an early draft for historical accuracy. I will never forget, Jody, that Gaelan Erceldoune of the Borderlands would never—ever—drink whiskey with an "e"!

I also want to thank my good friend Denise Dorman of Write Brain Media who has been my sounding board and muse all through the writing and beyond during our long coffees at the Deer Park Starbucks. Thank you for your support and your complete belief in *The Apothecary's Curse*.

I owe so much thanks to my wonderful agent, Katharine Sands, of

Sarah Jane Freymann Literary Agency in New York. She has been with me on the journey of this novel since I e-mailed her my first chapters and outline a couple of years ago and asked, "What do you think?" Her feedback and support while I was writing, and her tireless enthusiasm in finding Gaelan and Simon's story a perfect home, her friendship on this and other projects make her more partner than agent.

Mostly, I want to thank my amazing mensch of a husband Phil, whose undying support really made it possible for me to find the time and space to write, never complaining about dishes undone, floors unswept, and clothing not put away. As a reader, he critiqued *The Apothecary's Curse*, his keen eye pointing out ways to sharpen the story, and making suggestions (some of which I even incorporated!) along the way.

Lastly, I would be remiss without acknowledging Sir Arthur Conan Doyle, whose works, from his Holmes novels to his essays and his non-Sherlock stories, inspired me at every turn.

ABOUT THE AUTHOR

Author photo
© Cilento Photography

Barbara Barnett is publisher and executive editor of Blogcritics (blogcritics.org), an Internet magazine of pop culture, politics, and more, for which she has also contributed nearly 1,000 essays, reviews, and interviews over the past decade. Always a pop-culture and sci-fi geek, Barbara was raised on a steady diet of TV (and TV dinners), but she always found her way to fiction's tragic antiheroes and misunderstood champions, whether on TV, in the movies, or in literature. (In other words, Spock, not Kirk; Han Solo, not Luke Skywalker!) Her first book, *Chasing Zebras: The Unofficial Guide to House, M.D.* (ECW Press), reflects her passion for these Byronic heroes, and it was inevitable that she would have to someday create one of her own.

She is an accomplished speaker, an annual favorite at Mensa's HalloweeM convention, where she has spoken to standing room crowds on subjects as diverse as "The Byronic Hero in Pop Culture," "The Many Faces of Sherlock Holmes," "The Hidden History of Science Fiction," and "Our Passion for Disaster (Movies)," and "The Conan Doyle Conundrum."

A life-long resident of the Chicago area, she lives with her husband Phil not far from the beautiful Lake Michigan coast of Chicago's North Shore that serves as the modern-day setting for *The Apothecary's Curse*. She is the proud mother of Shoshanna (Mike) and Adam, and the loving *savta* of Ari.